FLANAGAN'S LEGACY

Preface

Flanagan's Legacy was in fact my second novel written and set in 1994. It went via an agent to a mainstream publisher but was rejected on the grounds that the Irish troubles were no longer a fashionable topic. The typescript sat in my computer for twelve years unread. I was occupied with my mystery thriller series involving the Simpson family and their daughter, Emily. When I looked again at Flanagan's Legacy, I found it intriguing with its mystery tour around the English Channel and then on to Southern Ireland.

We now live in happier times regarding relations between Britain and Ireland. My two characters, Clare and Michael may strike sparks off each other but they represent two nations that sometimes misunderstand each other. The third character, their ship *Quadra,* is based on a classic design by the veteran writer and yacht designer Maurice Griffiths.

Dedication

To all who sail and enjoy Chichester Harbour and West Cork, the places where much of this story takes place.

Credits

Once again I would like to thank Michael Glanister who read and corrected the text and Jo Smith who set it into shape for the printer.

Author

Jim Morley has sailed and raced small boats all his life. He spent forty years in farming and forestry, combining this with a career in freelance writing.

He has published several novels, reflecting his interest in boats and also rural matters. He lives near Petersfield in Hampshire and sails a small family cruising yacht on Chichester Harbour.

Cover design: moonlight and the Fastnet Rock by Guy Nicholson.

FLANAGAN'S LEGACY

James Morley

Flanagan's Legacy
First published 2011

Published by Benhams Sea Mysteries, 1 Fir Cottage, Greatham, Liss, Hampshire GU33 6BB

Typeset by John Owen Smith

ISBN 978-0-9548880-5-3

Printed by CreateSpace

PROLOGUE

GUISSENNY, BRITTANY, APRIL 1919

It was eight o'clock on a cold spring morning. The watchers in the field could hear the seas breaking on the rocks half a kilometre away. It would be an idyllic everyday scene, apart from the large aeroplane being towed across the pasture by a horse.

Edwin McGee could have laughed at the bizarre vision, but he was not at his best in the early morning and he was frightened. He was about to take his first flight as a passenger in this same aeroplane. It was not to be a short ten-minute joyride, but an epoch making flight across three hundred miles of stormy Atlantic water.

'There she is, Ed. One new assembled DH 9. Gas tanks full and rarin' to go.' Jim laughed. 'Whad'ya think?'

To a Bostonian like Edwin, Jim O'Dwyer's Southern drawl could irritate, but he was too much in awe of the man to comment. If he had to make this flight he could hardly have been given a better pilot. Jim was the all-American hero, the ace flyer who had fought in the terrible war just ended. It was a war that had mercifully left the nineteen-year old Edwin unscathed. Three convoys dodging U-Boats during 1918 had been the sole war experience of this young merchant navy navigator. Now he was to put his skills to a different challenge. The alleged record attempt had a double agenda. Everything would depend on his navigation this day; including both their lives. Colonel Flanagan had told them they would be making history. The dispatches they were to carry would strike a blow for their ancestral land and free a nation from the bonds of its rapacious overlords. He shivered a little and tried to say a prayer, but the words wouldn't come.

'Ed, time to be goin'. You got ya' charts?'

Edwin held up the leather case and the little box with the sextant.

O'Dwyer looked at the latter and frowned. 'Say Ed, see that cloud base?' He pointed at the murky sky. 'That crud could extend to several thousand feet. Above it there's ice. Can't guarantee you a sun sight at noon or any other time – sorry.'

Edwin's stomach felt as if it too had just swallowed a block of that ice. They were due for take-off in an hour's time: nine o'clock. He had plotted a course to take them north-west over the Scillies in order to make their planned landing in County Cork. But for the last leg he needed a noon sight with his sextant. God alone knew what cross winds and currents would set athwart their course.

He tried to appear calm. 'Could this ice really do damage?'

'Gee, I'll say. Ice on the wings would give this bird the dynamics of a railroad car.'

'I see.' Edwin knew his face was a picture of melancholy.

'Hey there, don't fret – we'll make it. Say Ed, you still set on being a priest?'

'Sure.'

'OK, you get on the line to your boss. Tell him that today I'd sure appreciate a squadron of his guardian angels to watch my tail.'

Edwin smiled weakly. 'I can try.'

'You do that. Y'know, after what I've seen in this war I kinda' envy your vocation.'

'Ever thought of becoming a priest yourself?'

O'Dwyer threw back his head and roared with laughter. 'Oh sure…sure…'til I got to the bit about poverty and chastity. No Ed, sorry but sorry.' He laughed again.

Edwin looked at his companion. Jim was a big man: tall and athletic with the build of a football player. His natural good looks augmented by his hair: blond, like a Viking, but also flecked with little strands of flame red. He had to agree, celibacy and self-denial were not this man's forte. Jim swung round, placed both hands on Edwin's shoulders, and looked him in the eyes. The power of the man was infectious. The dark eyes seemed to read Edwin's thoughts. 'C'mon – It'll be OK. Maybe we'll make our own bit of history.' Jim released him with a slap on the back. 'Let's go look at the ship.'

The Breton farm-men had unhooked their carthorse from the towing ring on the underbelly of the fuselage. They were surly and introspective. It seemed that nothing these mad Americans did could surprise them, but they were happy enough to take the lavish money that Colonel Flanagan offered. It was money that bought silence. The Colonel had hinted that a rival team seeking the record was not far away.

'Here we are,' O'Dwyer walked to the aircraft and patted the propeller lovingly. 'Ironical ain't it. This is a British-built ship, but she's none the worse for that. We've put in extra gas tanks. They'll take up the weight where there'd have been a bomb load.'

'Here comes the Colonel,' said Edwin. He could see the battered Model T Ford slithering its way across the wet grass. The Colonel had paid daily visits for the last week. The DH 9 had been delivered in parts on two motor trucks. The air mechanics who had assembled it had now departed. They had done their work well without knowing the real object of the flight.

The car stopped on the edge of the field. Colonel Flanagan stepped down leaving his driver sitting at the wheel. He was carrying a garment over his left arm.

'Where's O'Farrell?' asked Jim.

O'Farrell was a friend of Jim's, another pilot. It was he who had found them this aeroplane.

'He's in England – in Cornwall,' Flanagan was dismissive. 'This is the moment, gentlemen. How d'you feel?' The Colonel was a short stocky fellow who always seemed to have difficulty keeping still. Edwin sometimes wondered if the man was wholly sane.

'Now, Jim, put this vest on next to your skin. The dispatches are sewn inside.' He handed over the coat to O'Dwyer and with it a slip of paper. 'This is the address in Dublin. Memorise it and destroy the paper.'

'Say, Colonel, maybe I should eat it?'

'No just tear it up,' Flanagan replied sharply.

As Edwin had suspected, the Colonel did not have a sense of humour. O'Dwyer grunted as he slipped off his flying coat and then his jacket and shirt. He put on the waistcoat and hurriedly replaced his outer clothing. 'It'll be cold up there,' he remarked. 'We'll start up in twenty minutes. Maybe you can swing the prop for us Colonel.'

O'Dwyer had tested the controls and checked every inch of the aircraft before declaring himself satisfied. Then the Colonel had insisted they pose beside the machine while he took a photograph. The engineers had removed the circular gun mount in the rear cockpit, leaving it with a roomy but draughty feel. Edwin whispered another prayer, pulled the flying helmet over his head, and drew on the fleece-lined gloves. He handed Jim the paper with their first compass course. O'Dwyer had already shown him the speaking tube that was their only means of communication once the engine started.

'Ready Colonel?' O'Dwyer called from the front cockpit.

'Ready Jim – God bless Ireland.'

'And all of us.'

Edwin could hear the propeller rotate as the Colonel wound it by hand to prime the system.

'Contact,' called O'Dwyer as he pressed the ignition switch.

The Colonel swung down the propeller and the engine started first time. The sheer volume of noise even inside the helmet startled

Edwin. He felt the machine move, taxiing into the takeoff position.
O'Dwyer pulled the stick back to hold down the tail as he opened the
throttle wide. The noise was deafening and made worse by the
bumping and jolting as the aircraft sped across the field. Edwin could
see the rigging wires stressing and the wings flexing. Surely this
strange contraption would fall to pieces around them. Then came that
moment of magic. The jolting stopped, suddenly everything was
smooth. The engine was still on full power but its note had become
almost musical; they were flying. The cold wind was exhilarating.
Edwin watched in wonder as the ground disappeared beneath them.
He looked back to see the Colonel standing on the grass, arm raised in
farewell.

PART ONE

CHAPTER 1

SUSSEX, ENGLAND, MARCH 1994

Mike never saw what happened, but the sounds he heard stopped him in his tracks. Out of the darkness came a shout, a scuffle and a gasp of pain; then running footsteps making for the public footpath that skirted the edge of the boatyard.

So they were back again, once too often, but this time he was ready. He stepped into the shadow of the main shed. He wore dark clothing and the walls were painted with black bitumen. He stood tense, waiting. The runner was sprinting towards him. Mike could hear his short gasping breaths. Now he could see the figure clearly in the reflected light from the water. Just right: an easy rugby tackle from the left side. Three carefully timed steps and he launched himself catching the runner round the upper thighs. The quarry gave a frightened gasp and then a louder yelp as his face ground into the cinder path. Mike put his knee into the intruder's back and gripped the right arm in a lock. 'Who the hell are you?' he snapped.

'Mike, you got him?' The voice belonged to Peter Blair, Mike's business partner.

'It's the one who came out of the yard. Did you see what he was up to?'

'Not exactly, the bastard hit me on the head.'

'The hell he did. You OK?'

'I think so.'

Mike turned to their prisoner. 'You, up – let's see you.' The man climbed stiffly to his feet. Mike still held his arm in a lock while Peter shone the torch. Their captive was around thirty-five-years old with black shoulder length hair. He was a nondescript individual dressed in dark overalls and black trainer shoes. He was still breathing heavily and there were beads of sweat on his unshaven features. His dark eyes gleamed as they blinked in the beam of the torch. To Mike he some-how seemed an unlikely villain. But then these days who could tell?

'Who are you and what are you doing in our yard?' Mike spoke slowly and menacingly in his captive's ear. There was no reply.

'I saw what he was doing,' said Peter. 'Vandalizing a rudder with this.' He held up a cordless electric drill. 'Then he hit me on the head with it.'

11

'What've you got to say to that?' said Mike. He looked the man in the eye. There was neither fear nor truculence just a blank stare.

'All right, play it that way. You've been caught damaging property and you've assaulted my colleague. I'm within my rights making a citizen's arrest. I intend to hold you until the police arrive.' The face remained wooden.

'Pete, you got the key to the paint store?'

'Yes.'

'Good, he can cool off in there while we fetch the law.'

When Mike had started his business at Cottons Hard in 1990, the footpath had seemed harmless enough. It skirted this lonely corner of the harbour and was popular with walkers in summer and bird watchers all year. Mike could understand that. From the very first he had fallen in love with this place. It had that stillness when the tide receded and left behind broad acres of mud-flats to delight the curlews and gulls. Then for a few hours the tide would surge up the main channel to reclaim a vast lake, visible, it was said, to astronauts circling the earth. It was now the end of March. Their yard was full of laid up boats and the path had become an open invitation to the lawless. This winter had seen eleven incidents of theft and not one of the intruders had been seen, let alone caught.

The police were prompt. In a little more than twenty minutes a patrol car arrived with two officers. Peter and Mike made brief statements in the yard office. Peter was still dabbing an eyelid with a none-too clean handkerchief.

'Suspect do that to you?' asked one of the PCs.

'Too right – hit me with this drill. I couldn't duck – never saw it coming.'

'That's just as well, sir. My superiors don't take kindly to citizen's arrests. Much better leave things to us.'

'Oh that's great!' Mike was angry again. 'It just so happens that we were here when you weren't. What's more, this place has been broken into enough times and your superiors have done bugger all.'

'I hear what you say, sir. This time I'd think you were just about within the rules. Now we'll take a look at this man, please.'

Mike led the way to the paint store. He unlocked the door and their prisoner stood blinking at them in the torchlight.

'He's not one of our regulars,' said the PC. 'Right, who are you and what are you up to?'

'I've nothing to say here – not in front of these people.' It was an educated voice but the tone was arrogant, almost commanding. The policemen were clearly irritated. The constable who had been doing the talking turned to Mike.

'We'll take this man to the station and charge him. I don't think we need scene of crime officers to crawl all over your place. Please could you both call round tomorrow morning and confirm your statements with the duty officer? By the way I didn't catch your names.'

'Peter Blair and I'm Michael Walters. Peter and I run this yard.'

They watched the police car bump its way up the unmade road until its lights vanished.

'Come on, Mike. Let's see what damage he's done.' Peter led the way through the yard and shone his torch on a squat shallow-draught sailing yacht.

'It was this one, the American boat. That's what really pisses me off. She's finished except for a coat of antifouling. Let's see what he's done.'

Mike watched as Peter played his torch, inch by inch, over the yacht's hull. Peter was a fully qualified yacht surveyor. Repairing and refurbishing small craft was his side of the business. He was a tall man of substantial bulk. As he prowled around the yacht he reminded Mike of an ungainly bear.

'Nothing to worry about on the hull, thank goodness. Let's check the rudder. That's where I caught him drilling.'

The rudder was a broad wooden blade hung over the stern in traditional fashion and hinged to the keel.

'Bloody hell – look at that!' The rudder was perforated with a dozen quarter-inch holes. 'Why do that?' He sighed and began a closer inspection. 'Doesn't look too bad, but I'll have to unship the whole thing and take it into the workshop. Could be worse. I think all it needs are some plugs and a repaint.'

'How long will it take?'

'Couple of days.'

'OK, I'll ring the owner in the morning.'

'Who did you say this one belongs to? Some woman wasn't it?'

'Clare O'Dwyer – she's Irish, lives in Cork. What's more, I'm contracted to deliver this boat by sea. So you check everything. No keel bolts sawn through or loose chain plates.'

'You're letting your imagination run away with you. That guy was a vandal, pure and simple.'

'Possibly, but he didn't strike me that way.'

Peter went home leaving Mike to lock up once more. Peter lived in Chichester with his wife and three children dependent on the uncertain profits of the yard. Mike lived on the site, in an apartment built from an old barn. It lay adjacent to the farmhouse that shared the same entry road as the yard. As he opened the front door the familiar feelings of desolation enveloped him. It was six weeks since Annabel had moved out. The apartment in spite of his best intentions was untidy. He dragged the Hoover from its cubbyhole and began to dab listlessly at the carpets.

Annabel was beautiful. Annabel was stylish. Annabel was sensual. She had skills in bed that took their love making into realms that Mike could scarcely have dreamed of. He sighed miserably. Yes Annabel and her Daddy. Daddy was rich. He maintained a Maxi class racing yacht. It had been two years ago at Cowes Regatta that Mike had been recruited as an extra crewmember. After the racing he had been invited to a fashionable ball in one of the higher-class yacht clubs. Annabel had been there. She was dark-haired and lustrous; her tanned skin glowing against the line of her lowcut dress. Mike had liked to think that he had won the power play for Annabel. In retrospect he knew this was naïve. He had been coolly selected, cut out from the crowd – entranced and seduced.

Annabel's Mummy and Daddy had been polite but distant. To describe Daddy as an estate agent would be rather like describing Buckingham Palace as an elegant town house. Daddy's company bore his own name. It was not a name one would see on suburban billboards. Daddy handled country estates and top industrial sites. His name could be seen in the pages of Country Life, and the business sections of broadsheet newspapers. He had made it transparently clear that a no-hope boat builder was not his choice for a son-in-law. That apart, there was Mike's ambivalent background. He was that socially rootless individual, the working-class public schoolboy. In the stratified caste system of Southern England his face did not quite fit in any group or social situation.

It was not that Annabel disliked sailing. On a sunny day in the Mediterranean she could helm a yacht competently enough, and she was a fair navigator. But her notion of the sea was still, designer clothes, or sunning herself on deck in her bikini. Life at Cottons Hard Yacht Services was often dirty and disagreeable; the long hours had a poor financial reward. This second winter Annabel had had enough. She told Mike that Daddy had issued an ultimatum. He had most generously offered to train Mike in estate agency prior to giving him a post in the firm's Chichester office. Having accepted these terms Mike would be expected to marry Annabel within three months. His reply had been two unprintable words. There had been a blazing row, their first and only full-scale fight. The next day a tearful Annabel had summoned two taxis to carry herself and her nine suitcases. For Mike the ultimate humiliation had come four days later. He had received a letter from some smart solicitor warning him that any attempt to contact Annabel could lead to an action for harassment. He threw the letter on the fire. He had no intention of ever seeing Annabel again; the relationship was over.

It was bitterly cold outside and he turned up the heating a couple of notches. He was going to need a good few contracts in this coming spring just to pay the expenses of this place. For the hundredth time he wondered what he was doing with this rundown boatyard at the height of a recession. Most of his contemporaries had secure desk jobs and happy families. He had gambled everything to follow his dream. That included giving up a university place to take a job in a grubby design office. There had followed five years sailing around the world as a yacht crewman. Finally he had invested every penny he had in this crazy venture. Spontaneously Mike walked across the room and stared at his face in the mirror. It had been Annabel's mirror, one of the last reminders of her presence. His short-cropped hair was almost bleached white by sun and wind. His features were equally weathered. He was just twenty-eight years old, but the face that looked back at him could be that of a forty-year-old ageing failure.

A light was flashing on the answerphone, an extension of the one at the office. He pressed the play button and waited.

'This is Clare O'Dwyer. I'm inquiring about my yacht. Would you ring me please? The time is seven-thirty.'

Mike looked at the machine with distaste; he had an inbred dislike of bossy women. It was an abrupt message but at least the voice was attractive. Well he had news for Miss O'Dwyer, so the sooner the better. He rang the number.

'Yes?' The voice was curt – nervous perhaps?

'I'm Michael Walters from Cottons Hard. You asked me to ring.'

'Of course, I'm sorry, I thought you were someone else.' She sounded relieved.

'That's all right, Miss O'Dwyer. I was going to get in touch with you anyway. I'm afraid we've had a break in at the yard tonight and there's been some damage done to your boat. Nothing serious, but it'll set us back a day or so….hello!' Mike paused; the other end had gone very quiet.

'No, please go on, Mr Walters.'

'We'll make a full estimate for your insurance in the morning.'

'Yes you do that. What happened exactly?'

'We caught a man tampering with a rudder.'

'Do you know who he was?'

'No, but we caught him. He's in police cells at the moment.'

'Mr Walters, I want you to do something for me.'

'Yes.'

'I want you to hire a security company – the best around. Put a watch on my boat round the clock.'

'It'll cost you a fortune.'

'Don't worry. I'm paying. I'll transfer two thousand pounds sterling to your account tomorrow as a deposit. Spend what you need but I want my boat secure.'

'Understood, Miss O'Dwyer. If you say so.'

'I do say so – and, Mr Walters?'

'Yes.'

'You were recommended to me as a thorough-going professional and the man also said you were as honest as the day is long. So you can call me Clare.'

'I'll be happy to – and I'm Michael.' There was not much else he could say.

'Good, Michael. I guess we'll be working together for a while. Don't worry, there's nothing wrong with the boat, no drugs aboard,' she laughed softly. 'So you sleep easy. I'll be coming over in a day or so and we'll talk then.'

For ten minutes Mike sat bemused. This odd conversation, added to the events of the last hour, had unsettled him. On the spur of the moment he pulled on his fleece jacket and slipped out into the cold night. The tide had ebbed. The moonlight shone on the mudflats and the little trickle of water that marked the centre of the channel. The night was still, not a breath of wind. It was cold now and his hot breath floated in the air. He could hear happy voices from the direction of the village pub and the rumble of traffic from the motor-way three miles distant. The O'Dwyer yacht stood shored up close to the main slip with the yard's mobile crane towering above her. She had arrived from the United States the previous October as deck cargo on a freighter. An agent had approached them with a lucrative repair contract, and the yacht had been trucked in from Southampton. She'd been in a pitiful state of neglect but they had rolled her into the building shed and Peter had spent the best part of the winter replacing rotten timbers and rebuilding the cabin joinery. Now she was back in the open air her new paint gleaming. She was a sturdy traditional wooden sailing cruiser, just thirty feet in overall length. A modest craft, he thought, to need a security guard more appropriate to an America's Cupper. Strange too that she seemed to have no name. There had been faint traces of one when she had arrived but nobody could read it. He'd better ask this Clare what she wanted written there.

Once more he puzzled over this Irish client. She had always been something of a mystery. Tonight was only the second time he had spoken to her. She had never visited the yard. Her dealings had come via a string of emails and faxes. He'd had eighteen of these, enough to see that the lady had a good working knowledge of yacht construction. He had a mental image of a no-nonsense fifty-year-old professional woman: lawyer perhaps, or head teacher? She had a delightful voice: Irish, soft and lilting, with crystal clear diction. That night as Mike slept uneasily it was that hypnotic voice on the telephone that invaded his dreams.

CHAPTER 2

The next morning Mike telephoned the Portsmouth branch of a national security firm and a representative had arrived within the hour. Mike, more accustomed to the casual attitude of his own trade, was impressed. The security man suggested a daytime guard working in shifts. At night there would be a watchman with a dog. If Mike wished, the firm would install a floodlight system on the yard that day.

In the office Mike's answerphone was winking at him again.

The voice was young female, with a Sloane debutante intonation. 'I'm calling on behalf of Dawson, Watts and Partners. We are a London legal practice. Our junior partner, Sir Charles Venner-Harris would like to call on you around three o'clock this afternoon. We are acting on behalf of clients and we have information that could be to your advantage. Please ring and confirm. Our number is…'

Mike frowned. What the hell would this high-class lawyer want with him? Cottons Hard customers were mostly strapped for cash. They owned pocket cruisers and small racers. This wasn't the Hamble or Cowes. Then there was that name, Venner-Harris. By coincidence Peter and he had known someone with that surname fifteen years ago and the memory left a bad taste. He rang the number and confirmed the appointment.

'Thank you, Mr Walters,' the secretary's voice would have cut glass. 'I must ask you to be available on the hour agreed – Sir Charles is a very busy man.'

'So am I!' Mike snarled into the phone and hung up. The call had disturbed him; awoken old insecurities that he thought he had buried. He walked down the yard to find Peter.

It was ten o'clock, time they visited the police. Mike removed the toolboxes from the passenger seat of his ageing Vauxhall Cavalier and Peter eased in his sixteen stone bulk. Mike told him about the phone call.

'Is it the same V-H?' Peter asked.

'Can't be – you have to achieve something useful to earn a K. Our Venner-Harris wouldn't qualify in a hundred years. He's too young anyway.'

Peter laughed. 'You know what day this is?'

'Friday.'

'More than that, it's April the first.'

'Hey, d'you think that call was a wind-up?'

'I don't know,' said Peter. 'Would your rugby club mates try that?'

Mike laughed. 'It wouldn't surprise me, but no – that call was genuine, I'm certain.'

The police station was a dour, subdued place. It smelt of floor polish and paper files. Long, echoing corridors led out from the reception area.

'We've come to make statements about the break-in at our boatyard,' said Peter.

The desk constable looked blank. 'Did you report this, sir?'

'I think we're at cross purposes,' said Mike. 'The intruder was caught last night. Two of your people arrested him and brought him here.'

'Are you sure? I don't think we're holding anyone at the moment. Hang on I'll check.' The PC vanished through a door behind the desk. Mike whistled irritably and looked at the wall posters. The cold wind that blew outside the building had somehow filtered inside. The PC returned with a sergeant who pointed them to a side room. He was a little man with a thin face and slicked-down black hair.

'Sit down,' he said. 'I understand you're the people from Cottons Hard.'

'That's right,' said Peter.

The sergeant stared at them unsmiling. 'You two have been making waves with this incident.'

'Why?' asked Mike. There was something about this man's attitude that made him uneasy. 'It was a clear act of vandalism. We caught him red-handed. What's more he assaulted Peter here.' Mike pointed at the plaster on his friend's face.

'Your word against his,' said the policeman coldly.

'Oh come on,' implored Peter. 'He hit me on the head with an electric drill. I never even saw it coming.'

'So you say. But you've no proof, and don't interrupt please. It seems Mr Walters manhandled this fellow and locked him in a room with toxic materials.' The policeman's attitude was hard and un-friendly. Both Mike and Peter were momentarily speechless; neither had expected this.

'Now listen,' the sergeant leant forward. 'You two are both well-known and respected local business people. We've taken that into account, and because of it, we're taking no further action. But you could, should perhaps, be facing serious charges. So take it you've been warned.'

'Bullshit!' Mike snapped. 'He was trespassing. We caught him. He's done two hundred quid's worth of damage to one boat alone and we haven't had time to check all the others yet. Never mind what we did, are you going to charge the man?'

'He was released without charge last night.'

'What the hell?' Mike was standing up glowering.

'Mike, sit down – cool it!' Peter tugged at his arm and pulled him back down onto the chair. He turned to face the policeman again. 'We've had a dozen break-in's at our yard in the last seven months. At some other yards it's been worse. Not one of those thieves has been caught, not one single one, until last night. And then...you... you...let him go. What are you here for God's sake? Whose side are you on?'

'We have our procedures. As I say we've been lenient with you this time,' the sergeant replied.

Mike stayed outwardly calm as he fixed the sergeant with an icy stare. 'First thing,' he stated. 'I'm going to report this to the local newspapers. Secondly, I'm going to call a meeting of all the water-front businesses where I shall propose a vote of no confidence in the divisional police...'

Peter intervened. 'I endorse that, but first I demand to speak to your superior officer.'

'I'm afraid he's in a meeting.'

'And how long will he be in this meeting?'

'I really couldn't say.'

'Very well. You can inform him, as soon as his meeting is over, that I intend to trace last night's intruder and bring an action for assault and criminal damage.'

'I wouldn't advise that, sir,' the sergeant's brow furrowed. This time he looked worried.

'To hell with your advice,' growled Mike. 'I want to talk to the two officers who brought that guy here. Where can I find them?'

'I really couldn't say, sir.'

'Come on, Peter. We'll handle this our way.' Mike stood up and stormed out of the room through the front door and into the street. Still fuming, he set off at a cracking pace, tight-lipped, and seemingly oblivious to where he was going. Peter had to half run to keep up.

'Mike, slow down! Come on – cool it – you're not doing any good like this.'

'Bastards!' Mike shouted angrily. He was conscious of startled passers by gaping at him.

'Come on, in here and we'll talk.' Peter led the way into a coffee shop and sat down at an empty table. Mike followed breathing heavily.

'Now,' said Peter. 'Let's have a think.'

'Sorry,' Mike sighed with a wry grin. 'That copper riled me – can't do his job so he blames us.'

'Look,' Peter stared back. 'You were dead set to have a brawl in that police station and get us into real trouble. That copper knew a lot more than he was telling us. He was stone-walling – it stood out a mile.'

'How so?'

'I don't believe for one moment they wanted to let that bloke go free. No, something happened.' Peter paused while the waitress delivered their coffee. 'Drink this, count to fifty, and then listen to me.'

'Go on,' Mike grinned; he'd learnt to respect Peter's intuition on occasions like this.

'OK, first, I've changed my mind about one thing. Remember you said that guy wasn't an ordinary vandal? I didn't agree with you, but I've done some thinking since.'

'I thought he was a cocky sod considering the circumstances.'

'Agreed, but think about it. All the other break-in's we've had to date have been thefts. The police told us it was kids, artful dodgers, and the stuff was passed straight on to receivers. None of them hung around to do damage just for the hell of it.'

'So who was that bloke?'

'I don't know, but I intend to find out. I meant it when I said I'd sue him. Don't you think it was odd the way that copper reacted when I told him so?'

Mike laughed. 'I wouldn't advise that, sir,' he mimicked.

'Yes,' said Peter. 'And he meant it. For some reason I had him rattled. Could our thief be a bent copper?'

Both of them felt better as they drove out of town. The sun was shining and early spring flowers were blooming in suburban gardens. The tide was flooding into the harbour, filling the main channels and lapping into the creek below the yard.

High water was at six o'clock so there would be enough depth to start launching yachts at four. The keelboat racing fleets would be starting their summer season on Sunday and all twelve of Cottons Hard boats must be ready. With each yacht worth twenty thousand or more pounds it was work requiring the utmost precision. Soon they lost all track of time until Mike saw Leanne coming towards them with mincing steps, as she avoided the puddles left by the overnight rain. She wore a mini-skirt over lurid purple leggings. Leanne was the yard's, nineteen-year-old self-styled secretary, although Mike secretly rated her as a dumb bimbo. Leanne was a member of the adjacent sailing club. At weekends she crewed her boyfriend's Fireball dinghy and for that reason alone she was an asset to the business. As Mike admitted, she could talk to a customer on the telephone, knew port from starboard and what a sheet was. However in the last few weeks she had been making him feel uneasy. She would fuss around him in the office worrying about his comfort and fetching him unnecessary cups of tea. Increasingly he had caught her staring at him with melting doe-like eyes. Peter had made ribald comments, but Mike did not find the situation funny. He was not inclined to make space in his bed for immature teenagers. Apart from that, Leanne's family was Polish and Catholic. They had encouraged the girl to take this job because they felt she would be morally safer than in a big company.

'Bloke in the office,' she said. 'Says he's got an appointment – right snotty git.'

'OK, tell him we're coming.' Mike looked at his watch: it read three twenty five. It was now that he remembered that irritating phone call. This supposed titled lawyer who had, "something to your advantage". It was fast turning into one of those days.

He and Peter walked back to the buildings. In front of the office was a Range Rover with the current year's registration. On the passenger's seat was a folded Barbour jacket and a copy of The Financial Times. The yard office was a spartan place with the usual office furniture and some stack-up plastic chairs for visitors. On the edge of one of these perched a large man, with an expression of distaste on his florid face.

'Oh I don't believe this!' said Peter. 'Look who's here.'

The visitor had risen to his feet and was staring open mouthed. 'God, Peter Blair and 'Oiky' Walters, still playing boats.'

'Hello Chazz,' said Peter. He carefully wiped his hand on the seat of his overalls and extended it. 'What are you doing here you old snob?'

The newcomer limply took the proffered hand. 'A professional visit, I really had no idea.'

Mike stared. He had had enough shocks in the last twenty-four hours, but this one had rendered him speechless. Mike had sprung from honourable but humble roots. His late father had been a foreman in the railway works at Eastleigh and his mother was still a primary school teacher. At thirteen Mike had won a scholarship to Westborough, a minor public school. There he had met Peter and made many other friends, but if there was one Westbrovian he might have hoped never to meet again it was Charles Venner-Harris. Chazz, as he was known, had never quite fitted in at Westborough. It had been rumoured that V-H had failed the entrance exam for Eton so catastrophically that even his noble connections could not work him a passage there. Westborough was a friendly unpretentious place. Most of its pupils came from middle-income families who had made dire sacrifices to pay the school fees. Such people Venner-Harris held in lofty contempt. His family had lands in Ireland and an estate in Cheshire, or maybe Cheshire was in the Venner-Harris estate. Mike never really knew nor cared. After a few weeks even Westborough's easy tolerance had snapped and Chazz was thrown in the lake. In the intervening years the man had hardly changed. Broad shoulders, and round faced, with a shock of untidy blond hair, he always projected a sense of awkwardness at odds with the aristocratic poise.

'I was told to expect a Sir Charles,' said Mike.

'I am Sir Charles Venner-Harris,' said Chazz. He slapped a business card on the table. Mike picked it up.

DAWSON WATTS & PARTNERS
SIR CHARLES VENNER-HARRIS Bt.

'My uncle died, and the baronetcy passed to me. It's an ancient title attached to our lands...'

'I know, in bloody Cheshire,' said Mike wearily.

Charles gave him a withering glance. 'No, from our Irish lands as it happens. I'm sure Blair will appreciate what I'm saying. His father is at least a gentleman. I wouldn't expect you to understand, Oiky.'

Mike grinned. There had been no venom in these exchanges; they'd been a remembered ritual. Grown men had let slip time until they were seventeen-year-olds again. 'Right,' he said. 'Business. What brings you down among us hoi-polloi, Chaz? Your office said you had a proposition?'

'Yes,' replied Charles. 'We have clients who wish to purchase a

23

yacht, a rather special yacht. We're informed that you have it here in this er…place.'

'Yachts are she, never it,' said Peter. 'And this place is a boatyard. For heaven's sake, Chazz, have you never done any real sailing?'

'I'm a member of the Royal Thames…'

'That's not an answer to my question,' broke in Peter. 'Which yacht had you in mind? We've over sixty laid up here.'

'It's…er…she's called, the *Mary Elizabeth Chester*.'

'Crikey, what a mouthful. Sorry, never heard of her. What about you Mike?'

'I couldn't say. If she's here, she's not under that name. Sounds a bit Yankee.'

'The yacht is American,' said Charles. 'Our information is she was shipped over from the United States and that you have her here.'

'Oh, I don't believe this,' groaned Mike. 'That bloody boat is becoming a jinx.'

'Ah, so you do have her here.'

'There's only one that's been shipped over from the States,' Mike explained. 'She's got no name painted on her, but she belongs to an Irish woman. I'm due to deliver her, the boat that is, at the end of the month.'

'Miss O'Dwyer of Crosshaven. That would coincide with the information furnished by our clients.'

'Yes, that's the woman who hired us to rebuild the yacht. But Chazz, shouldn't you deal with her direct? It's nothing to do with us. We're only doing the work – we can't sell the boat.'

'I think I'd better explain my brief,' said Charles. *'The Mary Elizabeth Chester* was the property of the late Senator James O'Dwyer. It was designed by the Senator and he did much of the construction with his own hands. I understand she was named in honour of his late wife. Our clients are The Irish-American Cultural Society. They wish the yacht to return to the United States as a memorial to the late Senator O'Dwyer.'

'Hang on a minute, Chazz,' Peter interrupted. 'Are you saying that this O'Dwyer woman isn't the legal owner? We've done around ten thousand pounds worth of work. If we don't get paid it could break us.'

'I can certainly reassure you on that point. Miss O'Dwyer is the Senator's granddaughter. There's no doubt about her ownership. She inherited a trust fund and bringing the yacht to Ireland was one of the pre-conditions. Having said that, once she's completed the conditions of the legacy there's no impediment to Miss O'Dwyer selling the yacht.'

'Once again, Chazz, old mate,' said Mike. 'I say you should be talking to her, not us; we can't sell the boat. Why tell us all this?'

Charles frowned. 'That's the point I'm coming to. Miss O'Dwyer has been approached several times but has refused all our offers. Our clients have recently raised their price to five hundred thousand American dollars...'

'What!' Mike was startled. 'Look Chazz, this *Mary Elizabeth* whatever is a nice conventional family cruiser. She's a lovely boat of her type, bit of a classic, but you say she's amateur built. Thirty grand, sterling, that's what she's worth, and that's maximum.'

'It's not a question of market value. The offer is a token of our client's esteem for Senator O'Dwyer...' Charles raised his hand. 'Please let me continue. I've come to the point where you might assist, and, I might add, to your advantage.'

'How?' said Peter.

'Our proposal is this. Persuade Miss O'Dwyer to accept our client's most generous offer and a commission of four per cent of the purchase price will be paid to you.'

'Twelve thousand five hundred pounds,' said Peter, punching the buttons of a calculator. 'That's assuming one dollar sixty to the pound.'

Mike nodded. 'We could do with the money, but if your clients can't persuade the woman, what chance have we got?'

'Expertise, expertise,' Charles repeated. 'We thought perhaps if you could convince Miss O'Dwyer that the yacht is in some way faulty – un-seaworthy is your term I believe...'

'But she is seaworthy, I've already signed the certificate,' said Peter.

'But suppose, just suppose, you were to change your mind. If on reflection you were to discover something seriously wrong?'

'No chance. I'm a professional small ship surveyor. I've got ethics as well. What's more I'm surprised at you; all these years of preaching about officers and gentlemen and now you ask me to pull a mean stunt like that. Sorry, but no.'

'I see,' Charles nodded. 'But how about you, Walters? Such scruples shouldn't trouble one of your background.'

'If Peter says the boat's good, she's good, nothing changes that.'

'There's a lot of money at stake,' said Charles.

'Agreed, and I guess there's a lot more in it for you, eh?'

'I cannot reveal details of our fees but a successful resolution would benefit our practice.'

'OK, Chazz,' said Mike. 'We'll talk to the lady, but it'll be straight – no hanky panky. Anyway, she might decide she doesn't like the boat. As far as I know she's never seen it.'

'It…it,' Charles smirked. 'Blair says boats are always she. Caught you there, Oiky.'

They saw their visitor off the premises and watched the Range Rover bump its way up the narrow track, skirting the black watery morass of mud flats.

'Two-faced sod that,' said Peter. 'Why should we do his dirty work?'

In the office Leanne stood glaring at them. 'Is that creep coming here often?'

'Not unless we're really unlucky,' replied Mike. 'Hey, what's the matter?'

'Cos he pinched my bum, that's why. And stop laughing – it's not funny.'

By eight o'clock they had launched all the remaining racing yachts. It had been a close thing against a falling tide, but they had made it with ten minutes to spare. Back home Mike had showered, put on a change of clothes and pushed an instant meal into the microwave. He had that relaxed, smug feeling of a job well done. Almost he forgot the frustrating meeting in the police station. He sat down in his armchair and broached a can of beer. It was warmer tonight, the wind had shifted into the west and he could hear it moaning in the leafless trees behind the farm. He turned the television on to catch the ten o'clock news. Then the doorbell rang.

For twenty seconds it rang joined by a frantic knocking and a continuous high pitched scream. Mike ran to the entrance hall and pulled open the front door. A bedraggled form fell inwards and crumpled on the carpet. It was Leanne.

CHAPTER 3

Leanne was shaking and sobbing as she crawled through the doorway. She had obviously been in the water and her body was covered in mud and slime. Her long blonde hair hung in her eyes and her shoes were missing.

'Leanne, for God's sake! What happened?' He was appalled by her condition.

'Men,' she gasped. 'Two men, I couldn't stop them.' She began to cry again with her breathing in deep gasps. 'I couldn't get away. The one in the back had a knife. Then I crashed the car. I went over the wall into the creek.' She convulsed with a fresh bout of shivering.

'All right, love. All right, it's over, you're safe now, come on, stand up.' He tried to be calm and rational. He leaned down, grasped the girl by her arms and lifted her to her feet. 'Come on over here and sit down.'

'Oh, I can't, I'm all filthy. I'll spoil your chairs.' For a moment the voice had returned to something like normal.

Mike steered her into the kitchen where she sank gratefully onto a stool with her head on the table. He poured some milk into a saucepan on the stove and stirred in a spoonful of sugar and a slug of brandy. He heated the mixture, poured it into a mug, and gave it into her folded arms. 'Drink it,' he ordered.

She sipped the drink cautiously, and then finding it was good, downed it in three gulps. Tears still streamed down her face, but she was quieter.

'Take it easy, love. Tell me in your own time. Two men you said. Did they hurt you?' He looked anxiously at her. All her clothing was in place except her missing shoes. Hopefully the car crash had happened before the bastards could molest her.

'They were waiting behind a hedge when I got home. They jumped into the car. The one in the back had a knife.' She was trembling again. 'Then the other one told me to drive here.'

Mike stood up and paced the floor fists clenched. He was possessed by rage. Like everyone, he'd read about such people, but incidents had always seemed remote. One read about these things, but they happened elsewhere. The victims were other people's wives and daughters. Now it was happening here, to him, to one of his people and it called for vengeance. He strode into the sitting room and rang the mobile number of Benny, the yard's new night guard. Mike had met him for the first time that day. The man was an ex-marine and a Falklands War veteran.

'Benny here,' the man answered.

'It's Michael Walters. Benny we've intruders.'

'Yes Mr Walters. My dog's got wind of something. I was just about to ring you myself.'

'Benny, it's worse than that. You know Leanne from the office? She's been molested by two men – I reckon they're still around.'

'I thought I heard a car a while back, near your place.'

'That was Leanne's. It went over the edge into the creek, she says. She escaped from them but she's in one hell of a state. Listen, that Rottweiler of yours. What's his form, would he do damage?'

'Only if I tell'm to.'

'All right, I'll take responsibility, but I want to give those bastards some retribution before we hand them to the law.'

'I get the message. I'll work round the footpath and you come down the road from the house. That way there's no place for 'em to go unless they swim. By the way, you got a mobile phone?'

'Yes.'

'Take it, ring me and we'll stay on open line.'

Mike replaced the phone. Leanne was watching him from the door. 'I don't want you to go,' she said thickly.

'Lock yourself in the kitchen. I'll lock the front door. Don't move from here until I'm back.' He rummaged in his desk for his mobile phone, then pulling a balaclava over his head he let himself out into the night.

He rang the watchman's number. Benny answered at once. 'Mr Walters? I hope you don't mind but I've rung the law and they're on their way. Had to do that – company rules.'

'OK Benny. Can you see anything?'

'No, but Target, my dog; he's still upset about something. My suggestion is that you come down the road quiet as you can, 'til you're in sight of the yard, then you stop, take cover and wait. There's someone out there for certain and we'll see 'em if they move.'

'Right, I'll do that – keep listening.' Mike dropped the mobile into his pocket and began to move down the edge of the road towards the yard.

On his left was a fringe of thorn bushes skirting the fields. On his right the road ran along the old sea wall with a drop of two or three feet to the water below. The tide was ebbing again. He could hear the song of the marshes: that musical sighing and gurgling as the water ran out of hundreds of folds and runnels back into the main channel. He could see the entrance to the yard and he was almost within range of the new security lights. For twenty minutes he stood still listening, eyes straining across the mudflats to the line of the shore beyond.

'Peter…Peter! Is that you?' The voice was so close it seemed to spring from the ground itself. Mike stiffened in shock. 'No it's me…' he said cutting himself off in mid sentence. Of all the bloody idiots, he'd answered instinctively and now he'd blown it.

He could see the man now. Seemingly he'd risen from the water. He must have been crouching below the creek wall. Now he was standing upright looking wildly about. Mike put his head down and charged. But this was not going to be a repeat of last night. Mike's quarry saw him, dodged, and sprinted away up the track. It seemed he was a fit man for Mike found himself struggling to keep up. He gritted his teeth for one last effort when something bowled him over from behind. He hit the rough stone track and lay there half winded. Whoever or whatever had felled him bounded away in the dark. There were two gunshots, then silence. Mike pushed himself against the hard surface. This was a new experience and he was genuinely scared. Somewhere out there in the night was a man with a gun.

'Mr Walters, are you all right?' It was Benny, but the watchman sounded tinny and disembodied. 'Mr Walters, are you all right?' It was the telephone still switched on lying a few inches from his head.

'Yes, Benny, I'm OK. Someone's shooting and something knocked me over.'

'That was Target. You were in his way. The man you were after, he lit off across the fields. I'm worried about my dog. I reckon it was Target he took a shot at.'

'Is the coast clear? I'm lying on the ground here.'

'Yes I can see you. You can get up now. I'll be with you in a minute.'

Mike scrambled to his feet. He could see the corpulent figure of Benny striding along the road from the yard. He could hear cars coming down the track and soon he could see headlamps and flashing blue lights.

'Here's the force, and about time,' said Benny as he came up to him.

There were two police cars. Benny ran to the first and held an animated conversation with the occupants. Two men climbed out and followed by Benny began to run across the field towards the main road. Seconds later the other car pulled up beside Mike.

'You from the boatyard?' asked the driver.

'Yes, I'm Michael Walters. There's someone around here with a gun.'

'We've got the situation in hand. You'd better go back indoors.'

'I've got a girl in there who's been assaulted.'

'We understand that sir. We'll deal with it in good time. You go inside and keep the lady safe. We'll speak to you when this incident's over.'

Mike shrugged and walked back up the track to the farm. He looked at his watch and was startled to find that he had been out here for over an hour and a half. Concerned for Leanne he ran the remaining yards. He called out softly as he put the key in the door. To his surprise Leanne was not in the kitchen. She was on the settee, her bare lugs tucked under her, apparently bathed and rejuvenated, and wrapped in his spare bathrobe. A strong aroma of alcohol pervaded the room, and on the table beside her a stood tumbler and a newly opened bottle of whisky.

'I'm better now – wanted a drink,' she slurred.

'That's all right, you've had a bad shock.'

'What happened? You were a long time.'

'Everything's fine, the police are out in force – you're safe now.'

'Have they caught them?' Her small voice had a tremor.

'Not yet, but they will.' He sought to sound reassuring.

Leanne was trembling again. Her apparent calm was disintegrating. Mike sat beside her and she clung to him weeping, her face twisted and anguished. 'They made me drive the car. I was to take them to the yard. Then I was to talk my way past the guard. They said if I tried to warn him they'd cut my throat.' Her words were little more than a whisper. 'The man in the back had a knife. He scared me and he spoke funny – he was evil.' She paused and downed the rest of the glass. Mike quickly retrieved the bottle and shut it in the cupboard. At least a quarter of the contents had gone.

'You need some rest,' he said.

Leanne scarcely heard him. 'He scared me. I couldn't think what to do, so I turned the wheel and went over the edge into the creek.'

'On purpose?' Mike was startled.

She nodded. 'It was the only thing I could do. I just wanted him to drop the knife.'

'That's why you were soaking wet?'

'I had to swim. The car fell over and the water came in, but the window was open and I swam out.'

'Christ girl, you must have a cool head.' Mike stared at her with a newfound respect.

'It was a bit like capsizing. You keep your eyes open and swim clear. I've done it before.'

The doorbell rang and Leanne gave a frightened gasp. Mike picked up the poker from the fireplace. 'Who is it?'

'Police, Mr Walters. We'd like a word.'

He opened the door to find the police constable who had spoken to him from the car. 'We've tracked one of them to the head of the creek but he's gone in the water and our dog's lost the scent. What's more there's a bloody great Rottweiler rampaging around. Your security man's trying to catch it. We think the thing's got a flesh wound and it's gone crazy.'

'What can I do?'

'Stay put. Don't go out. Keep the door locked. The intruders could be anywhere.'

'What about Leanne, she's the girl they tried to kidnap?'

'She'll have to make a statement before she can go home. Where does she live?'

'Her parents live in Midhurst but she's got a bedsit in the town here.'

'May I speak to her?'

'Of course – through here.'

Leanne was still sitting on the sofa. The room stank of alcohol although the policeman seemed not to notice.

'Look, Miss,' he said, 'We're doing our best to catch these men. We're arranging for a woman PC to talk to you as soon as the emergency's over. Do you want to sit in our car or are you happy to stay here?'

'I want to stay here.'

'Are you certain about that?'

'I don't want to go to my flat. That's where they found me.'

Mike went to the door with the PC. 'Look,' said the copper. 'I didn't want to say too much in there, but until the emergency's over the woman will have to stay with you. You understand I don't like leaving her here...'

'She'll be safe. She works for me and I've known her family for years.' Mike was annoyed at the man's implication.

'Very well, it seems she trusts you. We'll send a WPC over as soon as we can, although...' he looked at his watch, 'Christ, it's nearly one am. It may be daylight before she's here.'

The policeman disappeared into the night and Mike locked the door. He turned to find Leanne watching him while clinging unsteadily to a table.

'Did you hear that,' he said. 'You'll have to stay here. Bedroom's upstairs. You can use it tonight. I'll kip on the couch here and keep watch.'

'You must be ever so lonely now Annabel's gone,' she said.

'I'll survive.'

Leanne walked to the foot of the stairs. Slowly she untied the bathrobe and let it fall gently to the floor. For ten seconds she stood facing him naked. He could see how shapely she was. Her small neat breasts, the little shock of blonde pubic hair and the faint line of last year's bikini tan on her firm trim figure. Despite all Mike's good intentions he was almost lost; overwhelmed by raw hot lust. He hadn't had a woman for weeks, over two months in fact. In the tension of their last days together Annabel and he had ceased physical contact.

'You can sleep up there with me,' Leanne said quietly. 'I'd like that.'

Mike slowly asserted his willpower. Recovering his poise he took a deep breath and smiled tactfully. 'You've had a bad shock; you need sleep. You did brilliantly tonight and I shan't forget it.'

'Spoilsport,' she smiled.

He watched her, still naked, walk unsteadily up the stairs and heard the bedroom door shut. He went to the sitting room and poured himself a drink. It had been a long day.

Mike and Peter stood on the sea wall gazing into the murky waters of the Swatch, a creekside pool that remained partially full even when the tide had retreated. It was the following afternoon and the water had ebbed to the point where Leanne's battered Fiesta car was visible again. Above them drummed the yard's mobile crane, with Kevin the yard hand in the cab. Another ten minutes and they should be able to put a towline on. Watching, a short distance away stood the police forensic team. Both wore white overall suits. The one in charge was a talkative character with a permanent grin on his face that Mike considered uncalled for in the circumstances.

'Of all the places to go over the edge. She must be born lucky that one,' the man said.

Leanne had understandably been shocked and subdued that

morning. Mike had been relieved when a policewoman had called early. He had left them alone in the kitchen, and half an hour later a police car had arrived to take Leanne to her mother in Midhurst. The police had to admit that they'd lost all trace of the fugitives. The Rottweiler had been subdued with a tranquilliser dart. A bullet had carved through the skin of his neck and he was with a vet in town.

The water had fallen another foot. Mike and Peter donned waders, and carefully traversing the muddy water, shackled a tow chain to the front bracket of the car. The crane pulled the Fiesta back on land. The car, glistening with mud, bumped over the bank on its rear wheels.

'That'll do you,' Mike called to Kevin.

Once more the car stood on its four wheels on dry land. The police team moved forward and peered inside.

'Christ!' exclaimed the forensic officer; his grin had gone. 'There's a bloody body in the back.'

CHAPTER 4

A vanload of police arrived within twenty minutes and erected a screen around the Fiesta. More cars were arriving, all customers of the yard. Mike and Peter took turns to reassure them. Yes, there had been accident, but it was over now. There was nothing to worry about. This last sounded rather hollow as by now an ambulance was on the scene, its crew unloading a body bag. Mike managed a brief glance at the casualty. He had seen a drowned man once before; it had been seven years ago during his spell with a lifeboat crew. The body then had been that of a young fisherman, one of a family crew, all lost when their boat had foundered. The boy's face had stayed with Mike ever since, sometimes invading his more troubled dreams. He had unkempt curly blond hair and an odd enigmatic, almost sleeping expression. The sight had troubled Mike. Boats and the sea were his profession, his whole life. He loved the boats that he sailed and built, but he knew he could never love the sea; it was cold evil and treacherous.

This time he had felt no pity for the wet and slimy corpse that lay on the ground by the roadside. He felt nothing; neither hate nor disgust, only morbid curiosity. It was an unusual face: a shaven head, as bald as a baby with thick rather sensual lips. A full-face black balaclava had slipped off and lay by the side. It had only been a glimpse before Mike had been brusquely pushed away by the ambulance men.

At half past twelve Mike left them to it. He was due to play Rugby at two thirty and he needed to change. Back home he snatched a quick meal of scrambled eggs and a glucose drink. He had no enthusiasm for today's match, and Leanne's filthy togs still littered the bathroom. He drove the eight miles to the ground slowly. Other drivers sounded their horns impatiently behind him. Mike ignored them; he was lost in thought. There seemed to be some fate at work. His secure world was collapsing around him. Annabel's angry departure was only the beginning. He had done nothing to deserve any of this. Sailors are superstitious by nature, Mike would never admit such a thing, but perhaps he was no different from ten thousand others. All his ill fortune had coincided with the arrival of the O'Dwyer boat. Could there really be such a thing as a jinx? Of one thing he was certain; the sooner he was shot of Miss O'Dwyer and her bloody boat the better. He arrived at the rugby ground in a strange mood. He didn't want to be there. For once in his life he shunned convivial company; he wished he could be alone.

Mike's team was depleted by injury and the lads had been arguing among themselves as to who should play out of their normal positions. Mike had snarled at them. As team captain he had bluntly dictated who played where and defied them to argue. The others were startled. Poor old Mike; girlfriend trouble they speculated.

The match was as dire as his worst expectations. Today's opponents were a team from Bognor Regis, so the game was by way of being a local derby. It ended with Mike's side going down 56–7. In the changing room Mike caught sight of the opposing side's scrum-half. The man was standing stark naked in front of a mirror drying his hair. His right ear lobe was missing. Coincidence or not, Mike had seen the same disfiguration two nights before. He walked straight up to him.

'Hi, are you a copper?'

'Yes,' he looked evasive. 'Yes, I am as it happens.'

'I thought so. You arrested a man causing criminal damage at Cottons Hard – two nights ago, remember?'

'Maybe,' the man replied warily. He was hardly at an advantage in his undressed state and Mike was clearly angry. 'I know, you're Michael Walters, and you're pissed off because our Superintendent let him go. But it wasn't my fault.'

'All right, get dressed, then have a beer on me and explain.'

The policeman reappeared fully dressed and Mike steered him to a corner of the bar. Yes, he was a police constable and his name was Garry. Mike sat him down and ordered two pints. The noise of the match post-mortem-cum-singsong was deafening.

'For God's sake don't repeat what I'm going to tell you,' said Garry. 'You see we were in a Catch-22 with that little jerk you caught.' He downed his pint in three bites and looked sorrowfully into the empty glass. Mike nodded to the barman. Garry grinned and cradled his refill.

'Well, we got the guy back to the station. Then he starts on about how he's not talking to anybody except the chief.' Garry repeated his three-gulp trick with a satisfied sigh.

'The prisoner wouldn't give us a name; then he tried to say he was a Customs man. That really made the chief mad. You see we hate those bastards; they're always in our way. The Super says, 'Right that's it – put him in the cells'. Then the little squirt says he's Security Service. You know MI5 or 6, or something of that ilk. Brings out an ID, says it gives him crown immunity. We put him in the cells anyway and the chief rings London. They order us to let him go – no choice.'

'Why would the Intelligence Services want to bore holes in an old sailing yacht?' Mike was baffled.

'God knows. Look we civilian police, we've a rulebook a mile long. If any of us puts a foot wrong in any way whatever, we get the media, the do-gooders, and a shower of bloody politicians all over our backs. But the spooks, they don't answer to anyone. They can do what the hell they like. They can break the law whenever they claim the national interest and nobody's got the right to question a thing they do. No, those sods are out of control, I'll tell you that for nothing.'

'Your sergeant said it was our fault. Told us he was thinking of charging us for assault.'

'That's Ray, he's a buck passer. I'd have been more subtle.'

Mike bought the man another drink and left it at that. He'd at least had an explanation. He left the gathering and drove home as soon as he decently could. He wanted to find Peter, and if the truth was told, he was rather pleased with himself. Almost he could see himself as a detective. Didn't Sherlock Holmes say that having eliminated every possibility what was left, however implausible must be the truth.

In the privacy of the yard office Mike told Peter what he'd learned. Peter was unimpressed. 'I saw the solicitor this morning. I don't care who that vandal was. We're going to trace him and throw the book at him. Solicitor says he'll start formal complaint proceedings against the police as well.'

'Have you heard any more from the police about last night? Who were those men, and have they identified the dead'un?'

Peter shook his head. 'They're playing it very close at the moment, but they've been back to see Leanne – I rang her mum.'

'How is the poor kid?'

'She's all right, relieved if anything. Apparently that man in the back seat was a nutter. He really scared her. She was convinced he'd kill her, that's why she drove the car over the wall.' Peter stood up and closed the window. It had been a fine spring day but nightfall was bringing a chill. 'Anyway,' he continued, 'it got him killed and good riddance I say.'

The phone rang. Mike leaned over and picked up the receiver.

'Cottons Hard Yacht Services.'

'Good evening Michael. It's Clare O'Dwyer. How are you and how's my boat?' It was the same lilting Irish voice. Mike wondered again who this enigmatic woman really was. Frankly he wished he'd never heard of her.

'Hello Miss… er, Clare. Your boat's fine. We've got the security men in place and they're doing a good job. Actually we had an incident last night: nothing to do with your boat as far as we know, but the system worked.'

'Good, I'm glad to hear it. Now I've some news for you. First, I'm coming over tomorrow on the ferry with my car. I'll stop near Swansea for the night and drive up to see you on Monday around midday.'

'Great, we look forward to meeting you and showing you your boat; we're almost ready to step the mast and launch her.'

'Good, I'll be looking forward to that too. Now, Michael – my other bit of news. I had an Englishman arrive on my doorstep this afternoon – says he's an old friend of yours.'

'Really?'

'Sure, calls himself, Sir Charles Venner-Harris. Do you know him?' She seemed to be stifling a giggle.

'Yes we know him from way back, but old friend is stretching it a bit.'

'I'm relieved to hear it,' she was laughing openly now. 'Holy Jesus, Michael; I thought Brits like him went out with World War One.'

'I think he's probably one of the last of the dinosaurs,' Mike grinned.

'Oh well it takes all sorts as they say. Now, Michael, I want my yacht's name painted on her stern – all right? You can choose your own design but I want the work done by a real sign writer – no tacky transfers.'

'Yes we can do that. What do you want us to write?'

'Her name's *Quadra*,' she spelt it out for him. 'And she's Royal Cork Yacht Club.'

'No problem, Clare. Weather permitting we'll have it done by the time you arrive.'

'That's good. I'll see you on Monday. Goodbye, Michael.'

Mike put the phone back and whistled. 'Well I never. Chazz must've been booked to fly to Ireland the moment he left us. He's bloody anxious about something, that's for sure.'

Peter changed the subject. 'Could you drive over and see Leanne tonight? Her mother said she'd been asking for you.'

Mike winced. 'Must I?'

Peter shot him a questioning glance. Inwardly Mike groaned. They had known each other since boyhood; there wasn't much he could hide from Peter. 'I'm sorry for the kid, but I'm worried about her. Pete, I'm serious, not boasting; it's not the time for it.'

'Did she make a pass at you?'

'Yes, last night, in spite of everything she'd been through. Mind you, when I got back to the flat she'd drunk herself nearly legless with my Scotch.'

'What happened?'

'Nothing, I swear to God. I told her how impressed I was with the way she'd handled things and told her to get a good night's sleep.'

'All right, I believe you, though most of your mates wouldn't.'

'Pete I'm not interested. She's not even twenty; and I'd feel a real shit if I had to face her family.'

'I know, but tread carefully with the kid, it's probably only a phase. Anyway, will you go and see her tonight?'

'Why not you?'

'There's no way I can drive to Midhurst tonight. I've got a parents evening at my youngest's school.'

Mike left the office and began to walk back to his house. He stopped to pass the time of day with the security guard. He was Benny's relief; a cheerful little man with a Midlands accent.

'There's a car over there, been parked up for the last hour.' The guard pointed to where the road branched off to the sailing club. 'D'you want me to take a look?'

'No I'll go,' said Mike. 'It's probably only walkers.'

The tide was ebbing again, building up speed as it raced towards the harbour entrance and the open sea. The Cottons Hard Sailing club was five hundred yards down its separate entry road. It was not a glamorous affair, consisting of two wooden cabins and an old barn that served as a gear store. Beside it was a level area with forty or so assorted racing dinghies and below by the water was the "hard", which gave the whole place its name. As he turned a corner in the track Mike had his first proper look at the car that the guard had reported. It was pulled over tight against the grass verge facing him. It was a new black Ford Mondeo with this year's registration. It wasn't abandoned since there appeared to be two people seated in the front; two people who dropped their heads the moment they saw him. Mike supposed they were probably guilty lovers, although this was still a rather public spot. Mike was twenty yards away when the car's engine started. What happened next was unexpected. The car drove at him. The driver changed gear, put his foot hard on the throttle and despite the rutted surface drove straight at Mike. As he leapt for safety he saw the front wheels turn and swerve away from him. Mike fell into a shallow ditch beside the track. He crawled out and stood up muddy and shocked, his right hand tingling from nettle stings. The Mondeo had vanished.

There was nothing to be done but walk home. It had been an odd incident to end a traumatic day. Mike could not understand it. He doubted if this crazy motorist had seriously meant to harm him, but he had certainly succeeded in scaring him. Probably it was just another example of loutish manners. He tried to remember the registration number, he thought he could recall letters, A and Y and two digits but the rest was gone.

The Micalczyk family: Stanislaus, Linda and Leanne, lived in an isolated period cottage among gorse and heath-land to the west of Midhurst. Mike liked them. Stan's father was an elderly Polish war veteran who still lived in Chichester. Like many second-generation immigrants Stan had studied hard and prospered. He had his own accountancy practice and it was he who audited the yard's books. The Micalczyk house stood in the middle of their own chaotic small-holding. It was their attempt to hold onto their heritage and their peasant roots. Mike parked his car, stepped out, and wished he had brought his rubber boots. The gravel in front of the cottage was muddy and the geese that surrounded him were aggressive.

It was Leanne who opened the front door. She showed not one hint of embarrassment; it was as if the naked incident the previous night had never happened. She was friendly and welcoming, and Mike had to admit, she looked entrancing; in black jeans, a cropped top, and barefoot. This casual attire suited her far more than the short skirts and lurid colours she wore to work.

Leanne's mother Linda had almost overwhelmed him. She was a large bubbly lady, a local girl, whom Stan had married when he started his business in the town. He had done his best to teach Linda Polish so the family could talk that language in private, especially when Leanne's grandfather was with them.

'We can never thank you enough for what you did last night,

Mike.' Stan shook him warmly by the hand. 'We owe you.'

Mike was embarrassed. It was almost as if they thought he had rescued Leanne. He wondered uneasily what story she had told them. They ushered him into their living room. There was a scent of wood smoke from the roaring log fire whose flames reflected on the white walls and wooden beams. Soft orchestral music filtered from the stereo system.

'That's Górecki, isn't it,' said Mike anxious to please.

Stan positively beamed. 'Of course, we've gone Polish tonight. Fancy you recognising that.'

'I'm a fan, I've got that recording at home.'

Mike declined a drink; he was driving and he didn't fancy some Polish fire water. Linda brought him a cup of coffee and a large slice of cake. Mike was ravenous; he hadn't eaten since midday.

'Come upstairs,' said Leanne. 'I want to talk.'

Mike sat on a tattered armchair while Leanne squatted cross-legged on the bed. It was a typical teenager's room, with pop posters, and a dressing table littered with, lipsticks, bottles and spray cans.

'The police have been here twice,' she said.

'I know.'

'It was difficult, talking to them – I sort of dried up.' She stared at the floor. She wasn't playing with him now, she was serious. Mike could only guess at her inner state of mind. 'I've been thinking about it all day. I can't help it. Anyway it keeps coming back; like a replay on the telly.'

'Talk to me,' he said gently. 'It'll maybe make things better.'

'I know; that's why I wanted to speak to you private.'

'Take your time. Start from the beginning.'

'Mike,' she looked at the floor. 'I don't think they were after me,' she stammered. 'You know, not rape or nuthin'.'

That was probably true; the girl's instinct would have told her. 'All right,' he said. 'What do you think they were after?'

'There's something in the yard. Something they were prepared to kill for and it's in a boat.'

'Did they say so?'

'I couldn't understand them at first. They spoke foreign. They told me I was to talk my way past Benny. I was to tell him I'd left something behind. Then I was to take them to a boat, but…but, they didn't say what boat.' Suddenly she was shaking and there were tears on her face.

Mike said nothing. He stood up, moved across, and took her hands in his. Slowly she responded and the tears dried.

'They spoke funny,' she said. 'Some of it was in some foreign language and I couldn't make it out, but it wasn't Polish or Russian or anything like that.'

'The one who got out of your car saw me in the dark and thought I was his friend – he called me Peter, it sounded like. He might have been Scottish but I'm not sure.'

Leanne shivered. 'I know the one in the back with the knife was Peter. That's what the other one called him when they weren't talking that funny lingo.' She lay back on the bed. 'What's it all about, Mike?'

'It's that bloody American boat again, that's my guess. The sooner we get that thing out of the yard the better. Have you told the police about this?'

'Not about the boat. I wanted to tell you first.'

'OK, I'll call in at the police station on my way home and tell them. I can check if they've caught the missing man.'

'They still hadn't when we spoke to them at five o'clock. I've got to stay here until they do.'

'We'll collect you for work when you feel ready and run you back afterwards. When all's safe we'll see about getting you another car.'

Leanne clapped her hands in delight. 'Thanks, Mike,' she smiled happily. Mike was impressed with her resilience. It would be a lucky young man who eventually made his life with her.

'I'd like to come back tomorrow if that's all right?' She tilted her head sideways and switched on her most seductive smile. Mike lifted her to her feet and quickly left the room. Leanne followed him humming happily to herself.

Mike said goodbye to the Micalczyk family and drove back down the sandy track to the road. The moonlight glinted on a car parked in the pinewood opposite – another black Mondeo? He turned right and headed south for Chichester. He was worried now, or was this some stupid paranoia? Could it be the same Mondeo he had seen hours earlier? Had it followed him? And why was it now parked within a hundred yards of the Micalczyk house? He wondered whether he should turn back. He knew the police had promised to keep an eye on Leanne, but the occupants of the earlier car had not behaved like normal police. As he rounded the next bend Mike switched off his lights and coasted into a layby. A car was coming from the Midhurst direction. As it passed, Mike gunned his engine and pulled out behind. He switched his lights to full beam and read the number of the car in front. It was the Mondeo; the same one that had driven at him by the yard.

CHAPTER 5

It was ten o'clock when Mike reached the police station. The bright moon cast an eerie light over the nearby canal basin. Inside all was quiet. Mike wondered if he was due for another confrontation. He was glad when the desk officer turned out to be a young woman PC. There was no sign of Friday's officious sergeant.

'Earlier this evening someone tried to drive a car at me.' Mike described the incident. The constable looked baffled. After a whispered conversation on the intercom another sergeant appeared. Thankfully he was younger and much more polite than the colleague with whom Mike had clashed.

'May I ask why you didn't report this at once?' he asked.

Mike explained that he had had only half a glance at the car's registration number. He then told the man about the events at Midhurst. How he had been visiting the girl who had been held hostage and that he was convinced the Mondeo had followed him. Lastly he handed over a slip of paper with the registration number on it.

'Thank you sir, we'll check it with our computer.' The sergeant offered Mike a seat and then vanished.

When he reappeared he looked uneasy. He assured Mike that he had nothing to worry about, and that inquiries would be made in the morning. It wasn't satisfactory. The copper had developed an odd shifty look. Mike suspected the man knew a lot more than he was telling him. Mike asked about protection for Leanne. The sergeant assured him smugly that the situation was in hand. Mike left it at that and went home. Indoors he poured himself a giant slug of whisky and almost surprised himself with seven hours of deep dreamless slumber.

At half past nine on Monday morning, Peter and Mike had a call from the police. The caller this time was polite to the point of deference. A senior police officer would like to meet them. Could they hold themselves at readiness in their office. The police, he explained, were now in a position to give them some details of their investigation into the events at Cottons Hard.

Twenty minutes later their guest arrived, chauffeur driven, in a police BMW. Here was plainly a very senior officer, in a blue tailored uniform, complete with medal ribbons and badges of rank.

'I'm Jim Rowlandson. I'm Assistant Chief Constable of this county. I think we owe you gentlemen an apology.' He was a genial character and Mike liked him.

'It's true,' said Peter, 'that my solicitor is starting complaint proceedings, but we don't have to go through with them. Just give us a logical explanation why you let go the only boat thief anyone's caught this year.'

'I can certainly do that, but first I must ask you to drop what you're doing and come with me. You will then have your explanation and an apology.'

'It sounds like you're arresting us,' Mike was suspicious.

'Oh perish the thought. I'm asking you to come with me to my house and meet some colleagues of mine. It'll take about an hour.'

Mike knew that in the nicest way they were being given orders. The BMW whisked them out onto the main road and then onto the leafy suburbs North of the town. Ten minutes later they were turning into the drive of a sturdy Victorian house. The lawns were trim and the borders bright with daffodils. Four cars were parked on the gravel by the front door.

'Come in,' said Chief Rowlandson. 'My wife, I think you know.'

Peter was smiling as he shook hands with a round jolly-looking woman. 'Mrs Rowlandson teaches my two youngest,' he explained.

Mrs Rowlandson turned to her husband. 'Your people have taken over the dining room.' Mike thought he caught a note of disapproval.

The room they were shown into was well proportioned, with tall windows through which the sunlight shone, lighting the scene within. Four people were seated along one side of a highly-polished rect-angular table. Mike glanced at Peter. He was already feeling uneasy. This place had the feeling of a sinister committee meeting. He looked at the people opposite. On the right hand was an elegantly suited black man. On the other end sat a large man in a rumpled blue suit. His features reminded Mike of Benny's Rottweiler. Next to him sat an elegantly suited late middle-aged man with dark hair and olive skin with a distinct angular nose. Directly opposite Mike, sitting in the centre of the row, was a woman. He looked at her and his unease deepened. She was small in stature and aged, he would guess, mid thirties. Her short-cropped black hair only served to highlight her paper-white complexion. She wore a dark suit with no adornments, no earrings, no finger rings. For half a second he caught her eye and it was chilling.

It was she who spoke first. 'Mr Rowlandson, you may brief these men.' Her voice was cultured: secure background, good school. Mike felt a wild compulsion to run out of this awful room into the sunlight and the fresh air.

'Gentlemen,' Rowlandson began. Mike could have sworn the man was nervous. 'Gentlemen, as you know things have happened at Cottons Hard over the last few days that are obviously troubling you, if not mystifying you.' He glanced at each of them but neither spoke. 'We've decided after much discussion that it's in everyone's interest, especially the national interest, that you be put in the picture. Are you agreed?'

'Of course we are,' said Peter. 'It's our business. We've a right to know why we're being got at.'

'Very well, but first a small formality. You are required to sign these.' He handed each of them two sheets of paper and a pen. 'You will have your explanation, but you will be bound by the terms of The Official Secrets Act. That means that you must never reveal anything you hear in this room under pain of criminal prosecution. Do you understand?'

Both of them hesitated; then Peter signed, followed by Mike.

'Both copies please,' said the woman. It was she who collected the papers and snapped them into her document case.

'Good,' said Rowlandson with forced heartiness. 'Now I can make the introductions. First on your right is Clarence Fairbrother. He is attached to the United States Embassy in London.' The black man nodded and grinned at them. 'Next to him,' Rowlandson continued, 'is Senor Perez, who represents the Spanish government. The gentleman facing you is Inspector Brogan of the Irish Garda Siochana. The Irishman grinned and nodded.

'I am enchanted to meet you,' said the Spaniard.

'Finally, the lady in the centre represents British counter-intelligence and for that reason cannot be named.'

Mike was not going to be intimidated. He looked the woman straight in the eye from four feet. The face was dominated by these eyes. Eyes like dark pools, cold and unmoving.

'Do your men make a habit of vandalising boats, and when they do who picks up the bill?' he asked.

'And I've still got a black eye as you can see,' said Peter. 'That was the work of your man.'

Not a flicker of emotion registered on the woman's face. Ice maiden, Mike thought.

'Very well,' she said. 'It's true the incident was caused by one of our field agents. I will only say that he exceeded his instructions and that we, as a service, do not encourage glory seekers.' The voice was cold and emotionless. 'I personally interviewed this man and reprimanded him. You may take it from me that at this moment he will be wishing he'd never been born.'

Mike could believe that. 'OK, will you tell us what all this is about?'

'I will ask the questions,' said the ice maiden. 'You must understand that you have been partially vetted, both of you, and we are satisfied for the present.' She glanced at her notes. 'Tell me about Miss Micalczyk?'

'Eh?' Mike was caught off balance. 'What are you on about?'

'Micalczyk. That name occurs three times on our East European files, but none are linked to the one named here.'

'You can't mean Leanne? You're not serious?' said Peter.

'Leanne Micalczyk. Aged nineteen, employed by Cottons Hard Yacht Services. Now tell me more.'

'The Leanne who works for us has a grandfather,' said Peter. 'I know them; I used to live near them. Old man Micalczyk is Polish. He was in the Eighth Army. Get him in a pub and he'll tell you how he won the war. Later he drove a refuse cart for Chichester Council. He's retired now, and there's nothing sinister about him except that he's a miserable old git and he understands English better than he lets on.'

Mike pitched in. 'As for the lovely Leanne. Not only does she have no political associations. I doubt if she even knows the name of the Prime Minister. She's a plucky kid though; she put up a bloody good show the other night.'

The ice maiden nodded. 'On Friday afternoon you had a visitor, Sir Charles Venner-Harris…'

'Oh come on!' Mike interrupted. 'You lot must be more paranoid than I thought. Chazz Venner-Harris is as dumb as they go, and he's a true-blue Tory – we've known him for years. No, lady, you're barking up the wrong tree there.'

'We shall see. Who did he say he was representing?'

'Some Irish American group, he said.'

'The Irish American Cultural Society?'

'Yes, that was it.'

She nodded again. 'You will have your explanation, or as much of it as you need to know.' She turned to the thickset man on her right. 'Mr Brogan, please proceed.'

'I tell you for nothing,' said the Irishman. 'Your little Polish girl did a better job than she knows.' The man spoke with a pronounced Dublin accent but there was nothing comic about him. 'The dead man in that car was Peter McManus, which will be the sweetest news for most of the police of Europe. He has been the leader of a Provisional terrorist cell for ten years. He's killed a few in his time I can tell you.'

'What would these people want with Leanne?' Mike asked.

'Nothing personal to her. We think they needed her to bluff their way past your security. We believe there is a race on to find something.'

'Is it to do with that American yacht?' asked Mike.

'In our view that is so.'

'But why?' said Peter. 'She's only an old cruising boat. There's nothing special about her, certainly no drugs aboard. I would know because I've just rebuilt the whole of her down below.'

'No, not drugs,' it was Clarence the American. 'We believe there is something hidden in that boat. Did you find nothing? A small package, a sealed container? It's documents we're after.'

'No I'm sorry. There was nothing like that, not in the parts of the ship I've worked on.'

'Clarence,' said the Spaniard Perez. 'You'd better tell them the whole story.'

Clarence looked at the ice maiden. 'How much can I tell these guys?'

'We have clearance for everything up to and including the death of Senator O'Dwyer,' she said.

Clarence grinned cheerfully at them. This must be a real CIA man thought Mike, although Clarence seemed a likeable fellow for such a sinister tag. 'Now, either of you ever hear tell of Senator James O'Dwyer?'

'Yes,' said Mike. 'He's a dead American politician.'

'Hey! That's H.L. Menken's definition of a statesman.' Clarence laughed. 'Well now, I guess not even the Senator's best friends would call him a statesman. I'd say he was what you Brits call a chancer. You know a character, a joker and a darned scoundrel with it.'

Clarence explained. James O'Dwyer was a native born American by the narrowest of margins. His Irish immigrant mother had given birth on the dockside within half an hour of arrival in New York. 'The old man used to joke about that,' said Clarence. 'Said it meant he could run for President.'

The young James had got himself a college education and a law degree. Then he had found a place with an attorney in Wilmington North Carolina. From then on his career had blossomed.

'Just like W.S. Gilbert,' said Clarence. 'You know, "I cleaned the windows and I swept the floor and I polished up the handle of the big front door...". Jim did even better than that, he married the boss's daughter and when old man Chester became a judge, he made his son-in-law head of the firm. Then came 1917 and America entered the war, the First War of course, and Jim volunteered for the Air Service.'

Clarence explained that Jim O'Dwyer's exploits had made him a national hero. Then in 1919, while awaiting transport home, Jim had gone absent without leave. As he was due for formal demobilisation nobody had taken much notice. In fact he was in Ireland, a member of Michael Collins' Republican forces. Following the signing of the Irish Peace Treaty, James O'Dwyer had returned to a hero's welcome in the United States and a dubious career in law and politics.

'OK,' said Clarence, 'this is where your boat comes in. O'Dwyer was a sailing nut. He raced yachts and he designed 'em. Just after World War Two he designed and built the ideal boat for his old age. She could take ocean voyaging, but mostly he just wanted to swan around the Chesapeake and Pamleco sound. This is the boat that's in your yard right now.

'The old man had kept on sailing into his eighties until failing health forced him to lay up his yacht. Jim O'Dwyer had died the previous July: he was ninety-eight. It was on his deathbed that he played his final joker.

'He told the people around him that he had a document; it was a copy of one that was already in the archives of the British, United States and Irish governments. He said he kinda' reckoned it was dangerous. He was going to tell them some more but he relapsed into semi-consciousness. Not long afterwards the old man died. All the witnesses say the same though. He mumbled something about his boat. "My boat, it's all there in my boat". That was it, they all agree the wording.'

'There's no documents in that boat now or I'd have found them,' said Peter. 'You say he was a joker. Couldn't he have been winding them up?'

'Fair question, but no. Apart from being on the edge of death the witnesses knew him too well to be fooled. No, whatever he was trying to say he meant it. They all agree the same. There was Jim's wife's cousin, Judge Chester junior, two of his staff, a priest and lastly his granddaughter Clare. They all say the same. Reckon the old boy was hanging onto life until he cleared his secret.'

'Why is this document so dangerous?' said Peter. 'I mean if it's history how can it affect things now?'

'Not so,' said Brogan. 'In my country, we live and breathe our history. Five hundred years is as real as last week.'

'To put it bluntly,' said Clarence. 'If this document were to surface in public, I'm not sure you British would ever trust us Americans again.'

'I would second that,' said Brogan. 'Not that we care about Great Britain's relationship with the United States. It's the repercussions in Ireland that trouble me.'

'I also agree,' said Perez. 'In Spain we have many troubles in our north. We have terrorists, ETA, who are allied to those in Ireland and who would much like to discredit America.'

'If it's that bad, how come you let the boat out of the States?' asked Mike.

'Yes,' said Clarence, 'that's the question. Jim O'Dwyer told them nothing but he gave his cousin a file number in the State Department archives. He didn't say what was in it, only that it was dangerous and that nobody knew that he had a rogue copy.'

'A boat's a funny place to leave documents,' Mike was sceptical. 'The environment would be hopeless, they'd fall to pieces eventually wherever you stowed them.'

'You'd think so, but there's no doubt what the old man said: "in my boat". They were near about his last words but all the witnesses agree he was lucid and in control.'

'Then why didn't you pull the boat to pieces?'

'We didn't know at once. It was weeks before Chester thought to do anything about it. He went to the Department in Washington but nobody took him seriously. He persisted, so they had a look. Luckily the researcher had enough sense to realise what he was reading. The whole thing was handed to us within the hour.' Clarence frowned. 'By the time we'd gotten round to searching for the boat it'd been shipped and in your yard two months. Then my lords and masters took another two months deciding whether to tell your government.'

'All right,' said Mike. 'You're asking us to search the boat?'

'It's being searched now, by experts,' said the woman.

'What!' Mike was really angry. 'You mean you've been hacking that boat apart behind our backs? You've no right...'

'We have every right. We have a search warrant.'

'What about damage?'

'There'll be no damage. We have the most modern imaging equipment. Only if we detect something will we penetrate the boat, and it is you who will be required to do the work.'

'Miss O'Dwyer, the owner, is due here this afternoon,' said Peter. 'What are we supposed to tell her?'

'You will say nothing.' The ice maiden gave them a bleak look. 'You are under the authority of The Official Secrets Act – remember that. You will watch this O'Dwyer, her words, her behaviour, and those with whom she associates. You will do that, you will observe total secrecy, and you will report to me.'

'Nothing doing,' said Mike.

'I agree,' Peter concurred. 'We don't spy on our clients.'

Mike glanced around. He avoided looking at the ice maiden but searched the faces of the others. Rowlandson was embarrassed; Mike could have sworn the man was nervous. Brogan caught Mike's eye, frowned, and shook his head. Perez looked inscrutable, Clarence had a sardonic smile. Then Mike looked at the woman. He did not stare in her face from choice; he was drawn to her. Her dark eyes seemed to have enlarged and her face shrivelled. Here was a personality who did not stomach acts of defiance from puny men in mundane jobs. She said nothing; there was no need. Mike could not believe his own ears as he heard himself mumble an apology and promise the woman his co-operation. It was involuntary; something that was drawn from him by some means he knew not. Slowly he broke away from the ice maiden's stare. There was another surprise, for the first time in years he saw Peter, white faced and confused.

CHAPTER 6

Clare left Swansea at half past ten. She felt relaxed and at peace for the first time in months. For nearly a year in fact: the time it had taken even to begin to sort Granpapa's tangled affairs. Her eyes still misted when she thought of her grandfather. She had lived in Ireland, three thousand miles from the old man, but they had always been close. Of course she had long known that he was something of a rogue, but discovering the full scale of his deviousness had unnerved her. Granpapa had been a big man in every sense and his death had caused more than a ripple in Ireland and America – Spain as well. The Irish press had made quite a splash. *James O'Dwyer among the last surviving volunteers....* But this was Ireland and the past would not let go that easily. It seemed that Michael Collins' Free-Staters were still not everyone's flavour of the year; among the letters of condolence had been a vivid hate mail. Much the same in the States; it seemed the old Senator's friends and enemies were about evenly balanced, while his heroics in the Spanish civil war brought more controversy.   Latterly, the Irish American Cultural Society had pestered her with their obsession with her boat. Not that she had ever knowingly met a member of this group. And why on earth should they wish to be represented by that comic Englishman, Charles, with his patrician posturing, and his Irish granny?

'Daughter of Lord Clarina of Limerick,' he'd said.

Charles had departed the previous morning to search out his Ascendancy roots. She guessed that right now the astute Limerickers would be parting Sir Charles from his ready cash.

Her attention drifted back to the scene ahead. She was on the approaches to the Severn Bridge. A quick glance below and she could see the tide ripping over the shallows. One day she would sail her boat under this bridge and on up the estuary to Lydney and Sharpness. These were just the challenging tidal waters for which Grandpapa had designed *Quadra*. Why had he insisted that she rename the boat and why *Quadra*? For years she had been the *Mary-Elizabeth,* or just the *Mary-Liz.*   She smiled as she remembered the family cruises to Annapolis; such happy memories. Then years later she had sat beside the old man when he knew death was near.

"The ship's all yours. Just two conditions. Take her to Ireland with you and she's to be *Quadra:* my name for her." He had reached

51

out and taken her hand. "Look after her – there's a secret in her."

What was the secret? One thing was for sure, there were no bits of paper. She also knew that nothing she said would persuade those CIA men, or Sir Charles and his mysterious backers. Offering half a million dollars for God's sake. "A measure of our client's esteem for your grandfather."

"Horse shit," that's what Grandpapa would have said. Nobody would pay that sort of money out of esteem for James O'Dwyer. Sure there was a secret, but they were all forgetting how deceitful and devious the old man had been.

The car-phone was bleeping. Now who on earth? Clare grabbed hold of the handset. 'Hello.'

'Clare, hi there…'

'You!' she frowned. 'What now?'

'The Brits have searched your boat – nothing found.'

'I could've told you that.'

'Sure, now a warning. Those two boat builders, Blair and Walters. Delia's got 'em on a string. She's told 'em to watch you.'

'Bloody hell!'

'I know, but their hearts ain't in it. The bitch, she stitched 'em up good. I guess they'd've agreed to anything to get out of that room.'

'OK, I'll be careful. Hell, you know I can do without all this. I only want to sail my boat.'

'You know, Clare. If you want my advice I'd do just that. Sail away into the sunset and the sooner the better.'

'Oh yeah, I didn't ask your advice and even if I had I doubt if I'd take it.' She slammed the phone down. The line of the M4 lay ahead. Pursing her lips angrily she swept majestically into the fast lane and pushed the accelerator to the floor.

Mike hardly spoke on the return journey to the yard. His over-whelming sensation was anger. Never had he felt such humiliation as he had suffered at the hands of this Security Services woman. There had been no spark of humanity about her; only those dark eyes that had telegraphed superior intellect and deep contempt for him as a male with his way of life.

In the road to the yard they pulled over for another oncoming police car and a British Telecom service van. 'Playing at BT men,' their driver snorted. 'Who do they think they're kidding?'

'Who's kidding?' asked Peter.

'Spooks,' the man replied.

Kevin the yard hand was outside the office looking flustered.

'What's going on?' he asked.

'I was going to ask the same,' said Mike. 'I see you've had the police here.'

'Too right, they had a warrant. They made me stay in the office. What are they looking for?'

'Stolen property in one of the boats,' Peter lied. 'It doesn't involve us so don't worry. It's publicity we could do without so keep your mouth shut.'

Mike ran to the O'Dwyer yacht and scrambled aboard. He pushed open the main hatch and dropped below. He rummaged from end to end of the cabin and then crawled into the engine compartment. If he had not known of the search he would never have suspected the recent intrusion. The spooks were thorough; one had to give them credit for that. He went on deck and looked down at Peter who was searching the undersides of the hull. 'I don't think they found anything below decks,' he said. 'There's no damage – nothing.'

Mike released a long sigh. 'Let's hope this is the end of it.' Some hope that. Deep down he knew there would be no closure until they'd removed this wretched craft a hundred miles and hopefully gone for ever.

It was half past four. The lights were on in the main building shed as Mike and Peter examined the damaged hull of a newly hauled out sailing yacht. Peter, who was facing the door, nudged Mike's elbow. 'We've a visitor,' he murmured. He pointed to the open door. Silhouetted against the fading light was a woman.

Mike stiffened, then relaxed. For two seconds he was convinced she was the ice maiden.

'Yes, what d'you want?' he asked brusquely.

'There's a fine warm welcome for sure, Michael. It is Michael isn't it? I know your voice from the telephone.'

She had stepped out from the shadows and was standing in the full glare of the overhead lights. She faced Mike and held out her hand. 'I'm Clare and I'm very pleased to meet you.'

Mike took the hand. It was small but the grip was firm. 'I'm sorry I snapped like that,' he replied, 'but I've had a lousy day. Welcome to Cottons Hard and meet my colleague, Peter.'

As Peter in his turn shook hands Mike stared. His preconceived notions were shattered. Clare was young, far younger than he had expected. What on earth had made him imagine a middle-aged spinster? She really was a most attractive girl, in her mid twenties he would guess: slim with a pleasing round face already with a touch of suntan. Her hair was blonde but he could detect a trace of flame red reflecting in the overhead lamps. What could have made him mistake her, even momentarily, for the ice maiden. The only similarity was in the eyes. But these eyes were soft and laughing; as they fixed on him again they washed away the morning's anger and resentment.

'Right,' she said. 'Show me my boat and tell me when we can go sailing.'

CHAPTER 7

'Go on, Leanne,' called Mike. 'This is your moment.'

Clare had arranged a bottle of champagne and six glasses. This was to be a renaming ceremony, with no wasteful destruction of a bottle. Etiquette required a toast from all aboard and one glass for the ship. Leanne picked up the extra glass and walked gingerly forward trying not to spill a drop. On the foredeck she stopped, stifled a giggle, and drew a deep breath.

'I name this ship, *Quadra*. May God bless her and all who sail in her.' She ended in a rush, tipped the contents of the glass on the deck, and collapsed in wild laughter.

It was one of those prematurely hot April days. Half an hour earlier the yard tractor had rolled *Quadra* down the slipway on a wheeled launching cradle. She lay floating, rocking gently against the yard pontoon. Now was the magic moment: the culmination of months of work. Mike turned the key and pressed the engine starter button. The big twenty horsepower diesel fired. He gave a quick glance over the stern to see the cooling water pouring from its duct. Peter took the tiller while Leanne released the bow spring. Wind and tide took Quadra slowly from the jetty and pointed her towards the centre of the channel. Mike released the back spring and they were away. Clare was busy unrolling a flag from a shiny new ensign staff before fixing it in its mount on the stern. In a sight rarely seen at Cottons Hard: the Irish tricolour streamed in the wind.

Quadra lay to her mooring in the channel. Mike relaxed in the cockpit and took stock. Below decks Clare was preparing a champagne lunch for the yard staff. He liked Clare. He wished all Cottons Hard customers were as precise and businesslike as this energetic twenty-four year old. And she was attractive with her long flaxen hair and those surprising dark eyes. She had told Mike that she was an artist. She also wrote and illustrated children's books. She produced some copies for Peter's children. Peter told him how she had read some of them to the kids and they had sat spellbound by the soft lilting voice. But Mike had noticed a bitter sad reflection in those dark eyes that had disturbed him.

Something was not right. Mike sensed that behind the happy extrovert was a troubled inner being. Once, unexpectedly, he had found her sitting by the sea wall looking wistful as she stared across the water. She had turned round and he had asked if she would like to walk with him along the path to the top of the harbour. She had jumped to her feet and accepted with genuine delight. They walked in silence for a while, past the boat yard, and out into open country. It was half an hour short of highwater and the harbour was full, with the marshes and mudflats transformed into one vast lake.

Mike opened the conversation. 'I understand your grandfather built *Quadra*?'

'Who told you that?' The reply was sharp and momentarily unsettled him. It was as if the question was an intrusion. He turned and caught a flicker of uncertainty in the dark eyes. She quickly looked away from him and stared over the water. 'How did you know about my grandfather?

Mike had to think fast. He had heard the full story from the American, Clarence, but he could hardly tell her that. 'It was Charles Venner-Harris,' he said, remembering in the nick if time.

'Of course, I should have guessed that.' For the first time since he had met her Mike watched Clare's face change to a happy grin. It was a surprisingly mobile face. Suddenly it felt good to be walking with her.

'Is Charles really an old friend of yours?' she asked.

'Peter and I went to school with him. But I wouldn't call him an old friend. He moves in a higher class than I do.'

She pursed her lips. 'We don't exactly have class in Ireland – or not like you do. But having met the man I think I know what you mean.' She stared at him. 'Was Annabel high-class?'

Now it was Mike's turn to feel offended. His friends had learned not to mention Annabel. 'Her father is not upper class,' he replied. 'He likes to think he is. He mixes with them, but I would say they see him as a money grubbing little shit.'

Clare nodded and said no more. They walked on in silence. 'It's true,' she smiled. 'Grandfather built *Quadra*. He did some of the building himself and all the designing. I've inherited his papers and things and there's some plans among them, I'm told.'

'What plans?' Mike had not meant to be so abrupt, but he had remembered Clarence's story and the words had slipped out.

'Yacht drawings, of course – what did you think I meant?' She was eyeing him now with suspicion. Mike regretted his mistake, and he didn't care for the way she was staring at him; her eyes reminded him more than a little of the ice maiden.

He said no more after that; by common unspoken consent they both
turned and walked back to the yard in silence. He wished that Clare
had never mentioned plans and papers. It had put a barrier between
them. He was sure that she knew something she was not prepared to
speak of, while he knew things about her grandfather that he was not
allowed to tell her. He was more than ever certain that they were all
living in a web of deceit.

Mike awoke from his daydream. Clare was refilling his glass. He
looked up and smiled.
    'I want to take *Quadra* on her trial cruise,' she said. 'Are we
ready?'
    'Yes, we only need to load the stores and you can sail away. Are
your papers in order?'
    'Yes, the ship's registered and tax paid. We've both got passports
I presume?'
    'You want me to skipper for you?'
    'Yes, definitely. I'd like your help for this shakedown cruise and
the trip to Cork. What d'you say to three hundred pounds a day?'
    'Jesus,' Peter exclaimed. 'You do realise that could be eight or
nine grand by the time he's finished?'
    'Who cares, I'm spending my grandfather's ill-gotten gains.'
    'We'll need up to date charts,' said Mike. 'Where do you want to
go?'
    'Any chance we could go to Etaples?'
    'Why there?' Mike was surprised. 'It's a long way east and it's a
tricky entrance – very shallow.'
    'I know, I've been there. You see this is a sentimental journey. I
used to spend some of my school holidays there with grandfather, and
I've a good friend there still.'
    'All right, but I suggest we start with a straight crossing to
Cherbourg, or better still, St Vaast. Then we'll watch the weather and
take it from there.'

With the party over everyone dispersed to do more mundane jobs.
Mike had driven over to Bosham, to collect *Quadra's* new sails, and at
five o'clock he had taken Leanne home. The girl was still nervous
though she put on a brave show. Nobody chose to mention that the
second gunman had still not been caught. The police were being
especially coy. Mike was certain they knew the identity of the
Mondeo car that had tried to run him down. As for the missing

gunman: they told Mike that he had escaped and was almost certainly overseas. It was unsatisfactory and hard for Leanne.

Clare returned to the yard at six, her car laden with stores for the voyage. Mike gave her a hand to stack them in the office.

'There we are,' she said. 'All ready for tomorrow.' They walked outside into the evening twilight and Mike locked the door.

'I'll wish you goodnight, Michael. I'm tired and I'll go back to the hotel for a night's sleep.'

Mike was puzzled; something was wrong. She spoke projecting her voice, almost as if she was addressing the world at large. Mike saw her to her car and watched as the taillights disappeared past the farm. He decided he would collect his gear, lock up the flat, and spend the night at anchor in *Quadra*. It was his custom to sleep one night aboard before the start of a voyage. He liked to absorb the feel of the ship, particularly a strange one. He suspected that whatever the problems on land, *Quadra* was a friendly ship, one to trust their lives to. She would understand the sea and she would look after them.

Mike locked the office door and walked back along the line of boats. He stopped for a brief look around.

'Mr Walters.' Mike stiffened as he felt the hair on his scalp tingle. A figure had walked out of the shadow. 'You may report now,' said the woman he thought of as the ice-maiden.

'Where the hell did you spring from?' Mike had been startled and his anger was beginning to burn.

'I was waiting for O'Dwyer to leave. She has done so. Now you can report.'

'There's nothing to report.'

'Don't prevaricate.'

'I'm not, it's just that nothing's happened. We like Miss O'Dwyer. We've launched her boat and tomorrow she's leaving.'

'For where?'

'She's off on a trial cruise and if you must know I'm going with her.'

'Port of destination?'

'Damn you, I will not submit to this.'

'Answer my question.'

'Well it's no secret. I'll inform the coastguard when we leave anyway. We're aiming for St Vaast; then it depends on the weather.'

'Good, these are your instructions…'

'Oh sure to hell they are!' Clare's voice came out of the shadows. The carefree young woman who had left minutes before had been transformed; her voice blazed with hate. It was all too much for Mike. He stood rigid with shock – gaping.

'Hello, Delia, would you be making a pass at my friend Michael? I wouldn't do that, Delia.' Clare had moved within a foot of the other woman. She stood hands on hips, face bent forward. Mike caught the cold glint in her eyes reflected in the security lights.

'Oh yes, Delia. You're not as smart as you think. I drive in here an hour back and what do I see? A nice shiny black motor car parked up in the bushes.' Clare's voice was hard and the Irish accent vivid.

'So I say; who is it that I wish I didn't know who has a liking for shiny black cars? So there it is, Michael. I drove out of here just far enough, and then I ran all the way back. And as I expected there's a nice young fella like you caught by a wicked witch.' Clare had half turned towards Mike. Her face was smiling but it was a smile of pure hatred and it shook him.

'Yes, Michael, this one's more than wicked. I think evil is the word. When Adam met Eve I guess she was the snake.'

'O'Dwyer,' the woman's voice cut through Clare's tirade. 'You are a foreign national acting in a suspicious manner. You'd be advised to watch your attitude.'

'Attitude!' Clare laughed. 'I've heard it all now. See, Michael, here's proof of why you British are the stupidest people on earth. You so love paying your sworn enemies to guard your security…' Clare gasped in pain as the woman hit her in the face with a slashing half slap, half chop. Clare staggered and collapsed to her knees clutching the side of her face.

Mike dived at the woman. She saw him coming; side stepping deftly, she began to run. Two strides and he handed her a slap to the head with the full power of an arm muscled from heavy lifting. With savage satisfaction he heard her scream. 'So you've got some feelings then you bitch.' He shouted.

Seizing her by the armpits he lifted her slight form and crashed it against the topsides of a yacht. He felt the breath crumple out of her.

'Now you listen good…' He never finished the sentence. A tongue of flame roared inside his head. He dropped his captive, staggered and fell headlong. In his fury he had failed to watch behind.

CHAPTER 8

Mike lay prone. He felt dizzy and for a moment he thought he would vomit. Someone or something had struck him a sharp blow to the head, behind his left ear. He could hear shouts, running footsteps and a man's cry that changed to a scream of intense fear. Silence, then a car started. The engine gunned, as with tyres spinning wildly on the loose gravel it sped away up the entrance road. Mike tried to ease into a sitting position. Nausea and giddiness engulfed him and he lay down again.

'Michael…Michael, can you hear me? Are you OK there?' It was Clare; he could feel her kneeling beside him.

'Think so, yeah, I'm all right. Someone hit me. I'll lie still for a minute.'

'Shall I call a doctor?'

'Oh God no. It's not that bad.' He tensed as more footsteps approached. There was something odd about them. One set was regular, heavy booted, the others sloppy and shuffling. A huge form was standing over him and a warm wet jowl was slobbering and licking his face.

'Whoa there, Target. Back off boy.' It was Benny.

Mike sat up in alarm, his injury forgotten. 'That bloody great dog!' he gasped.

'Target won't touch you,' said Benny. 'Anyway he's had his sport for tonight – look.' Focusing with difficulty Mike could see Benny holding a long strip of cloth.

'Ripped the back out'a that heavy's jacket, 'e did. The bugger shit himself – did you hear'im yell?' Benny chuckled. 'Them two's hopped it, but I got a good look at the motor. Mondeo; nice one – jet black – this year's plates. The geezer was driving. The girl, she was in a bad way – he had to half carry her.'

'What happened?' Mike asked. He took a series of deep breaths. His head still hurt but his vision was clearing.

'Delia's minder was behind you,' said Clare. 'He must have been there all along but I never saw him.'

'I don't know how the hell they slipped past me.' Benny sounded mortified. 'It was like they was invisible. Sorry, Mr Walters.'

Mike squinted at Clare. 'How are you? That woman hit you a hell of a crack.'

'Oh, I'm fine. I was a bit off balance. But my, what a temper she has in her. And you Michael, are a hero. That hiding you handed her is one she's been asking for these thirty years. Never mind me – that holla she gave was sweet music to my ears.'

'You seem to know her.' Mike was fully conscious now and his mind was a torrent of questions.

'Delia – sure I know her – worse luck. Look, Michael, I don't want to talk right now, but I'll tell you more when we're at sea. Are you sure you're fit to sail tomorrow?' she sounded anxious.

'Yes, I'll be fine. It was a clever disabling punch, martial arts stuff. That bloke was a professional; he knew what he was doing.' Mike staggered to his feet and stood giddily, putting out a hand to support himself. He leant against the yacht hull, the same boat against which he had battered the luckless Delia.

'Will we be allowed to sail,' he asked. 'I've just assaulted a top national security officer. They could lock me up and throw the key away.'

'They'll not do that. Delia will keep her mouth shut so long as I'm around. You see, I don't know the half of all the truth about her, but I know enough and she knows it too.'

A wave of exhilaration washed over Mike as he felt the little yacht respond to the pull of her sails. He was in his element once more. All life's insecurities; Annabel, the bank manager, the police, that Delia woman, and a dozen other traps for the unwary, were left far behind. At sea he was in his own world. He was in control.

'Clare, come and steer her. She's your ship – tell me what you think.'

Clare walked aft along the deck to the cockpit. She released her safety harness and sat down at the tiller. It was a cold grey morning and both of them had dressed in foul weather gear and gloves. Clare wore a dark balaclava pulled down over her ears, with her long blonde tresses tied in a ponytail. She turned to Mike, her eyes shining.

'Head for the Nab Tower,' he said. 'When we pass it we'll alter course for France.'

Mike studied the set of the sails. This was a different rig to the one old man O'Dwyer had used. His had been a solid wooden mast with a cutter rig of two small headsails. Mike had changed this to a modern alloy spar with a sloop rig. 'What d'you think?' he asked.

'She's great, I reckon she handles easier than in the old days, but I was only a kid then, so I expect the tiller seemed heavy.'

'It'll be seat of the pants navigation this trip. We've left in such indecent haste that I forgot the GPS.' Although Mike was only twenty-eight, he was something of a traditionalist. Electronic gadgets were fine when they worked, but these gizmos tended to fail when they were most needed. Murphy's Law, they called it, and he smiled: this was an Irish ship.

At seven thirty it was full morning light. Mike made a radio call to the Coastguard reporting their departure and their intended destination, St Vaast. 'It's sixty miles to Cap Barfleur and the tides should cancel out.' He glanced at the chart. 'St Vaast's another six miles or so, but if we maintain our speed we should get there with enough water to pass the lock.' St Vaast, he explained, was an artificial harbour with lock gates, so timing was important. He didn't intend to hang around outside at night in a rising wind.

Clare echoed his thoughts. 'What if we don't make it on time?'

'Divert to Cherbourg, no problem.'

It was glorious sailing despite the bitter cold. Two miles south of the Isle of Wight they began to feel the full force of the south-westerly breeze. Mike pulled down a reef to reduce the area of the mainsail. How sweet the air smelt here at sea, how very unimportant the world he had left behind. Suddenly even Annabel seemed trivial. He couldn't resist a whoop of joy.

Much steadier now, *Quadra* began to eat away the miles. Mike's respect for this little yacht was growing by the minute. In spite of her shallow draft she was clearly a staunch sea boat. A fair Channel swell was running, but she rose to each wave with a natural grace, and her decks were almost dry. With a beam wind she was pushing towards six knots; there could be no better conditions for a trial trip.

'Your grandfather knew what he was at when he designed *Quadra*- doesn't she go!' Mike was sitting beside Clare. The electric auto-helm was steering the ship and its whirring and whining accompanied them as they ate a late breakfast. Clare was ebullient, no trace of seasickness.

'Yes, that was like Grandpapa. If he tried something he'd do it well.'

'She's an interesting design,' he said. 'There's a touch of a Maurice Griffiths about her.'

'You're right,' she laughed. 'I remember Grandpapa saying the British must have some soul. They produced Maurice Griffiths, Uffa Fox, and Erskine Childers.'

'I thought Childers was Irish?'

Clare laughed joyously. 'Well, I guess he had an Irish granny, but then everyone in the world has an Irish granny.'

'That must be true,' Mike grinned. 'Your national football team is living proof.'

'Watch it boy, that's fighting talk. Anyway, Michael, have you got an Irish granny?'

'Sorry, no.'

'Your friend, Sir Charles has. Did you know that?'

'No I didn't.'

'She was the daughter of Lord Clarina of Limerick.'

Mike groaned. 'He'll never join the real world. I'll tell you something. That bloody woman, the one you call Delia, she was asking about him. Have you any idea why?'

'No, but I'm not surprised. Charles called on me at home. Look Michael, there's some funny business going on there. Charles doesn't know his ass from his elbow, but he's mixing with some strange people.'

'I know, Irish-Americans of some sort. He tried to bribe Peter into certifying this boat as unseaworthy. Pete wasn't amused I can tell you.'

'That was a low trick for an English gentleman.'

'I agree, but I suspect there's a tidy sum being dangled and that stretched even Chazz's code of honour.'

Clare stood up and wound a few turns on the jib winch. She looked at the sail, then satisfied sat down. 'Are you sure you're OK?' She had been fussing over him all morning. It was the third time she had asked.

'I'm fine, stop nagging,' he forced a grin as he felt the bruise on his head. 'Say, did you get a look at that thug who hit me?'

'Sure, big fat slob, with a shaved head. I never saw him either until he moved. He had the look of one of your arrogant army boys.'

'They've a job to do,' Mike answered coldly.

'Is that so?' Her face was inscrutable, but her eyes were challenging. In a minute they would be enmeshed in a blazing argument about history and politics. Mike was not falling for that one.

He swung round to face her. 'Clare, it's about time you came clean. Who is Delia and how do you come to know her?'

'I never had a choice in the matter. You can't choose your relations. It's family – Delia's my aunt.'

CHAPTER 9

Clare would not be drawn further. For some time she sat silent with brooding. Mike left her there while he tried to absorb this latest revelation. In a way he wasn't surprised. He remembered Clare's arrival at the yard. That first instant he'd seen her in the half-light of the shed. He'd thought she was the ice-maiden then. Certainly in those amazing deep eyes there was a resemblance. He wondered where the relationship came from, mother's side or father's. One thing was for certain: the hostility between the two women was mutual and deep.

For the next few miles they had busy shipping lanes to cross. The wind was rising and the yacht was becoming overpowered again. Mike decided to pull down a second reef. Soon both of them were lost in the delight of the moment. Mike was a professional skipper. Usually a delivery trip such as this would be a routine job in a standard production yacht. *Quadra* was different. She was a beautiful classic design with a unique will of her own. They were averaging far more than the projected six knots. A little after half past five that evening they caught their first glimpse of land with the tall tower of Cap Barfleur lighthouse.

'There we are,' said Mike. 'We're on time and up tide of where we're making for.'

They passed the lighthouse some five miles off, and the long coastline of the Contentin Peninsular began to open up to starboard.

'Keep looking ahead, Clare. You should see a sort of castle.'

'Is that it?'

'Yes, that's the one, Isle de Tatihou. Used to be a jail; sort of French Alcatraz.'

Clare grimaced. 'This doesn't seem much of a fun place to me, Michael.'

'Wait until we're in port. It gets a bit crowded in summer, but it's a lovely place.' He shot a quick glance around. 'See that light over there, that's the end of the harbour wall. We'll get the sails off and motor in.'

They passed the lock gates with still an hour of flood tide. Clare was looking around. They could see plenty of activity among the fishing boats, but the yacht marina to starboard was barely a quarter full.

'Early season,' said Mike. 'It'll be packed out come July.' Turning *Quadra* in midstream he glided her gently into a visitor's berth. Clare jumped onto the pontoon with the lines while Mike cut the engine – silence. Gradually their ears adjusted to new sounds; the wind in the rigging, the French chatter on the fish dock opposite; the bustle of the little town beyond.

Mike sighed contentedly. 'There you go, *Quadra* reborn, and a Channel crossing behind her. How do you feel now?'

'Great, Michael, It's worth all the aggravation we've been through. Tell me, should I report to customs?'

'I wouldn't bother; the French aren't heavy with cruising boats. They sometimes check documents and crew numbers, but that's about all unless there's a drug bust on.' He looked critically at the adjustment of the docking lines. 'I tell you what I feel like. Let's change out of this foul weather gear, snug down the ship, and then up to the town for a meal and some vino.'

Clare laughed. 'My thoughts exactly.'

Mike left Clare to tidy up the boat while he wandered down to the yacht club. The few boats in the marina were mostly local, but one stood out. She was a large motor yacht with a Dutch ensign. She was around sixty feet long and based on the design of a fishing trawler. Her paintwork, teak trim and decks were immaculate. It seemed odd that all her windows, including the enclosed bridge deck, were curtained.

At the yacht club he collected a weather fax. The outlook was promising. A freak high-pressure system was pushing up from the Azores and an above average temperature was forecast. Mike returned to find both Clare and her yacht transformed. The mainsail was stowed along its boom, with a precision he could never hope to emulate, and the French courtesy flag was fluttering from the starboard hoist. Clare he hardly recognised; she looked stunning. She had changed into an outfit of white trousers, a dark blue blazer and designer deck shoes. She had released her long hair to glow red gold in the setting sun. Feeling rather shabby, in his jeans and Arran jumper, Mike walked with her into the town.

They found an excellent restaurant in Rue Maréchal Foch. Clare studied the menu for a minute and then ordered for both of them in fluent French.

'I learned when I was a kid,' she explained. 'Grandfather sent me to school in Paris. I didn't speak a word when I went but you learn quick enough at that age.'

'I wish I could speak some languages,' said Mike. 'I can just get by with a bit of French and German, but that's it.'

She grinned. 'The trouble when you're Irish is that everyone assumes you're English, and is that aggravating.'

They made the most of six courses and two different wines. Life, Mike reflected, was good. Here he was on a busman's holiday in a superb classic yacht, and with this lovely girl paying all the bills. He was suddenly aware that someone was staring at them. A large slightly balding man, in a tailored suit had moved within a few feet of their table and was grinning down at them.

'Mind if I join you folk?' he said.

Mike did mind very much, but the stranger was already pulling up a chair and sitting down. Mike caught sight of Clare's face and a little ripple of communication passed between them; just enough to know that she was also put out.

'The name's Cassidy – Sammy Cassidy,' said the man. 'I saw you people sail in just now. It did my heart good to see the flag of Ireland.' His voice had risen a multiple of decibels and most of the people in the room were staring at them. It was obvious to Mike that Sammy was an Australian, and he was also very drunk.

'Nice to meet you, Mr Cassidy,' Clare lied.

'Call me Sammy, everyone in Oz knows Sammy Cassidy. In Melbourne, Sydney, Brisbane, they quote me. Not Adelaide or Perth, though – too many Poms.' Sammy belched.

'What's your line then, Mr Cassidy?' asked Clare.

'Me, I'm a writer – an 'istorian.'

'You're an academic?' said Clare open-mouthed.

'Watch it lady – you taking the piss?' Sammy lurched towards Clare belligerently. Mike carefully measured the distance. If this drunk meant trouble he would have to sort it himself; there was no one around who looked like a bouncer.

'No, not so, Mr Cassidy,' Clare smiled sweetly. 'I'm sure you're a most profound historian. Your people would be from Ireland I suppose – 'tis a fine name you have?'

'Too right, lady. My great-great-granddaddy came from Mayo.'

'Would you be on holiday then?'

'I'm travelling around. I'm hoping to find a boat or a plane for Ireland.'

'Sorry, Mr Cassidy, but we're heading eastwards tomorrow.'

'That's all right, lady; but would you know of a ferry connection from here?'

'In Cherbourg, there may be; but It'll probably be quicker to take a boat for Portsmouth and travel over via England.'

'England,' Sammy snapped. 'I ain't never been to that rot-gut country, never 'ave, never will.' He was looking dangerous again.

'You don't like the British?'

'Did Hitler like Jews?'

'Hey now – steady on!' Clare was startled.

'No, don't get me wrong, lady. I've nothing against Jews. Give'em a fair go and they're clever bastards. But Poms – I can't abide 'em.'

Mike's temper was rising as his fists began to clench. Clare threw him a warning glance and he relaxed. It was amazing the rapport that was developing between them. He knew exactly the words of her unspoken message. Keep your mouth shut, I'll handle this.

'See here, Sammy,' she said soothingly. 'Tomorrow's Sunday and all the British lords and ladies will sail over from Cowes in their fine yachts. So you go to bed now and you'll be in fine voice with your insults in the morning.'

'Lords, you don't say. Jeez, I'll give 'em some shit.' Sammy turned blearily and looked at Mike. 'Your 'usband ain't got much to say?'

'That is because he speaks when I tell him. Goodnight Sammy.'

'Goo'night, and allow me – my card.' Sammy handed Mike a white printed calling card.'

Clare paid the bill and they made good their escape. Sammy remained behind, head slumped on the table. Mike glanced at the card in the light of a street lamp. With surprised grunt he passed it to Clare.

S. P. CASSIDY. BA HONS. MELBOURNE.
Visiting delegate. Irish Australian Cultural Society.
Affiliated to
The Irish American Cultural Society.

Clare laughed. 'We ought to introduce him to your friend Charles. They'd get on like ten houses on fire.'

'If you say so.' Mike was still fuming. 'Another two minutes and I'd have thumped him.'

'I know; that's the stupidity of men – like children you are.'

'What the hell was biting him? What have we ever done to Australia to make him like that?'

67

'He's an Irish-Australian, Michael. He carries a grievance from his ancestors and very burdensome it is. Do you understand what I'm saying?'

'Not really.'

'Irish-Australians are like Irish-Americans. Their forebears never left Ireland from choice. They were driven out by famine and persecution, and they've not forgotten.'

'So you all hate us.'

'Now you're putting words into my mouth.' Clare had stopped walking and was standing with her hands lightly touching a metal railing on the edge of the quay. 'Look Michael, if you're an Irish-American, or ditto Australian, there's a good chance you or your parents will be near the bottom of the pecking order. You've got your community and the old religion, but you have to sweat bloody hard to get out of the ghetto. It's not as if you're black, that'd be much worse, but it's still not easy. You grow up with a sense that you're near the bottom of the heap and you blame it all on the English.

Mike was puzzled. 'Jack Kennedy was never an Anglophobe, despite his old father. I've dealt with Yanks with Irish surnames and they've been fine.'

'Of course, so are ninety-five percent; it's only a small minority where the grievance festers.'

'So what about you, Clare?'

'What about me? I'm a well-balanced Irish girl. I've a chip on both shoulders.' She laughed.

'So you hate us?'

'Oh, do me a favour, Michael. There's not a family in Ireland without some English cousins. Sure, we feel the humiliation sometimes, but the boot's on the other foot now. In the Republic we've higher average wages than the Brits these days.'

'Humiliation?'

'Of course, like everyone else in your stupid old Empire. Ask the Indians.'

'Ask them what?'

'Oh God, are you so thick that I have to spell it out for you? Look man, if you'd been occupied by Hitler's Germans or Genghiz Khan and his boys, you could at least take a pride in dying honourably.'

'I still don't know what you're on about.'

She swung round and grasped his arm. He jumped back at the force of her grip. 'How much self-esteem are you going to retain after seven hundred years of subjection to a lazy, incompetent, apathetic, uncultured race like the English? That's the humiliation: colonised by the English. Think of it, centuries of rule by clowns like Charles Venner-Harris.'

'Hey now, uncultured? I'm not having that, what about Shakespeare?'

Clare relaxed and laughed. 'When I was at convent school, the sister who taught us English insisted Shakespeare was Irish and his real name was Shaugnessy.'

It was Mike who laughed now. 'That would explain a lot.'

They walked on in silence. Neither wanted to continue this sterile bickering, nor would they let the odious Cassidy come between them. The water was lapping against the pontoons of the yacht harbour setting up a gentle rocking as they walked towards their boat. Loose halyards tapped on masts; somewhere there was a clink of glasses and a burst of happy laughter. As they walked their fingers brushed together and spontaneously they strolled hand in hand for a few yards, then mutually they parted and walked on.

'You know,' said Mike. 'Thanks to Mr Cassidy we never got our coffee. I'll light the stove and brew us a pot.'

CHAPTER 10

At seven o'clock next morning Mike came on deck to find fog. The town was invisible and he could only just make out the ghostly forms of the fishing fleet. He wondered what this would do for their chances of sailing. He hoped the promised high temperatures would burn off the fog before too long. Mike was restless; he wanted to be moving again. Another day in port risked a second encounter with Sammy Cassidy. Mike was not confident that he could restrain himself from chucking the obnoxious Sammy into the dock.

He went below and lit a burner on the galley stove. He would make them both a cup of coffee and then go to the yacht club for a shower. Outside on the pontoon he heard footsteps and a murmur of conversation. Mike looked up sharply. Someone was climbing aboard. He felt the yacht rock gently and heard the sound of movement in the cockpit. None too pleased he peered out of the hatch straight into the eyes of a French policeman; a gendarme in a peaked hat.

'Bonjour,' said Mike politely.

'Capitaine, I wish zee papers for zis ship?' The man's English was about on par with Mike's French.

'Right, you'd better talk to the owner,' Mike replied. The policeman looked uncomprehending. 'Oh hell, je trouve le proprieteur. Un moment, s'il vous plait.' Mike gave up and ran forward to bang on the forecabin door.

'Hey Michael, what's going on?' Clare called back.

'We've a visit from the law.'

Clare appeared sleepily, still dressed in the now rumpled white trousers and top. She had a brief conversation with the policeman.

'He says he wants to check our papers,' she said. 'He's also got a customs man outside and he's insisting on coming down as well.'

'Right, we'd better let them get on with it and go,' he sighed.

'I thought you said the French don't bother with yachts?'

'I've never seen this before,' he admitted. 'But it's early season. I suppose they want something to do.'

The policeman gave a call and a round-faced swarthy man in a leather jacket came down into the cabin. Clare handed them the ship's papers and their passports. Mike produced his yacht master's certificate. The customs man wandered around eyeing every nook and cranny but touching nothing.

'Madame, Monsieur, all is on order. When you leave?' asked the policeman.

'We'll sail this morning,' replied Mike.

'You stay in France waters?'

'For a few days, yes. We're making east towards Dieppe.'

'Merci, Capitaine – good trip.'

The customs man, who had remained silent throughout, followed the policeman on deck.

'Michael,' Clare was looking at him with an odd expression. 'Give it half a minute and I'll follow them.'

'Why, you can't be serious?'

'That policeman was never from these parts, and the uniform was wrong. It's a theatrical costume – I bet my sweet life on it.'

'How d'you mean not from here?'

'If I was to make an educated guess, I'd say he was a Basque from down South.'

'Does that matter?'

'No, but it's not likely, and I told you the uniform was wrong. Look Michael, don't just stand there in my way. I'm going out to have a look.'

'I'll come with you…'

'No you will not. It's stealth I need, not some flat footed Englishman they'll see a mile off – you wait here.' She ran on deck and dropped, barefooted, onto the pontoon. With a wave she disappeared into the mist. Mike shrugged and went below grumbling. It seemed clear the woman had an overheated imagination.

Clare was back within ten minutes. 'I was right,' she said triumphantly.

'What did you see?'

'Just as I thought. That copper was mighty quick to take off his jacket and hat, so quick I nearly missed them.' She flopped down on a bunk a little breathless. 'Well, off they go just as far as that big Dutch boat. There's three others waiting for them by the gangplank. They have a proper little chin wag, and then up they all go on deck and down below.'

'Are you sure they weren't checking her papers as well?'

'I don't believe it. That guy was no policeman and did you ever see a customs man like that one?'

'You're right,' he muttered. 'It's certainly odd.'

'Now listen, there's more. One of those they met; well I knew him. It's our friend Sammy from last night.'

'That idiot,' said Mike grimly. 'If I run into him again he'd better mind his manners.'

'Yes Michael, you know you've got one hell of a temper in you?'

'Only when I'm crossed by creeps like Cassidy or your Aunt Delia. You still haven't told me about her yet.'

'I'll tell you when I'm ready. It's not something I find easy.' A cloud seemed to pass over her. 'Michael I say we should get out of this place now. I'll feel safer at sea, fog or no fog.'

The little tower at the end of the harbour wall vanished into the murk. *Quadra* was at sea in a dank swirling mist. Clare, standing on the foredeck, sounded the fog signal: one long blast for a vessel under power. Mike looked at the tiny, hand-held foghorn with distaste; he'd seen better things at kiddie's parties. He was worried, because with no breath of wind he was forced to run under power. The drumming of the diesel blocked out all other sounds.

'Clare, keep your eyes open, concentrate and listen. If you see anything, yell.'

'Will there be many boats around?' she called.

'Bound to be fishermen. In a minute I'll stop the engine and we'll have a listen.'

Mike steered *Quadra* to an estimated position four miles north east of St Vaast and then swung onto a new course of 85 degrees. He aimed to cross the Baie de la Seine at a safe distance offshore but clear of the shipping lanes to the North. First he shut off the power. The yacht coasted along under her own momentum while he strained, listening. From astern came the wail of the fog signal on Cap Barfleur. Funny the way the mist played tricks. The lighthouse was sounding from the starboard quarter, completely in the wrong place. At that moment they felt the stirring of a breeze, not much but enough to move them cautiously on their way.

'Come on Clare. Let's get the main up, we'll sail. It won't be a speedy trip but it'll be a whole lot safer.'

For two hours they sailed on with a light breeze and maybe three knots through the water. Mike calculated that with the tide under them they would be doing even better. Every half-hour he updated their estimated position on the chart. Clare sat on the foredeck sounding the new fog signal – one long and two short blasts for a ship under sail. The fog was thinning and the breeze was picking up but more on their starboard side than he expected. They twice heard fishing boats and once passed close to a big one floating on the tide. Clare who had remained alert throughout gave a call.

'Michael, there's a good sized ship out there astern somewhere.'

'I agree, I've heard her. We're doing fine, but this wind's odd. It's too early for a proper sea breeze but that's what it feels like. I wish we had that Decca – something's wrong here.'

Another hour and the fog had thinned to around five hundred yards. They could still occasionally hear the engines of the strange ship somewhere not far away. Mike picked up the radio-direction finder. The big lighthouse was one of a number of radio beacons that put out a powerful coded signal for navigation. He swung the instrument to find the 'null', the quietest part of the signal, and read off the bearing on the built-in compass.

'Bloody hell, 310 degrees!' he whistled.

'What should it be?' Clare asked.

'265, or thereabouts.'

'Have you been watching the compass?'

'Of course I bloody have!'

'Hey there, you calm down. Isn't it funny how men will never admit it when they're lost.'

'Well I am now. I've done something really daft, and I can't see what.'

'Never mind Michael, fog's thinning – here comes the sun.'

She was right; he could feel the warmth of the sun as the bright rays burst through all around them. Somewhere close by came the rumble of heavy engines; the mystery ship again. For five seconds the sun opened a gap in the mist illuminating the vessel passing through.

'Christ, it's that Dutchman,' Mike exclaimed. They listened as the sound of engines receded and died away.

'Michael, they wouldn't be looking for us?' Clare looked pensive.

'What d'you think? I'm going to have a look at the chart.'

Mike sat at the chart table and puzzled. What the hell was going on? Fog was confusing but he was an experienced navigator and nothing as bad as this had ever happened before…

'Hey Michael, come up here quick!' Clare was yelling down the hatch at him.

'What's up?'

'I don't know; there's something right ahead. It looks like an apartment block in the middle of the sea.'

Mike scrambled into the cockpit, took one look ahead, and gave a whoop of relief. 'Thank God!'

'Michael what is it?' She was becoming angry as she stamped her foot on the cockpit floor.

Mike grabbed the chart. He was bubbling with joy and relief. 'Look, the chart says we're here, but we're not here, we're there… which means we're actually here, which we shouldn't be, but I know where we are.'

Clare looked at him and the ghost of a smile lit her face. 'Michael, are you quite sure you never had an Irish granny?'

He laughed. 'Quite sure. Come on let's move it. If that Dutchman's really looking for us, I know where we can hide away all day. Let's get the sails off and motor in.'

Clare, shrugged and did what she was told. They did a rough stow of the mainsail and Mike started the engine.

'Clare go forward and take a look ahead. You'll see a green channel mark and a red one almost in line.'

'OK Michael, I see them, I'll point you.'

'That's great, I'm going to leave the green buoy to starboard, then we'll turn sharp right and anchor in the pool behind those concrete walls. I want the anchor free and ready to let go, OK?'

The fog had nearly gone and they could see for over a mile. On their bows were the huge concrete walls that had so startled Clare. Beyond was a sheet of placid water with a sandy beach and the houses and villas of a little seaside town. Mike judged the distance, took a quick look at the depth meter and put the engine in neutral.

'Let go,' Mike called.

Clare released the anchor; there was a splash and the chain roared out behind. 'Better give it 130 feet of chain,' he called.

Mike put the engine astern to dig in the anchor; then satisfied he switched off. *Quadra* lay peacefully in a pool of warm sunshine and in deep clear waters. Beyond, to seaward, were the grim walls of concrete.

'Michael, where are we? What is this place?'

'I don't know how we come to be here, but we're at Arromanches. This is the 'Mulberry', the old D-day harbour, or what's left of it.'

CHAPTER 11

'Now we'll take a look at that compass.' Mike glared at the main steering compass on its pedestal in the cockpit. He and Peter had checked it through 360 degrees before the voyage. It had performed perfectly during the Channel crossing; so what was wrong?

'You investigate, I'll get us some lunch,' said Clare.

For the third time in five minutes Mike picked up the little hand held compass and checked its heading against the main one. There was no doubt; the big compass had an error: a deviation big enough to take a fogbound yacht straight into the North French coast. He hoped he was wrong, but with an awful feeling of certainty, he ran his fingers around the bowl of the compass and its mount. Then he found it. Taped in the recess of the moulding was a tiny piece of metal no bigger than a pound coin.

'Clare I've found it. We've been jinxed, sabotaged – somebody's trying to hi-jack us.' He held up the offending object.

'What is it?'

'Magnet, placed where we wouldn't think to see it. Done deliberately to throw us off course. What's more, I stake my reputation it was done by an expert. We were sent on exactly the course someone wanted.'

'That guy in the leather jacket?' she said. 'I bet he did it while that sham copper kept us talking.'

'That's what I think. I crashed out last night. I was fast asleep but I reckon I'd have woken if anyone climbed aboard. No, it's got to be them. Clever too, it must have been a spur of the moment plan when they saw the fog.' That still wasn't an explanation though. He was thinking fast now. The Dutch yacht had been waiting for them. Someone knew they were going to St Vaast. Only two other people knew that information; of that at least he could be sure.

'What are they after, Michael?'

'I should think that's obvious. Here's another lot of people who think this ship's full of hidden treasure.' He watched her face carefully.

'But there's nothing like that in this boat. There never was. At least nothing tangible like bits of paper.' Clare was adamant.

'So you do know something about this.' There was a change in his manner, a flash of hostility. He could see that he had startled Clare and her reply went unspoken. 'Clare, what happened today is the final straw. I've had three weeks of continual trouble and aggravation from this boat. I want very good reasons why I shouldn't up anchor now, take you back to St Vaast, and leave you there to take whatever comes.' That was the crunch, either this woman told him the truth, or...

'No Michael, don't do that...'

'Why not?' he interrupted. 'You and your grandfather's conspiracies are nothing to me. Right now most of my life is before me and I want to live it. I'm not going to put myself at risk for causes I know nothing about – Wait!' he waved away her interruptions. 'What's more they are causes which I believe you know much more about than you pretend. You level with me and I'll see what I can do. At the moment I can't help you – the trust we had is gone.'

Clare had sat down on the opposite side of the cockpit. For the first time some of her self-assurance had gone. She seemed smaller; vulnerable. There were tears on her face and her lower lip trembled. 'What did Delia tell you?' she asked quietly. 'That time her people searched *Quadra* and she told you to watch me.'

Mike fixed her with a cold unwavering stare. 'Good, now we are making progress. How would you know I was told to watch you?'

'I heard you report to her two nights ago, didn't I? It seems you weren't averse to spying on me. Yes, me, who was paying you good money and never done you harm in her life.' Clare's spirit had returned with a bang, her voice glittered with anger and her accent was vivid.

Mike remained unmoved. 'So you know that the boat was searched. Now how is that, I wonder?'

'When I was on the road from Swansea a friend rang me. No, I'm not saying whom, but an old friend of my grandfather who works with Delia. He watches her because grandfather asked him to – for my sake, see.'

Mike didn't see, but he let it go. 'Now you've said this much, I'll level with you in my turn. This Delia made Peter and me sign the Official Secrets Act. That means I mustn't repeat anything she told me to anyone on threat of prosecution. What's more I'll be repeating it to you, and you're a foreign national, which I guess makes it ten times worse.' He caught her eye forcing her to look at him.

'I'll never betray you, Michael, least of all to Delia.'

'Thank you. Now a week ago, the same day you arrived at Cottons Hard, this Delia briefed Peter and me. She was with an American, a

CIA man we think, a rather scary Spaniard, and one of your under-cover police from Dublin. They told us that your grandfather had hidden a copy of a secret document inside this boat and if it ever saw the light of day it would just about kick off World War Three. That appeared bloody unlikely to us but they seemed to think so. I might have been a bit more co-operative if that bloody woman hadn't given me the creeps. What is she, some sort of zombie?'

'The living dead? Not her, she's alive all right. She has to be alive to work her hate. I guess one day she'll work it from beyond the grave as well.' Clare's voice was almost a whisper, barely audible above the sounds of the ship.

'Michael, what do you know about the Spanish Civil War?' At last she had lifted her head and was staring him in the eye.

For the moment Mike wondered if this was a calculated evasion. He took one look at her face and knew she was serious. 'It was a prelude to the big war, that's all I know.'

'Granpapa was a drinking pal of Hemingway and others. He was out there in the thick of that war advising the Republic and helping build up their air force. That got him into big trouble politically because he crossed the Catholic Church, and that's a risky thing for an Irish politician.'

'Why did they mind?'

'Because the Church hierarchy backed Franco. Typical of them, they couldn't see the wood for the trees.' She was wandering now, gazing outside the ship. She wasn't evading him; that strange telepathy had returned between them. There was something she must tell him; something she never spoke of and would hurt her to reveal.

She sighed. 'Anyway the Republic was beaten and Franco's men were shooting people for sport. Granpapa smuggled out a leading Government politician and his family. Felipe, Carla and Maria, Lazarraga. He settled them in London, helped Felipe find a trans-lator's job and paid for little Maria's schooling.' Clare faltered for a few seconds and Mike nudged her gently.

'Has this something to do with Delia?'

She nodded. 'Yes, but there's no honour in it. When Maria was nineteen, Grandfather sponsored her for Yale medical school. You see she was already at Oxford and doing well...' Again she hesitated. 'If you must know, my grandfather was a terrible old hypocrite. Women – young one's at that. There must have been a dozen of them that I know of, and there were others, even into old age. This Maria was very beautiful, she still is. She became Grandfather's mistress for two years. Then she fell pregnant and Grandmother Chester put her foot down. Maria was sent packing back to England.'

'I still don't see the connection with Delia.'

'All right, let me finish, will you? Maria was a good Catholic girl and she wouldn't have the foetus aborted, more is the pity. So she had the baby born in England. She was christened Chechu, which is a Basque name, seeing that's the country where her mother Maria was born. But in England she's always been Delia Lazarraga, now of Her Majesty's Secret Service, and Her Majesty's harbouring a snake in the grass there and no mistake.'

'What's made her like she is?'

'That nobody could tell, but she's Spanish and Irish and that can be a wild mix. Her mother Maria's as bad in her way but you can understand that. I don't know the details, but something happened to Maria in the Civil War. Something she saw as a very little kid. I don't know what it was and Granpapa would never say.'

'You say this Maria is still alive?'

'Yes, and on the face of it she leads a blissful life as a country doctor in Dorset. But she's still all eaten up inside by something she saw in Spain when she was three years old.'

'Wait a minute?' Mike interrupted. 'This Delia woman is definitely English by birth?'

'That's right, she was born four months after Maria arrived back in Britain. Grandpapa saw Maria all right for money. He bought her a nice little estate in Dorset, and he paid for Delia to go to a posh school and on to Oxford.'

'And now she's in government service?'

'That's right, another bright graduate with a sick mind. She wants to hit back at the world and you Brits are daft enough to give her the chances she needs.'

'Is she your only relation?'

'She is now. I had an uncle once but he died before I was born and both my parents are gone – my father when I was a kid and my mother six years ago. My father was in the Irish diplomatic service and he was always overseas. He died in South America. Michael, I hope you're not thinking I'm paranoid, but there's evidence that Delia had a hand in him dying...' Once more her voice faltered, clearly on the edge of tears.

Mike would not press her further. He could not believe ill of this girl, nor would he desert her for all his threats. Beneath the jolly extrovert face she had shown another self, deeply troubled and unhappy. They had a working professional relationship, but since their time at sea together they had developed another deeper understanding. It was almost as if the three weeks they had known each other had been three years.

'Come on,' he smiled at last. 'What was it you said about some lunch? Let's eat and we'll talk later.'

'You will stay with me – with the ship?' her lower lip drooped anxiously.

'Yes I'll stay. I think I've a score to settle with your Aunt Delia myself.' That was true, the woman had damaged his masculine pride, and he had retribution to hand out to the thug who'd hit him from behind without warning. He had a feeling that if he stuck by Clare he would be meeting both of these others again. He had also had an explanation of sorts. He was not sure how much of it he believed but he was satisfied, or rather he felt a reassuring gut feeling, that Clare was an innocent victim. For that reason alone he should stand by her.

Lunch was a more relaxed meal than it might have been. Clare was her normal self again as she looked round the scene outside the boat.

'Was this place the D-day harbour?' she asked.

'That's right. I've been here once before. I was hired to take a boatload of the real veterans. It was very emotional, kind of...' he hesitated trying to find the right words. 'No, you're Irish you wouldn't understand.'

'And what is it Michael that I wouldn't understand?' Clare's eyes were flashing dangerously.

Mike was surprised. 'You weren't involved in the war that's all – no offence.'

'Well Michael, let me educate you. If you took a percentage, there were more of our young men, and women too, who volunteered for your forces than any country in your bloody old empire.'

'Your government sent a message of condolence to the Germans when Hitler died, it's well recorded.'

'That was Eammon de Valera, all strict for protocol. I never liked that man and Grandfather hated him.'

Mike quickly changed the subject. 'What are your plans?'

'I want to go to Etaples. It's not a pleasure trip any more. There's a man there I need to see. He's an old friend of Grandfather's and I think he may have a line on our problems.'

'You could go overland. You'd be there in an hour or two.'

'No Michael, we'll go in *Quadra*. It's true I don't know what this secret is, but if it's not in the boat it's connected with her.'

'OK, if we catch some sleep we could make a night passage towards Dieppe.'

'I need to make a couple of phone calls. I tried on my mobile but it's one that doesn't work in France.'

'Make them with a link call on the ship's radio.'

'And have the whole world listening? Do me a favour.'

He nodded, that made sense. 'Let's take a run ashore.'

They pulled the little inflatable dinghy high up the beach to the tide line. The hot weather had brought out some early season sunbathers. Mike looked around with disappointment. These buxom Norman ladies were not the lissom maidens of the Riviera. He speculated as to how his employer looked in her swimwear.

Clare was squatting on the sand with an odd expression.

'What's wrong?' he asked.

'Do you not feel something?'

'No, should I?'

'You should. I think I see ghosts.'

'Eh?'

'That's because you're English. In a place like this it is much better to be Irish.'

'What ghosts, Clare?'

'Soldiers, the ones who came here.' She looked up at him with an enigmatic smile. 'Come on, you – let's find a telephone.'

They found a café with a pay phone. Mike sat outside in the sunshine while Clare made her calls. Two phone calls, she told him, although she was reticent as to whom. A quarter of an hour later she rejoined him, and they sat in the sun enjoying their coffee. Mike said nothing. He felt he'd asked enough questions. He could only remain wary and wait developments.

The tide was flooding, spreading out across the water to where the little yacht swung to her anchor dwarfed by the huge bulk of the Mulberry wall. Far out to sea Mike saw a power vessel away to the north on a course for Barfleur. Even at this distance there was something familiar about her. He ran across to a viewpoint with a coin-operated telescope. He swung it round on the distant ship. He said nothing but motioned Clare to look.

'Is it?' she asked.

'I think so. I doubt if there's another like that. I'd say she's our Dutchman.' They watched until the vessel dipped below the horizon.

'Come on,' he said. 'Let's get back on board.'

Mike sat at the chart table while Clare peered over his shoulder.

'I think we agree,' he said. 'That the people in that ship deliberately jinxed our compass and sent us down here for some motive of their own.'

'It wouldn't have worked if it hadn't been foggy – had you thought of that?' she replied.

'I think they planned it on the spot when they saw the conditions. What worries me is the cleverness of it, the skill and ingenuity. We're up against some formidable people.'

'Any of the people behind this would be clever – devious anyway.'

'All right, who are they?'

Clare was looking really worried. 'Worst case would be terrorists. We'll have to watch our step.'

'Could it be the French?'

'I'm sure they'd love to have the secret, but they could have searched us officially, like the Brits did. They had no need to go through all this pantomime.'

'What do we do?'

'We've no choice. We'll take *Quadra* to Etaples. There's a man there who's expecting us and I've arranged for someone to fly over from England to meet us tomorrow. Between the two of them we may have the answers.'

Right, let's look at the chart. We'll make a night passage. There's a good forecast and it'll be cooler so we shouldn't have fog.'

'Will that Dutchman still be looking for us?' Clare looked apprehensive.

'If she is, she'll find it a hundred times harder to spot us at night.' Mike sought to reassure her. 'I know the sound of her engines now. If I hear her I'll douse our navigation lights until she's out of the way.'

Mike started the engine and left Clare ready at the helm while he walked forward. *Quadra* had a lot of anchor chain out and pulling it in would be heavy work, even with the hand-cranked windlass. The anchor emerged from the deep coated in wet sand and a few wisps of weed. Mike waved to Clare who put the engine in gear and steered for the gap in the harbour walls. Mike stood on the foredeck, one hand on the mast as he watched the shoreline and the little town shrink in size and then merge with the oncoming dusk. He wondered how he would have coped had he been born into his father's generation. Fifty years ago he could have risked his life in this place, probably as a seaman, but possibly as a soldier or a pilot. How would he have acquitted himself? That was something he would never know. Kill or be killed. There was something pleasingly simple about war: easier to comprehend than the twilight world of Delia Lazarraga. Thank God that awful woman was out of their lives, for the present at least. For a few seconds Mike felt cold at the thought of her. It was humiliating and ridiculous that one thin undernourished looking woman should scare the living daylights out of him.

CHAPTER 12

Clare glanced into the cabin. The red light over the chart table was enough for her to read the clock. 0300 – three o'clock in the morning. Fifty-five miles run, nearly half way. By rights she ought to feel tired. Hell no, just the opposite. Never had she felt more vital or alive. Here she was, alone in the night at the helm of her very own ship. Well, not quite alone; she could see the huddled figure of Michael on the port side bunk. She guessed her skipper was more awake than he looked. She closed her eyes and drank in the sounds of the ship. The surging rush as she rose to each wave and the deep sigh as the water pushed past her sides and curled into the wake behind. She was helming her own ship sailing at night, beneath a clear starlit sky, with the moon dancing on the waves around her. Clare's romantic nature burned with the poetry of it all.

Compass; remember the course! 045 degrees; she had strayed slightly. Gently she pushed the tiller, and the compass card swung back on the heading. She shot a guilty glance into the cabin, but Michael slept on. She hooked the auto-helm back on the tiller and pressed the switch. The soulless robot would do a better job than she could in her present mood.

Michael had taken the first four-hour watch to see them past the busy approach to Le Havre. Clare could see the lights of the segregated traffic streams to the north. She looked around the horizon, each quarter in turn and a last glance to the north again. She looked down into the cabin. Oh, what was she to do about Michael? Chance had thrown her together with this wildly attractive man, only for all this trouble and anxiety to come between them. She was drawn to Michael in every way, physically and as a person. But did she mean anything to him? He was quietly self-assured, rock steady until his temper was roused, and then he would blaze with passion. He had fallen out with Annabel, his girl friend of two years. Peter Blair had warned her that Michael's quarrel with Annabel had hurt him deeply. She had seen how Michael's friends and colleagues liked and almost revered him. That pretty little girl in the office clearly adored him, though Michael seemed not to know it. Even the ludicrously snobbish Charles had spoken of him with a grudging respect. Clare had enjoyed plenty of lovers: French, Italian and of course Irish. None had lasted: all had been shallow men with huge conceits and a stone-age view of women. Michael was very different. But how was she to handle him? The fact that he was English didn't help. They really were the most peculiar people.

Clare had no ill will towards the British. Her generation could afford to be the first Irish to take a balanced view. She had read enough history to know that the English were never the rapacious master race of Irish myth, nor were her own people the saints and martyrs they liked to believe. British and Irish alike were the victims of geography as much as anything. Over sixty million people crammed into a small archipelago of islands; a crazy cultural mis-match.

'How's things?' It was Michael. He was standing on the cabin steps looking forward. Clare had not seen him get up, so absorbed had she been.

'I'm fine.' She was glad of his presence, even though she had been happy alone in her private world.

'Watch change – time for you to get some sleep.'

'Michael, I don't want to go below. Can't I stay here with you?'

He laughed. 'No way, come on – sea discipline. You get some sleep – I'll need you in good shape for the last lap.'

'I suppose so, but it's nice up here.'

'Never mind, tell you what, make us each a hot drink. You can stay until you've drunk it and then get your head down.'

Clare was startled into full awakening. It was daylight and the engine had started. She peered at the clock and then leapt from her bunk. It was nine-fifteen and she'd been due on watch an hour ago. Half guilty, half resentful, she climbed on deck.

'You never woke me,' she said.

'No need,' said Mike. 'I was alright here. You're not really used to this – much better get some sleep.'

'If you won't let me stand proper watches, I'll never get used to it.'

'I know, but don't take it to heart. I'd have called you quick enough if we'd needed a sail change.'

Clare looked around. To starboard was the French coast with the lights of a large town still visible in the morning light.

'That's Dieppe,' said Mike. 'I had to stay up here to see us past the crossing traffic.'

'How much further?'

'About twenty miles to Pointe Le Touquet. Then we have fun and games.'

Why?'

'Because it's a very shallow entrance, and I'd better warn you, I've never been in these channels before.'

'You're being modest, Michael. You'll get us there.'

The wind was dropping so they lowered sail. They motored on for a while then Mike pointed out the tall light tower on Pointe Le Touquet.

'It'll be another hour before there's enough water in the channel,' he said.

They had passed the Pointe when Clare spoke again. 'There's another boat coming up behind us fast.'

Mike trained his binoculars. 'Looks like a fisherman, or at least I hope that's all she is.'

'What's wrong, Michael?'

'She's bow on to us, so I'm not sure, but she could be our Dutchman.' He handed the glasses to Clare.

'Black hull, white bridge and red funnel, and she's too clean and polished to be a fisherman. No Michael, that's her, the same one I'm sure of it.'

There was a gasping sound from the VHF radio, then a voice. 'Yacht *Quadra*, this is the *Admiral Van Haagen*, over.'

Mike and Clare glanced at each other; neither moved.

'Yacht *Quadra*, d'you hear me? I have urgent messages for you.'

Clare gripped his arm. 'Michael, that's no Dutchman.'

Mike said nothing. The radio reception from no more than a mile was perfect. The man's accent was certainly not Dutch.

CHAPTER 13

Mike had made his decision. 'Clare, I'm going to cut the corner and go in over the sands.'

'Will we have the depth?'

'I've no idea but we haven't a choice. The channel is over a mile away and they'll catch us before then. I'd rather not have a meeting with those people out here.'

He made a quick calculation. *Quadra* drew a trifle over three feet and the big trawler at least eight. It was a flood tide and no wind; even if they did ground the larger vessel would be unable to follow. Mike turned *Quadra* and headed straight for the distant village of Camiers. At once the shallow-water warning began to bleep on the depth gauge. Eight feet...seven...five...four feet. The water around them had developed a yellowish shade. They were already in the shallows.

'They're following us,' said Clare.

'They can't possibly, we're barely going to make it – they haven't a hope.'

'Maybe they think we know a way in.'

'You could be right. No! look he's bought it – Christ! What a mess.'

The *Van Haagen* had hit the sand at full speed and the impact had swung her round showing her full starboard profile. The force of the impact had been enough to fell the crewmen. Mike could see distant figures scrambling up from the deck. He was aware that his heart was thumping. It had been a tense few minutes but they should be safe now. He pulled back the throttle and dropped their speed to a cautious four knots. He knew that hitting the sand at speed they could well damage their mast.

'They're lowering a boat,' said Clare.

'Laying a kedge anchor, I expect. I'm going to head up towards the channel.'

Clare was still concentrating with binoculars. 'There's another boat, an inflatable. Oh Michael, it's coming our way.'

'How many in it?'

'Three I think.'

Mike glanced at the depth gauge: seven feet. He pushed the throttle open wide and the big diesel responded with a roar. Seven knots was about the best they could do, a poor response to a high-speed rigid-inflatable. This was a development he hadn't anticipated. Seconds ago he had been convinced they were safe now he was scared. Whatever happened he would not show fear in front of Clare.

'Do we send a 'Mayday'?' she asked.

'And say we're being pursued by pirates? No, we'll have to sort this ourselves.' Mike had forced himself to think rationally and now he had a plan.

Their pursuer, a rigid-inflatable or RIB, was fairly flying – bouncing across the sea towards them. He could see her crew distinctly.

'Clare, under the chart table. There's a wooden box. Fetch it please?'

Clare disappeared below. 'Is this it?'

'Yes bring it up.'

The box was varnished, about two feet square and eight inches deep. Mike released the combination padlock and took out an object wrapped in an oily rag. Mike removed the rag to reveal a set of distress rockets.

'Michael, for God's sake what's that?'

'Flares, I keep them for distress.'

He laid out four rockets on the deck beside him.

'What are you going to do? Clare looked anxious.

'Call attention to ourselves if I have to. You get below and stay by the radio.'

Clare looked mutinous. She spared a glance for the approaching craft then meekly she climbed below and sat at the chart table.

The pursuing inflatable closed to within twenty yards. A man was kneeling in the bows. He seemed to be wrestling with some item of equipment. There was a crack. Something whined through *Quadra's* rigging. There was a twang as a wire parted. The RIB overtook them and began to circle ready for a second pass. It was coming closer this time. It was coloured orange with a central steering position. Two men stood in the bows in front of the helmsman. One carried a loud hailer and the other the gun. Mike knew little about guns except that this was a semi-automatic weapon.

'*Quadra*,' it was a tinny voice from the loud hailer. 'You are to stop your engine. Let us aboard and you'll not be hurt.' It was the same voice as the one on the radio. Mike saw the gunman aim and fire. Again two shots screamed through the rigging.

'Michael, don't stop! Don't let them near.' Clare called from the hatch.

'Get back below,' he snapped. 'Lie on the deck!'

He picked up a flare. The inflatable was moving up astern. It was coming really close this time. Mike could see the helmsman shaping to lay alongside. The gunman was down on one knee preparing to aim. Mike levelled the flare and fired. There was no way one could aim the thing; it was a signal not a weapon. The charge passed only inches in front of the inflatable. Startled, the gunman had fired early. Mike neither saw nor heard the shot. He was surprised how cool and rational he felt as he picked up another flare. The inflatable was five yards away its crew clustered in the bows. Aft of the helmsman the boat was empty. Mike aimed from point blank range and shot a flare into the empty stern. The most he could hope for was to create a diversion. What followed was different. There was a cracking popping noise, audible over the sound of the engines. Then a tongue of flame shot skywards from a cloud of oily black smoke. The helmsman let out a yell. All three men stood staring at the stern before as one they leapt overboard. Their boat powered on for another twenty yards; then with a loud thump, the entire craft vanished in a ball of fire. Seconds later there remained only scorched debris and a circle of burning water.

Clare was beside him clutching his elbow. 'What happened?'

'I'm not sure. It may be they were refuelling and forgot to replace the cap on the tank.'

'What do we do?'

'That motor launch of theirs is coming. I think we'll leave them to clear up.' He could see the crew of the inflatable floundering in the sea. The water temperature at this time of year was too cold for them to survive long. Unless they were rescued at once they could die. With relief he saw all three pulled into the launch.

'Hey, yonder's Sammy.' Clare was staring through the binoculars.

'That Cassidy?'

'The very same. He's not one of them that shot at us but he's playing the rescuer.'

'We'd better radio in and report all this. There isn't a single witness to say what really happened. We could be in trouble.'

'I've done it. I made a link call to my friend. He'll talk to the police and we'll have help waiting.'

They motored up the main channel to the marina at Etaples. On arrival Mike was surprised to see a reception committee. Six cheerful Frenchmen took their lines and secured them to the pontoon. They jabbered in high speed french to Clare who happily jabbered back.

'Who are this lot?' he asked. 'They look like a rugby team.'

'That's perceptive of you, Michael. They are a rugby team.'

One of the men climbed aboard. He was a burly character, with a swarthy Mediterranean complexion, and somewhat older than the others. Monsieur, Madamoiselle, I am Jean-Luc. I 'ave a car to take you to le Chef.'

The car was a Rolls-Royce Silver Shadow. Jean-Luc opened the rear door and ushered Mike into the plush interior. When Clare followed he made an attempt at a gallant bow. She laughed happily. With *Quadra* safe and the dangers behind them she was determined to enjoy the moment. Mike wished he could be so sure. Two more large men crammed into the rear seat one on either side of them. Another man took the wheel and Jean-Luc filled the front passenger seat. Clare continued chattering in French but Mike felt apprehensive. It was all too like the film scenario where the gangsters take their victim for a 'ride'.

The car sped past tall pines and luxurious gardens. This was Paris-Plage, the casino playground of the high societies of Paris and London. To live here one needed serious money. After eight minutes the car turned off the main road in front of a high wall and a pair of tall wrought iron gates. The driver hooted twice and a man emerged from the shadows, unbolted the gates, and swung them open. They passed through into a long gravelled drive. On either side were immaculate lawns and borders ablaze with spring flowers. The house was not as large as Mike had expected. It was a long, low building painted white with green shutters. They drew to a halt on a wide gravel sweep. Their escort piled out en masse. Clare followed and with a joyful cry flung her arms around an elderly man who stepped from the front door.

'Oncle Roger,' she said. 'Ici mon ami, Michael. Il est mon capitaine.'

Mike shook hands with the man who greeted him with a smile. He was tall, slim, and dressed in that casual elegance the British found hard to emulate. He had craggy features, with silver-grey hair, and striking blue eyes.

'Bonjour Michael, my little Clare has already told me about you and you're very welcome. Now both of you come in and meet the company. One of my guests you already know.' It was a relief to find the man's English was almost without accent.

'Oncle Roger, I have not introduced you properly.' Clare spoke to the old man with mock severity. 'Michael, this is Roger Peyron. I call him Uncle Roger though he's not really. His own father flew with my Grandpapa in World War One, and we've been close families ever since.'

Monsieur Peyron bowed happily to each in turn. 'Michael come and see my little house. It has associations with your country. Your King Edward the Seventh stayed here with my grandfather and later we entertained the Duke and Duchess of Windsor.'

The interior of the house was sumptuous but not vulgar. The furniture, the carpets and the pictures, spoke of old money and good taste. Peyron stopped in front of a small portrait. It was of a young man in uniform, with pilot's wings. There was something teasingly familiar about the face: the distinctive dark eyes and the blond hair.

'There you are, Michael. Capitaine James O'Dwyer, Clare's grandfather.'

'That was painted in 1917,' said Clare. 'Granpapa was in the United States Air Corps.'

'There is no doubt who Clare takes after,' said Mike.

'No doubt whatever – come and meet our guests,' said Peyron. 'We will have a little apertif, then business.'

They entered a book-lined study. Standing by the windows were two men with drinks in hand. One was a tall, sun-bronzed man, dressed in casual style. He was a stranger to Mike but his companion was not. The other was Clarence Fairbrother, the black CIA man.

CHAPTER 14

'Hi there, we meet again.' Clarence's handshake was warm. He indicated his companion. This is my Australian colleague, Craig Bilton.'

'G'day,' said the Australian on cue.

'Don't look so surprised, Michael,' said Clare. 'I've known Clarence for years. It was me who rang him yesterday.'

'And what she had to say brought me right over here.' Clarence had stopped smiling.

'Clare and Michael,' said Peyron. 'What refreshment can I offer you?'

'Uncle Roger, if it's all the same to you we'd like something to eat, or I would.' Clare glanced at Mike. 'We've had no breakfast.'

'That's true,' Mike agreed. 'Breakfast time we were otherwise occupied.' And bloody frightened, though he'd rather not admit that in this company.

'Ah yes, you were repelling boarders – a fine British tradition. Certainly I can offer you croissant and coffee.'

Peyron rang a bell and gave instructions. Then he indicated a semi-circle of leather bound chairs.

Mike had been bursting to speak and now he did so with urgency. 'That ship, the *Van Haagen*, is anyone doing anything?'

'Indeed yes,' said Peyron. 'The ship has been re-floated and is lying at anchor. Half an hour ago the police boarded her and released the master and crew. I'm afraid of the miscreants there was no sign.'

'Released – so the criminals were holding the crew under duress?'

'Oh yes, Clarence. I think you should put our friends out of their suspense.'

'That's true,' said Clarence. 'Michael, I've a story to tell. I've learned a whole lot since our last meeting.' He paused to look at Clare. 'Have you told him about Delia Lazarraga?'

'Yes.'

'OK, yesterday I found that agent of Delia's – the one you boys caught drilling holes in Clare's boat.'

'I know what I'd like to do with him,' said Mike.

'Not yet, I've got him on my side. You see, the guy's feeling pretty sore after Delia sucked the blood from him. He didn't take much persuading to talk.' Clarence gave each of them a sharp glance.

'See here, I'm taking you folks on trust. Roger and Craig are both connected with intelligence services. What I'm about to tell you mustn't go any place else – all right?'

The both nodded assent.

'Good. Now Delia's man had tracked a terrorist cell to Flushing in Holland. He thought they were planning some mayhem in NATO army bases in Germany. But no, they boarded a Dutch charter yacht, the *Admiral Van Haagen*. Charlie reports to Delia and she says, "get you back to England first plane, 'cause these are the boys looking for the Flanagan papers". You see Delia still reckoned the papers were in that yacht at Cottons Hard, and that's where the bad guys would likely show next.'

Mike was doubtful. 'Why should terrorists hire a plush motor yacht?'

'These are Provisional IRA and they knew every security agency was already staked out at every port and airport, but nobody would think to check a swank motor yacht in a marina. That's where the *Van Haagen* was – in the yacht basin not two miles from your place.'

'Expensive deception?'

'No, take it from me these people ain't short of bucks,' replied Clarence. 'So, Delia ordered Charlie to stake out the boatyard and then wait for her. But Charlie had other ideas. Why not find the papers first and replace them with a false set for disinformation? So that was the point where he started a bit of free enterprise.'

'Drilling holes,' said Mike.

'That's it, but there was a method in it. You see Charlie'd been in the States. He's seen the U.S. Coastguard at work on drug runners, and with drug boats the number one hiding place is in the rudder. So he sets to work only to be jumped by you.'

'Don't expect me to say sorry,' said Mike.

'Sure, but you can see why Delia was mad. She'd planned to stake out the place, let the terrorists find the papers, and then take them in one swoop.'

Clare spoke. 'May I ask, who is Flanagan, and what has he to do with my boat?'

'You'd better explain, Roger,' said Clarence. 'You know more about the man than me.'

'Just so,' said Peyron. 'But now we go back in time to the Great War: to my father's time and, Clare, to your grandfather and to Thomas-Jefferson Flanagan.'

'He couldn't possibly be called that,' Clare spluttered with laughter.

'That was his name. He was Muster-Master to the United States Expeditionary Force.'

'I like that title, Muster-Master,' said Clarence. 'I guess they'd call him a Logistics Officer these days.'

'Clarence, these papers?' said Peyron. 'I understand you've seen the originals?'

'Sure, I had a sight of 'em as soon as the State Department handed copies to us.'

'What was your impression?'

'They prove there was one hell of a conspiracy hatching. There's no telling what might happen if the truth surfaced even now.'

'As bad as that?'

'Yes, this is Ireland remember, and right now couldn't be a worse time.'

'Why?'

'Sorry, Roger, I can't tell you that.'

'What about the IACS?' said Craig the Australian.

'If they find those papers they'll milk 'em all they can,' said Clarence.

'Please,' Mike intervened, 'You've lost me. Who are the iacs, or whatever you said?'

'There's several branches,' said Craig. 'But the one that concerns me is the Irish Australian Cultural Society.'

'Sammy Cassidy again?' said Clare.

'How d'you know that name?' Craig looked startled.

'We met the man in a bar in St Vaast two days ago,' said Mike. 'He's a pain in the rear if you want my opinion.'

'There's more to it than that,' said Clare, 'He was on the *Van Haagen* yesterday and again this morning. We saw him in their launch.'

'Lady, are you quite sure of all this?'

'As sure as I'm sitting here.'

Mike pulled out his wallet and tossed across Sammy's card.

'Well well,' Craig whistled. 'Sam Cassidy the Pom basher. What was he doing?'

'Dolan was seen with Cassidy in Holland,' said Clarence.

'I'm in a fog again,' said Mike. 'Who is Dolan?'

'He was an IRA cell commander,' Clarence explained. 'His number two was the late McManus, the guy your secretary drowned in the creek. We think he was the other one in the car – the one who made it back to the *Van Haagen* under the noses of the Sussex Police.'

'You're right,' said Mike. 'I heard his voice that night and again today. It's the same man, I'm certain.'

'It still doesn't explain why Sam Cassidy was aboard that ship,' said Craig. 'You see Sam's all wind and piss, I doubt if he'd even shoot a rabbit.'

'Who is he?' Clare asked. 'He told us he was a historian.'

'Well, he is to an extent. He wrote a couple of books in the Seventies – all about the early squatters crossing the mountains. They weren't bad stuff either, you know, popular but well researched, even scholarly. Then somehow Sam slipped off his trolley. He started a third book on the Eureka Mine. This time it was hysterical anti-British propaganda. Complete bullshit – no reputable publisher would touch it.'

'But it was published on the internet,' said Clarence. 'We've some printed text on file, I've seen it.'

'Yeah, Sammy gave it to a small circulation paper 'The Hibernian', they serialised it. You see we've a big Irish community in Australia. It includes some of our oldest families and a lot of top names: sport, politics, business, you name it. Ninety percent of them's totally reasonable mature people, but not all. There's latent support for the IRA and we don't tolerate terrorists whatever their cause.' Craig paused it was as if he were weighing his words. 'Michael, you ever been to Oz?'

'Yes once for a yacht race.'

'How d'you find us?'

'Fantastic, to tell the truth. All the people we were with were great.'

'Did they slag you off for being a Pom?'

'Yes, but it was all good-humoured. You learn to get your dig in first.'

Craig nodded. 'That's the way it's always been 'til now. It's what happens in a family; we exchange insults because it's fun.'

Mike agreed. 'That's how we found it.'

Craig nodded again. 'But in Australia it's like the old song, "the times they are a-changing." I'll be straight with you, I'm a republican. I think we need our own identity, but I'm not a nationalist with a big N. To be that you've got to find people an enemy to unite against. Someone they can blame for all their own mistakes – someone to hate. Put it this way, I don't want IACS and Sam Cassidy stirring the pot with some conspiracy theory about Poms.'

'How much success are IACS having?' asked Peyron.

'At the moment nil. Sammy's the kind of bloke you invite on a TV chat show when you want to give folks a laugh. But that could all change. If IACS can come up with some revelation about the Brits in World War One, they could stir things.'

There was a knock on the door followed by an elderly woman with a food trolley.

'Michael and Clare,' said Peyron. 'Your breakfast arrives and enough I see for all of us. I think we should cease discussion for ten minutes.'

Mike sank his teeth into a croissant. This wasn't his usual choice of breakfast but the bread was superb and the coffee excellent. Beside each plate was a folded newspaper. 'English early editions,' said Peyron. 'It is one benefit of living near an airport.'

'Thank you,' said Mike. He was genuinely touched by the gesture.

The paper was The Daily Telegraph. He was about to turn to the sports page when an item caught his eye. It was the centre of the front page.

BY-ELECTION SHOCK
TORY CANDIDATE MISSING.

With nominations due to close for the North Worcester by-election, Conservative Party officials are desperate to trace the whereabouts of their prospective candidate, Sir Charles Venner-Harris. There has been no word of Sir Charles since he left on a private visit to Ireland ten days ago...

Mike grunted with surprise and handed the paper to Clare. 'Well now, there's a turn up.' She passed the paper to Peyron while Mike explained Charles's connection with them.

'I would not expect a Conservative Party politician to be involved with these people.' Peyron looked questioningly at Mike.

'I wouldn't know, but I can't see Venner-Harris succeeding in anything devious. He's got nothing between his ears, I know him of old.'

'You say this man visited you at home?' Peyron looked at Clare.

'He said his clients wanted to buy my boat. He offered big money too.'

'With a large percentage for Sir Charles?'

'Exactly so,' Mike agreed. 'He admitted it.'

'I think we know why the "Culturals" were after your boat,' said

Clarence. 'Michael here knows why, and I guess so do you, Clare.'

'There's nothing in the boat,' Clare protested. 'Nothing at all and I don't believe there ever was.'

'I think we are all agreed about that,' said Clarence. 'But I believe these documents exist, and Clare,' his change of tone made her start. 'You've got them. You may not know where yet, but they're yours by inheritance, and you'll have no peace until they're found.'

Midway through the morning Clarence and Craig left for the airport. Mike and Clare went with them in the Rolls-Royce driven by Jean-Luc. Mike asked Jean-Luc if he really was a rugby player as Clare had said. The man's face lit with a mighty grin. Indeed yes; he was a Southerner from Provence where rugby was an obsession.

At the airport was Clarence's own Cessna. Mike gathered this was a CIA perk granted only to a very few top agents. Half an hour later they watched the plane climb away over the estuary. Clare had asked Clarence where he was going, but he only smiled and said Holland. They would be back for dinner with maybe some of the answers. He winked at them and left it at that.

Mike spent the rest of the morning with the local rigger replacing *Quadra's* broken stay. Now the ship could face anything the sea was inclined to throw at her. Roger Peyron had delayed lunch until their return – French seafood at its most glorious with a dry white wine. Mike caught Clare's eye across the table. She looked lovelier than ever as her golden hair cascaded over her plain white jumper. Once again there was this strange telepathy between them: 'Glad you came with me? It was worth it wasn't it?' Not a word had been spoken – he just knew. He smiled and mouthed the word, 'Yes'.

After the meal Roger had coffee served in his study. On the table lay some deed boxes and a long cardboard tube.

'Michael, Clare and I must talk in private for a while. You see, I am her grandfather's executor for all his estate in Europe. This is my first chance to speak with her since her return from America.'

'Of course,' Mike stood up to leave but Roger called him back. He handed Mike the cardboard tube.

'A moment, these will interest you. They are the original drawings for the yacht, *Mary Elizabeth Chester*, now renamed, *Quadra*.' He looked at Clare. 'There must have been some reason for Jim to change the name.'

Eamon Clarke was ninety-nine years old and he lived in two rooms off a back alley in Amsterdam's infamous, 'red light' district. Eamon had left his native Ireland sixty years ago to wander the highways and byways of the world. He had never returned home and he had no wish to. The only Ireland he knew was deep in his imagination; deep in his spiritual being. It was that green land of saints and scholars that he had fought for in his youth. That dream had died amidst the greed of politicians and the humbug of clerics. He was an old man now, but once he had been young; an idealist who had killed men for his dreams. Hundreds more he had killed across the length of Europe; men, women and children too; all for the highest motives. Would that be held against him in the next life? He fingered the rosary on his lap. He could still feel and, miraculously, he could still hear, but his sight was gone; only light and shade now: the sun through the window or the bright light bulb in the ceiling.

Old as he was, Eamon's mind was still sharp. Who were all these people beating a path to his door? All these questions about Jimmy O'Dwyer; Jimmy the aviator. He'd been more forward in telling the men who'd come today. He had liked the Yankee who had done most of the talking, and the Australian; great fellows the Aussies. But that woman yesterday had frightened him. It wasn't her English accent; Eamon held no spite for the English as people. It was her manner; she'd been as cold as the chill of winter wind. Once more he seemed to be back in 1920 facing the interrogators in Dublin Castle. He'd known real fear then. Shut your mind, shut out the present. Resist, resist; you are a soldier with a cause and they shall not break you.

He heard the door open. The young couple in the rooms above had befriended him and little Anna would come and cook him a meal and tidy his few possessions. He half turned in his wheel chair. Instinctively he had known something was wrong. The iron bar shattered his frail skull with its first blow. It killed him outright but that was not enough for his attacker. For a frenzied half minute the bar rose and fell as the old man's head was systematically beaten beyond recognition. Blood seeped into the carpet and spattered the table and chair.

Clarence had left the Cessna at a NATO airfield near Utrecht. He and Craig had taken a taxi into Amsterdam. Expensive travel, but he wasn't picking up the tab. They had found the old man, chair-bound and sightless, but still lucid. A most satisfactory interview had followed. Craig had stuffed the tape recorder back into his briefcase and they had left in excited good humour. That had been a mistake. If Clarence had used his normal caution he would have spotted the figure in the arched doorway across the street.

At the airfield they received clearance and the Cessna had taken off for the return trip to Le Touquet. Clarence eased the control column back until the altimeter read three thousand feet. He had been given an easterly track, taking him clear of the main airport at Schipol. The commonplace remark he was about to make to his companion never left his lips. The bomb in the tail ripped the aircraft apart and the wreckage fell, a ball of fire, into the water of the Ijsselmeer.

CHAPTER 15

Mike awoke to find himself still lying among the sheet drawings of *Quadra*. He was worried that he might have damaged them. However all was well, and he slid off the bed, picked up the drawings and laid them in a neat pile on the table. He looked at the clock; half past six. He had slept for three hours. There was a knock on the door; it was Clare. 'I looked in an hour back,' she said, 'but you were still out for the count.' She sat on the bed beside him, throwing her long hair over her shoulders.

There was a further knock on the bedroom door. It was the elderly housekeeper. 'Please, telefon pour Mamosielle.'

Clare went with her. After a few seconds Mike followed, walking quietly down the wide stairway. He had no wish to pry, but he was puzzled as to who might be ringing Clare here. He met Roger in the hallway just as Clare ran out of the study, rather breathless.

'Michael, we've got to go to a place called Billancourt.'

'What's going on?'

'That was Craig. He says he and Clarence have landed at an airfield near a place called Billancourt. Clarence has had engine trouble. He's going to fix it and go straight on to England, but he must talk to us first – urgent.'

'Where is this place?' asked Mike.

'I know it,' said Roger. 'It's over near Amiens, but I doubt if Clarence will have his engine fixed so easily. The last I heard of the place it was a ruin.'

'What sort of airfield?'

'It's an old wartime Luftwaffe strip. Later it was used by a crop spraying firm, but I do not think they still exist.'

'Is it still on the map?'

'Of course, a moment please.' Roger went into his study and reappeared with a road atlas and an ordnance map. 'Here we are, past Abbeville on the N35. Turn left at Mouflers. Now look at this large-scale map. There is a ruined chateau here. Go up the avenue, round the back of the house and voila...' Roger marked the airstrip with a pencil.

'We should find that all right,' said Mike.

'I will ask Jean-Luc to drive you.'

'Hey,' said Clare. 'No need to be bothering him. Have you still

99

got the little 'Visa'?'

'But of course, it is in the garage. Certainly you may use it.'

They were on the road in the little Citroen. Clare drove and Mike sat beside her, staring at the flat countryside in the falling light. He had enough knowledge and imagination to know that this undistinguished land was steeped in history. They were nearing the battlefields of the First World War. Mike's own late grandfather had been there and had never fully recovered from the resulting trauma. Clare's grandfather had flown above the battle in a conflict scarcely less brutal.

'Who is Roger Peyron?' he asked suddenly.

'His father was with my grandfather in the Great War. He was Olivier Peyron.'

'Another pilot?'

'That's right, Olivier was with the Lafayette Squadron. He was French, of course, but most of the pilots were American volunteers with the French Air Force.'

'Including your grandfather?'

'No, that was much later. He was with the American forces, but Olivier was sent to help train them for battle.'

'It's Roger who intrigues me. I've never met a Frenchie who speaks English as well as he does.'

'He was in England as a boy. He told me he went to school there. What I do know is that when the war started he was in Senegal. In 1940 he hitched and walked over a thousand miles to join the Free French forces. He fought in the desert in North Africa.' Clare stopped her face troubled. 'When he came back from France after the war he found his wife and child had vanished. Anne-Marie, his wife, was Vietnamese. Most people think she was swept up and sent to a concentration camp.'

'And Roger?'

'He will not accept that they are dead. I can tell you he's spent a fortune trying to find what happened.'

It was dusk now as they approached the village of Billancourt. They saw the entrance posts of the chateau; grim stone pillars which once supported ornate gates. The drive was an avenue overlooked by dark trees. The road was weed-infested and potholed. The Citroen bumped and drummed over its uneven surface.

'Not many people come this way,' Mike grunted.

They had reached a fork. To the left the drive curved round

towards the house. To the right was a branch road hardly better surfaced but laid in concrete sections.

'That'll be our way,' said Clare as she steered onto this new turning. They circled round a thick belt of trees until they could just make out what must be the airfield. In reality it was a large field of young growing wheat with a hard runway visible in the middle. At the edge was the outline of an aircraft.

'Where the hell's Clarence?' muttered Mike. 'Hey slow down, I don't like this – something's wrong.'

'Why?'

'That plane's not Clarence's Cessna. It's a Piper Twin, about twice the size.'

'Oh Michael, are we in trouble?'

'Could be, stop and turn round.'

Clare slowed and began to make a U-turn. 'Look out,' Mike yelled. 'Put your foot down – here's the trouble.'

Another vehicle, high sided and square, had shot from the trees and was coming at them on a collision course. Mike recognized a Toyota Land Cruiser. Clare stamped on her brakes and in a cloud of dust and pebbles struck out into the cornfield. The Toyota followed, overtook, swung wide, and deliberately rammed them, T-bone style, sideways into their engine. Mike was half stunned by the impact; Clare screamed. The engine died and the Citroen subsided into a cloud of steam. Mike heard the Toyota stop. Painfully he twisted his head as the door was forced open. Clare screamed and swore with fury as she was dragged out. Strong arms grabbed Mike and threw him to the ground. He fought back with all he knew, but it was no good. He was rolled over face down into the black dirt. Someone had hold of his wrist. He felt a slight pain. Then all faded into a warm darkness.

Mike could hear voices. A rumble of background conversation but no clear meaning. His eyes opened to a subdued light. He tried to move; nothing happened. His brain no longer seemed to control his limbs. As if in some surreal dream he could move neither hands nor feet. He was paralyzed. Semi-conscious now he began to panic.

'Any luck Tommy?' He could hear this voice, a male Irish accent, and only a few feet away.

'Negative.'

Mike felt his throat tighten. It was that voice again. The gritty Belfast accent he'd heard at sea, and on that night at Cottons Hard.

'No good, the girl knows nothing.'

'Would she be bluffing?'

'No way, the Doc gave her a full shot and she answered everything like a little kiddo.'

'How good is that stuff?'

'The best, the real McCoy truth drug. The Doc gets it from some fellah who used to be in the Stasi in East Germany.'

'What did she say?'

'Nothing, she knows no more than we do. There never was a thing in that boat. Her granddaddy was only hinting at it when he died. Anyway she says Delia took the boat apart a week back.'

'Oh shite.'

'One thing she told us. O'Dwyer gave her some names to look up, and guess who?'

'Tell me?'

'Eamon Clarke in Amsterdam.'

'That bastard, is he still alive?'

'It seems so, and did that name excite the Doc. There's a score there for the Basques to settle it seems. Their memories are almost as long as ours.'

'Do we eliminate?'

'That's a decision for the high command, but I wouldn't think it a good idea. O'Dwyer's a big name in the South. The old man fought in the independence war.'

'Sure, but he was a treaty man – they were all traitors.'

'Jesus but I could use a drink,' said Tom.

'Bottle of Jack Daniels in the cupboard.'

There was a clink of glasses and a muttered greeting in a foreign tongue, probably Gaelic. Mike was fully awake now and beginning to recover some feeling. He could have shouted with relief when he found he could move his finger tips and slightly wiggle his toes.

'Brendan, there's another thing,' said Tom. 'I'm not for eliminating those two with that dumb Australian around.'

'Let's finish him too?'

'Jesus sake, Bren, use your head – we've been ordered to play the Culturals along.'

'Sure, I know, but that Sammy riles me.'

'He makes me laugh. All that stuff about, Ireland and Australia, both being persecuted Imperial victims.'

'The Englishman?' asked Brendan.

'What about him?'

'We eliminate him don't we?'

'Not without orders. See Bren, you're a sight too keen on eliminating. You know the rules, indiscriminate executions get us bad publicity.

'It was that man's office girl who killed Peter?'

'She's only a kid, Peter scared her witless and she panicked.'

'She still killed him – one of the best we had.'

'Forget it, Peter was a soldier. He died in action and there's honour in that.'

Mike heard a shuffle of footsteps. He shut his eyes. He knew someone was looking at him.

'He's still out cold.' It was the man called Brendan. 'What did the Doc give him?'

'Another drop of something from the Krauts. Doc says it'll keep him out for another six hours.'

Mike smiled inwardly. Well, the Doc had his calculations wrong. He was feeling stronger by the minute. He had no idea what time it was, but by the way these men talked it seemed his recovery was premature. Mike was fairly certain he could sit up if he tried and in another ten minutes he would be near to standing. He could hear more muffled voices, then the sound of a door opening.

'Here, make way for the lady,' said Tom.

'Michael!' it was Clare's voice. 'What've you done to him you murdering bastards?' Astonishingly she was sobbing. He felt her clasp his hand and his whole body suffused with a glow as she crushed her lips against his cheek and he felt the wetness of her tears.

'Shut it, you silly bitch,' said Brendan. 'You're fellah's OK – he's only sleeping it off.'

'How do I know that?'

'You have my word as a commandant of the Provisional Irish Republican Army,' said Tom pompously.

'What army?' her voice sneered scornfully. 'There's no cause on earth that's worth the slaughter of little children. None of you respects democracy and proper law.'

'You'd be with us if you were true to your country,' said Tom.

'I don't believe I'm hearing this,' Clare's voice had reached a new timbre of hot rage. 'You're bloody bacteria leeching on a sick body. One day, God willing, somebody will cure the sickness and there'll be nothing for you to feed on.'

'Let me teach her some manners?' Brendan's voice had risen in anger.

'No, leave it,' said Tom wearily. 'She's only a woman – they've no understanding.'

There came a distraction. Close at hand there was a drumming clanking sound. 'What's Juan up to?' asked Tom.

'He's refueling the plane, 'case we have to get out in a hurry.' Mike recognized the voice of Sammy Cassidy.

'Sure – that's sense.'

''Ere – 'ows the Brit?'

'Still sleeping.'

'Is he now?' Sammy chuckled. 'You call yourself an Irish woman? What are you shacking up with a Brit for?'

'I'll not dignify you with a reply, Mister Cassidy.' Clare's voice would have cut glass.

Mike sensed someone was leaning over him. This time he caught the fumes of Bourbon.'

''Ello Pom, y'know where I' been today? I've been on a tour. A tour of the battlefields of the First World War. That's when your bloody King George fell out with 'is cousin Billy, so millions 'ad to die to settle it.' Sammy's fume filled breath had shifted to Mike's nose. 'But there's more. King George says to 'is generals, "Put those bloody colonial Aussies in the first wave – they're expendable. Then we Brits can claim the victory. But if there ain't no victory we'll blame it on the Aussies and say they can't fight."'

Bullshit, thought Mike. He was becoming angry again. He remembered his old grandfather's incoherent tales of the trenches. Thousands of men died in an ill-directed cause, but to slant history, as Cassidy was doing, was to dishonour them all.

'I'll tell you straight,' Sammy continued. 'We're finished with Poms. Time's coming when they can choose. Support the Republic of Australia, keep their noses clean, and we might just tolerate a few of 'em. As for the bloody bulk, we'll track 'em down and ship 'em out – all the way home to bloody Pom land.' Mike gritted his teeth as Sammy belched.

'Would you put a sock in it, Sam? He can't hear you.'

'Only rehearsing, wait 'til the bastard wakes up.'

Presently there were fresh footsteps and Mike heard more people enter the room.

'Aircraft, we have refuel – she is ready.' The man spoke in heavily accented English in a voice that was somehow familiar. 'That man, he still asleep?'

'Flat out, Doc,' replied Sammy.

There was a babble of conversation that stopped abruptly as Tom's voice cut through it. 'Quiet…quiet I say! Will you listen?'

'Chopper,' said Brendan. 'It's coming closer.'

Mike could hear it himself now. The droning rattle of a helicopter moving at speed towards them.

'Shite, she's carrying spotlights!' Brendan's voice had an edge of panic and it sparked off a chaos of shouting and running feet.

'Still,' roared Tom. 'Stand still. You are soldiers. I will have discipline!'

Despite everything Mike was impressed. The man was a terrorist with a twisted mind and very probably a psychopath. But he could keep his head, and in a perverted way he was a born leader.

'Will you make your way to the airplane in good order. Juan you go first and start up. Brendan bring the girl.' There was no reply only the scraping of footsteps. The whine of the approaching helicopter was overwhelming now.

'Get your hands off me,' Clare screamed. Mike heard the slap of her palm connecting with Brendan's face.

For the past two minutes Mike had been flexing his muscles. Mentally he was preparing himself to climb off the rickety bed. He lifted his head and shoulders. Instantly he felt a wave of nausea. Could he stand? He struggled to his feet and with a glow of elation found all working normally. Brendan was struggling with Clare. He was a short, slightly built man, and by no means having the best of the battle. As he tried to pin Clare's right arm behind her back he was oblivious to all else. He never saw Mike. At that moment Clare gave a viscous back heel into the man's shin. Brendan gave a yelp and swore. Mike caught him by the collar of his jacket and pulled him back. Brendan gave a startled gasp and swung round. As he turned Mike measured the blow. He was not at his sharpest, his head ached, he felt sick and dizzy, but his blood was up. In his youth Mike had been an indifferent boxer, but this time he was desperate. The first punch slammed into Brendan's face. It was a round freckled face with thinning red hair. As he stumbled Mike hit him again. This time it was a wild swinging right-hander that missed the head but connected with the side of the throat. Brendan sank to his knees. Mike stood back for a second as he aimed again. His right foot honed by a season of rugby crashed into his opponent's face. Brendan howled, collapsing on the floor spitting broken teeth.

Mike found Clare clinging to him, she was crying as she pressed against him burying her wet face in his jumper. Gently he kissed her on the forehead and pushed her away. Brendan was crawling on all fours towards the door. Mike kicked him again through the legs and into the groin. The man curled up in a ball of silent agony.

Mike ran to the door and looked through. Beyond was a deep cavern with a glimmer of light framed in a square at the far end. As his eyes adjusted he saw he was in an old aircraft hanger, and the light was the gleam of the moon outside. In front of the hanger was the aircraft, the Piper Twin. Its engines were beginning to turn. There was a roar as the first one fired. Even above the noise he could hear the helicopter, now almost overhead. Its ground sweeping spotlight was dazzling as it played over the stationary aircraft and lit it in a cold pool of light. The pilot of the Piper was in trouble. One engine was running; Mike could see the shining disc of the propeller. The second motor was turning slowly on its starter, jerking as it failed to fire. Then both engines stopped. The door opened and the four men jumped out and ran round the side of the hanger. Tom was yelling orders to the others while the rotund figure of Sammy struggled to keep up. Mike followed them staying in the shadow of the building. He guessed they were making for the Toyota. The four reached it and piled inside. The car was moving out into the field and onto the runway. The helicopter followed very slowly, keeping pace with its quarry only a few feet below. Nine times out of ten such intimidation would have worked. This time it faced disciplined but desperate terrorists. The roof hatch of the car was open. From it came three short bursts of automatic small arms fire. The spotlight went out. The helicopter jerked and banked away to land heavily in front of the buildings. The Toyota turned across the cornfield and vanished.

Mike watched men jumping from the chopper; eight of them. At the same time he could see headlights. Another vehicle was speeding towards them from the approach road. Who was it now? Should he hide? He was sick and dizzy. Now he was on his knees vomiting as the ground swung mistily up to hit him in the face. Strong hands were lifting him and rolling him over. He looked up into the concerned eyes of Roger Peyron and Jean-Luc.

CHAPTER 16

Mike sank back on the pillows and closed his eyes. Thank God the headache was fading, though his limbs still twitched crazily. He couldn't help thinking about Clare. How she'd grasped his hands and clung to him throughout the homeward journey. He knew the pair of them had drawn closer through the bond of shared experience and that odd telepathy that kept recurring. Clare was beautiful, and she was sensitive and clever. She was a fine seaman. That was the word. Mike refused to use the politically correct "seaperson". His mood swung between elation and depression. He was already very fond of Clare and God alone knew what the future held for them. The deaths of Clarence and Craig had shaken him as nothing had in his life before. Roger had confirmed that a skilfully planted bomb had destroyed the Cessna. Whether this was the work of the IRA or the Basques, as Roger suspected, was at this stage conjecture. It was clear that there were still dangers to be faced and he felt resentful that Clare had not told him everything. Logically why should she? He only knew he wanted Clare; yearned for her physically as much as he craved her companionship and love. Was he only lusting after this girl as a reaction to the loss of Annabel? He had better decide soon or risk more hurt. A week ago he had lived in his own dull world. He never expected to find danger or excitement. Now he had faced both, even death, and had emerged the stronger for it. He felt smug and rather pleased with himself. Secretly he was thankful for the experience. Above all it was the bond he shared with Clare.

He suppressed the memory of Annabel and his thoughts of Clare, and turned instead to Senator Jim O'Dwyer. What sort of man was this who could manipulate events from beyond the grave? By some accounts O'Dwyer had been an accomplished scoundrel. But to those really close to him he had been a loveable rogue. To his credit he had generosity and a willingness to take risks when moved by a cause. Roger had told him of Clarence's father, Lincoln Fairbrother, a black civil rights lawyer whom O'Dwyer had befriended. This alone was a near suicidal act for a Southern senator in the Nineteen Fifties. It said much for O'Dwyer's standing that he had won through and survived. His bravery in war was beyond dispute but what idealism had drawn him into the bloody guerrilla conflict of post-1918 Ireland? Mike was also baffled as to why half the people of Southern Ireland regarded

O'Dwyer as a hero and the other half saw him as a traitor and an appeaser. That all this seemed totally logical to Clare only served to heighten the racial and cultural gap between them.

Peyron's doctor had taken blood tests and then ordered him to bed. He was feeling better now as the effects wore off. As his strength returned he craved company: Clare's company. He stepped into the corridor and tapped on her door. She called out cheerfully for him to enter. Clare had also been ordered to rest although she showed no obvious side effects from the 'truth drug'. She was sitting propped up against the pillows of a vast Empire period double bed. Mike froze in the doorway. He felt uncertain and shy as his eyes fell on the golden hair cascading over her bare shoulders. She had demurely drawn the sheets around her, but he had seen enough to know that she was naked.

'Well,' she said. 'Come in and shut the door or it'll be draughty in here.'

Mike obeyed, though he felt tongue-tied and rather foolish. Her voice was softer and more musical than ever and her eyes shone with laughter as they met his. Suddenly he relaxed as Clare started to giggle. He walked slowly to the bed, sat down and reached to take both her hands.

'Where did you get that terrible thing?' she pointed at the mock oriental bathrobe he wore and made a grimace.

'Roger lent it to me.'

'It's awful – take it off.'

'I can't, I've nothing on underneath.'

'Michael,' she spoke firmly. 'I'm an artist, a professional painter. You're not wearing that colour-clashing monstrosity in my presence. Take it off and come in here with me.' She sat up and threw aside the bedclothes. For the first time he saw the full line of her nude body. She reached out and grasped both his wrists. He felt how strong she was and how hard her seaman's hands. Gently she undid the single cord around his waist.

She must have known all along that he would come to her. It was the instinctive telepathy that had worked between them almost since the day they first met. Her eyes shone and her face flushed in the dim light of the room. The drugged lethargy that had so recently consumed him was gone; driven out by the force that swept through him. Slowly he ran his face and chest along her body, nuzzling her, and licking the hardening nipples. She was in control now as he slid inside her. It was if they had made love a hundred times before in another world.

Mike sat on the bed while Clare knelt beside him her head on his shoulder and her arms around him. Freshly showered and fully dressed they awaited the call for dinner.

'Clare,' he asked suddenly. 'What is Roger's job – he must be something pretty big around here?'

'Mon Oncle Roger?' she giggled softly and pressed against him. 'You know he looked round the door while we were in bed.'

'Oh my God,' Mike gasped. 'When was this – I never noticed.'

'That's because you were crashed out asleep.'

'Oh hell, what'll we say? Have we abused his hospitality?'

Clare groaned. 'Now you really are being bloody English. Of course not, I should think he'll be pleased. He's a Frenchman remember, and still one hell of a lover I wouldn't be surprised.'

For five minutes Clare said nothing. Instinctively Mike knew something else was troubling her.

'Michael,' she spoke in little more than a whisper. 'Roger's told me about Clarence and Craig. I feel awful, I can't believe they're dead. I feel I'm to blame.'

'No you're not. Roger told me what happened. His people don't know who planted the bomb. He thinks it was the Basques. He's upset too, but he says Clarence must have been careless.'

Clare dabbed at her eyes with a tissue. 'I've known Clarence for years, his daughter Delphine played with me when I was a kid. Poor Delphine she loved her Dad.' She drew a deep breath and wiped her eyes again.

Roger had briefly told them of his own horror on receiving the news of the destruction of Clarence's plane. He had at once alerted the security forces and then set out for Billancourt with Jean-Luc.

'Michael, I've still no idea what I told those Provos. I've tried to remember but it's no good – it's all a blank.'

'You're not meant to remember. They put some smart drug in you. I heard a little when they thought I was out stone cold.'

'Was it about me?'

'Yes, they said you had a list of names…'

'Oh hell!'

'I wouldn't worry about it. They weren't that interested. All they wanted was those mythical bloody papers.'

'But there are no papers. Why can't everyone see that?' Clare's voice had risen a pitch.

'Wait a minute,' Mike intervened. 'What's happened may be a good thing. You told them Delia had already searched *Quadra* and they sort of took it as a fait accompli.'

'Did you hear any of the names?'

'They mentioned one, some man in Amsterdam. They were really excited about him. They said something about being surprised he was still alive.' He hesitated, and gently freed himself from her embrace. 'You know, I wish you'd told me about those names before.' He tried not to sound resentful but it was the last real barrier between them.

'Michael, please believe me. If that's what's worrying you then forget it. I only learned about them yesterday. The names are in a book my grandfather left. Roger gave it to me – here I'll show you.' She went to the dressing table. From a drawer she fetched a small book and handed it to him.

It was an address book, expensive with hand-tooled leather binding and a lock. Inside was an imprint.

Published by J. Schuster. Philadelphia. 1934.

It was a well-thumbed little book packed with the everyday memos one would expect.

'The addresses are in the second half,' said Clare.

Mike leafed through the pages. The late senator had enough contacts. The addresses section was full of names from Adams to Ziegler, all written in the same sprawling hand.

'Now Michael, what strikes you?'

'I dunno, you tell me.'

'I'll give you a clue. Look at the European entries.'

'They've all got reference numbers. Is that it?'

'I think so. I'm going to tell you what I told Roger earlier. So you and he'll be the only one's who know it, OK?'

Mike nodded.

'On the day grandfather died, he told everyone there was a secret in the boat. All right that's the story everybody's heard. Now listen to my story that I've never told. Two days before he died he saw me alone. He said to me, 'there's a secret in that old boat. Take her to Ireland and see if you can find it. Roger Peyron's got an old address book of mine. Find the references, all the eighty-sevens. Find them and talk to them. Don't delay or one or two of them will be gone along with me'.

Mike began to search the pages. Some of the addresses were as old as the book and many had been deleted with a single line. Each one had a reference number, although at first he could see none with a code: eighty-seven. On a whim he looked up Peyron.

Peyron. Olivier. Ref 87. Entry erased. 2nd February 1951. New entry. Peyron. Roger. Ref 8 'I've found Roger, for a start,' he said still turning the pages. And here's another…

'Clarke. Eamon. The address is in Amsterdam. Entered May 1989, that's much more recent.' Mike was excited now. 'That's the name they mentioned. The one they thought was dead.'

'I had a quick look,' said Clare, 'and there's a couple of names I knew. Here give the book to me.'

Mike handed over the volume and Clare began to skim through the pages. 'Here we are, Edwin McGee, in County Waterford; and the other one's, Colonel Carl Newhoffer, in Galway.'

'Any idea who they are?'

'Sure, McGee's a Catholic priest. He must be a fair old age though 'cause Granpapa knew him back in the Nineteen Twenties. I don't exactly remember him but he signed my baptismal certificate.'

'And the other one?'

'I've met Newhoffer and so has Roger. He's an American businessman who owns a lot of property in Ireland. He was some sort of protégé of Grandfather's – he seemed a nice guy.'

'And there's one more; Michael O'Farrell, but it just says, 'living Falmouth Cornwall, 1952.'

'Is this all in your grandfather's handwriting?'

'Of course – why?'

'Just wondered. It matches some old scribbles on *Quadra's* plans. I couldn't make out what they meant. It's no matter – just professional interest.'

He returned the book to Clare. 'D'you know exactly what Roger does in French intelligence? He's obviously a big wheel to be able to mount that rescue.'

Clare seemed uneasy. 'You're right, but officially he's retired. All I know is that he used to be the head of something called Bureau Soixante-Neuf. He never speaks about that and I think he still works for them in some way or other.'

There was still half an hour until dinner and they found Roger in his study. Mike hung back sheepishly but Clare marched up to his desk and slapped down her grandfather's book.

'I've shown Michael the list,' she said.

'Good,' he replied. 'The trouble with your grandfather, Clare, is that he could do nothing in a straightforward manner. Sending you on this trail is exactly the kind of chicanery he loved.'

'You name's on the top of the list,' said Mike.

'Quite so, I'm not surprised, but of all these names I would say I know least about this.' Peyron motioned them to sit down. His manner had changed. He had an air of authority that made him seem distant.

'Tomorrow my young friends, you and I will be making a visit to Paris.'

'Paris!' Clare looked annoyed. 'We don't want to go to Paris, we want to get sailing again.'

'It is not a matter of choice,' Peyron was unmoved. 'I am ordered to conduct you to Paris. There are people there who wish to talk with you.'

'Well, too bad Uncle Roger, we've only just escaped with our lives. We've had enough.'

'No Clare, you did not escape, you were rescued at my instigation by French Special Forces. At this moment there is a wounded man in hospital and a valuable helicopter out of action. Worse there is a dangerous group of terrorists still on the loose. Be sensible, young lady, of course you must be interrogated.'

'I half expected as much,' said Mike. 'Be reasonable, Clare.' He turned to Peyron. 'If we co-operate, will we be free to sail?'

'Most certainly, and you will be under the protection of France. I promise you that.'

'You can't say fairer than that,' Mike laughed ruefully. 'OK, we agree.'

It was a cold bleak outlook at eight o'clock the next morning. The fine weather of the previous few days had given way to low frontal cloud and a cold penetrating drizzle. Mike could have done justice to a better breakfast than the croissant and coffee on offer. He said nothing to Clare, but he knew she also had a twinge of unease about the promised day. Why this trip to Paris? He had expected from the start that they would be questioned. He was more than willing to help, especially if it led to the capture of the gang that had held them captive. Why were the French wasting valuable hours when they could easily have talked to them here?

Jean-Luc had parked the Rolls-Royce by the front door and they all piled aboard. Roger Peyron and Mike sat in the back while Clare opted for the front passenger seat. Jean-Luc completed the two hundred and twenty kilometres to Paris in a little more than two hours.

It was a display of driving that Mike could only describe as inspired arrogance. The freeway had been crowded with heavy transport of all nationalities as well as a multitude of private cars. The big Rolls had stormed through the lot with a panache that made Mike blink and confirmed his view that Jean-Luc had nerves of steel. Eventually, just twenty kilometres short of Paris they had been pulled over by a highway patrol car with two surly police officers. Jean-Luc had growled at them and Peyron had produced an ID. His demeanour had been that of a duchess offended by some unwashed plebs. The police had taken one glance at the papers and then backed off saluting vigorously.

At ten thirty they had reached the capital's northern suburbs. Clare looked around excitedly. She had expressed surprise when Jean-Luc had turned away from the Police Prefecture and the administrative quarter and had headed towards a particularly seedy and run down area of old Paris. What had once been a street of elegant eighteenth century houses was now in multi-occupancy with North African migrants and European hippies. The car pulled up at a tall grey building with an archway completely filled with heavy metal doors. The surrounding walls were covered in graffiti and vandalized posters for the Front National. The few people on the street had stopped to watch this alien exotic vehicle with openly hostile stares. Jean-Luc left the car and walked across to an intercom on the front door of the house. The very sight of the man was enough for the small crowd to shrink back. Three minutes later, two burly janitors appeared and swung open the doors to the archway. Both were dour characters, with stubbly unshaven faces and wearing jeans and leather jackets. Jean-Luc drove the Rolls through the arch into a large central courtyard. Waiting to greet them was a little man with at least a superficial likeness to Groucho Marx.

He pulled open the rear door of the car, bowed to Peyron and addressed him as 'Patron'. He stared a trifle lecherously at Clare before formally bowing. Mike he completely ignored. They all followed Groucho into the building through a decrepit revolving door. Inside, the place reminded Mike of a hospital. They passed through a labyrinth of corridors all signposted in French. The walls were lined with doorways, some led to large open-plan offices with staff at work with computers; others led into smaller, more secretive cubbyholes. It was into one of these that they were finally shown. Behind a desk sat a man who rose to greet them. He was casually dressed in sports slacks, a polo-neck sweater and stylishly cut jacket. He was aged around thirty-five, with the same swarthy Southern appearance as Jean-Luc. He greeted Peyron respectfully and then sat down again. He offered no recognition to Clare and Mike beyond an indication as to where they should sit. They complied and pulled up the wooden chairs, which seemed to be the room's sole furnishing, apart from a table in the corner with a video screen.

'My colleague will transcribe these proceedings in French,' the man behind the desk indicated Groucho who was fiddling with a tape recorder. 'I will proceed in English to facilitate matters.' Their interrogator stared at Mike and Clare coldly, as if seeing them for the first time. 'Monsieur Walters, M'moiselle O'Dwyer, I think you are both lucky to be alive.'

'Too right,' said Mike, 'and we appreciate our rescue. Perhaps you could convey our thanks to the people involved.'

'Certainly I will do that. Now will you tell me about the men who held you?'

'Yes,' said Mike. 'There were two IRA men, one Australian, and two others: nationality I couldn't say.'

'Will you describe these others?'

'One claims to be a doctor,' said Clare. 'He's late thirties, Mediterranean in looks, bit over a metre and a half height. The other's called Juan and he's the pilot of their aircraft they left behind.'

'We'd already met the pair of them in St Vaast,' said Mike. 'They tried to kid us they were French police and customs. The one called Juan sabotaged our boat's compass.'

'I'd say both of them were Basques,' Clare added.

'And, M'mselle, you would be correct.' He brushed back his fringe of dark hair. It was an irritating gesture. 'And now we turn to you.' He stood up and glared down at Clare.

Mike was not impressed. As an interrogator this fellow was not in the same league as Delia. Clare seemed unfazed.

'What were these people looking for?' asked the man.

'Looking for?' Clare's face was impassive.

'M'mselle, we think you know very well what they were looking for.'

'Clare,' it was Peyron. 'You already understand that we know about Flanagan.'

Clare flushed angrily. 'And who in hell is Flanagan? You talked about him but you wouldn't tell me who the fellow was or what he had to do with my boat.'

'Thomas Jefferson Flanagan, late of the United States Army, and his associate James O'Dwyer. We are not entirely sure what their association meant, but we need to know.'

'My grandfather never mentioned anyone called Flanagan.' Clare's tone was final.

Peyron caught the inquisitor's eye. 'I think she is telling the truth, Henri. I know her well.'

The man, Henri, brushed his hair back again. Mike was beginning to find the gesture infuriating. He turned and pointed at the video screen with a remote control. There appeared a grainy black and white film of aircraft taking off from a grass field. Mike recognized an old film of World War One combat aircraft. The film cut to a group of pilots. All dressed in heavy flying gear. The camera highlighted a man in the centre. He was a tall man with fair hair and a cocky grin. 'Granpapa – that's granpapa,' Clare was half standing in her excitement.

The film changed scene. Mike couldn't follow the commentary but the picture was modern in full colour. It showed a very old man, face weathered by wind and time. He spoke slowly in guttural French that Mike didn't even attempt to translate. Only one word made any sense: 'Flanagan…Flanagan'. The name was spoken clearly three times in one minute. The picture faded to that of a presenter speaking to camera. Henri held up his remote control and the screen went blank.

Clare spoke, clearly she had understood more than Mike. 'I've never heard a word of any of this. My grandfather did once claim to have flown to Ireland before Alcock and Brown, but he was drunk at the time and I thought it was all bullshit.'

'No Clare,' said Peyron. 'Your grandfather was telling the truth. That old man we've just seen is a Breton farmer. He's one hundred years old this year and he helped Jim set up his aircraft.'

'What was that film?' Mike asked impatiently.

'It is a television feature about the early flying record attempts leading up to Charles Lindbergh.'

'If Granpapa held a record it wasn't like him to hide his light under a bushel.' Clare was decisive.

'On the contrary,' said Peyron. 'We think your grandfather was involved in a conspiracy that he would never dare refer to until the end of his days.'

'And M'mselle,' said Henri. 'The Americans know exactly what he was up to, so do the Irish, and the British. They are all very frightened my friends.'

'I still don't see how anything that happened seventy years ago can influence matters today.' Mike was tired of all the game playing; he wanted out of this place.

'Perhaps I can convince you,' said Henri. 'There are some secrets that men will die for.' He had an odd cryptic expression. 'Come with me. I will show you a very brave man.' He stood up and beckoned them to follow.

More dreary corridors, shabbier and paint peeling, led to a dead end with a lift. Henri ushered them all inside and pressed the descent button. They emerged in a basement. Mike speculated that it had probably been a vast wine cellar. Now the space had been divided into cubicles bricked up from cheap concrete blocks.

'In here,' said Henri.

'Do you think this is such a good idea?' Peyron spoke; he looked worried. He whispered some more words to Henri in French.

Henri half smiled. 'Indeed yes, Patron. Unlike the English we hide nothing. Our ways are no different from theirs. It is right that our friends here learn how seriously we are taking their case.'

They entered one of the small rooms. It was bare, no furniture whatever; just four walls and a concrete floor. The left-hand wall was almost completely filled with a long rectangular window. Mike thought it was probably a two-way mirror. Through the glass they could see another similar room. In it was a man seated in another of those hard-backed chairs. His arms were pushed through the wooden slats of the chair back, and his wrists were handcuffed. There was blood and bruising on these wrists. Mike felt himself suffuse with horror as he looked at this figure. It was slumped forward, probably no more than semi-conscious. There was blood on his face, the lips were cut and swollen, as were the eyes. His red hair was matted with blood where it had fallen across his face. Mike knew him, it was Brendan the terrorist he had grappled with at Billancourt. The man the French special forces had captured.

'No! No! Why?' Clare had turned on the three Frenchmen; her face was white and her fists clenched.

'M'mselle, we are not sadistes,' said Henri. 'We only wish for information that will save innocent lives. This man knows the things we wish to know...'

'Yes, and you have ways of making him talk,' said Clare with biting sarcasm.

'On the contrary, it seems that we do not,' said Henri. 'As I say, this prisoner is a very brave man. He says nothing. A brave man may

have a bad cause but he is still brave. He walked to the door. 'Come,'
he commanded. They followed Henri meekly into the main passage.
Mike was trying to sort his own emotions. He was worried because he
felt nothing. No disgust, certainly no pity, nothing. It was unreal, a
bad dream. Perhaps he would wake up in his own bed, safe and home
in Sussex.

CHAPTER 17

They were all in the passage outside the macabre viewing room. Peyron and Henri had moved a few yards away. Peyron was whispering urgently. Henri nodded respectfully. Groucho lit a disgusting Gauloise cigarette. It was so pungent that Clare found herself coughing. She was on the verge of tears but unable physically to cry. She wanted to scream but she was damned if she would show such weakness in front of these males. She wanted more than anything else to run from this place into the fresh air and be done with the lot of them. She glanced at Michael. He showed no obvious emotion, but his face was taut and his eyes, when she caught them, looked hurriedly away. He was making a show of his English, old-school, stiff upper lip, but it didn't fool her. It was satisfying in its way that Michael was the most transparent of all her lovers, as well as by far the most interesting.

Roger Peyron had finished his harangue. Clare had half listened but could hear little of it, except for Henri who repeated his, 'Oui Patron…oui Patron…' sycophantically every few seconds. Clare tried to suppress the nausea she felt and to think logically. It was clear they were in Le Directoire of 'Soixante Neuf', the shadowy intelligence agency of which Roger Peyron had once been, Le Chef. It seemed that Roger still held a great deal of sway in this place. She wanted to think that he was disapproving and revolted by what they had witnessed. That was wishful thinking because he clearly regarded the happening as routine. Uncle Roger, Granpapa's friend; the same Roger who had laughed as he pushed her in the garden swing when she was six years old. The same Roger, who a few years later, had introduced her to the wonderful canon of French literature. The same Roger who had lost his wife and child to war. She remembered the torment she had seen in his face on one occasion when she had caught him unawares.

Of course she and Michael had no reason to fear these people. But Roger and Michael knew nothing of one childhood memory that had now surfaced from her subconscious. She was barely three years old, standing alone, and completely ignored, in a room at Madrid airport. Her mother had just been arrested and taken for questioning. It appeared that Granpapa was still on the Franco regime's blacklist. Nothing had happened; Mother had returned within half an hour and they had been allowed to continue their holiday with a warning not to discuss politics.

'Come,' Henri commanded. He turned and led the way back to the lift.

They were in civilized surroundings again; sitting in comfortable chairs in some sort of boardroom. The French had produced cups of coffee, although Clare could barely sip hers.

'We have good news,' said Roger. 'Your two Basques have been caught. The police picked them up in Perpignan at eight o'clock this morning. Henri has applied for them to be transferred to him, but that may take some hours.'

'What about Cassidy?' Mike ground out the name. The venom startled Clare.

'Unfortunately no. Men answering the description of Cassidy and the Irishman, Dolan, boarded a private airplane at Le Bourget last night. The aircraft was a Learjet belonging to an Irish air charter company. We have made contact with Dublin. They have questioned the company concerned. Apparently this aircraft was returning empty, but was chartered at short notice, by an American.'

'But are you sure it was them?' Mike interrupted.

Groucho tossed two photographs across the table. 'These are the men.' It was the first time he had spoken.

'The pictures were taken by the security cameras at the airport,' said Henri.

Mike took a look and passed them to Clare. 'That's Cassidy,' he said. 'I can't identify Dolan. I heard his voice but I never properly saw him.'

Clare looked at the pictures. 'Yes, that's them. So they're in Ireland.'

'It seems likely,' said Roger. 'The Irish themselves want Dolan and so do the British. I think it will not be so easy for us to claim him back, but we have an Interpol warrant for Samuel Cassidy.'

He was looking at both of them now. 'You must understand, we will not tolerate Irish terrorists operating on our soil. We will always co-operate with the British and Irish. It is not our quarrel, but we are a civilized democratic state. We deplore terrorism anywhere, but the more so when it is aimed within our borders.'

Clare was not certain where this lecture was leading; she was more concerned that Groucho had lit another Gauloise.

'The man you have just seen,' Roger continued, 'is Brendan

Williams. We know that he is a specialist bomb maker. It is of real concern to us that he may be sharing his knowledge with ETA. If so there could be innocent French lives at stake as well as Spanish. Now perhaps you will understand why we do not deal so gently with Monsieur Williams.'

They were aboard the car again heading back towards the city centre. Roger Peyron spoke at last. 'We may wish to talk with you again. So you will remain in Paris for tonight at least. I will find you an hotel, after that you will be free to enjoy yourselves.' He paused. 'But please remember it is I who am standing surety for you. Do not disappoint me by trying to abscond.'

Mike was not happy, but it was clearly no good arguing. When all was said the French could easily have held both of them in custody.

'Why look so sad?' Peyron smiled. 'This is Paris. You are young. Enjoy it while you can.'

Roger Peyron had found them a small hotel. Mike was both amused and relieved that he had booked them into one room as a couple. Mike was alarmed when he remembered that they had no luggage, no clothes, not even a toothbrush between them. Clare laughed. 'My credit cards – we'll spend some more of my grandfather's ill gotten gains.'

Mike had one more question for Peyron. 'Why are you interested in this Flanagan? All that stuff was seventy years ago. It may excite the Irish but it's nothing to do with you.'

'No Michael.' Peyron was emphatic. 'You miss the plot. We are not concerned with Flanagan, but the British are. The British are, of course, no more than bag carriers for the Americans these days.'

'I dispute that.'

'Maybe, but the Americans are also very concerned about the misdeeds of Colonel Flanagan. Now we have a good exchange of intelligence with America, Britain, and Ireland. But not this time, they are all hiding something about this Flanagan that they refuse to share with us.'

'I must say that seems odd,' said Clare.

'Now my friends, we do not carry bags for the Americans. We are watchful of the United States; we know they harbour dreams of world hegemony. So if the British and Americans are frightened of something,' Peyron spread his hands. 'Then we will move heaven and earth to discover this secret for ourselves.'

Mike was still dressed in his jeans and shabby seaman's sweater. Clare had been scornful. 'You cannot wear those rags in Paris. Come on we'll shop.'

Mike had greeted this suggestion with dread. He had memories of trailing around behind Annabel. He remembered hours of waiting while Annabel dived in and out of changing cubicles demanding his opinion of one outfit after another. He wasn't competent to judge, except for the miniscule bikinis that she had favoured. This would have been the one enjoyable part had not the snooty shop staff regarded him as an intrusive voyeur.

In the end it was not too painful. Clare's schooling in Paris had ended at the Sorbonne only four years before and the city was little changed from the one she remembered. Mike had been to Paris once, to watch an international rugby match. It had been a convivial all male occasion of which he recalled little after visiting the second bar of the evening. Today, with Clare in charge, things were to be sophisticated and ordered.

She steered him through two boutiques and watched over his choices critically. His dread that she would equip him in some truly ghastly gear was unrealised. He emerged dressed in narrow dark trousers, a stylish black jacket and a gaudy but tolerable soft shirt. Then he had taken a deep breath and crossed his fingers as they moved through a series of fashion shops. Clare had tried on a dozen outfits; but in the end she knew her own mind and had not asked his opinion of anything. At last she was satisfied and appeared preening herself in a short black halter-neck creation. Mike was amused to see that it revealed as much Clare as dress. To guard against the cold night she completed the ensemble with an outrageously expensive stole.

Mike had been horribly embarrassed when the shop girl had asked him if he wanted to choose lingerie for Madame. 'No need,' Madame had replied, 'Tonight we will be, 'au naturel'.

'Il est anglais,' said Clare, as both girls had laughed at his discomfiture.

The last call had been to a shoe shop. Clare had ignored the strappy high-heeled evening footwear, and had chosen instead some elaborately decorated flat shoes.

'Tonight,' she said, 'we go dancing.'

At eight o'clock they dined in La Fontaine, a discreet little upstairs restaurant. Clare remembered it as a favourite eating place for the better-off students. It was dimly lit and quiet. A place where one could eat well and talk seriously without disturbance.

Mike had been feeling increasingly hungry. He and Clare had ignored lunch; they were both feeling queasy after the things they had seen in the torture cells. As they reached La Fontaine the scent of spice and garlic triggered off a craving as desperate as Mike could remember even from childhood. He couldn't help smiling as Clare slowly removed her stole to reveal the dress. A group of happy young people, boys and girls, stopped eating. The boys had openly stared and grunted their approval. Clare smiled back. Mike wondered if the audience would applaud. It was an incident unthinkable in politically correct London. She spoke to the headwaiter and he directed them to a table in a tiny alcove. Once again Clare studied the menu and ordered for both of them.

'Happy?' she asked her eyes sparkling.

He met her glance. 'Yes, I'm happy – happier than I've been in years.' He said it slowly and seriously and he meant every word.

'No Sammy Cassidy to spoil it tonight?' she answered. She was serious but there was mischief in her eyes.

'Clare,' he asked, 'your grandfather was American but you're all Irish – how come?'

'Oh that's easy. My father was born in the States but he always wanted to return to Ireland. He was a bright lad, and the Irish Government offered him a diplomatic job. He married my mother in Dublin and I was born seven months later. I was an Irish premature baby.'

'Why specifically Irish?'

'Because the Church, and Mam's snooty relations could kid themselves the couple hadn't slept together before the wedding.'

'So you weren't that premature?'

'God no, I weighed seven and a half pounds.' She sipped her wine. 'Say Michael, are you a Catholic?'

'No I'm not.'

'Protestant then?'

'I'm not sure about that, aren't they the lot who say you can't play games or have sex on Sundays?'

'What are you then?'

'Anglican, I suppose, you know C of E.'

'And what do they believe in?'

'At Westborouigh they told us God was an Englishman and a

gentleman. Sounds fair to me.'

'That's about the level of intelligence I'd expect. Anyway, "She's" Irish, all the world knows that.' Clare laughed and changed the subject. 'How did you come to be in the boat business?'

'With some grief to my parents. I was set to go to university when I got offered this job out of the blue.'

'The job you're in now?'

'No, I was hired as personal assistant to Red McDonald. He's a Canadian yacht designer and a big name. He opened a design office in Lymington and I worked there. It was really just a general dogsbody's job, but I learned the technical side and I got loads of racing.'

'And now you've your own business?'

'That's right. I knew Peter at school and when he asked me to be a partner I jumped at it.'

'They told me your father's dead?'

'Yes, five years ago. But he was getting on. You see he married late. Mum's twenty years younger than him and he was nearly sixty when I was born.'

'That sounds like Ireland,' she smiled, then looked thoughtful. 'Both my parents are dead. I told you I'm sure Delia had a hand in killing my father. Then my mother died two years ago. She had breast cancer.'

'I'm sorry.' There was nothing else he could say.

'That's life,' she said. 'She remarried after father died. Her second husband was a shite – still is.'

'It's natural not to like step-parents.'

'No it wasn't that. She went and married Noel Shaw-Mulligan. TD.'

'What's TD?'

'In your country that'd be MP. I tell you, Michael, there's not a more slimy politician in either the Dail or Westminster. Mother was well connected; I think marrying her was part of his climb up the greasy pole.'

'Tell me about your grandfather?'

'Oh, Michael, now you're asking. I wouldn't know where to begin.' She leant forward and took another sip of wine. Mike watched as the light shone on her bare shoulders and lit the little strands of flame red in her hair.

'Granpapa intruded into a lot of people's lives and some of them got hurt. I told you how he saved Felipe Lazarraga from being shot by

Franco?' She glanced at Mike. He nodded fascinated by the mood shift that his question had brought in her.

'That was brave and selfless,' she continued. 'But then he seduces Felipe's only daughter and their child is born with a hatred for him that I have to face as well.'

'It's Delia you're talking about?'

'The same.' She drummed the tablecloth with her fingers. 'He was a rogue but I loved him.' She looked Mike straight in the eye. 'I loved him. You see my parent's marriage was a sham. My father, Bobby O'Dwyer, was always away and Mam didn't care. I don't think he meant a thing to her. It was Granpapa who raised me. I was his favourite. It's very strange – kinda' scary in a way, but he used to say he saw something of himself in me.' She laughed and rolled her eyes. 'That would say I have the potential to be a lying two-faced bitch.'

'Well, you're not,' he said. 'I'm a good judge of character and I say you're an open generous, lovely, intelligent, sensual woman.'

'Yeah, maybe you don't know me so well.' She looked at her watch. 'Come on man. Let's pay the bill and go dancing.'

On Clare's instructions the taxi dropped them outside a shabby building on the left bank. A growing crowd was on the sidewalk, youngsters all: a complete mix of every ethnic group.

'Say, the kids in this place are young these days,' said Clare.

'How long since you were here last?' asked Mike.

'Four years, but it's great to see it's still going.'

Mike laughed. 'That means you're four years older. I bet these kids are the same as you were then.'

She looked rueful. 'I'm sure you're dead right. What music d'you like?'

'I'm really into serious, you know classical, but I like rock as well – sixties to early eighties mostly.'

'Then you're in for a culture shock.'

The room was a darkened basement. It was crowded and there was a hush of expectation. Smoke, tobacco and cannabis, hung in the air like incense. Clare nudged Mike. 'This is modern African music,' she murmured. 'From Senegal and Mali – real cool stuff...' Her words were drowned in a roar as the band sidled onto the platform. They were all black Africans: five musicians and a girl singer. In most other ways they were an orthodox western rock group: lead, rhythm and bass guitars, a keyboard, and a drummer. Tom noticed the drummer had a second kit of wooden drums, with stretched skin surfaces. There were other instruments, marimbas and a primitive lute. The music began. Mike had drunk a fair quantity of wine, his head was mildly muzzy; he stifled a yawn. Such feelings were swept aside, buried and forgotten. It was strange music, haunting and wild. The drum beat pulsated and the little girl sang, her shrill ethereal voice lilting eerily above them. The crowded hall began to ululate in thrall to the sound that washed through them. Mike was carried away with the rest, nothing could resist the music; it seemed to leach his mind and take control of his limbs. Clare was swaying to the dance, her lithe form gyrating, arms raised, her body almost rubbing against him. Then her eyes caught his. For a second he shivered. They were like the ice-maiden's eyes, like Delia's eyes. No, not like Delia; these eyes were benign. They washed through him like warm sunshine and they said, 'I claim you, you're mine'. Suddenly the music ceased. Clare put her arms around his neck and pressed against him with the whole line of her body.

'Let's go back to the hotel,' she whispered. 'Let's make love.'

CHAPTER 18

The intruders came at three o'clock in the morning. Asleep in each other's arms neither Mike nor Clare heard the click of the duplicate key that unlocked the bedroom door. Then came the lights, dazzling white, converging to spotlight the naked and defenceless couple in the bed.

Caught in the twilight world between waking and dreaming, Mike tried to stare into the light. Then he buried his face in the pillows, the pain of the beams was burning his eyes and drilling into his half sleeping mind. Clare at his side screamed and clung to him, her fingers digging into his bare flesh.

'That's 'em,' said a detached voice.

Mike's mouth was dry. Never in his life had he felt so vulnerable. Half conscious and naked, apart from the thin duvet, they were helpless.

'Who in hell are you?' It was Clare. She had found her voice. 'How dare you burst in here?'

Mike was at least as startled as their visitors. He doubted if they had expected a reaction like this from a frightened woman. Clare was wide awake now, releasing her grip on Mike she sat up in bed clasping the duvet around her breasts. 'Get out! What perverted shites are you anyway?'

'Lady, we're the United States Central Intelligence Agency,' replied the disembodied voice.

'The bloody CIA.' Clare spat the words. She was incandescent with rage. 'I'm not talking to you. You evil murdering pile of horse shite. Get out!'

Mike's courage had not exactly returned, but he had to do something to regain his self-respect. Slowly he slid out of bed and stood shading his eyes against the light. His normal sight was beginning to return; he could just see the outline of three figures in the shadow behind the glare.

'Say, you're a well provided fellah,' said a second voice. 'I can see why the dame likes you.'

'Shuddup, Herman,' rasped the first voice. 'Say, Mr Walters, you'd better know my colleague here's gay and you're kinda exciting him.'

'What d'you want?' Mike snapped.

'Just a little talk. You play truthfully and we'll go.'

'All right, get out while we dress.'

'You got three minutes,' replied the voice. The men turned off their spotlights and walked through the door.

Mike turned on the bedside lamp. Clare was already up and pulling on the scanty evening dress over her head. She turned to Mike, put a finger to her lips, and held up a tiny object. It was a mobile phone. Mike shook his head vigorously. This was plain stupid. The men outside would be listening; she would have no chance of even calling a number. A smile flickered around her eyes and she slipped the phone into a half open bedside drawer. Mike was impressed. It seemed he'd found himself a girl with a cool head.

'Come in then,' he called with as much sarcasm as he could muster.

The CIA men stepped quietly into the room. The second man was carrying a roll of cloth and a box. The last man shut the door and locked it. Mike felt much easier now. Without the benefit of surprise these men were as nondescript a trio as one could find. Two were youngish fellows of about his age. The man, obviously the leader, was older and attired in a shiny grey suit. He held out an ID badge. 'I'm Agent Jonathan Van Outen. I'm empowered to ask you questions regarding the late James O'Dwyer and the late Colonel Thomas-Jefferson Flanagan.'

'Empowered.' Clare laughed. It was an ironic tinkling sound that must have been profoundly irritating to those on the receiving end. 'I don't have to answer a sodding thing. You're on French soil and neither of us are bloody Americans anyway.'

Agent Van Outen grinned although his eyes remained hard. 'Miss O'Dwyer, I can't make you reply to anything. I think we'll have a little picture show.' He indicated his two colleagues. They had unpacked the bag and were assembling its contents. Mike saw it was a colour slide projector. The rolled object was a projection screen. The other man hung it from the picture rail on the far wall. The second trained the projector and plugged it into a wall socket. Van Outen walked across and turned out the light. The sole illumination was the beam of the slide projector and the square of light on the screen. There was a click and the first picture appeared. Clare gasped.

It was a colour photograph of a group of people in holiday mood beside a swimming pool. In the foreground were two girls, age mid teens, sitting on a diving board. One was a white girl, the other black.

Both were dressed in swimming costumes and had clearly just emerged from the water. In the background stood an elderly man, who none the less looked bronzed and remarkably spry. He wore only a lurid pair of Bermuda shorts and flip-flops. He stood with an arm around a much younger woman. Her almost wild beauty moved Mike. She was wrapped in a beach robe but her face hands and feet were all heavily tanned. Standing beside the couple was another elderly man. This one was fully clad in a lightweight tropical suit and a Panama hat. Mike was drawn to the white girl; there was something familiar about her. Then he realized he was looking at Clare. Clare aged about seventeen, still to develop the lissom body that he had devoured all that night.

'Tell us about the picture, Clare.' Van Outen looked coldly at her.

'She's Miss O'Dwyer to you,' Mike snarled.

Clare waved him into silence. 'We were in Mexico,' she said. 'The guy in the Bermuda's is my grandfather, the old fellow in the Panama is Luis Esquilada – we stayed with him. The pool's by his house in Acapulco. Grandfather knew him in Spain in the Civil War. Luis was a war pilot like grandfather.'

'Yes,' said Van Outen. 'What would an American lawyer be doing flying missions for a communist regime?'

This was evidently ground that Clare knew. 'It was a democratically elected Socialist government.'

'If you say so.'

'And Mister,' Clare's eyes flashed angrily, 'if you think you've some blackmail mileage in that picture, forget it. The lady with my grandfather is his daughter-in-law, my mother. And the little girl on the plank is Delphine, and she's just lost her dad, two days ago, not that you care.'

Momentarily Mike saw a flash of anger cross Van Outen's face. 'Lady, of course we care. Clarry Fairbrother was one of our finest. There's no hiding place for the people who killed him. You can take it they're as good as dead.'

'Then why don't you people go look for them and stop pestering us?' Clare fixed the man with her eye contact and Mike watched him wince.

'Don't give me that smart-ass. Suppose you tell us who took that picture. You ain't seen nothing yet. We've a dozen more and some of 'em's real tasty.' Van Outen's face creased in malice.

Mike intervened. 'If you're really after these terrorists, aren't we all on the same side?'

'Is that so, Mr Limey?' Van Outen sneered. He pressed the remote button and the projector displayed a fresh picture. Mike was shaken, gobsmacked was the term he used later. The picture was a copy of one from a four year old yachting paper. It showed a young girl in a Topper class dinghy, a popular starter boat for children. Mike remembered the incident. He was the adult instructor holding the boat; the fourteen year old child was Leanne Micalczyk. The screen put up a second picture. It showed Mike standing in the yard at Cottons Hard holding a sheet of paper with some plans drawn on it. Leanne stood beside him. She had put her hand on his waist and had nuzzled her head against him. Mike remembered that day. It had been a week ago, Leanne's first day back at work. He had shown her *Quadra's* rig plan and for a few seconds she had leaned against him. How the hell did this bloody Yank come by a photograph when Mike knew none had been taken. Mike was now very angry. The implication was clear, he was being set up. Before he could make an angry comment the scene changed. The next picture was of a woman standing in a field with binoculars to her eyes; it was Delia. He could see now that both pictures had been taken with a telephoto lens; probably from the far bank of the creek.

The three CIA men laughed. 'That lady was watching you, Mr Walters, and we were watching her,' said Van Outen. 'Now, how say we look at some real pictures? See what Clare here was up to at sweet seventeen.'

'I don't care,' Mike snapped. 'Why are you watching me and what lousy construction are you trying to make with completely innocent photographs?'

'Hey, cool it man. We don't make no constructions, but the Lazarraga says you've been seeing the little girl.'

Mike ignored him. 'Come to the point. What d'you want?'

'Clare knows,' said Van Outen. 'Papers – Colonel Tom Flanagan's letter – April 1919.'

'I haven't got any bloody papers,' said Clare. 'There's nothing in my boat. Delia pulled it apart last week. She found nothing. Even the Provos accept that so you might as well too.'

Van Outen was about to say something but now his attention was elsewhere. There were noises in the passage outside the bedroom. Without warning the door splintered to matchwood as a metal ram destroyed the lock.

There were people in the room; men with handguns. It was all too much for Mike. His eyes took in the scene but his brain refused to function. He had no idea what was happening and, for the first time, he mentally gave up. Not so Clare. She seemed unsurprised by the new arrivals. Someone had switched on the main light. There were two newcomers in the room and one of them was Henri. 'I think,' he said in English, 'that we deserve an explanation.'

'We don't trade secrets with Bureau Six-Nine,' Van Outen replied sourly. 'We've just lost one of our best men and he was working with you.'

'Every war has its casualties,' said Henri. 'I wish to know why the CIA are harassing two young visitors who have been offered the protection of France.'

'Protection!' Van Outen was coldly furious. 'What've you told these punks, Clare? If you've told 'em about Flanagan...'

'I haven't told anyone about anything,' she shouted, 'because I don't know a bloody thing about anyone called Flanagan. Up to two days ago I'd never heard of him. So why can't you stupid men get that into your puny brains.'

'In this case, Jonathan my friend,' Henri was smiling sadistically. 'Mam'selle is telling the truth. We questioned her and we are satisfied she knows nothing.'

Clare stood up and crossed to the slide projector. She pulled off the circular carrier and tipped out the contents. 'I'll have these,' she said. The two Frenchmen grinned as she slipped the cardboard squares into the cleavage of her dress. 'Now all of you take yourselves out of here.'

It was a tone not to be argued with. The CIA picked up their equipment and left without a backward glance. Henri waited for half a minute and then turned to follow.

'I regret the delay, Mam'selle, but we also were interested in what you had to say. These Americans are really very stupid.' He bowed politely and left.

'Christ,' Clare sighed and threw herself back on the bed. 'That means the French must have this place bugged.'

'Is that why Henri and his mate showed up?'

'Oh no, I called them.' She withdrew the mobile phone from the bedside drawer. 'Roger gave this to me. It looks like a phone but it's a panic button. Press the 'send' key and you alert the fuzz.'

Mike had had enough of this alien world. 'I want out of here. Tomorrow we put to sea.'

'Yes,' said Roger Peyron. 'I think that would be the best plan for you.' He sat, face inscrutable. 'Will you be taking *Quadra* to Ireland?'

They had returned safely to Roger's house. *Quadra* was ready for sea. Mike had worked on her checking every piece of rigging, buying and loading stores, filling the fuel tank. He had visited a yacht equipment dealer and bought a Decca position finder. He was taking no chances of a repeat of the incident with the faulty compass. By mid-day he pronounced himself satisfied. They were ready to go.

'Yes,' said Clare. 'We're taking her to Ireland. That's where she belongs.'

Peyron looked pleased. 'I think that is the best plan for you. I must say I will be happier if you are both at sea for a while.'

Clare looked at him. 'Tell us straight, Uncle Roger. Are we in danger?'

Peyron seemed to be weighing his reply. 'You have escaped dire peril once. I am inclined to think these terrorists are no longer interested in you, but it would be better if you were beyond their reach.'

'What about those CIA men?' Clare sounded bitter.

Peyron looked grim. 'Not only the Americans. Believe me you will have to be very cautious. You must be watchful for MI5 and MI6. Irish 'Special Section' of the Garda, and also my Henri and Bureau Soixante Neuf, not to mention the Spanish.

'Why them?' asked Clare.

'Simple, the two Basques we arrested yesterday have been identified as ETA activists. Informed opinion in the intelligence community believes some joint action is planned between the Provisional IRA and ETA. We are uncertain as to what this action entails but it will be soon.' Peyron poured another glass of wine.

'We'll never make Ireland in one passage,' said Mike. 'Even with a fair wind it'd take over a week, and we'll be battling against the prevailing winds. We'll have to take shelter sometime.'

'May I make a suggestion?' said Roger.

'Of course.'

'Take Jean-Luc with you. He is a seaman, and more important, he is a man to guard your lives as he has mine more than once.'

'Seaman?' Mike was doubtful. 'I thought he was a rugby player?'

'He sailed with Claude Coty in the first of the world-girdling races.'

'The hell he did.' Mike was impressed. Coty was one of the great long distance sailors and a French national hero. He caught Clare's eye and knew neither of them was happy, however much they liked Jean-Luc.

Roger smiled. 'Jean-Luc is a Frenchman, he understands the virtues of tact.'

Clare blushed nervously and they both laughed.

'Will he want to come?' she asked.

'It was his idea.'

PART TWO

CHAPTER 19

Mike and Jean-Luc had been sharing the watch keeping between them, leaving Clare to cover for a couple of hours in between. Clare was a handy seaman but these conditions were something outside her experience. Hanging on tightly to the grab handles Mike lowered himself into the cabin and shook the water from his foul weather gear. Even as he did so *Quadra* gave a mighty lurch, almost burying her lee rail. Mike grabbed a nearby ledge and hung on as the ship slowly righted. A dozen unsecured small objects had showered across the cabin. He saw a broken bag of sugar mixing its contents with the water puddling the floor.

His eyes met Clare's and he smiled reassurance as he carefully picked his way to the table and sat down beside her. He kissed her cheek and put his arm around her. She was cold, her skin was cold to touch, and she was shivering despite her thick layers of clothing. He was cold; Jean-Luc, iron man though he might be, was cold. Worse, they were tired. They had completed three and a half days at sea, all to windward in a rising gale. Two hundred miles of the busiest waterways in the world with only two qualified watch keepers. He had to make a decision.

'Where are we?' he asked.

Clare handed him the Decca plot.

'We're eighteen miles south of Portland,' he said. 'Tide's going west. In this wind we must be picking up the tail of the Portland race.'

Quadra made another huge lurch and once again lay over on her beam ends. Above them there was a roar of slatting sails. Clare gave a squeak as she clung to him. He kissed her again this time full on the lips. 'Come on,' he said. 'We're changing course for Poole.'

Mike had seen it all a hundred times before but he was still amazed how peaceful everything had become. They had turned the ship around and were now running before the gale. The wind, that minutes before had been an icy blast, was almost tame. Suddenly the sun broke through, lighting the confused broken seas. Above them a blue sky was flecked with clouds. Morale soared by the second. They no longer felt cold, especially after Mike managed to boil some eggs and make coffee. Half an hour later they shook out a reef. They were on a broad reach now with the wind at ninety degrees to their port side. This was *Quadra's* best point of sailing. Speed increased by a knot and a half as the ship sped on her course with almost dry decks. Two and a half hours and they sighted Durlstone Head near Swanage. Beyond was Studland Bay and the entrance to Poole Harbour.

'Do we report ashore?' asked Clare.

'Afraid so,' Mike grunted. 'We're a ship with a foreign flag and a mixed nationality crew and this is our first port since France.'

Poole Town Quay was almost deserted. The early season and the south-west gale had combined to keep most yacht crews in harbour. Mike went ashore with their passports and the ship's papers. He was uncertain of the procedure as the master of a foreign vessel. In the event the customs were uninterested, though the man checking the passports gave Mike an odd interrogative stare.

'Normally I'd go into the town and celebrate,' he told the others. 'But if it's all the same to you I think we'll slip away and to find a nice quiet anchorage.'

They motored across the harbour and anchored off Shipstall Point. The wind was funnelling down from the hills and blasting over the ground in short vicious squalls. Mike and Jean-Luc laid a second anchor.

'This is a nice place,' said Clare. 'I like it, it reminds me of Ireland.'

'Over there's Corfe Castle,' said Mike. 'It's a ruin on a hill top. Cromwell blew it up.'

'Did he now?' said Clare meaningfully. 'Always was breaking things that man – when he wasn't killing poor folk, that is.'

'They say he was a Welshman,' said Mike grinning.

'That doesn't surprise me,' she replied. 'From all I've heard he was a mighty clever fellow, so he couldn't have been an English general.'

All that day the wind blew. *Quadra* rode securely to her anchors although she rolled uncomfortably as the tide turned. For the first time in weeks Mike and Clare felt safe. Not so Jean-Luc. He paced the deck like a disgruntled bear glaring at the town, at walkers on the shore and at a solitary light aircraft.

Night came and Mike suddenly realised how tired he was. It was a satisfying tiredness born of three gruelling days at sea. At nine-thirty Jean-Luc stood up and announced he was going to bed in his quarters in the fore cabin.

'I go sleep,' he said. 'If I go on deck in zee night I use zee 'atch. You both OK – I not see you, I hear nothing.'

'I think that was a bit of French tact,' Clare giggled. 'What does he think we'll be getting up to?'

Mike sat on the settee and put both arms around her. He eyed the berth; it was two and half feet at its widest. Clare followed his gaze and laughed.

'It's an awful hard mattress,' she said mournfully.

Mike kissed her goodnight. He crossed to his own bunk and wriggled into his sleeping bag.

'Michael,' she whispered, 'are we really safe at last?'

'I wish I could be sure of that. At least the penny's dropped that there's nothing hidden inside the ship.'

'I love you, Michael.'

'And me you.'

'What about Annabel?'

'Who's Annabel?' Suddenly he laughed. He realised with a warm glow that he hadn't thought of Annabel for almost a week. How trivial that woman seemed compared with Clare.

Mike awoke next morning to the sound of engines. A motor boat was alongside. He could hear voices on deck. One of them was Jean-Luc, but he could make nothing of what was being said. Mike pulled on his outer clothes and opened the hatch. An official harbour launch was alongside. With the helmsman in the cockpit was the incongruous sight of a uniformed policeman in heavy black boots. A third man in civilian clothes had climbed aboard *Quadra*.

'I'm looking for Michael Walters?' he said.

'That's me.'

'I know,' said the man with a cheerful grin. 'I recognized you. I'm Detective Sergeant Jolly – Dorset Police.' He held out his ID. Mike examined it carefully; he had not forgotten the bogus French copper in St Vaast.

'How can I help you?' he asked warily.

'We would like you to spend the morning with us. We believe you may be able to help us with our inquiries.'

'And what am I supposed to have done?' Mike had a perfectly clear conscience and he was not pleased.

'I wasn't aware that you had done anything.'

'You said I was to help you with your inquiries. The inference is plain.'

'No sir, not so. It's just that someone wants to meet you.'

'Michael, don't go! It's a trick. It's Paris all over again.' Clare was standing beside him, her blonde hair awry and blowing in the breeze.

'No Madam, no tricks, just routine. Someone wants to pick Mr Walters' brains on a technical matter. He's a public spirited yachtsman and I think he'll be glad to help.'

Mike softened a little. Jolly was a good name for this man. He had a round tanned face and an easy smile. As he stood rock steady on *Quadra's* rolling deck.

'You said you recognized me?'

'Seen you at Cowes and Lymington. I crew for my father-in-law – he's got an X-boat.'

'OK,' said Mike wryly. 'I'll come quietly.'

As the launch crossed the harbour, Sergeant Jolly told Mike about last year's Cowes regatta, and of the family cruiser he hoped to own one day. The launch ignored the Town Quay and instead motored on up the channel to the marina at Cobbs Quay. Waiting ashore was another policeman.

'This is my colleague,' said Jolly. 'Inspector Lamont, Special Branch.' Mike shook hands. This man was tall, thin and careworn. In normal circumstances Mike would have taken him for a school teacher.

'Mr Walters, thank you for your time. If you'll come this way we have a car.' The voice was deep and surprisingly cultured.

The car was a nearly new Ford Escort. Lamont drove with Jolly beside him; Mike climbed into the back. He gazed at the passing countryside with interest. It was familiar ground, for they were less than twenty miles from Westborough where he'd spent his schooldays with Peter Blair and Charles Venner-Harris. Past Blandford they left the main road and plunged into a maze of back lanes, twice stopping to give way to crossing herds of cattle. Now they were climbing into the wilder hill country before they turned into a little lane leading down into a valley far below. At the bottom they forded a shallow stream and before them stood a chain link fence. Jolly left the car and walked to the gate. He opened a box and took out a telephone. Five minutes later a Land Rover appeared on the other side. Two men unlocked the gate and pulled it open. They drove through and Mike saw the gate close behind them.

'What's all this for?' he asked.

'Don't worry about it,' replied Lamont. 'It's to keep the menagerie in, not people out.'

For a quarter of a mile they drove through scrubby pastures and copses of birch and conifers. The drive began to curve round between high banks. These were neatly trimmed with rhododendrons well in bud. At the end of the drive was a surprise, or rather two. The build up had led Mike to expect a mansion. What he saw was a picture book half timbered cottage with a thatched roof. It was really very small no more than five rooms for a guess, but it had a twinkling charm with its whitewashed walls and little dormer windows beneath the thatch. The cottage had maybe half an acre of garden, again surrounded by a chain link fence.

Lamont parked the car on the gravel by the gate and they all climbed out. The surrounding land was covered by heather and gorse bushes already ablaze with yellow flowers. The whole place had a sweet scented freshness and Mike stood drinking it in. Lurking among the bushes he saw squat shaped figures like ungainly children. Mike stared in surprise; these were apes, or were they chimps? He wasn't sure. His eyes were drawn back to the house. A woman had walked down the garden path and was standing by the open gate. She was tall and slim with flowing black hair. He would guess she was already well into middle age, but this hardly mattered. She had a presence and a pure physical beauty such as he had rarely encountered. So spellbound was Mike that momentarily he forgot where he was. Something pushed against his trouser leg. Without thinking he brushed it away. An excruciating pain seared through his wrist. He gasped aloud and shot round to see an ape scuttling into the bushes. He stared at his hand. The skin was broken with a jagged rip and blood was dripping on the flagstone path.

'Mr Walters,' exclaimed the dark woman. 'I must apologize, I should have warned you. 'Diamond's behaviour is becoming insufferable. You are the second guest he has bitten.' The voice was soft, not unlike Clare's, but the diction was flawless, well bred English. Mike was startled; his preconception had been that the woman was foreign.

'Come through here, Mr Walters. I'll treat your hand and when my daughter comes we'll have tea.' She opened the gate and Mike walked through followed by Lamont. Jolly remained by the car grimacing at the apes.

'Inspector,' said the dark woman, 'you haven't introduced me.'

For a second Lamont seemed disconcerted. 'Mr Walters, may I introduce Doctor Maria Lazarraga.'

CHAPTER 20

In the shock of the moment Mike forgot his throbbing hand. Suddenly he was tense. There could only be one Maria Lazarraga who would have an interest in him. This must be the Basque girl, Maria, one time mistress of James O'Dwyer, and the mother of his daughter Delia. He felt a chill of irrational fear, not of physical danger, but something other that he couldn't define. Everything that Clare had told him suggested these women were bad. He took a deep breath. Nothing could happen here on this lovely spring day and in this beautiful garden. He suppressed an overwhelming desire to run from this place back to Clare, to their boat, and to the mundane predictable world he understood.

'How did you know we were in Poole?' he heard himself ask.

'My daughter received a call from Immigration last night. You're a celebrity, Mr Walters. Your arrival has been awaited in every port on our coastline. You know it was really most convenient of you to drop anchor so close to us here.' She was staring at him, eyeing him from head to toe. She had soft eyes, quite unlike Delia's, but her expression was enigmatic. Mike felt as if he was an unruly child standing before his teacher. Then the face softened and there was the flicker of a smile. Suddenly he felt dizzy. He was aware his pulse rate had risen and his arm throbbed worse than ever.

'Come along,' she said. 'I'll dress your wound. I cannot say what will happen to Diamond. As I grow older I find it in myself to be forgiving, but my daughter does not.'

She led the way indoors. The interior was shadowy with low ceilings and darkened beams; old ship's timbers he thought. There was a scent of cut flowers and wood polish, mixed with cooking spices. Anywhere else it would have been welcoming and pleasant. Maria washed and dressed the wound. She was swift and efficient. Mike shrank back as she produced a loaded syringe.

'Mr Walters,' she said sharply. 'I'm a doctor. This is an anti-tetanus injection, nothing more. Be sensible and co-operate.'

The injection was skilfully performed and painless. 'Now,' said Maria, 'we shall find my daughter.'

Delia was in the garden. He saw her the moment they came into the sunlight. She was walking towards them with something in her arms. It was a small bushy tailed monkey, a Marmoset. She cradled the creature as if it was a baby and it lay passive and trusting, resting its tiny head on her chest.

A jumble of impressions raced through Mike's mind. It was only the second time he had seen the woman in daylight. She had the same dark hair as her mother, but beyond that there was little resemblance. Perhaps Delia took after her father. He remembered the ill defined pictures of O'Dwyer he had been shown in Paris. The resemblance between the man and Clare had been striking, Mike had seen it instantly. Those disturbing dark eyes, apparently possessed by all the family, must come from him. Delia stood a few feet away, as swaying gently, she murmured to the creature in her arms. She wore a black ankle length skirt and a black jumper. A green body warmer provided the only dash of colour. Some people might have supposed the scene had charm and pathos. To Mike there was nothing; just a cold caricature of a Madonna and child.

A man came round the corner, one of those who had opened the main gate. He was a sturdy, well-groomed fellow; Mike took him to be an ex-soldier. Delia handed him the marmoset and she watched intently until both were out of sight.

'Inspector Lamont,' she said. 'Thank you for bringing Walters. I will question him in private. There is no operational need for you to know what is said.' The voice as ever was flat and expressionless.

Lamont nodded and walked away down the path to the garden gate. He did not look pleased. Mike fought down another spasm of panic as Delia faced him. Suddenly he felt very vulnerable and alone.

'Come in, Mr Walters,' said Maria. Leaden-footed Mike followed her back into the cottage. He knew by the soft footfall that Delia was close behind.

'Tea or coffee, Mr Walters?' asked Maria.

'Nothing, thank you.'

'Oh nonsense, have you had breakfast?'

Mike was suddenly very aware that he had not breakfasted. 'I would like a cup of coffee,' he conceded.

Maria nodded graciously and went into the kitchen.

'Walters, sit down – you make the place untidy.' Delia's voice was as flat and neutral as ever.

Mike sat down on a soft floral patterned sofa and waited. How would Delia respond to the man who had given her a personal battering at their last meeting?

She sat down opposite. 'Walters, you are an impulsive, uncontrolled individual and I don't like that. It seems you always act before you think. If you continue somebody will kill you.'

'Such as you?'

'If necessary, yes.'

'Why?'

'Because you, to coin a phrase, are a loose cannon. Unwittingly you've become a danger to state security.'

'What danger, what on earth could I have done…?'

'You've done enough in the last fortnight for me to seriously consider eliminating you.' Delia's voice had a cold edge as she cut off his attempt to reply. 'I suppose I can attribute your stupidity to some infatuation for Clare O'Dwyer. An excess of testosterone is making you an expensive liability.'

Mike's temper was beginning to burn. 'What've you got against Clare except some stupid family vendetta?'

'O'Dwyer is not what you suppose, Walters. Do you really think you are the first?'

'I've no idea. I don't care, and it's none of your business.'

'My business is the security of the state. Walters, I gave you information in confidence and immediately you travel to France and consort with undesirables.'

'You have no idea where.'

'Don't waste your breath. You've been with Peyron. Before you reached him you waged an unofficial war with ETA. Now you've seriously compromised me with the French and if that were not enough you are travelling with one of their field agents in your yacht.' Delia paused. Her eyes were very like Clare's, only these eyes were cold, calculating, and probing. They were eyes that would unlock his innermost thoughts if he allowed them. He tried to respond but his mouth was dry and no sound came.

'You are a damn fool, Walters, and that is why I say you may not live long.'

Relief came as Maria returned with a tea trolley. Mike gulped the coffee thirstily and accepted a second cup.

Delia spoke. 'Mother, please leave us.' Maria retired and Mike took a deep breath. Delia's eyes were on him again.

'Where is Charles Venner-Harris?' she asked.

'How in hell should I know?'

'O'Dwyer has not mentioned him?'

'Only that he called on her in Cork, but that was a month back.'

'As I expected she knows more than she trusts you with.'

'What does that mean?'

'Walters, if you are to redeem yourself you will find Venner-Harris.'

'Why, because he's some sort of politician?'

'I wouldn't waste the resources of the state to rescue any politician.'

'Shouldn't you respect your masters?' Mike's inner courage was reasserting itself. This verbal fencing was something two could play.

'James O'Dwyer was a politician...'

'Your father?' Mike interrupted.

'Stop being provocative, Walters. You make no impression on me. As I said, James O'Dwyer was a politician. He was devious, contemptible and in my experience typical of the breed.'

'Not so,' said Mike. 'What about the civil rights movement? He put his whole career on the line.'

'You mean Lincoln Fairbrother? Yes, and Fairbrother died violently as has his son.'

'Someone blew up Clarence's plane, was it you?'

'No, it was ETA. They've admitted it.'

'Did you kill Clare's father?'

'Her father?' For the first time there was a flicker of a smile. 'He vanished in Argentina. It's generally supposed to be the work of the Junta, O'Dwyer knows that well.'

'She says someone nearer home fixed it.'

'The man was a meddler. Another muddle-headed individual driven by compassion. You remind me of him, Walters.'

'Why d'you want Charles?'

'I don't want him. We think he holds the key to what we're after, but the fool doesn't know it. We never realised his importance until IACS took an interest in him.'

'Who are these IACS? I've met their Australian spokesman and he's a prize prat.'

'What Australian?'

'Sam Cassidy, we met him in St Vaast.'

'Really? The French never told me that.'

Interesting, Mike noted. It seemed there were gaps in Delia's information. There was a good chance the French had told her nothing about his and Clare's involvement in the events at Billancourt.

'Bernard Anderson...' Delia began.

'Eh?

'I said Bernard Anderson, Professor of Modern European History at Patrickstown College.'

'Is that in Ireland?'

'No, New York State. Anderson is the founder of IACS.'

'So his writings are on a par with Sam Cassidy's?'

'In intent, yes, but Cassidy is a buffoon and Anderson is a scholar.'

'What's this to do with Charles?'

'Anderson is an Anglophobe and a propagandist. Isn't it strange that such a man should engage the services of Venner-Harris? We suspect he knows Venner-Harris has more to offer than legal advice.'

'What can I do about it? I've been press-ganged under threat by you. I'm not trained for any of this. I wouldn't know where to begin finding Charles. Why don't you use your own people?'

'Believe me Walters, I'm not employing you from choice. However, you know Venner-Harris personally. More important you are with O'Dwyer. Stay with her and she'll lead you to Venner-Harris.'

'What if I refuse to have anything to do with this?'

'You've no choice. I've already warned you what will happen. Also your file is clean. You're a patriotic Englishman, you will serve the state and rescue your friend.'

'I'm not sure I'd class Charles as a friend. What's happened to him anyway?'

'He's certainly being held under duress. He's forfeited his chance to be an MP – his party are fielding a substitute.'

'All right, supposing I come across him, what then?'

'Tell him to keep his mouth shut.'

'About what?'

'Tell him if he values his life, let alone his political career, he'll forget he ever had an uncle.'

'Can't you be more specific?'

'He will know exactly what you mean. I am not giving you details that you do not need to know. Just tell him that.'

'All right, I suppose so, but I'm not sticking my neck out to rescue him.'

'I don't want him rescued. Frankly he's more use to us as a murdered martyr.'

Mike gave Delia a hard stare. 'Miss Lazarraga, what is it that really drives you? What do you really believe in?'

'Order, Walters. An ordered society directed by those who have proved their excellence.' Delia's eyes were drilling into him again.

Unworried Mike stared back. 'You're saying dictatorship by bureaucrats and for the rest of us it's tremble and obey.'

'Walters, your file says you won a scholarship to Westborough

School and while there you achieved six A-levels, two of them at grade A. You never went to a university. Why is that?'

'I went to work in a yacht design office – it's what I wanted to do.'

'It's fortunate not everyone is like you.'

'And it's a bloody good thing there's not too many like you.' Mike's temper flared.

'Walters, you are over-emotional and undisciplined. I don't like that. It's time you understood what I mean by order.' Delia stood up and gestured him to follow.

She led him into the garden. Mike followed her along the winding path. It was certainly a fine garden, meticulously laid out and lovingly cared for. Beyond the stock fence was the scrubby heathland through which they had driven. Beyond that was the line of the Downs.

Delia stopped and turned round. 'James O'Dwyer settled a sum of money on my mother and gave her all this. I doubt if it was to salve his conscience. No, money buys silence.'

She pointed. 'Within our ring fence we have twenty protected species. Here they are safe, far safer than they would be in the wild.'

'Do they breed?'

'Obviously, but no overstocking is permitted. Over twelve years our numbers have remained the same.'

'So anybody surplus is eliminated; that's the word all you people seem to like.'

'The elderly and infirm are culled humanely, as are the inadequate and those who lack discipline.' The ice had returned to Delia's voice. 'Tell me, Walters, have you ever witnessed an execution?'

'What d'you mean?'

'Follow me.' Delia turned on her heel and strode to the garden gate. Standing there was the dour gardener, the one who had taken the marmoset.

'Walters, this is Corporal Henderson. You've already met him to your disadvantage.'

'When?'

'Aye, two weeks back, over Chichester way. Ye assaulted this guid lady and I gi' ye a hiding.' The man addressed him direct. His accent was Glaswegian with undisguised malice.

Mike remembered. 'You crept up behind me in the dark and then you wet your pants when the dog jumped you. Not much of a soldier are you?'

'Ye shut your foiking mouth!'

'Henderson enough, you will show restraint,' Delia snapped.

'Aye Maam.' Henderson obeyed but his face was venomous.

'I intend Walters to witness the execution. Are things ready?'

'Aye Maam.'

'Carry on then.'

Henderson opened the gate and they all filed through. With alarm Mike saw the police car had gone. 'Where's Lamont?' he asked.

'Inspector Lamont will return in half an hour. Don't worry Walters. I've had enough of your company and you have a mission to return to.'

Mike followed the others along a sandy track. There were fircones under foot and heather to either side. At the end of the track was a wall of earth evidently heaped up by a mechanical digger. On the flat ground in front of the wall was a wooden cage occupied by a single dark haired ape.

This is Diamond,' said Delia. 'He bit your hand for which I apologise. You're not the first he's attacked. We do not tolerate such behaviour. Walters, I intend to illustrate your lesson. Here in our community we have freedom, but where there is freedom there must also be order and discipline.'

Mike's attention was drawn to the ape. It crouched on the ground with a puzzled grin on its face as it searched the sand. It seemed a spiteful trick to imprison a dumb animal for something it could barely comprehend. Henderson had vanished. Mike looked round and saw the man coming out of a wooden hut. Casually swinging in his right hand was a gun; an automatic weapon.

'What's he got that for?' asked Mike. With rising horror he began to understand the purpose behind this charade.

'Don't worry,' Delia had an icy smile. 'He's not going to use it on you,' she paused, 'this time.'

'You're going to kill that poor monkey, just because it bit me. Let it go.'

'Walters, you are even softer in the head than I supposed. It all fits your file. Despite your education it says you come from the lower classes. Clearly you lack moral fibre.'

Mike's fist came up as he lunged at her.

'Back off, Jimmie, or I'll blow ye awa!' Henderson was standing his gun leveled inches from Mike's chest.

'Keep him there, Henderson.' Delia walked to the hut and returned with another gun. Snapping the magazine in place she walked to the cage. The ape looked up at her with a childish and pathetically trusting expression. Delia fired a full clip of ammunition into the twitching body. The shots echoed on the hills and a smell of cordite wafted over the scene. A pool of blood began to seep into the yellow sand.

Regardless of the gun pointing at him Mike walked away. At the edge of the track he vomited on the ground. Then he ran. Down the track he sprinted expecting every second to be his last. No bullets came, only a peal of mocking laughter.

In five minutes he was at the main gate; it was locked. The fence was no problem for a fit man. Mike pulled off his sweater and threw it over the barbed wire top. He swarmed up and over dropping to the ground. Then he ran hard and fast up the steep lane to the road above. Only when he reached it did he pause for breath. An ancient Cortina car was cruising slowly down the road. He looked up in surprise as it stopped beside him.

'Michael, it's you. Thank God you're safe!' It was Clare and sitting beside her was Jean-Luc.

CHAPTER 21

For Clare the day that had started so brightly had become a nightmare. She had not worried overmuch when Michael had left with the police. Despite her first misgivings she doubted whether the matter had anything to do with their troubles. Not so Jean-Luc. It seemed Peyron had instructed him not to let either her or Michael out of his sight. By instinct and upbringing Clare was suspicious of British officialdom, but her doubts were as nothing compared with Jean-Luc's.

'I not like it,' he muttered. 'The mad woman, Lazarraga. It is she who takes him – I know it.'

The morning dragged by. Clare busied herself about the ship, cleaning and tidying. Jean-Luc had prowled around on deck muttering and glaring at the shore. Clare told herself not to be stupid. How could Delia know they were here of all places? Of course Michael had reported their arrival but that had been routine. Would such information find its way to Delia in London? Was she in London anyway? The weekend was coming; more likely she would be in her country retreat. Clare had gone with her grandfather just once to the cottage to visit Maria. Delia had been there that day. Delia was ten years older than Clare. Throughout the visit Delia had stared at her with cold unrelenting hate. Clare remembered the utter joy and relief as she and Grandfather had left that awful place and driven back to Poole to go shopping.

'Oh God, Poole!' she shouted the words out loud. Clare strove to stay calm. Delia lived in Dorset, maybe only a few miles away, but where?' In the countryside near some place with a funny name: Tarrant Welcome; that was it. She remembered because it sounded silly and so totally inappropriate.

'Jean-Luc,' she was on her feet yelling in French. 'We've got to get over to the town. You're right – Michael's in trouble.'

It took them an hour to recover the anchors and motor over to the Town Quay. They found the police station. The police were friendly and helpful but knew nothing of Michael. Sergeant Jolly? Yes, he had gone on a job that morning, up Blandford way. At Tarrant Welcome? Could be; no one knew for certain.

With Jean-Luc in tow Clare found a bookshop and bought the local Ordnance map. Ignoring surprised glances she knelt down and opened it on the floor of the shop. Every second village seemed to be a Tarrant. There Was Tarrant Gunville, Tarrant Hinton, Tarrant Rushton. At last he found, tucked away in the hills, Tarrant Welcome. They left the shop and Clare ran down the road to a garage they had passed. Would they hire her a car?

The garage man was a dour, unshaven, xenophobe. Clare's Irish accent and Jean-Luc's Gallic appearance had aroused all his prejudices.

'What be you a wantin' it for?'

'I need it to fetch a friend, that's all'

'I don't like Paddies. You're all the same, planting bombs and the like.'

'Jesus,' Clare muttered, cutting off the rebuke she had in mind.

Grudgingly she was let loose with the most decrepit car in the yard. She paid the extortionate cost in cash.

All this Clare explained to Mike as they drove back to Poole.

'Worst moment was just now,' she said. 'We heard shooting in there.'

Mike nodded. 'That was Delia, the woman's completely barking mad. She murdered a pet ape. It made me sick. It was like watching a child killed. After that I didn't wait – I legged it.'

In Poole they returned the car and Mike led the way to *Quadra*. He ordered the diesel tank to be topped up along with their water supply.

'I'm not touching another main port this side of Ireland,' he told the others. 'If we need to hole up we'll find somewhere quiet.'

At six o'clock that evening they motored through the harbour entrance and anchored for the night in Studland Bay. There was little or no wind so Mike decided to wait for morning and the west going tide. Jean-Luc retired to his fore cabin leaving Mike and Clare facing each other across the cabin table.

'Clare love – thanks.'

'What for?'

'For sussing out where I was.'

'I'd have been a lot sooner if I hadn't been so stupid. I knew Delia lived near Poole. I knew it all the time and it never clicked.'

Mike crossed over and sat beside her. He put his arms around her and felt her warm response.

'Clare, I once heard you say that the British always hire their enemies to guard their security.'

'I said that to Delia and she nearly hit the head off my shoulders.'

'I seem to remember I repaid her with interest.'

'Sure, and then you got laid out yourself by that gorilla who shadows her.'

'I met him today. He's a thick jock called Henderson. I deliberately riled him and came as near to being shot as I'll ever be.'

'That temper of yours was it?'

Mike said nothing. For three minutes he seemed lost in his own thoughts. Clare,' he said softly. 'Whose side is Delia on, and how did she get where she has?'

'Delia joined your Home Office straight from Oxford. She controls a section of your spy service. I've heard she could be on her way to leading the whole shebang.'

'But how? Hasn't anyone noticed she's crazy?'

'I doubt it. That's the trouble with you Brits. You've no control over these people and you recruit them almost entirely from clever misfits. Once it was gays from Cambridge, now it's psychos from Oxford. They can do what the hell they like and it's ever so bad form, "old chap", to ask questions.' Clare mimicked an exaggerated English accent.

'I'll tell you one thing,' said Mike. 'She's not sure what happened to us in France and she talks of Peyron as if he's an enemy. She says Jean-Luc's a French spy.'

Clare laughed softly. 'Nobody trusts Delia. Not the French and the Americans anyway. Clarence was watching her for the CIA. It was Clarence who told me Delia had recruited you to watch me.' Clare shivered in his arms. 'I feel terrible about Clarence. I can't help wondering if he was killed because of me.'

'I asked Delia that. She says it was ETA – they're Spanish aren't they?'

'Basques, not Spanish. That's almost as bad as saying the Irish are English.'

'Perish the thought,' Mike laughed.

'It matters not whether it's ETA or IRA these days,' Clare explained. 'They work together. Half that gang that held us were Basques.'

'Have you ever heard of a Professor Anderson?' Mike repeated what Delia had told him about the man.

'Yes I've heard of him. They say every lecture he gives in the States, he rouses the rabble and then they pass the hat round for NORAID.'

There was silence in the cabin. For several minutes the two of them clung together. Outside the water murmured against the hull and a loose halyard tapped against the mast.

'Clare,' he said at last. 'Delia's ordered me to find Charles Venner-Harris.'

'Ordered?'

'That's right, or at least if I don't go through the motions I'll be found face down in some canal. That's what she hinted.'

'Does Charles matter in all this?'

'Delia seems to think so. She believes he's a link to the Flanagan riddle without knowing it.'

'In that case she's probably right. Delia may be crazy but she knows what she's at.' Clare was close to him now whispering in his ear. 'Michael, I want those answers. I'll never really know Granpapa until I've found the truth. I'm sure now that he meant me to follow this through.'

'How'll we do it?'

'You really mean we?'

'From now on where you go I go. I say we follow up those addresses.'

'What about the Amsterdam one?'

'We'll phone Roger Peyron. The Irish names are for us.'

'Michael,' she whispered gently licking his ear. 'Is Jean-Luc still being tactful?'

Mike chuckled. 'He made quite a point about leaving the anchor watch to him.'

'We don't want to let him down, do we?'

'No,' he said. 'That wouldn't do at all.' Already his hands were softly sliding under her clothing, pulling off her woollen sweater and then the loose cotton shirt. She wore no bra. Her breasts and the nipples gleamed in the subdued light as they hardened to the caress of his fingers and tongue. With a gurgle of pleasure she lay back on the bunk kicking off her remaining clothing. Mike now stripped of his own clothes knelt above her. Oblivious to everything he kissed her breasts and lips and ran his hands under her thighs. Then he slammed his head against the underside of the bunk bookshelf. Muttering a single expletive he fell forward heavily on the naked girl. For half a minute they lay together laughing happily and a little hysterically.

'Jean-Luc must've heard that one,' she whispered. 'Come on boy, on the floor for us.' She slid off the bunk onto the carpeted surface of the cabin.

'It's the deck,' he said. 'Never call a deck a floor, it's always...' He never finished as Clare grabbed his arm and heaved him off the bunk.

'Oh God, this carpet's like a doormat,' she gasped. 'It's etching a pattern on my bum.'

'It's an offcut,' he replied. 'Peter got it in a carpet sale in Chichester.'

'Oh did he?' she giggled. 'Any cheapo remnant for that stupid paddy woman, eh?'

Mike had no chance to reply. Clare had seized him by the shoulders and pushed him to the deck. Now it was she who sat straddling him, reaching between his legs to push him deep inside her. He caught his breath as he looked up into her triumphant flushed face, and then gasped as she leant towards him and her long blonde strands brushed lightly across his chest.

Jean-Luc lay on his bunk in the fore cabin smoking a cheroot. He listened with approval to the girl's spasmodic cries of ecstasy. The noises went on for half an hour and then, following an interval of silence, resumed again louder than ever. He smiled; that young man Michael had seemed a dull fellow but already he was rising in Jean-Luc's esteem. An Englishman who knew the art of pleasing a woman must be a rarity indeed. He reached into the locker for his transmitter. With his shipmates otherwise occupied this was a perfect moment to call his control.

CHAPTER 22

There were footsteps on the deck overhead. Clare yawned and looked at her watch. It was six a.m. She wondered what was happening. According to Michael they would not be moving until daylight. He had pointed out that there would be a foul tide to work against as well as a westerly wind.

It had been frustrating for Clare that after their wild bout of love making both had to return to their single bunks. Clare had wanted to spend the night lying snuggled close to her man soaking in a long, luxurious afterglow. Modern yachts provided double berths, but *Quadra* was a ship of her era. Clare wondered how her grandfather had coped with the succession of bimbos he had taken to sea, even into his eighties.

She sat up and pulled a jumper over her head as Michael dropped down into the cabin. He walked across and gave her a hug. 'Forecast was wrong,' he said. 'Wind's changed, there's high pressure building east of us and it looks like a fair wind after all.'

'That's brilliant,' she shouted as the implication sank in. 'We'll make Ireland non stop.'

'Not so fast,' he shook his head. 'It's only a force four – good chance it'll die midday. It's cold as well, so I doubt we'll get a sea breeze either.'

'When do we start?'

'Jean-Luc's getting ready to weigh anchor now. Breakfast on the move, I think.' Even as he spoke the starter on the diesel whirred and the engine drummed into life.

It was cold, the wind that came out of the east had an icy tang to it. Clare had come on deck dressed in yesterday's jeans and jumpers. She had instantly scuttled below again and pulled on her full foul weather gear plus balaclava and gloves. Michael was dressed the same, while Jean-Luc was arrayed in his old fashioned oilskin suit complete with sou-wester hat. The Ancient Mariner, she thought. The wind was strong enough to push *Quadra* along at four knots despite the foul tide. The sky was obscured by a blanket of grey cloud. Clare stared across to the coastline and the town of Swanage. Even as she did so a snow shower blotted out the scene. They sailed on for twenty minutes in a swirl of tiny ice particles.

Mike set a course to take them out to sea, well south of the race at Portland. He explained that they would have four hours good sailing when the tide turned. He aimed to anchor for the night in Devon at Salcombe or Dartmouth. Although they were all experienced sailors they were still short-handed for a long continuous passage. As for those who might be monitoring their progress; he would play it safe and on no account would he go near main ports like Plymouth.

At nine o'clock Mike told Clare to go below and rest. He would take the first watch, alternating with Jean-Luc, four hours on and four hours off. Clare could stand two hour shifts to help whichever of the men was on watch at the time. She was not inclined to argue. This was not Clare's notion of sailing. She liked warm seas and sunny skies. This masochistic, freezing cold stuff had no appeal.

She lay on her bunk and listened to the sounds of the ship. She shut her eyes and started to think. She needed to think her way into the mind of her grandfather, James O'Dwyer. Clare had read modern European history during her time at La Sorbonne. She had dropped out with no degree, but the experience had given her a working knowledge of the subject.

So what was this secret from seventy years ago that was so damning that it could panic governments today? Colonel Thomas-Jefferson Flanagan was a logistics officer. Smart move that; a soldier who avoided fighting: a man who organized rations and transport. He was an American with the American army in France. Much to the irritation of the French and British they had needed the Americans to arrive in force to turn the tide and end the war. Why were the Americans in the war anyway? Some German conspiracy to do with Mexico. Granpapa had no connections with Mexico. Roger Peyron had said that Granpapa had carried a letter from Flanagan to Michael Collins. Now this was nearer home. Grandfather had known Collins. He would wax lyrically about his admiration for this ruthless guerrilla leader. Collins had been the strategist of the Irish resistance during 1919 to 1921; the only period when Britain and Ireland had been formally at war. It had been a bloody business that had ended in stalemate and eventually a compromise treaty. The treaty had created the six-county state of Northern Ireland and with it a trail of calamity that was with them to this day. Whatever this secret, it must be bound up with the treaty. The treaty had split Ireland and triggered a second tragic civil war. Like other revolutions this one had devoured its children. Collins had died, cut down in hail of bullets, in an ambush near his home village; while the writer, yachtsman and romantic

Erskine Childers, was executed by firing squad. So what could all this have to do with the present day? Well, it was interesting, but hell, the world had moved on since 1921. Who outside Ireland remembered or cared a jot about any of these events? Michael and Peter had been told that this alleged missing document was so compromising, that even today it could damage relations between Britain and America. The Irish intelligence man had told them it could destroy any hope of long-term peace in the North. These spooks, Delia included, were not fools; they certainly did not deal in fantasy.

It was true what she had said to Michael. She wanted these answers too. Her grandfather had set this time bomb ticking. She remembered the last words he had spoken to her a few hours before he died. "Take my boat to Ireland. There's a secret in her". For the first time Clare believed she knew what he meant. Grandfather had never hidden his chicanery from the world. This was the one secret he had kept to himself because – and the thought was incredible – because he was afraid to reveal it. Yes, Grandfather who feared no one. Heavens, he had crossed people as varied as de Valera, Franco, the Catholic Church, General MacArthur, Richard Nixon, the Ku Klux Klan, Senator McCarthy, the Mafia, the CIA, the list was endless. What had he to be afraid of from this obscure Colonel Flanagan or his memory? Clare knew only one certainty. Granpapa wanted her to know this secret. He had left her the boat and the clues, such as they were, she would follow. Follow regardless of the danger? She shivered a little and pulled her sleeping bag around her. Her one regret was involving Michael. He too was in danger. There was this odd mission that Delia had condemned him to. "Find Charles Venner-Harris." Who on earth would want to find that, fat pompous Brit? At this point she gave up. If Clare believed in anything it was fate. She would go where fate carried her.

Mike was sitting in the cockpit, a mug of tea in his hand. It had just passed midday and with the tide under them they were making better progress. They had passed Portland Bill, out of sight below the horizon an hour ago, and were well out into Lyme Bay. How peaceful, almost dreamlike it all seemed. He knew well that in the days of sail this was one of the most treacherous coasts in Britain. Square-rigged ships that ventured too near the land in an onshore gale would become 'embayed', trapped between the headlands of Portland and Start Point. Caught in a desperate struggle to escape they would lose ground little by little until, maybe days later, they would be driven ashore, sometimes with huge loss of life. Mike pushed such morbid thoughts from his mind. *Quadra* had modern rig, an engine, and an emergency radio. They were running before the wind now with all the sail they had which wasn't much. *Quadra* didn't like it. She was wallowing painfully in the disturbed sea that had built between the Portland race behind them and Start Point somewhere in the haze ahead.

He smiled at Clare as she appeared on deck. He would hardly have known her in the bulky foul weather gear, had it not been for the wisp of golden hair that protruded from under the hood. At that moment the mainsail shivered, slatted and then hung useless.

'That's it,' he said in resignation. 'Wind's gone. Time to use 'the iron topsail'.

'The what?'

'That's the name the old-timers called an engine. It's a term of abuse, or irony anyway.' He turned the key and pressed the starter button. The big diesel roared into life. Once again they were moving, eating away the miles to nightfall.

'Come on,' he shouted. 'Let's get the sails stowed. We won't need them now.'

'Where are we going?' she asked.

'We'll put into Dartmouth. We'll rest up tonight. Then another early start tomorrow.'

'I think we might risk a drink ashore,' Mike had appeared in his shore-going clothes. 'Come on, let's hit the town. You coming, Jean-Luc?'

'Non, I stay with zee ship.' The man was gloomy and emphatic, so Mike didn't argue.

Quadra was securely berthed in the Dart marina not far from the Navy college. Security was good here and Mike was fairly confident their stay would be quiet. Clare changed into her favourite designer jacket. 'Say, we'll do better than drink. My credit card'll stand us another meal.'

They wandered hand in hand leisurely down the Embankment Street as far as *The Carved Angel* restaurant. It was early season and that famous eating house was quiet.

'This time,' said Mike, 'I'm going to order for both of us in the Queen's English.'

'What's your Queen got to do with it?' she grinned. 'You don't sound anything like her.' She signalled to the waiter. 'My boyfriend and I would like to peruse the menu.'

'You don't sound like her either,' he laughed.

Mike was secretly delighted that the food was every bit as good as that in the restaurant at St Vaast, and in *La Fontaine* in Paris. He ordered a second bottle of wine. They were in no hurry and God knew when the opportunity would occur again. Clare was watching a group of men eating heartily at a nearby table. They were all around Mike's age, but there was something about them that set them apart.

'Navy men,' said Mike. 'Probably instructors from Britannia College.'

'What sort of place would that be?'

'It's the training school for the Navy's officer corps. The best in the world.'

'It's your navy you're talking about?'

'Yes, it's still the best. A bit short on ships these days but still great on achievement.'

'Is that so?'

'What's the matter with you?' he stared at her surprised at the tone.

'How, Michael, would you like it if you heard a German boasting of the achievements of the Luftwaffe?'

'I'd laugh. They took a hiding in 1940, just like the one Nelson handed out at Trafalgar. Both battles saved Europe from military dictatorship.'

'Nelson's no hero figure to us. His battle may've saved you, but it kept us under foreign rule for a century.'

Mike looked at her coldly. 'If the Germans or the French had conquered Britain, would they have left Ireland alone?'

'I don't know.' She in turn was surprised at his vehemence.

'Would you rather be ruled by Napoleon, Hitler or the likes of Charles Venner-Harris?'

'I told you before,' she snapped. 'We could've died with honour.'

'The trouble with you lot is you're a sight too keen on being saints and martyrs. I'm interested in living.'

She smiled. 'Sure – I'm sorry. It's just my gut reaction. My logic tells me you're right.'

They walked slowly back along the waterfront. They were in no hurry, glad to be alone together.

'I like this place,' she said.

'It's beautiful in summer. I wish I could show it to you. It runs for miles all the way to Totnes. *Quadra* would be in her element.'

'Why is Jean-Luc so grumpy?' she asked.

'He's only being tactful.'

'There's more to it than that. I think he's got his own agenda. Roger asked him to be our minder, but I know he's up to something else.'

'How come?'

'This morning I saw him with a sort of two-way radio. He was talking into it, not much above a whisper. I couldn't hear a word above the noise outside.'

'Did he see you?'

'No, I'm sure he never.'

'Delia told me he was French Intelligence.' Mike did not know what to make of Clare's news. Then with a shock he remembered. 'Clare, we've never contacted Roger Peyron about that name on the list. You know Clarke – in Amsterdam. He was going to check it out for us.'

'Michael,' she released his hand and swung round to face him. 'How the hell did I forget? We'd better phone him now, my mobile's in the ship.'

'Mobile's not secure; we'll find a pay phone.'

They found a phone booth. Mike gave Clare his BT card and left her to make the call. He walked back to look over the water. Fifteen minutes later she rejoined him. 'Any luck?' he asked.

'No good, the man Clarke's dead. He's been dead nearly two weeks.'

'Oh well, these things happen,' Mike was philosophical.

'You haven't heard the half of it,' she replied grimly. 'He was an old man, nearly one hundred years old, and someone beat him to death with an iron bar.'

'Oh hell no!'

'Oh hell yes. There's more, Clarence and Craig called on him that very day.'

'You're not saying they did it – no way.'

'No, I'm not saying that. Will you listen until I'm finished?'

'Sorry, go on.'

'Roger says that just across from where the old fellow lived there's an upstairs flat. Two ladies live there, both hookers – it's a rough part of that city you understand.' Clare stopped as two passers by walked within earshot. Then she continued. 'These two ladies keep their eyes open – it's second nature to them. Roger says they told the Dutch police they saw Clarence and Craig go in and leave half an hour later.'

'How did they know it was them?'

'They didn't, but it seems Clarence had informed the Dutch Intelligence people before he went. Protocol you see.'

'OK, just wondered.'

'Anyway, now the important bit. After they'd gone a woman went into Clarke's place. It was getting dark but the two ladies reckoned they'd seen her earlier that day.' Clare paused and seemed to stare reflectively into the middle distance. A large motor yacht was passing up river, slowly stemming the ebb tide. 'Go on,' said Mike. 'What then?'

'This is the cruncher, not that it proves a thing. You see, they describe a thin dark woman with a white face...'

'Delia?'

'Could be, but we mustn't let our imaginations run away to meet the facts.'

'Who was Clarke?'

'Now there you have it. Roger says the Irish press and TV were swarming all over the place. It seems Mr Clarke was an old IRA man – one of the last alive.'

'IRA?'

'No, old IRA, there's a distinction. The boys who fought the Independence War in 1920 were The Irish Republican Army. They were a guerrilla force, hit and run, completely legitimate. Any man, or woman for that matter, could honourably join and plenty did.'

Mike was only half listening. '1920 and Ireland again. Your grandfather and Flanagan. This Clarke was supposed to know the answers and now he's dead.'

CHAPTER 23

'Course 275 degrees,' Mike called to Clare. 'Hold it as near as you can while we fix the preventer.'

Clare grasped the tiller. She felt just a little nervous. The two men had gone forward to set the preventer tackle. Its purpose was to stop the sail boom swinging across the boat in an unplanned gybe. A slight wind change could do this to the point of damaging the rigging or even injuring a crew member. Whatever happened, she Clare, must not be the cause of such a gybe while the men were working forward. They were speeding at six knots towards their next port of call, the Helford River, a few miles west of Falmouth.

The job complete, Michael and Jean-Luc were making their way back to the cockpit. She began to relax.

'Clare, have you looked astern?' called Michael.

'No,' she hastily swung round. Hell, there was a bloody great ship overtaking them. Where could it have come from?

'That caught you out,' Michael was grinning in a most irritating and chauvinist way. 'Don't worry, doesn't matter out here. Remember to look behind as a matter of habit. When we get to Cobh and Ringiskiddy there'll be ferries and big craft all over the place.'

Clare took another glance at the ship; she was closing fast.

Michael had a look through the binoculars. 'This one belongs to the "Andrew".'

'What's that?'

'Navy slang for the Admiralty. You know, like I said last night, best in the world.' He focused the glasses again. 'She's only a fishery protection boat though. That's all we'll have left soon.'

'Then our navy'll be the best,' Clare smiled.

Michael roared with laughter. 'You have definitely got to be joking.'

Clare let it go. She wished she knew why mention of the Irish Navy caused people to fall about laughing; even the Irish themselves. This British warship was very close; she could hear the beat of her engines and the sound of her bow wave.

'She's an Island Class patrol boat.' Michael was leafing through a reference book. 'I wish she'd keep her distance – there's no need to pass this close.' He sounded annoyed.

The ship surged onwards passing within two hundred yards. Her wash sent *Quadra* pitching and rolling as Clare struggled with the tiller.

'Nosy bastards,' said Michael. 'There's civilians up on her bridge. One of 'em's taking a good long look at us.'

'Arrogant as always,' Clare joked.

'Let's hope that's all it is.'

That was the last incident of note on their passage. It was still daylight when Jean-Luc steered *Quadra* up to the visitor's buoys off the Helford Sailing Club. Mike leant over with the boat hook and caught the ring in the top of the float while Clare threaded a mooring line through it. Mike signalled and Jean-Luc cut the engine.

'Look at that,' said Mike pointing. He was gazing at a magnificent motor yacht. She was moored to a large buoy a hundred and fifty yards upstream. She literally shone in the evening light. Her hull was devoid of the slightest speck of dirt. Her woodwork was immaculate, her metalwork gleamed.

'Gi'me the binoculars,' Clare demanded.

'In the cockpit,' he replied. He wished he could get to grips with her sudden mood swings. Something had angered her.

Clare picked up the glasses and trained them on the motor yacht. The tide was flooding, so the other ship was pointing at them. Then the wind caught her shallow draft and she swung gently in the tideway. They could just see her stern. 'Irish ensign – same as ours,' said Clare. 'I thought I knew her.' She sounded disgruntled and Mike wondered why.

'I'd have thought you'd be pleased?' he said.

'Well I'm not. What's it the man said in that film. "Of all the gin joints in the world she has to walk in here".'

'I take it you know the people in that bimbo-carrier?'

Clare giggled. 'What a great name – I like it.'

'That's what we call them in the Med. You see them in St Trop', with naked starlets sprawled all over the decks. Anyway who is she?'

'She's called, *Shy Colleen of Howth,* which is a bloody silly name, Howth's her home port, and she's joint owned by Nicolai Constantinescu, and Noel Shaw-Mulligan.'

'Your step-father?' Mike gaped in surprise.

'The same, they say it's a small world and it is sometimes, especially when you don't want it.'

'Who's the other name? He sounds like a Greek pirate.'

'Nicolai's Rumanian by birth. Irish by adoption.'

'What a great mix.'

'All contrived though. Great advantage to travel on an Irish passport, everyone love you. Granpapa told me that. If you've an American one you get spat at all round the world.'

'They've seen us,' Mike was looking through the glasses now. There was a young man standing on the flying bridge of the yacht staring at them. He was joined by another, shorter and stockier. He handed the binoculars to Clare.

'That short-assed jerk is Noel,' she said. 'The other one is Toni, he's Nicolai's son.' She looked really alarmed now.

'Clare darling, what's the trouble?'

'Oh shite, I'd better come clean – I don't want to hide anything from you…'

'Nor me from you,' he replied quietly and waited. She put her arms around him and buried her head in his chest. Jean-Luc walked past ignoring them.

'Michael,' she was hesitant. 'I used to know Toni in Paris. We had a bit of a fling when I was seventeen. If you must know …I…I lost my virginity to him. I think you ought to know that.' She looked at him pleading.

Mike kissed her. 'You certainly lost it to someone, I've already noticed.' He laughed at the relief in her face.

She in turn laughed and cried at the same time. 'It's just that if we bump into Toni I don't want trouble.'

'Why should there be. What d'you take me for?'

'Oh thank you, Michael. I do love you.' She paused and kissed him again. 'I'll tell you something else. Toni's a lousy fuck.'

Mike sat at the chart table writing up the log of that day's passage. He gulped a mouthful of lager straight from the can by his elbow. No gourmet meal or fine wines tonight. This was a quiet spot; the bright lights might be a taxi ride away in Falmouth, but Mike had no appetite for them. He had been more disturbed than he admitted by the close scrutiny they had received from that warship. It was something that had never happened to him before on any yacht, British flag or foreign. He closed the log book and put it back on the shelf; he wondered if he was going paranoid. He could hear Clare's voice and a muffled reply from outside the ship. Mike climbed up the four steps to the cockpit. Looking over the rail at him was a man. He had a round, rosy-cheeked, almost cherubic face, with short curly black hair. He was holding onto the rail with one hand, in the other he held a full whisky bottle.

'Hi there, skipper. I'm Noel from *Shy Colleen* over yonder. Would you care to be joining us for a jar or two?'

'I'm sure we'd be delighted,' was Mike's instant response. Clare looked daggers but he didn't care. He only knew that he liked this Noel.

'That's dandy,' said Noel, there was no disguising his pleasure. 'The night's young and we'll have some grand craic.' He disappeared into the rigid inflatable craft he had arrived in. The engine started and with a jaunty wave he sped towards his own vessel. He turned and called. 'Don't bother with your dinghy. I'll fetch you in this one – seven o'clock.'

'Thank you very much Michael.' Clare eyed him balefully. 'Thank you very much for nothing.'

'Oh come on. In harbour you never refuse an invitation like that one. Anyway I rather like the guy.'

Clare continued glaring at *Shy Colleen*. Someone had switched on the lights in that ship's glass enclosed after-deck. 'Toni's got a girl with him,' she snorted.

Mike was amused. 'Who was it that talked about me being jealous?'

'I'm not jealous. I only said he's got a girl on board.'

'So what, he's not going to sit around moping over you.'

'It's not that. I'm watching them through these glasses. She's wearing a clingy strapless gown and she's swilling something in a wine glass. The gown's red – the trollop.'

'Never mind, they won't expect us to dress up. Not coming off a boat like this.' Mike started to coil the mainsheet.

Clare's cheeks had a flush. She turned on him bristling. 'Like hell they won't. I'll not be shown up by her.' She stamped away below. Jean-Luc turned an impassive face to Mike and winked.

Mike wandered around the deck for a while. Satisfied he went below. It was time he had at least a shave and a quick wash. Clare was standing in the cabin. She looked totally incongruous in the designer dress she had bought in Paris.

'That's a waste of time,' he grumbled. 'Now I'll have to go formal.'

'And so you will,' she grated. 'I'll not have either of us shown up by these people,' she paused. 'I can't help but wonder why Noel was not the least surprised to see me here? He *knows* something.'

They waited by the rail as *Shy Colleen's* boat travelled the short distance. Mike was dressed in his best shore-going slacks, and a blazer with a yacht club tie. Clare had pulled her foul weather top over the dress for the duration of the boat trip. The boat was piloted by a crewman. He was a cheerful, bearded individual who welcomed them in a strong Dublin accent. It was almost dark as they powered towards the brightly lit super-yacht. Mike looked wistfully back to *Quadra.* He knew which ship he preferred.

The boat came alongside a platform with steps leading upwards. Clare led the way and Mike followed. Noel Shaw-Mulligan greeted them at the top. 'Into the saloon with you. Drinks, dinner, and more drinks.'

Mind-blowing was the only word that Mike could think of for the plush centrally-heated lounge area. The furniture, fittings and décor would not have been out of place at the Ritz. Noel relieved Clare of her jacket and waved them both towards the young couple standing by the bar. Mike had never seen the man in his life, but he knew the woman. He had at once been as close to her and as intimate as it was possible to be.

'Hello Annabel,' he found himself mumbling the greeting while the room and its contents spun around him.

'Would you two know each other?' asked Noel.

'We have met.' Annabel took a tiny exquisite sip from her glass. She turned back to Mike. 'I thought I recognized your boat. It's that heap of junk that sat in your yard. Are you really telling us you sailed her all the way here.' She had cocked her head on one side in her most alluring attitude, but the smile was all malice.

Mike felt oddly elated. This was the moment he had been dreading. He knew that sooner or later he would bump into Annabel in the company of another man. It was joyous to discover he didn't care. That compared to Clare, Annabel was a vapid nonentity and that he was free of her for ever.

'That heap of junk is our ship, Annabel – Clare's and mine.' He stared back. He had no need to react to her taunt, her opinions meant nothing.

'Michael,' said Clare. There was a bite in her tone. 'You seem to know this person. Would you have the manners to introduce us?'

Noel who was looking increasingly embarrassed intervened. 'No, it's me who should be remembering his manners. Please, Miss Clare O'Dwyer, meet Miss Annabel de Boulliet.' Noel made an apologetic bow; his short stocky figure looked faintly ridiculous.

The girls advanced to within a foot of each other and stared eyeball to eyeball. They reminded Mike of two boxers being introduced in the ring.

'So you are Annabel,' said Clare. She was smiling but her body language sent a wholly different message. 'I rather like my heap of junk. She was built by my grandfather.'

'The senator, you mean. Toni was talking about him.' Annabel's perfectly enunciated Home Counties vowels were clearly meant to cause maximum irritation. This was not her sloppy Sloane Ranger speech that Mike remembered.

'Has he indeed?' Clare swung round to face the second man. 'Hello Toni, have you nothing to say to me?'

The young man in question had shrunk slowly backwards until he was firmly wedged in a corner of the bar. He was tall, with Mediterranean features, and had dressed himself in a white evening suit that looked out of place, as did the next-to-nothing dresses worn by the girls. Mike thought the whole scene would have been better played out under a tropical sun.

Toni advanced took Clare's hand and kissed it. 'Of course I remember, Clare. I didn't recognize you at first, it's been so long, and you are more beautiful than ever.' His voice was soft, cultured Irish; pleasant but featureless.

Clare laughed. 'So you're still full of blarney. Now Toni, what is it you've been saying about my grandfather?' She had gripped him with that awesome eye contact; the thing she seemed to share with all her family. Toni said nothing, and despite himself, Mike felt sympathy. He remembered being similarly skewered by Delia Lazarraga. He also had been too tongue-tied to reply.

'Toni says your grandfather was a two-faced egomaniac.' Annabel replied for him; she was bending forward relishing the contest.

'That's interesting,' said Clare sweetly. 'Michael says your father is a speculative land dealer and he's a money-grubbing shite.'

Annabel bristled as the shot struck home. 'My father is a respected property adviser. As for Mike, I bet he hasn't told you his father was a common railway worker.'

'Did you tell me that, Michael?' Clare grinned at him. Mike was rather shocked to see that she was enjoying herself.

'Yes, I did tell you. He built locomotives.'

'Of course I remember. Well, that seems a useful profession.'

'Tell you something else,' said Mike. 'Annabel's surname is de Boulliet, but her grandfather's name was Bullit.'

'Don't you dare sneer, you common little oik,' Annabel was furious. 'We're Norman descent, Bullit was a corruption. My father revived the true name.'

'Say, Noel,' said Clare, 'don't you sometimes wonder at the strange ways of the English?'

'I never cease to,' Noel replied. 'Now you ladies, you're not performing in a Sheridan play. So will you please be nice to each other and not spoil the party.' He spread his hands and turned to each protagonist with such a disarming grin that Mike could not help but like the man. He wasn't sure why Clare so detested Noel. He was her step-father, so maybe there were things, family secrets, unrevealed. Otherwise he would have said this devious politician was not unlike grandfather O'Dwyer.

'Noel, what would you be doing in these parts then? Don't try telling me you're on holiday – Cornwall in May isn't St Trop?' Clare shot the question across the dinner table.

Noel grinned, wholly unfazed. 'You could say I'm on a fishing expedition. Did your grandfather ever mention the name O'Farrell?'

'Why?' For the first time Clare looked evasive.

'It's no matter,' Noel positively smirked.

Clare shot back at him. 'What can you tell me about The Irish American Cultural Society?'

Mike felt slightly resentful. He was on the point of scenting an enormous glass of brandy. Apart from this he had absorbed enough alcohol this evening to anaesthetize him from all their troubles. The dinner had gone surprisingly well. Clare had remarked on the coincidence of both ships arriving at Helford on the same day.

'I've been here for a fortnight,' said Annabel airily. 'Cornwall's ripe for expansion.'

Mike, already on an alcoholic high, had laughed at her. 'It can't expand, it surrounded on three sides by water.'

'That is exactly the kind of puerile remark I would expect,' she snapped. 'I mean Daddy is planning three upmarket developments in this area. We've had nothing but grief from the local peasants. They're brain-dead morons all of them.'

Clare's question to Noel had come out of the blue towards the end of an evening that had been mostly anecdotes and small talk. Toni and Annabel had left the dining saloon to fetch another bottle of liqueur. For the first time Clare was alone and private with Noel Shaw-Mulligan.

'Ah, the Culturals,' said Noel. 'Basically they're trouble and misnamed too. American yes, cultural I wouldn't know, but there's nothing Irish about them. No sense of humour for starters.'

'But who are they?'

'Their big cheese is Anderson, Dr Bernard Anderson. I must admit I've never met the fellah but they say he's got the charisma when he speaks to a crowd.'

'We've met their Australian man and he's a complete pillock,' said Mike.

'Maybe, but it wouldn't do to underestimate Anderson. The man's a historian, he's well thought of.'

'I'm told he doesn't like us British?'

'Sure he's an Anglophobe, but as I say he's no sense of humour.'

'All right,' said Clare. 'If he hates Brits so much, why does he use a British lawyer to hassle me into selling my boat?'

Noel's jaw sagged for a second. 'What's this Clare? Sounds like you've a tale to tell us?'

Clare told him the story of her visit from Charles Venner-Harris.

Noel's whole demeanour changed; he looked troubled. 'Venner-Harris, now there's a name.'

'What d'you know about him?' Clare held Noel in an intense stare.

'I wish you wouldn't look at me like that. You're as bad as your grandfather,' he grumbled.

'Tell me about Charles Venner-Harris. Delia Lazarraga says he's been kidnapped.'

'Of course, the Tory party man who's gone missing. I saw a Garda report about that. There was no suggestion of kidnapping.' Noel sucked noisily at his brandy glass. 'T'was another of that name I had in mind.'

'Who?'

'Only a name that's cropped up from the past. You might as well know – it's from your beloved grandfather's past as well.'

'Flanagan again?'

'Now we come to it. I wasn't going to spoil the craic by mentioning that business.' He looked at Clare. Every trace of the folksy populist had vanished. Noel Shaw-Mulligan was a worried man. 'Clare, I'm speaking to you as your poor mother's husband, so it's family. A warning, don't take after your grandfather. Stop being stubborn. If you've got those documents, give 'em to me now. If you don't trust me, give 'em to Judge Brennan in Cork.'

'Noel,' Clare held him in the full force of her eye contact. He shrank back as if he had been stung. 'Noel, we have been harassed the length of England and France by terrorists, the French, the CIA. Worse Michael's taken a grilling from Delia. I'll tell you what I've told the bloody lot of 'em. Until a week ago I'd never heard of Flanagan. There are no papers in my boat. If there's anything in Grandfather's house, the CIA will have been there. So what's your problem? I know nothing.'

Noel drained the last of his brandy. 'Let's hope they don't exist, but Special Branch say they do.'

'But Noel, what's the deal? Jesus man, it's stuff from seventy years ago.'

'I know that, but this is Ireland and time's not always a great healer.'

'Noel, don't you dare hold out on me, and don't patronize me neither. What's in those papers?'

'I'm not patronizing you, Clare. I've seen them. We've got the original in the ministry. My lord and master, the Taoiseach, showed me the photocopy. I've been sworn to silence, life or death, seal of the confessional, whatever you like. If you knew what I knew you be shite scared as well.'

'All right, give us a hint?'

'If this get's public there'll be no peace in the North, not this year, not for many a year to come. The Yankees'll look a lot of darned fools and the Brits'll be spitting their teeth at them.'

'I know, that's what we've been told all along the line – it's crazy.'

'I can only repeat what I've said, Clare. I'm shite scared.'

CHAPTER 24

Henri had been looking forward to this trip to Bilbao; but now it was raining and the place was as depressing as Dieppe in January. Henri had rather resented Chef Peyron's intervention. That old man was too sharp by far. He still did not miss a thing. It had been Peyron's work that had led to this grand intelligence coup. The former Chef de Bureau had been called back to investigate the Flanagan mystery. This opportunity to embarrass the British and Americans was too good to miss. However, Henri had no personnel to spare and a puzzle such as this was very much Peyron's specialty. Moreover he had known the American O'Dwyer and his granddaughter. The matter of this Irish girl and her English lover would have been a low priority for Bureau Soixante Neuf. It had been Peyron who had made the right connections. Interrogation of the two Basques had confirmed his intuition. Now, if Peyron's theory was right, they had a crisis on their hands, and only he, Henri, could contain it. So it was that he had abandoned his desk in Paris and returned to the field. Today he was Michel Charron, insurance assessor, dressed in his dark bourgeois suit and raincoat and clutching his cheap document case. Yesterday Henri was, or liked to think he was, a Paris sophisticate; a former graduate of Le Lycée and La Sorbonne. Now he was back with his southern Basque roots. The sensitivity of this mission needed a fluent speaker of Euskera. Henri was pleased to find his native language returning so quickly. It was a revisiting of his childhood, to the little village near Bayonne. Herding the pigs and geese with his schoolmates; kicking a rugby ball into le curé's garden.

'I think your chief may have it right.' It was Perez. So deep had Henri been in his reverie that he hadn't heard the footsteps.

'Not Le Chef, the ex-Chef – I am le Chef de Bureau now.' Henri was surprised how easily his pride was stung now that he was a Basque again. Peyron had been an outstanding intelligence chief and his was a hard act to follow.

'Of course, my friend,' Perez was soothing, 'and between us we shall have a result to be remembered.'

'You look pleased with yourself.' Henri was studying Perez's gaunt face. The Spaniard was tall and amazingly fit for his sixty years. He had a true hauteur, with his long greying hair and sharp features. Perez was no Basque, he was a Castilian, but Henri suspected there was something of the Moor in his ancestry. Perez had seen a lot of trouble in his life. He could just remember the Civil War. His Catholic priest uncle had been shot by the Republicans. Perez's trade unionist father had been shot by Franco. France had seen her share of brutality, but the casualness with which Perez and most Spaniards regarded these happenings puzzled Henri. In Franco's time Perez had been a journalist. He had worked on a censored paper by day, and edited a subversive underground one by night. He had been banned from working and twice been imprisoned. In jail he had met other political prisoners. Later he had constructed an anti-government intelligence network of his own. Then Franco had died and democracy had been restored. It had been an inspired decision by the new government to recruit Perez into its legitimate service.

'Yes, Henri. The lady flew into Madrid this morning.' Perez cut the end off a cigar and attempted to light it. He looked in disgust as the rain destroyed his matches. 'Always it rains when I come to this country.'

'You think she will come here?'

'If your former chief is correct, yes we shall see her.'

'Will you arrest her?'

'Certainly not,' Perez was appalled. 'First rule of intelligence, Henri. Wait, follow, and then spring the trap. Besides there are other considerations. Lazarraga is a big name in these parts. Felipe Lazarraga was a man the Fascists feared. The people remember O'Dwyer also.' Perez sighed. 'Tact Henri, my old friend. There are sensitive-ities here, and we must respect them or face even more trouble.'

Henri had no argument with that. Perez was talking about the infamous Poz massacre. It was fifty years since, but there were lesser atrocities from five hundred years ago and the Basques still remem-bered them.

'We will have time on our hands tomorrow,' said Perez. 'Would you like to see where it happened?'

They abandoned Perez's car at the end of the track and walked the final kilometer. The road was crumbling and part of it had long since slid into the ravine. Perez was not inclined to drive up it. The rain had passed, the sun was shining, and the grass was green. The sheep by the roadside looked content, the birds sang and a warm drying wind blew over the landscape. Henri was happy, this was his country too. He was consumed with a deep inner 'joi' he did not attempt to explain to Perez. They reached the summit and paused for breath, or at least Henri did. Perez might be thirty years older than Henri but he was leaner and fitter.

'Round the corner and you will see,' Perez said cryptically.

Ahead of them was a stone cross, or rather a crucifix, about a meter in height standing beside a white obelisk. Surrounding both was a gravel square built from particles of crushed rock. Henri moved closer. There were little bunches of flowers at the foot of the obelisk and framed photographs, worn and weathered, but still recognizable. The obelisk had thirty names carved on it. The inscription was in Euskera.

The fallen of Poz
June 2nd 1937
Vengeance lies with God.

'Very short and simple,' said Henri. 'This is almost like a British graveyard in Northern France.'

'James O'Dwyer raised this memorial and paid for it. He brought Felipe Lazarraga's body here for burial after Franco died.'

'I wonder what he meant by that inscription?' said Henri.

'I understand that some of the perpetrators were still alive. O'Dwyer didn't want the villagers to seek retribution in kind.'

Henri nodded. 'Probably kill the wrong people and get themselves into one hell of a lot of trouble.'

'Exactly.'

'I find this place spooky. Where was the village?'

'After the massacre the Nats razed it to the ground. The bodies were in a mass grave but the people reburied them later when the dictatorship fell.' Perez led the way to the top of the mound and pointed. In front of them was a cemetery, all grass and lines of crosses. Beyond were the crumbling stones that had once been houses.

Henri felt depressed. These were his people too. If it had been his village he would never have left vengeance to God, whatever O'Dwyer might think. He turned his back on the scene and returned to the present.

'Perez, this man we are to meet. You trust him?'

'Yes, implicitly. We have turned several ETA activists and this man, Carlos is genuine. He has infiltrated the group we are interested in and his intelligence has been good.'

Henri grunted. 'I hope you are right. Is this him now?' A motor

171

bike was grinding cautiously up the track as its rider avoided the worst of the potholes. He rode straight to them and dismounted pulling off his helmet. The man was young, no more than twenty five, with a round, cheerful face. Henri wondered what it must be like to walk with danger as this man did. Retribution would be horrible if the terrorists had any inkling that he was betraying them. Carlos propped his machine on its stand and walked to the memorial. He stood for a few seconds, crossed himself, and walked back to them.

'You're sure you weren't followed?' asked Perez. He spoke fair Euskera but with an appalling accent.

'No, they are all with the ship. Anyway, nobody comes here, to this accursed place.' Carlos shrugged and began to pull off his motorcycle leathers.

'This is my colleague from France.' Perez introduced Henri. 'He is in the role of an insurance man. The law requires a fishing vessel to be insured. We have arranged that our friend here will do the inspection this afternoon.'

'Shouldn't be any trouble with that,' Carlos replied. 'I tell you something though. The bill of sale shows the purchasers name as Lazarraga.' Carlos seemed pleased with himself.

'Isn't that a bit blatant, arrogant even?' said Henri.

'I'm surprised,' said Perez, 'but I suppose it's a clever move. As I told you, Lazarraga is a big name in these parts. The people would resent a move against her.'

'So this ship, *El Juanita,* is leaving on a legitimate fishing excursion?'

'Unless we find her stuffed with Lebanese guns.' Perez replied grimly.

'Tell me, my friend,' said Perez. 'Do you know the first thing about insurance and ships?'

'I know enough to tell you that thing is a rustbucket,' Henri replied. 'I would not chance my life to her across the Baye all the way to Irelande.'

They were on the fish dock at Bermeo. Perez was crouching in the anonymity of his car. He suspected that some of the ETA might know him by sight. This was as far as he was prepared to go. From henceforth Henri would be on his own. They were looking at their objective. She was, *Juanita,* a thirty-year-old tuna boat converted to a conventional stern trawler. She was bulky and her rusty plates had been repaired more than once.

'I understand she is registered as seaworthy?' Henri asked.

'Yes, they say her engines are modern and good, and that is what counts apparently.'

Henri sighed. 'I'd better keep my appointment.'

Carlos met him at the gangway. He was stonefaced; no one would have had a suspicion that they had met before. Carlos took Henri to the captain who took him on a tour of the ship. The captain had produced a certificate of seaworthiness and made great play with the state-of-the-art radar. As Henri had suspected, *Juanita,* was a crumbling wreck. Not even her smart new diesel engines could compensate for that. Henri passively viewed everything, made no comment, and assured the captain of a favourable quotation for a Biscay fishing voyage. Nothing was said about other destinations, nor did Henri comment on the wooden pallets that were laid on the floor of the fish hold. He doubted they were for fish boxes. On a pretext of buying cigarettes, Carlos walked part of the way along the dock with Henri. 'I am to sail with the ship to Ireland,' he said quietly.

'Sooner you than me,' Henri grunted.

'Tell Perez we are shipping empty crates. We are bringing arms out of Ireland, not in. That's all I know.'

Henri nodded and walked away. Peyron had been right.

CHAPTER 25

'Ireland,' said Clare. 'She's near – I can feel her, smell her.' She was standing in the cockpit staring into the early morning mist.

'I can't say I can feel anything,' Mike yawned. 'What am I supposed to smell – a pint of Murphy's?'

'Oh God, you Brits. Don't you ever feel the emotion when you return to your shores?'

'No, quite the opposite. I'm always wondering how many letters are waiting from the bank manager and the tax man.'

'Hopeless,' Clare sighed.

'You're right about our position though. The Decca plot makes us twenty miles south of Mine Head. We'll be in Crosshaven by early afternoon.'

'Michael, there's just one problem.'

'Let's have it then?'

'I say we don't go near Cobh or Crosshaven. Why don't we go on to Kinsale or Glandore?'

'Sure, if you like, but why?'

'Because this may be Ireland, but Cork's a main port. There's customs men, there's our police, the Garda, even our Irish Navy that you Brits like to take the piss from.'

'So what?'

'Because we've got enemies. Don't think me paranoid, but our Special Branch police are as thick as thieves with MI6. I'd wager within half an hour of us mooring Delia will be informed. There's Noel as well.'

'What about him?'

Suddenly she was angry. 'Oh yes you like him, but remember, you don't know him – I do. I tell you if it's to his advantage he'd betray us to Delia as well.'

'Yes, I remember what he said. He wanted you to hand over the papers…'

'That's right. I told him I hadn't got any papers, but he's such a liar himself that he didn't believe me.'

'You know *Shy Colleen* passed us in the night?'

'You never said that. How d'you know?'

'I don't for certain, but I heard her engines and saw her lights. I'm sure it was her. She was doing twenty plus knots on the same course.'

'If he's making for Cork that proves my point. He'll have all the authorities waiting for us. I say we go on elsewhere.'

'Right, point taken. It's your country – I'm in your hands.'

'Good man, I say we go on to Glandore. It's nice and quiet there and near my summer cottage.'

Mike went below to the chart table. Glandore was a backwater with a tricky unlit entrance. Even if they made the passage under power it would be dusk when they arrived. He called Clare down and pointed to the chart.

'Don't worry about it,' she said. 'If there's a glimmer of light I'll pilot us in.'

In the event there was more than enough daylight when, a little after seven-thirty that evening, they passed the bleak rocks of Adam Island and made their way up the Glandore inlet to drop anchor off the little village of Unionhall. For a few minutes all three of them stood there, drinking in the scene and living the magic of the moment. The moment when a small yacht swings to her anchor after a long passage is always special. The noises of the ship, her motion at sea; those things that had dominated their lives were suddenly missing. All was quiet as they stood and looked across the water to the welcoming lights of the village.

The next morning Mike overslept. It was almost a tradition following a long passage. Half sleeping, he heard footsteps and then the noise of an outboard motor. Sometime later he heard the same motor return and guessed that Clare had launched the dinghy. When he finally awoke it was to a delicious smell of frying bacon and the sight of Clare sitting at the chart table. He climbed from his bunk and shuffled across the cabin rubbing sleep from his eyes.

Clare was studying a large ordnance map. She looked up and smiled. 'While you've been sleeping I've been ashore. I've brought you bacon, eggs, fresh bread, and there's coffee on the stove.'

'Well done, brilliant.' That had been thoughtful of her. He gave Clare a hug and a lingering kiss. She responded and then pushed him away pointing at the map on the table. 'I've borrowed this from the pub.'

'What area is it?'

'This bit of coast and a fair way inland. It's time we ran my Granpapa to earth. We've a whole lot of riddles, but I fancy we'll find the answers here.'

'You think so?'

'Yes, as I see it this business has its roots in the Irish Independence War, seventy or more years ago. This district is steeped in it. Michael Collins now – you heard me and Roger talk about him?'

'The guerrilla leader?'

'That's him. Did you know Britain and Ireland were formally at war in 1920?'

'Well yes, you were talking about it the other night. I take your word for it, but we were never told about it at school.'

'I bet you weren't, and you Brits blame the Japanese for not teaching their kids what their grandfathers did in the last war.'

'I fail to see any connection.'

'War by retaliation and atrocity. A competition to see who can kill the most innocents.' There was a gleam in her eyes.

'Tell me about Collins,' Mike intervened quickly.

'He was the strategist of the Irish resistance. Look Michael, I'm against war and I don't say I approve of all his methods. You know he practically wrote the rule book for modern guerrilla warfare.'

'Rule book?'

'Basic theory anyway. You hit the enemy where he's blind. He doesn't know where you're coming from or where you're going to strike next. So he lashes out at random on the local population. That only stiffens their resolve and you get more recruits joining the guerrillas. The whole thing spirals into a bloodbath.'

'Was this the same Collins that your grandfather was carrying messages to?'

'That's him; Collins was born here, or not far away, at Woodfield over the hill there. It's only a few miles from where he met his death.'

'Did we get him, the British?'

'Not likely; he was too smart for you to catch. No, it was later, in our own civil war. He was shot in a piffling little battle. Killed by some of his old school mates, though they never knew 'til afterwards. That's the stupidity of war for you.' Clare stared straight ahead her expression inscrutable. 'You know,' she went on. 'Grandfather lived a long life. He knew Churchill and Roosevelt and Martin Luther King…Hitler too, for that matter. But he always said Collins was the most charismatic man he ever met.'

Clare said no more but went back to studying the map. Mike served breakfast for all three of them.

'Where you go today?' asked Jean-Luc.

'First we make a phone call to your Chef Roger. I want to know if he's found anything more about that man in Amsterdam. Then we'll go hire a car and drive up to my cottage.'

'Which address book names do we try first?' Mike asked.

'That's got to be the old priest, McGee. This place he's in, St Brigid's, is for geriatrics, so without seeming unkind, I guess we should find him before his God takes him.'

'Have you any idea what his connection is with Flanagan?'

'Sorry, not a clue.'

'How do we approach him? If he's hiding something he'll be suspicious. He could tell us to go to hell.'

'I doubt he'll do that,' she laughed. 'Not if he's still in the business of saving people. No, I'll come straight out with who I am and I'll say you're a British historian.'

'Come off it. Do I look like one?'

'You look more like one than Sammy Cassidy,' she paused. 'You know I've a nasty feeling we haven't seen the last of him.'

After breakfast they took the dinghy across the water to Glandore village. Mike and Jean-Luc waited outside the Glandore Inn while Clare disappeared to make her phone call to Roger Peyron. Twenty minutes later she returned at the wheel of an ancient Morris estate car.

'This is the best I could hire at short notice,' she said. 'Get in, you boys, and we'll be away.'

'What luck with Roger?' Mike asked.

'No more hard facts, but it seems this Clarke was a really bad lot – suspected war criminal.'

'When? What did he do?'

'Roger wouldn't say,' she replied grimly. 'He wouldn't discuss it with me. What's your chief playing at Jean-Luc?'

'Who knows?' said the Frenchman with an expansive shrug. Clare muttered an expletive but did not probe further.

They had arrived at a junction with a main road. A large bilingual sign pointed to somewhere called, Skibbereen. Clare turned left and followed that direction for a couple of miles before turning into a side road. There were small patchwork fields dotted with herds of newly turned out cattle. They passed a couple of farms with small whitewashed dwellings and surprisingly modern buildings.

'God bless the Common Market,' said Clare when Mike commented.

They drove through a village, with one long wide street; rather like a Western film. Here the road surface ended abruptly. Clare picked her way through the potholes for another quarter of a mile until she turned into the driveway of a house, this time a small stone bungalow.

'Here we are,' she said happily. 'This is my hidey-hole in summer.'

Mike looked around. The house was a long, narrow, single-storey building. It looked neat and trim with its white walls and green window frames.

'It's over a month since I was last here,' said Clare. 'My, that lawn needs mowing; there's a job for a strong man.'

'I thought there'd be a catch,' said Mike.

'Come on,' said Clare. 'We'll go in round the back.' She led the way round the side of the cottage.

She stopped so abruptly that Mike almost bumped into her. 'What's wrong love?' He put his arm around her shoulders. She was shaking; he'd never seen her so distressed.

'Oh no…no…oh Jesus!' she gasped.

'It is zee writings, I think,' said Jean-Luc quietly. He pointed at the gable end of the house. The white wall was disfigured with ugly graffiti, daubed in red paint. Two lines of lettering in some foreign language.

'What on earth?'

'It's in Gaelic,' she muttered.

'What does it say, Clare?'

'There's two messages. That one says: O'Dwyers always traitors never forgiven.'

'And the other one?'

'O Michael, I don't know how to say it,' she broke down sobbing against his chest.

'Go on, love; words can't hurt us.'

'It says – O' Dwyer – Englishman's whore.'

Inside the cottage all was ruin and destruction. Someone had gone from room to room rending and smashing everything in sight. Furniture, chairs, tables, had been pulped with a sledgehammer. The curtains were torn from the windows and thrown on the floor among little fragments from ornaments and willow pattern plates.

'Was any of this valuable?' Mike asked for the sake of something to say.

'No,' she said. 'I never kept much here in winter, but they were my things – some from childhood.' Clare slumped down on a beanbag that had somehow survived the onslaught.

Mike for once did the right thing. He found a broom, a shovel and a waste bin, and began to clear up the mess. At the end of twenty minutes he had restored some sort of order. Outside Jean-Luc was up a ladder trying to scrape off the graffiti.

'Paint dries too well,' he muttered. 'Two days gone, I think.'

'We'll need some stripper and some wall paint,' said Mike.

'Michael,' Clare was standing behind him again. She was subdued but calm now. 'Take the car and go down to the village. There's a hardware store in the street. Willie and Shona Morrison run it. They're friends of mine. You'll find all you need there.'

'All right,' said Mike doubtfully. 'Will the people be friendly? I mean is it someone from around here who's done this?'

'No way!' she was clearly shocked at the suggestion. 'I know everybody here. No, this was done by outsiders. Tell Willie what's happened, not many strangers come this way and he doesn't miss much.'

Mike drove the car back down the track. He felt a touch nervous. What he had just seen was behind his comprehension. All his inbred English prejudice was beginning to surface. Whatever Clare might say this remote village had suddenly become cold and sinister. What sort of reception could such an obvious Britisher as he expect from these people?

The third house on the right of the village street had a shop window with a fading sign. *Morrison. Agricultural Engineers.* A larger building with a corrugated iron roof rose behind. Mike parked the car and went in. The room was dingy, but there was a pleasing smell of oil, tar, and rubber. It reminded Mike of a ship's chandlers before the days of plastics and synthetics. A marmalade coloured cat sat on a wooden workbench. It stared haughtily at Mike, eyeing this English intruder in a none too friendly way. A large man in jeans and work boots was counting nuts and bolts from a shelf of display boxes.

'Would you be telling me?' he addressed Mike, 'why these have to be changing sizes every dozen years?'

'I've been asking that in my own business,' said Mike with a grin. Nut and bolt sizing was a sore point and it seemed he'd found a kindred spirit in this farmer.

'No need to be looking for an answer,' said the other. 'There'll be someone making a fortune at our expense, of that you may be sure.'

'I don't doubt it,' said Mike.

'Where's the man gone?' said the farmer. 'Willie!' he peered into the gloom at the back of the shop. 'He's going deaf – never mind, he'll be back. From England are you?'

'Yes,' said Mike warily.

'Well you mustn't mind Willie there sleeping. Everything's a hurry in England, but God made a lot of time in Ireland.'

'Do you know Miss O'Dwyer…er, Clare?' Mike asked cautiously.

'Miss Clare? We're all knowing her. Is she back from England?'

'Yes, but only this morning – I drove up with her from Glandore.'

'So you'll be her fella' then? You'll not think me rude when I say we've heard talk of you.'

'You mean from that eejit the other day?' A new voice had entered from the back of the shop. Out of the gloom came a small, middle-aged man with a shock of curly red hair.

'That's the one, Willie. The fat Aussie.'

'Australian?' said Mike quickly.

'That he was. Nothing against him for that. We've any number of Aussies and Yankees coming here – looking for their forbears and rightly so.'

'Not that one,' said Willie.

'Indeed no; threw his weight about and the shite he talked.'

'Did he say his name?'

'Yes, but it escapes me now – it'll come back though. Said he was a famous history writer. Told us we should be at war. Said the Brits were ready to send the 'Tans' back at an insult's notice. Then he said…' the farmer almost doubled up in a rolling guffaw of laughter, 'he said we should be burning Willie here out of town on account of his reelegion. Bluidy eejit, for Jesus sake, this isn't the bluidy North!'

'I guess his name was Sammy Cassidy?' said Mike.

'Yes, now you say it, you're right – that's it, Sammy.' Suddenly the farmer looked thoughtful. 'There's some more you should be knowing. He said we should be driving out Miss Clare. Said her family were traitors from the Free State days. Then he said she'd taken up with an English fella' as if that was a crime.'

'That near caused a fight,' said Willie.

'True,' said the farmer. 'You see Con McArthy was there and his wife's English. She comes from Basingstoke – would you know that place?'

Mike smiled. 'Yes, I know it well.'

'There, who's for saying it's not a small world?'

'I think you'd better know,' said Mike, 'that someone's been to Clare's house and vandalized it. There's paint all over the walls and all her things smashed.'

'You don't say,' the farmer looked startled. 'Have you told the Garda?'

'Not yet, we've only just found it.'

Mike drove back to the cottage with a bottle of paint stripper and a can of masonry paint. Clare sat and listened intently to his report.

'That Sammy. I said we hadn't heard the last of him – I'll have his balls out if ever I catch him.'

'We'd better contact the Garda at once,' said Mike. 'There's an Interpol warrant out on him, remember?'

'We'll phone in the village,' she replied. 'Those bastards have cut the line here and I've left my mobile in the boat.'

'What does Cassidy have against these Morrisons? He said they should be burnt out because of their religious views – or something like that?'

'It's so pathetic,' said Clare. 'Sammy's in his own dream world. The Morrisons are Protestants, that's all. They're Scottish descent, but they've been in these parts as storekeepers for ever. It's not a thing we even think about these days.'

Clare used the telephone in the Morrison's office. She almost shouted in relief when the janitor of her apartment in Cork told her all was well and there had been no break-in. Then she rang the central Garda station and relayed a description of Sammy Cassidy. The duty officer had never heard of him and was inclined to be suspicious. He read Clare a lecture on the perils of wasting police time, and then grudgingly promised to pass on the information. Clare made a face at the telephone, called out her thanks to the Morrisons, and led Mike outside.

'Come on,' she said. 'We'll take Jean-Luc back to the ship and then we're off to find the good Father McGee.'

Jean-Luc was not happy. His instructions, he said, had been to keep Clare under protection at all times. Clare was brusque with him. She was home now among her own people and she could take care of herself. She wanted *Quadra* guarded. She was not going to risk her ship being damaged by Sammy Cassidy and his friends. Jean-Luc should stay with the ship and put to sea at the first sign of trouble. They took the Frenchman, still grumbling, back to Glandore and watched him motor the dinghy out to *Quadra*.

At a nearby village they re-fuelled the Morris from a garage with an antique hand pump. Then they were on the road heading east.

'Where are we going?' asked Mike.

'To Dungarvan, or nearly there – say sixty miles.'

'This St Brigid's, what is it exactly?'

'It's a Catholic retreat house, but mainly it's a retirement home for old priests.'

'What could an old priest know about all this?'

'Plenty, I wouldn't be surprised. Priests hear more of what happens than most – they've a lot of pull in this country.'

'Sounds like you don't approve?'

Clare smiled. 'If so, it's not something I'd discuss with an Englishman.'

The old Morris trundled along empty roads at a steady forty-five. This was Mike's first proper journey through Ireland though he'd been to Cork for the annual regatta.

'Cork's one of the oldest cities in Europe – did you know that?' Clare asked proudly.

'It doesn't look that old.'

'That might be because the British burned it down in 1920.'

'Sorry, I didn't know that.'

'Oh don't be all guilty. I don't think it was ordered. It was the 'Tans' who did it.'

'Who were they?'

'Oh God! They don't teach you anything, do they? Look, the Tans were supposed to be auxiliary police but they were psychopaths who'd been twisted by the big war. They were recruited to commit atrocities.'

'Police, you say – surely not?'

'Not proper police and the regular British troops were mostly honourable. I tell you. There was a village somewhere near here where a British patrol caught two Tans raping a local girl. The soldiers brought the Tans to their own officer – told him what they'd seen. Then the officer pulls out his revolver and shoots both the Tans dead. So they dig a big hole and put them down there and no one, but no one, ever told. But they say anyone from that British patrol who went back to that village for the next fifty years was treated as an honoured guest and no one ever blabbed why.'

Ten miles short of Dungavan they left the main road at an unpronounceable signpost. Twenty minutes later they were at the gates of St Brigid's. They were impressive gates with an imposing white lodge, and in front of them blocking the way were two police cars.

'What on earth?' said Clare.

A portly gard waddled across as Clare wound down her window. 'Sorry, Miss, you can't go in there today.'

'But I want to see my old uncle,' Clare lied plaintively.

'Not today Miss – government orders.'

'What's happened?' Clare was suddenly anxious. 'No one's been harmed have they?'

'No, Miss, this is an anti-terrorist exercise – government orders.'

'A bloody exercise? Look man, I'm not a terrorist – Jesus, do I look like one?' She glared at the man who looked so confused and uncomfortable that Mike felt sorry for him. He seemed a decent, not over bright village 'plod' of a type rare in England.

'Government orders,' the gard repeated the words like a mantra.

'What's that army truck doing?' Clare pointed to an ash spinney fifty yards away. Sure enough there was a drab Land Rover that Mike hadn't noticed. Standing motionless under a tree were two soldiers. They wore combat fatigues and carried automatic weapons. Their camouflage-painted faces were half covered by balaclavas. Mike felt increasingly uneasy. There was a silent menace about these men that he didn't care for.

'Hey there, Rambo, have you a smile for me?' Clare called to them. Mike felt a touch jealous. She had thrown back her golden hair and her smile would have disarmed a thousand soldiers. Not these men. There was no trace of emotion, or any reaction whatever; they could have been cast in stone.

'Come on, Michael. Let's go back and think.' Clare turned the car around and drove slowly back down the road.

'We'll pull over here.' She stopped on a grass verge, climbed out and opened the back door. She rummaged in her overnight bag and retrieved a pair of binoculars.

'Come on,' she called. 'If I remember rightly there's a footpath that takes us in sight of the house.'

Clare led the way at a cracking pace along the side of a hedgerow. A hundred yards and they were walking in the bottom of a high-sided dry ditch. Mike could see nothing beyond the thorn hedge that crested the top. Clare stopped then scrambled up the bank. Finding a flat spot she crouched and levelled the binoculars. Mike sat down beside her.

'Christ,' he muttered, 'that's some house.' They were four hundred yards from a vast Georgian pile of a mansion with a wide gravel sweep in front.

'There's another of those soldiers,' said Mike. 'Over there by the gate.'

Clare swung her binoculars. 'Well spotted – we'd better be careful.' She handed the glasses to Mike.

The soldier was identical to the two they had just seen. He was standing motionless close to a garden wall. If the soldier was guarding something, he certainly didn't mind who saw him. Mike switched the glasses to the front entrance. A large, dark blue Range Rover was parked in front with a uniformed driver waiting beside it. There was a movement in the doorway and a small group of people came out. One wore the habit and cowl of a nun. Mike concentrated on the other two. With a sharp intake of breath he stared intently and then gave the glasses to Clare.

'Jesus,' she whispered.

'It's Delia,' said Mike.

'I know – I've got eyes. Who's that plug ugly fellow with her?'

'His name's Brogan. He's one of your special police from Dublin. I met him that time with Clarence. The time Delia told me to watch you.'

'Let's get out of here,' said Clare. 'Those three soldiers won't be the only ones. There'll be others. Back to the car – I've something to tell you.'

Ten minutes later they were in the car and on the move. Clare drove while Mike watched her. There was an odd introspective look on her face.

'Michael, we've got a pretty fair army in this country. Not in size, but great in quality. We don't fight wars but our boys have been all over the world with the UN.'

'I know that.'

'I'm glad to hear it. Now in the last twenty years there's been the Provisionals and all the other terror groups. Worse than that, these organizations are linked to the bank robbers and the drug mafias. The Army has been sucked into cross border action and that means co-operation with the Brits.'

'And that's something you find hard to swallow?'

'Well done, Michael – you're beginning to learn.'

'Thank you.'

'Now in the last year or so, there's been rumours of a new elite Army unit. It's not large, only a few dozen, but it's said they're programmed to seek out terrorists in their hideaways along the border.'

'In the circumstances, that's not surprising?'

'No, but here's the controversial bit. I heard tell from a journalist friend of mine that these boys were sent to England under maximum secrecy, and they spent time in Hereford.'

'OK, I get the picture; they were training with the SAS.'

'Correct, but with our paranoia about the Brits it's political dynamite. So here's the catch. I think these are the men we've just seen and if our government is prepared to risk showing them in daylight, in County Waterford of all places. Christ, Michael, there's something going on here!'

Mike was shocked; he'd never seen her so worried. Clare stopped the car. The face she turned to him was tear stained and utterly miserable.

'Michael, I've got to learn the truth. It's Grandfather, I know he's at the bottom of all this. It's something he did all those years ago. There'll be no peace for me until I know it all.'

'We've already agreed that...'

'Not any more,' she was crying now. 'Michael, go back to England. We've got ourselves into something very deep here, but it's my business only. It's all Irish – there's no place for you.'

'Have you done?' said Mike, gently but firmly. He sat with his arms around Clare who had buried her wet face in his sweater. She stopped shivering, but the tears still flowed in a slow rhythmic sobbing.

'Now listen,' he said. 'I'm staying with you because I promised I would.' He stifled her protest with a single eye contact. He felt a surge of relief. They were on the same wavelength again. 'Anyway what good would it do me if I went back to England now?' In spite of everything, he laughed. 'I'd be defying Delia when I've been ordered to find Charles. Most likely the next you'd hear of me was that I'd fallen under a passing truck.'

'Michael, don't say that!'

'Why not? I heard Delia and she wasn't making empty threats.' Gently he lifted her tear-stained face between the palms of his hands and kissed her. 'Neither of us is running away. I want the answers as much as you do, and,' he whispered, 'you crazy girl, I love you.'

'Me too,' she murmured and suddenly she smiled. 'If anything happened to you, Michael...' she shivered convulsively and began muttering in a foreign language.

'What on earth?'

'It's part of an old Gaelic song,' she said, 'all about the sea and the waves and lost love.'

'We stay together then?'

'Yes,' she took a deep breath. The tears had melted away and she was smiling. 'Forgive me for what I said.'

Mike kissed her again. 'I feel like a drink and a bite. Let's find a pub.'

'Hey look, there's an omen,' said Clare pointing. 'Flanagan's bar, that'll be the place for us.'

They were standing in the square of a little town not ten minutes from St Brigid's. Mike looked around with delight. In choosing a pub they were spoilt for choice. Every other house seemed to be a bar. He looked at Clare and spread his hands. 'Your call, lead me to Flanagan's.'

The bar was a single darkened room not unlike an English pub. There was a buzz of conversation from half a dozen or so customers, but no piped music, no gaming machines, and no pool table. It seemed that Flanagan's was dedicated to talking. Behind the bar was an elderly man in a striped shirt.

Clare gave him a winning smile. 'Mr Flanagan would it be?'

'That's me.'

'I thought so; would you be the one in the picture with the hurley cup?' Clare pointed to a faded photo of a sports team.

'Indeed it's me, but way back in the days of my youth – that's well spotted by you, Miss.' The man could not contain his pleasure and pride.

'Michael here's from England,' she turned to him. 'Have you ever seen our great game of hurling?'

'I've seen it on the telly. It was mayhem, it's a wonder nobody gets killed.'

'It might look that way, but we Irish are great survivors,' the barman laughed.

Clare ordered two pints of beer; she was listening to a conversation nearby.

'There's gardai all over the place,' said a rough-looking man. 'What could be happening? Have the old fathers got a poteen still?'

'Maybe they're hiding that Lord Lucan?' speculated the barman.

'I tell you they'll not stop me feeding my cattle – gardai – bluidy filth.' The speaker was a teenage boy in a leather jacket and close cropped hair.

'You don't like the law?' asked Clare.

The boy made a mock spitting gesture. 'Who likes those eejits? Always stopping you and asking questions – filth they are.'

Mike eyed the boy with disfavour. He was the familiar, arrogant, disaffected youth. He was surprised to find the type in rural Ireland.

'What's this about feeding cattle, if I might ask?' said Clare.

'There's beef cattle in the park at St Brigid's. The sisters keep a herd there and I feed them twice a day.'

'You don't say. What's your name?'

'Declan.'

'Well now, Declan. I'll pay you well to get us into St Brigid's. Can you find your way past the garda and into the house unseen?'

'Sure, I can do that. Let's see your readies first.'

Clare held out the notes. Declan examined them. 'These are British notes,' he said. 'The Punt's worth half a percent over the Pound.'

'Oh no it isn't you little shite. What d'you know about exchange rates anyway?'

'Not a lot,' the boy grinned happily; he was a likeable little rogue, thought Mike.

Clare dangled the notes in front of Declan. 'Will you do it?'

'Sure I will – it'll be a laugh.'

They could see nothing from their cramped position among the hay bales. The banging, swaying and jolting of the trailer seemed to last an eternity. The wagon in which they were concealed was bouncing down a farm track behind an ancient grey Ferguson tractor driven by Declan with the panache of a rally driver. Briefly the jolting stopped. Mike could hear their guide talking to someone. Now they were moving again. Further painful jolting and then the engine throttled back. They could hear squelching noises and the mooing of cows. There was movement among the bales, then daylight and the grinning face of Declan looking down on them.

'Next time I stop it'll be by the gardens. There's no gardai around this side. Run across the lawn and you're in.'

'Where are those soldiers?' asked Mike.

'Can't see them – maybe they're gone.'

'I wouldn't bet on that.'

'OK, good man Declan. Here's a bonus.' Clare handed him another twenty pounds.

'Thanks, Miss. Remember, next time I stop you both be over the side and legging it.'

They were moving again. They could see now without standing up. Declan had left the tractor to its own devices while he stood on the trailer pitching bales to the cattle. At the last minute he leapt to the ground, raced after the tractor and climbed aboard over the drawbar. Mike smiled; it was a scene to give a safety inspector a seizure.

'Come on,' he called to Clare. 'Go for it!'

He lowered himself to the ground and ran. Twenty feet and they came to a wire stock fence with a wooden railed top. Mike vaulted over, a second before Clare, and wriggled into the shadow of a thick hedge. He could hear the tractor behind them with Declan calling the cows. A couple of feet to their left was a low gap under the hedge. Mike crawled through it with Clare close behind. Thankfully the grass was dry.

'Well, well, what marvellous apparition have we here?' A rich Irish voice boomed down from above them. Startled, Mike looked up into the eyes of an elderly gentleman clad in black and carrying a golf putter.

'Now don't say anything,' said the man. 'You see, clairvoyance is forbidden to one of my cloth but if I were to make an educated guess young lady, I'd say your name is Clare.'

Clare climbed slowly to her feet. The baffled look on her face was so expressive that the old man was laughing. He was dressed in a black suit with a clerical collar and was even more wizened and elderly than Mike had at first supposed.

'Excuse me,' he asked, 'but you wouldn't be Father McGee?'

'No,' the priest laughed again. 'I most certainly am not. Sure I'm no spring chicken but it'll be fifteen years before I catch him up. No, Father Edwin is the grand old man of this house – he's ninety-five.'

'See here, father,' Clare looked at he old man. 'You're right, I'm Clare O'Dwyer but how come you know me?'

'Because my child, we've been expecting you.' He eyed her sharply. 'It seems Father McGee has a secret that he wishes to unburden before he goes. Someone told him to expect you and he's been waiting.'

'What made you so sure it was me?'

'Intuition. Please understand Father Edwin has been fading for some months. I think he's been hanging on in the hopes of you coming. God has a way of ordering these things, and when I saw you I put two and two together and it seems I have a four.'

'Will you take us to him?'

'Yes, but first may I suggest that both of you children tidy yourselves. It wouldn't do for the Reverend Mother to be thinking you'd committed mortal sin in a haystack.'

Mike and Clare stared at each other; both laughed. Their hair and clothes were covered in loose hay. Clare produced a comb and after five minutes they had made themselves reasonably presentable.

'Come now,' said the priest. 'Follow me.'

The room was on the ground floor of the great house. It was comfortable but plainly furnished and in deep shadow, with the heavy curtains still drawn. There were pictures on the walls; religious subjects mostly but among them was a picture of an aircraft. It was an enlarged sepia photograph of an antique biplane. Standing on the ground beside it were two men.

'You looking at the airplane picture?' A voice croaked from the direction of the bed. A shock, because Mike had begun to think that the room was empty. He looked at the bed. Yes, there was the faint outline of a figure propped against the pillows; what had once been a man but shrunken by time.

'She's a DH nine – great ship. We put extra fuel tanks instead of a bomb load. Did the trip in five hours, with enough gas left to have flown to Dublin if we'd wanted.'

'Was that with my grandfather?' Clare asked. 'He once told me that he'd flown to Ireland before Alcock and Brown.'

'Sure,' the man in the bed gave a wheezing laugh. 'That sounds like Jimmy talking.'

Mike and Clare exchanged glances. Both had been surprised, for this voice was no Irishman; it had the cadence of an educated New-England American.

Mike drew up a bedside chair, while Clare sat on the edge of the bed itself. The old man fiddled for a few seconds with a whistling hearing aid before laboriously fitting it in his ear.

'My eyes are good,' he said, 'but I can't hear a darn thing these days.'

'Father,' said Clare, 'do you know who I am?'

'I guess you're little Clare. You've grown some these last years, though I met you only once – I did the honours at your baptismal.'

'I'm afraid I don't remember that,' Clare laughed. 'Father, I've come a long way to talk with you, but it seems you've been expecting me.'

'I've been expecting you these last six months. I've carried some odd secrets in my life then, bless me, if last Christmas I get a letter from Jimmy O'Dwyer's attorney. He says the old rogue's in purgatory, but when his granddaughter visits me I'm to tell her the whole story of our flight to Ireland, and how we took Tom Flanagan's dispatches to Mick Collins.'

'Excuse me for a moment, Father, it's time I introduced Michael. He's my fiancé, you can speak freely in front of him.'

Mike was startled; fiancé was pushing things a bit. Presumably Clare wanted a respectable formula for his presence.

Clare continued. 'Michael's just sailed Grandfather's yacht from England.'

'So, young man, you're a sailor?'

'Yes Sir.'

'And a navigator?'

'I do my best.'

'That's good, because that's how Jimmy and me got together. That airplane – Jimmy flew it and I navigated.'

'You were an air navigator?'

'No my boy, ship's navigator. I was third officer of the *Boston Star,* under Captain O'Leary. I'd just earned my watchkeeping ticket, and O'Leary recommended me to Colonel Flanagan for the flight.' Father McGee emitted another wheezing laugh. 'Cap'n O'Leary was a Canadian and so were most of the *Star's* crew. O'Leary may've been strong for Ireland, but boy he hated Yankees – guess that's why he volunteered me.'

'Whose aircraft was it?' asked Clare.

'Air Corps guy called O'Farrell, got it from some reserve depot. We took it to pieces and trucked it to Brittany. We told the locals we were on a record attempt. We started for Ireland end of April. I can't remember the date – memory's gone...' He lapsed into silence. Clare and Mike waited.

'There was no sun all that day. Hazy cloud all the way to ten thousand feet. Jimmy wouldn't climb high enough to give me a sun sight – said we might ice up the wings. All I could do was work a rough compass heading, allow a bit for wind, and hope we hit land some place. It was kinda' scary. Then Jimmy says, 'Ed, you still set on being a priest?' I says, sure I am. So Jimmy says. 'That's great, you sit back and pray and I'll steer the ship'. That's what we did and we made it straight over the lighthouse by Kinsale – dead on track.' The voice faded, for a minute they wondered if he had fallen asleep.

'Father,' Clare prompted gently, 'what happened next?'

'Jimmy landed in the flattest field he could find. We no sooner cut the engine before we were surrounded by British soldiers.'

'Jes...sorry, I mean what happened?' said Clare.

'Nothing, Jimmy bluffed 'em good. Told 'em we were American airmen on a record attempt,' he paused. 'You know that's true enough. I guess we were the first to make that trip and we've never had the credit.'

'What happened to the plane?' asked Mike.

'Last I heard the fuselage was a goose house.'

'What happened to you and Grandfather?' asked Clare.

'When the Brits had gone we found a farmer. He passed us on to the commander of the Irish forces. They had a "flying column" operating in those parts. I guess they didn't trust us one inch. For a couple of weeks we were moved place to place, never more than one night and mostly in old barns.'

'What about the papers Grandfather carried?'

'Eh...oh you mean Tom Flanagan's dispatches? Yes we were to

take them to Dublin, but we couldn't escape from the men holding us. To be fair they were only farm boys, but Jimmy worried they'd take the papers and lose 'em.'

'Did you get to Dublin?' asked Clare.

'Oh sure we did. One day a guy came to see us. Jimmy showed him the papers and an hour later we were on a train and then straight to see the big fellah himself.'

'Michael Collins?'

'The very one.'

'What happened?'

'We weren't told, but I guess Collins was suspicious. I think he may have thought the British were setting a trap. I guess he checked us first through his spies.'

'They say he knew what the British were going to do before they knew it themselves.'

'That's true, he had listeners everywhere. Did you know he had a man in London, inside Number Ten Downing Street?'

'I've never read that, but I can believe it.'

'It's true, Jimmy devised the code he used.'

'Code?'

'Sure, that's the work they set Jimmy to do. He was our code cracker.'

'Good God.'

'Exactly.'

'Sorry father, I meant no discourtesy – but code breaking? Yes that would suit Grandpapa, everything he did was coded.'

'That's what happened,' McGee continued. 'They sent me to a seminary, but Collins kept Jimmy by him in Dublin.'

'What were these codes?'

'Collins had people inside Dublin Castle. Some of them had access to cipher codes. But there were other signals from London, political stuff, in codes our people couldn't read. They gave 'em to Jimmy and after a few days he'd cracked 'em.'

'Why has my grandfather never been credited with this?'

'I would say very few people knew about it, and as for Jimmy I've my own theory but there's no honour in it.'

'What theory, Father?'

'If you insist. Jimmy O'Dwyer always made great political play in the States. Told anyone Irish how he'd fought in the independence wars here – hinted at great heroics. Never said the main of his fighting was in a Dublin apartment playing with numbers.'

'Sure, it rings true,' said Clare grimly.

'I can tell you about the man in Downing Street. Jimmy met him ten years later. The man had retired from the British Civil Service, but it still wasn't safe for him to talk.'

'Was he English?' Clare sounded doubtful. 'I don't like that. It would make him a traitor however much he disapproved of his government.'

'No, he was Irish, but the British assumed he was one of them. You see he came from an old ascendancy family, he had a title...Sir Something. Jimmy told me it, but I can't remember. It was a two barrel name.'

'Like Lord Fanshawe-Smythe,' Clare giggled.

'Yeah, that style of thing. The name though? It's just there. No it'll come back.'

'How did he come to be working for Collins?'

'It seems the man had no loyalties either way before 1916. Then came the Easter rising followed by the executions – the shootings. That was the blinding light for our friend – like Paul on the Damascus road. Overnight he was faced by a choice and he chose the land of his birth.'

'Good man,' said Clare.

'But he stood a good chance of being hanged if the British caught him. So Collins asked Jimmy to make a code for him – just for this one man. He did it, and boy was it clever. If you'd read it you'd say it was just some paddy writing a letter home. Collins used to send one of his "squad" men over to collect these letters and bring them home for Jimmy.'

The "squad"!' said Clare sharply.

'The same,' said McGee. 'Though the cause was just, I must say as a priest, that I cannot always hold the end to justify the means.'

'Can someone explain,' said Mike. 'I'm lost.'

'The Squad was Collins' entourage in Dublin,' said Clare. 'They were hit-men. They assassinated key people in the British administration – counter intelligence men mostly. Some were killed in front of their own wives and children.'

'That's what happened,' sighed the priest. 'Nothing outside the rules of war and most of the men hated what they did. There again some did not – like Eamon Clarke.'

'Clarke!' Clare stiffened. 'The man who was killed last week?'

'Yes my child. The very same and when I heard the news I thought I might soon be seeing you.'

'Father, you'd better believe it was nothing to do with us. Why should anyone want to kill him so long after the event?'

'They say we Irish have long memories, but so I guess do the Spanish, the Dutch, and the Ukranians.'

'How come?'

'Because Clarke had a taste for evil. What is the word for one who is so corrupted that he enjoys the act of killing and feels no remorse or sense of sin?'

'Nowadays they call them psychopaths.'

'That's right, and Clarke, may God forgive him, was such a one. He became a mercenary soldier in Spain with Franco, and then with the Spanish Legion in Hitler's army. There could be hundreds of children and grandchildren of his victims. Perhaps it was a wonder he lived so long.'

'Father, I think you should know that his name was on Grandfather's list along with yours. The list of people who knew the truth.'

'That's interesting, but how do you perceive truth? What truths are you looking for?'

Clare's face puckered for a moment. This was the core of the riddle.

'Father, we've been told by someone who knows that there were things in those papers you and Granpapa carried from France. Things that could hurt us today even after so long.'

'Ah, those papers. I've often wondered what was in them.'

'You never read them?' Clare's voice was expressive in its disappointment.

'No, I never read them. I can only tell you that some mighty enterprise was planned. We were told our mission could lead to freedom for Ireland.'

'Who told you?'

'Colonel Flanagan. He told me I could strike a blow for Ireland without compromising my cloth and shedding blood.'

'Please Sir,' said Mike. 'Did you know that a copy of those papers still exists? You see, it's missing and that's why we're all in such trouble.'

'No, I know nothing of that. I thought the whole affair was buried long ago.'

'Not so,' said Clare. 'The papers exist. Grandfather told me so before he died. He said they could lead to big trouble and it seems other people think so too.'

'Other people?'

'Yes, the Provos for starters.'

'I see. If that is so you are right to suspect mischief.'

'Father, we think three people, including this man Clarke, have been killed on account of those papers.'

'I don't know,' said the priest wearily. 'I don't know what Eamon Clarke would have known. It was weeks after we reached Dublin before we met him. Jimmy worked with Clarke because he was one of the London couriers.' Father McGee was quieter now and it was clear that his attention was lapsing. Suddenly he closed his eyes.

Clare leant forward. 'He's asleep,' she whispered to Mike. 'Do you think he's told us all?'

'I think so,' Mike whispered back, 'but it wasn't as much as I'd hoped.'

They tiptoed across the room. Just as Mike put out his hand to open the door the frail voice came once more from the bed.

'Say there, the name…the spy in London. He was Fenner, no Venner…'

Mike froze in surprise. 'Not Venner-Harris?'

'Sure, that's it. Sir Christopher Venner-Harris.'

The Reverend Mother was a fat jolly lady. Clare and Mike paid their respects as soon as they had left the sleeping Father McGee. Mike had never been inside a house of any religious order. Apart from a devotional statue, the Reverend Mother's office seemed no different to that of large hotel. There were two telephones, a fax, and a flickering computer screen.

'You're the second pair of visitors for Father Edwin,' the nun said.

'Really?' said Clare. 'He never mentioned them to us.'

'Ah, but those others never got to see him. Father Edwin was resting and to tell the truth I did not care for the look of them.'

'Who were they?'

'There was a woman and a Government man from Dublin. She never said a word, and as for the man – a most rude and uncouth fellow. Do you know he told me that if I didn't let him speak with Father Edwin he'd report me to the Minister of Justice.' The nun's eyes flashed with the memory. She reminded Mike of some crusty old sea captain who'd been insulted on his own quarterdeck.

'Minister of Justice indeed,' the Reverend Mother continued. 'I wouldn't let the Cardinal Archbishop or the Holy Father himself disturb Father Edwin if he was sleeping.'

'What did they say?' Clare asked.

'Oh, the man went away in great dudgeon. Say's he's coming back with a warrant.' She radiated indignation. 'You know there was a time when the politicians deferred to the church – not any more. Do you know? When we opened our extension here the Dail sent that awful man, Shaw-Mulligan.'

Clare made a heroic effort to stifle a giggle. 'Have those Gardai gone?' she asked. 'You know they stopped us coming in here this morning?'

'Yes, my dear. I heard you came in by the back door in a somewhat unusual manner. As for the Garda, they can hardly arrest you for visiting us.'

'I wonder,' said Clare.

It was late afternoon as they walked back up the long avenue of lime trees to the lodge gates of St Brigid's. Mike cast a wary eye around. The police had gone and there was no sign of the military special forces.

'How did that nun frighten all these people away?' Mike asked.

Clare laughed. 'That's the power of the church. I warned you, they're still a dangerous force to cross in this country.'

'But Brogan'll be back with his warrant.'

'I guess so, but we were there first, and I can't see that old fellow giving much away if Delia switches on the intimidation.'

They walked on in silence their feet slapping on the rough tarmac drive. 'Clare,' he said, 'I gather you don't like the church?'

'I told you that's something I don't discuss with the English,' she replied sharply.

'You're not discussing it with the English, you're talking to me, Michael. It's exactly the sort of thing we need to clear the air on.'

'Hardly as strong as that.' She stayed silent for a full minute. 'Michael, it's difficult for me. You see rubbishing the Catholic Church... it's almost like I'm spitting on my culture. Like I'm laughing at all the poor souls who died for our independence.'

'Not if you don't believe in it?'

'Yes, that's just it.' She stopped dead still, catching Mike by surprise. He turned as she kicked a stone off the road and onto the neatly mown grass.

'That word believe,' she muttered. 'I'll tell you a true story. I've got a cousin, Aidan. He lived near us when I was a kid. I was a little sweet on him if you must know.'

'How old were you?'

'Both fourteen – but this is it. I was at convent school, but Aidan went to secondary school run by the Christian Brothers. They're a Catholic teaching order.'

'Monks?'

'No, they're lay people, but they're not allowed to marry. They work off their libido playing hurling and rugby, and beating shite out of their charges.'

'We had that at Westborough.'

'That's your English masochism. Look, Aidan was a clever kid, still is. He had a real crisis of conscience. So he went to the brothers and told them he didn't believe in God anymore. He was genuine about it. He wanted help, reassurance – and what did he get?' Clare's voice was hard.

'Tell me.'

'They said, he'd better recover his belief in Almighty God by five o'clock or get a taste of the strap.'

'I guess that incentive didn't work?'

'It just made two disbelievers instead.'

'You being the other.'

'That's right. Of course the nuns thought I was next thing to Satan's daughter anyway.'

'Eh?'

'Because of Granpapa fighting for the Republic in Spain. Did you ever go to Spain in Franco's time?'

'No.'

'I did as a kid. Church and State, and both ruling by fear – you could smell it.'

They had left the car in the same barnyard where Declan kept his tractor. By the time they reached it the sun was well down in the western sky. Mike looked at his watch. He was surprised. A lot had happened this day but it was still only half past three.

'God, I'm hungry,' he held a hand to his face and yawned. 'We never did get to eat at Flanagan's pub.'

'Never mind, it was worth the wait. We've learned things.'

'Not as much as I'd hoped for.' Frankly, Mike was a little disappointed. He had really hoped the old priest might have known more. He told Clare so.

'No we've got to be patient,' she said. 'We've still to contact this Colonel Newhoffer. I've high hopes that he holds the key.'

'That's if he even agrees to see us.'

'He will,' she said, 'when he knows it's me.'

'We know some more about Clarke,' said Mike. 'It explains why Delia's gunning for Charles. That's what she meant when she said he had an uncle and he wasn't to mention him.'

'Charles and his Irish granny,' she laughed. 'Trouble is, Charles being missing. Delia wants you to find him and so do I now.' Clare stopped suddenly and put a finger to her lips. Mike also heard the approaching footsteps. It was only Declan. The young man came jauntily round the corner, a cigarette dangling from his lips.

He grinned in recognition. 'Hello there, did you find what you was after?'

'Yes we did,' Clare smiled back. 'We made no trouble for you, I'm hoping?'

'Jesus no, I do what I like – Gardai sod'em.'

'Thanks again, we'll be off,' said Clare.

Declan was about to move towards his tractor when he seemed to remember something. 'Say Miss, there was a fella' looking at your car an hour back.'

'Who was he?' Mike was suspicious. Adrift in this strange country he was on the way to being paranoid.

'Couldn't say, never seen him before. Could've been an army man.'

'Whose Army?'

'Whose d'you think,' Declan laughed. 'He didn't carry a Swiss Army knife so I guess he was one of ours.'

'What about the IRA?' Mike was really worried now. Both Declan and Clare laughed.

'No way,' said Declan. 'This guy looked a real soldier.'

'But he wasn't in uniform?' Mike persisted.

'No, just jeans and that, but you can tell'em.' Declan waved and walked away whistling.

'I'm going to look underneath,' said Mike.

'Jesus, whatever for?'

'Might be a bomb.'

Clare groaned. 'Will you never learn? This is Wexford, not bloody Belfast. We don't do that sort of thing here.'

Mike ignored her. He lay down on the ground and slowly wriggled under the car. The chassis could do with a pressure wash but there was nothing remotely resembling a bomb.

'Can we be going now?' Clare gazed down at him with a look of affectionate mockery. Mike knew he looked ridiculous but he didn't care. He felt a happy glow. Hers had been the sort of banter that marked a happily bonded couple. 'Come on,' she said, 'you can drive us back to *Quadra*.'

Just after seven o'clock they reached Glandore. Mike parked the car outside the Inn and they collected their few belongings. Clare had hired the car for a full week, so it would be available tomorrow.

'I'll give Jean-Luc a wave,' said Clare.

She walked to the water's edge and stopped abruptly. Her mouth dropped open, her words unsaid. The anchorage was empty: *Quadra* had gone.

Jean-Luc had been forced to accept the fait-accompli that Clare had wished on him though he was still troubled. He was not happy with the way this mission was shaping. Worst of all his loyalties were divided. His priority must be the assignment ordered from his unit and for that reason he was not sorry the others were out of his way. But he was also pledged to Chef Peyron to keep an eye on these children; and children they were. Neither seemed to have the least idea of the dangers with which they walked. That little girl Clare was far too cocksure if she thought she was safe merely because she was home in Irelande. That young man Michael had no imagination. He was a superb seaman, Jean-Luc was impressed, and Michael had told him he was a rugby player.

Le Rugby was an English invention and the style they played was symbolic of their race. Brave and tenacious to the last they played to a rigid fixed plan. Sometimes this succeeded, but more often ground itself into defeat when a little imagination would change everything. A Frenchman facing a tight defence would seek to run round it. Faced with an extended line he would look for the gaps, confident that his teammates would also think with their feet. Why could the English never grasp these simple principles? This was not idle dreaming on his part. If the girl Clare was impulsive all Irish, Michael was stereotype English.

Jean-Luc surveyed *Quadra's* deck. Such tide as there was in these parts was ebbing. He watched the little bubbles sliding past the yacht and down the harbour to the Atlantic just a few kilometres away. He went below, opened his sailing bag and took out a small mock leather case. To the casual eye the contents would have passed for a mobile phone. Two years had gone by since the *Ariane* rocket had launched a communication satellite with a secret radio link. Added to the system was a scrambler claimed by its inventor to be safe from any decoder outside France. Jean-Luc switched on the set and activated the security button. The radio would self-destruct in ten minutes unless he pressed the button again. Paris answered within seconds. Jean-Luc had called his control three times this week. Each time control had no instructions for him; only that Chef Henri was in Spain following a strong lead.

This time was different. Control reported that both the Spanish and French warships were on station. A French frigate was in place one hundred kilometres West of Ile d'Ouessant. Why did the English always mispronounce this as Ushant? Control reported that the Irish navy was in port and the British were inactive, apart from one fishery protection vessel.

Control's voice was clear. 'The woman, Lazarraga, has arrived through Cork airport this morning. *Lamartine* is following her. We think she is making for destination *Quatre.*'

'Understood, confirm *Quatre.*'

'This is your briefing, as of 0800 hours, Le Chef de Bureau instructs that a most grave situation has arisen. When the ship enters your area, we will not – repeat will not – be arresting her. She must be allowed to proceed. Chef confirms she is unladen. We suspect the terrorists are planning the *Second Option.* We believe their destination will be within fifty kilometres of *Quatre.* It is vital that all our resources be used to locate this destination. If you can assist you are released from your current mission.'

Jean-Luc confirmed that he understood. Paris closed the transmission, and he switched the set to safe mode. He was in a real quandary now. Clare had told him that she and Michael might not return for a few days. His mission from Colonel Peyron was to take care of these young people, while at the same time learning all he could about the Flanagan papers. Nobody seemed to know what these documents contained except that there was matter there to embarrass both the United States and Britain. Such information would be most useful to France in her endless struggle against Anglo-Saxon hegemony.

His duty now must be with his mission from the Bureau. The two matters were linked of course and might now be about to converge. *Lamartine* was one of the best shadows in the business; he needed no back up from Jean-Luc. *Quatre* was a private house only a short distance from where this boat was anchored now.

Jean-Luc examined the chart. *Quatre* was near Glengarrif and close to the oil terminal at Whiddy Island – less than a day's sailing. The landing would not be there. It was too public and there was no access to the sea. There would be somewhere else, not too far away, and ready made for a clandestine operation. He made his decision. His mission from the Bureau must succeed. If the terrorists were going for *Option Two* there was no telling what mayhem, what killing of innocent life might occur if they succeeded. Jean-Luc went on deck and began to shorten up the anchor chain. Ten minutes later *Quadra* was underway and heading out to sea.

CHAPTER 29

'I've seen the Harbour Master,' Clare gasped. She had run the last hundred yards and was breathless. 'He says *Quadra* left about four o'clock. We've just missed her.'

'Do they know why he left?' Mike managed the words but he felt almost numb with shock.

'I asked him if Cassidy had been around, but nobody's seen anyone like him. There's been a man asking questions though.'

'About us or the ship?'

'Both. He showed the Harbour Master an official ID – Special Branch.'

'How did they track us so quickly?'

'I reckon I know the answer to that,' Clare's voice had an ugly rasp to it. 'Who knew we were bound for Ireland? Who knows that I live in these parts?'

'Lots of people, I imagine.'

'Oh sure, but who knew I'd be here, or could give them a good guess? I'll tell you, it's that little schmuck Noel.'

Mike hesitated before replying. Clare was clearly furious and momentarily incapable of rational analysis. 'It's true,' he said. 'I'm fairly sure it was *Shy Colleen* who passed us in the night. She'd have been in Cobh hours before us.'

Clare wasn't listening. 'He knows something; d'you remember how he asked if the name O'Farrell meant anything?'

'The old priest mentioned an O'Farrell just now. It's one of the names on the list, and your stepfather was in Falmouth which was the town in the book. Maybe we should have stopped longer and gone looking?'

'No, there's an easier way than that. I'll find Noel and beat the truth out of him. Come on,' she said. 'Back in the car. We'll talk to the man himself. It's only a half hour drive.'

Clare took the wheel and drove back over the same route they had just travelled. Mike was worried and depressed. He felt the loss of his ship. He was after all the skipper, the legal master. He wasn't blaming Jean-Luc. They had given him full scope to leave Glandore, to protect the ship. Jean-Luc was a fine seaman. *Quadra* was as safe in his hands as Mike's; safer probably. He was worried about Clare.

For the first time she seemed to have lost all sense of proportion. She was driving them towards some sort of confrontation with her step-father. Mike had severe misgivings. Noel was a government minister, a force in this country and not someone to cross with impunity.

'Where are we going?' he asked.

'Twenty miles or so. It's a country house.' She lapsed into a moody silence and Mike left her there.

They were turning into some narrow lanes. They reminded Mike of the Dorset countryside where Delia lived. They had reached a dead end. Before them was an archway with closed wrought iron gates.

'Why's he shut the place?' Clare muttered. 'Could you jump out and open them?'

Mike walked to the gates. They were fastened together with a padlock and a heavy chain. He looked through the ironwork; beyond was a stretch of parkland, but not a sign of life, human or animal. He walked back and reported to Clare.

'I'll not let that stop us,' she said.

Clare parked the car off the road under an oak tree. 'Come on.' She turned and began to climb over the surrounding pole and rail fence. Mike followed her; there was nothing else he could do. He didn't bother to ask what was happening because he knew her well enough by now to be certain of a dusty answer. Clare walked straight up the tarmac road. It ran through grassland that had recently been mown. Mike could see a sizeable house ahead of them through a thicket of young ash trees. At this point Clare cut across the grass. It seemed she had every intention of marching over to the front door when she stopped and drew back pulling Mike with her. The house in front of them was not a mansion, but it was a substantial Georgian style building, standing full-square amidst gardens and stables. Mike took this in with a glance, but he had also seen what Clare had seen. Parked in front of the house was a blue Range Rover. Its uniformed chauffeur was looking into the depths of a little ornamental pool; probably watching the goldfish.

'It's the same car Delia was in at St Brigid's,' she whispered.

'Looks like it,' he agreed.

'Come on – round the back.' She set off at a half run into the spinney. The trees formed a continuous belt passing within forty feet of a walled garden. Clare ran across to a gap in the wall that had once held a door. The enclosed garden contained only a hard tennis court and a few shrubs.

Clare gripped his arm. 'Press against the wall and they can't see us,' she hissed.

They reached the back of the house in seconds. Mike risked a peep through a window; it was the kitchen. He caught the delicious aroma wafting through an extractor fan and was reminded once more that he had eaten nothing since breakfast. Clare tugged at his elbow and he followed as she scuttled round a corner of the building. Here he saw more lawns and a breathtaking view across the countryside to a line of low hills a mile away. There were lights on in the house. Mike could see people sitting at a table in a conservatory. He instinctively ducked behind a bushy shrub. He knew all three of them. Noel Shaw-Mulligan, Inspector Brogan, and Delia Lazarraga.

'Deceitful bastard!' Clare muttered. 'Come on, out of here. Through the stables.' She seemed to know the ground and Mike followed again without question. Clare darted down a narrow passage that led to a yard with horseboxes and a fodder store. There was a pleasant smell of newly broken hay bales.

Suddenly Mike felt another presence. There were footsteps behind him. A dark figure emerged from the gloom in front. Something was gripping him across the mouth and around the neck. Choking, he couldn't breath. He cried out, but no sound came. He could see nothing but a blur of shadows and a glimpse of sky. He was being lifted bodily and carried as helpless as a baby. He didn't know how long the sensation lasted but it could only have been seconds before he was thrown on a hard metal floor. Half winded he could just take in the clatter of closing doors and an engine starting. Then whatever vehicle he was in was away, drumming steadily along a smooth road.

Slowly Mike opened his eyes. As he moved his head he could make out a pair of combat boots. A voice spoke three sharp words in Gaelic. A second voice made a monosyllabic reply. Mike felt his stomach contract as he vomited, and for a few seconds he passed out.

CHAPTER 30

Colonel Carl Newhoffer had been recalled to his country's service and he was not happy. But the summons had come from the President himself and could not reasonably be declined. That morning, while Clare and Mike had been driving from Glandore, Newhoffer was disembarking at Dublin Airport. He walked gloomily through the reception area. The man waiting for him stood out like a sore toe. He hardly needed the name card he was carrying. Typical CIA goon, thought Newhoffer; the guy was even wearing dark glasses.

'Colonel Newhoffer, sir? I'm agent Van Outen. If you'll come with me I have a car.'

Newhoffer had followed the CIA man, and his two equally conspicuous sidekicks, to the black BMW in the car park. It was an embassy car complete with CD plates. 'Do I get a chance to freshen up?' he asked.

'Sir, a meeting has been set up for twenty minutes from now,' Van Outen replied dourly. 'You're expected.'

'OK, it's your ball game,' Newhoffer sighed in resignation. He was not amused by all this melodrama. He had been in some real negotiations in his time in places that smelt danger. He remembered the first mission in the nineteen seventies. He had travelled in secret to Hanoi under safe conduct. He and his chief had started the first tentative peace negotiations. 'Talks about talks', they called it. He'd gotten himself something of a reputation for clandestine meetings. Always hole-in-corner trysts with the demons of the Pentagon and the political right wing. There had been a forest clearing in El Salvador, a village in Angola, a hillside cave in Afghanistan and several others. It hadn't always worked and it had been scary. It was easy to be brave in battle, in a soldier's war. It was another matter to be an American surrounded by trigger-happy guerrillas and Islamic fundamentalists.

Twelve years ago he had left the army and devoted his life to golf. He had a sizeable family fortune and he used it well. He had invested in seventeen golf courses in Europe, America and the Far East. Three of these he had designed himself. His favourite course in all the world was right here in Ireland on the shores of Bantry Bay. It was one of his most ambitious ventures with its golfing hotel and associated conference centre. It was this conference house, quiet and secluded, that he had in mind for tomorrow's meeting.

They made it to the United States Embassy with five minutes to spare. Van Outen hustled Newhoffer through the building to a small room set out as for a board meeting. There were two persons already there. One was a small man with a ferret face and a Nixon nine o'clock shadow. Van Outen introduced this character as Dowling: plain and simple, no birth name, no rank. Newhoffer assumed him to be a big wheel in Irish national intelligence. The second to be introduced was a tall gangling individual dressed in a tweed jacket with an English club tie. 'Pennington, Foreign Office.' The man had a refined accent and a limp wrist. Newhoffer shook hands with a sense of doom. The British had any number of talented young graduates in their civil service. Why did they insist on sending exactly the kind of 'Poo Bah' most calculated to offend the Irish?

'You MI6?' Newhoffer asked.

'That's not an appropriate question. I'm not allowed to say.' Pennington had the goodness to look embarrassed.

'Yeah, he's Six,' Van Outen confirmed.

They all sat down around the table with Dowling in the chair. 'What I would like to know,' he said, 'is why are you sending Miss Lazarraga? We have her listed as MI5 counter-intelligence. Surely, Mr Pennington, it would be your show, MI6, would it not?'

'Normally yes, but Miss Lazarraga is the only person on our side with whom the Provisionals will treat.' Pennington sounded unhappy and it showed.

'Why's she called Delia? It don't suit her,' asked Van Outen.

Newhoffer knew the answer. 'Her mother's from the Spanish Basque country. Her real birth name's Cechu, that's Euskera – the local lingo.'

'We all know who her father is, or was,' said Dowling.

'I don't,' Pennington looked puzzled.

'Say, you haven't been so well briefed.' Newhoffer was surprised. 'He was O'Dwyer – James O'Dwyer.'

'The Flanagan man – good God!' Pennington's eyebrows had risen almost to his thinning hairline.

'Are we any nearer to recovering those documents?' Newhoffer asked.

'Not a trace of 'em,' said Van Outen. 'I ain't sure the O'Dwyer babe's got 'em. She seemed genuine to me and that Limey she's shacked up with is as dumb as they get.'

'I knew Jim O'Dwyer,' Newhoffer intervened. 'Nothing he ever did was straightforward. The Flanagan papers exist somewhere. I think he meant this to be a puzzle.'

'It's one we could do without,' said Dowling. 'Are you aware of the contents of those documents?'

'I haven't seen the originals. State Department wouldn't let me have so much as a glance.' Newhoffer was still annoyed about this. How could he act as a presidential envoy if they didn't trust him with all the facts. 'I know the gist of the plot though.'

'I've seen the original,' said Dowling, 'they're dynamite.' He grimaced.

'Who has an interest in exposing them?' Newhoffer asked.

'Anyone who wants to keep the conflict boiling on this island.' Dowling suddenly became animated; for the first time the man seemed almost human. 'Look we're doing well in this country. We're riding an economic miracle. For the first time we've a higher standard of living than the British. We feel good about ourselves. It we're to hang on to this we've got to keep the North isolated at least.'

'Whatever happened to, "one land, Catholic, Gaelic and poor"?' muttered Pennington.

'Unlike the British, we move with the times,' said Dowling. 'Your motto seems to be, "isolationist, xenophobic and poor".'

'Not all of us,' Pennington replied.

'Mr Van Outen,' said Newhoffer, 'do I take it you've interviewed Clare O'Dwyer?'

'Sure, in Paris. Both her and the Limey.'

'This Walters?'

'Sure, we were interrogating 'em and then the goddam French crashed in and that was that.'

'We can't have the French getting wind of Flanagan. D'you think they've found anything?'

'We don't think so. Soixante Neuf seem to have lost interest. They're involved with something in Spain at the moment, but we're concerned. It seems O'Dwyer was a friend of Roger Peyron. One of his men is on that yacht with 'em.'

'Mr Dowling, Miss O'Dwyer and her yacht are in your jurisdiction. What are you doing?'

'We traced them to Glandore last night. They're under observation. If necessary we'll pull them in for questioning. They can't do a thing anyway. Because of your mission, Colonel, we've soaked the whole area with extra Gardai, and we've an Army special-forces unit covering the ground as well. We may even have some news about those papers, but I'm not promising.'

'You're not saying you've found 'em?' Newhoffer was sceptical.

'No, but we've traced a survivor of the Flanagan conspiracy, still alive in Wexford. We're concentrating security in that area until he's been interviewed.'

'He must be a good age if he was an eye witness?'

'He's ninety seven.' Dowling looked smug and Newhoffer didn't press for more. The man wanted the glory for himself, and who could blame him.

It was time to move on to the important business. Newhoffer looked around the table. 'Are the Provisionals on for the meeting tonight?'

'According to the Lazarraga, yes.'

'Good, now I've given orders for all my staff at the O'Driscoll Centre to go on three days leave. Move your people in soonest.' Newhoffer was satisfied; at least this wasn't El Salvador, and it was nice to find everybody so co-operative. It was all too easy to be true. His nose told him he was missing something. Listen between the lines, say nothing, trust no one. That was his code, and he was staying with it. Suddenly it felt good to be in the field again.

The coast by Mizzen Head was a dark line to the north west. Jean-Luc could see it clearly despite the glare from the setting sun. The bleeper on his radio was calling again.

'*Quadra,* numero sept,' he acknowledged.

'Number Seven, we have the target very near you and just entering Irish waters. Can you give us your position on GPS?'

Jean-Luc obliged.

'Merci, your target is a stern trawler, fifty metres in length, name *Juanita.* She has a dark hull, white superstructure, Spanish colours. Your instructions; find and follow with caution.'

Jean-Luc repeated the instructions. Control had given him the approximate position of the target and he quickly laid a new course. It was pure chance that he was here. If this trawler was the key ship they were looking for he couldn't be better placed. The information he had been given suggested the quarry was making for Glengarrif. The wind was inadequate so he started the diesel. The weather forecast was evil. An Atlantic depression was speeding in from the west. Already the sky was hazy with high cirrus clouds. Within twelve hours there would be a gale.

He sighted the target exactly where he had hoped. She was the only vessel in sight as she came up from the south, buffeting and rolling, in the already rising swell. Both craft were of comparable speed under power. Satisfied, Jean-Luc tucked *Quadra* into a parallel course a kilometre to the east.

The trawler forged on. If she saw the nearby yacht her crew would hardly associate her with threat. Shortly afterwards she switched on her navigation lights and Jean-Luc responded with his. As he expected, the trawler gave Mizzen Head a wide berth before altering course northward towards Bantry Bay. Jean-Luc was in strange waters now though he had done his best to read the English language pilot book and British Admiralty charts. Those Spaniards certainly had no catch to land. The ship steamed on past the fish dock at Castlehaven. Jean-Luc followed her stern light past Bear Island and on up the fjord. Careful to avoid suspicion, he throttled back and let his chase pull ahead. Both ships held their course for the next half hour before Jean-Luc was nearly taken by surprise. The trawler turned ninety degrees to port. He saw her white masthead light and her red port hand light moving fast towards the north shore. Then abruptly they vanished. He had the presence to take a quick bearing with the hand compass.

Very carefully he steered *Quadra* inshore, his eyes darting between the sea ahead and the depth sounder. He knew from the chart that the shoreline was rocky but steep and that there was deep water within a few metres of land. In this darkness the rocks seemed close enough to touch. Carefully he selected a sheltered spot and released the anchor in fifteen metres. For ten minutes he sat still watching the anchor and his transit marks on shore. Satisfied the anchor was holding he went below and put on the kettle.

When he returned on deck Jean-Luc was dressed in dark clothing, with black woollen gloves and a balaclava. His face was blackened and in a small waterproof bag he carried his night-scope. With this equipment one could achieve the miracle of night into day. He inflated the dinghy and dropped it into the water. Climbing into it he shipped the outboard motor and pushed off into the night. The moonlight shone on the water leaving *Quadra* a black silhouette relieved only by her white anchor light. He steadied the boat and took his bearings. According to the chart the array of lights on the far shore came from a golf hotel complex. He started the outboard and ran along the position line from where he had caught his last glimpse of the trawler. He wondered if he was wise to give his position away with the sound of the motor. On the contrary, by proceeding openly he should defuse suspicion. If the trawler men saw him they would assume him to be a local fisherman returning home. He steered the inflatable with one hand and with the other he steadied the compass. There was a nasty lop in the sea even this far up the bay, proof of a storm brewing way out in the Atlantic. It was nothing to disturb the dinghy but it made it harder to hold the course on the correct bearing. As he drew closer to the steep shoreline he could see and almost hear the slap of the waves on the rocks. He cut the motor and let the dinghy drift. He was convinced he was in the right place, but of creek or inlet he could see nothing. The coastline seemed to stretch unbroken for miles. It was time to try the scope.

The first thing he picked up in the eerie light was a thick belt of trees. He smiled in triumph: this was the place. The trees covered a promontory, beyond which he could see the continuing shoreline, but much further away. Between the two points there was clear water, an inlet. He restarted the motor and ran onto a steep, rock-strewn beach. He pulled the inflatable as high as he could and tied the rope painter to a bush.

For several moments Jean-Luc stood, unmoving, listening. Satisfied he slung the night scope over his shoulder and melted into the shadows. In front was a steep, tree-covered bank, mostly fir and birch. The ground was soft and there was enough moonlight to see where he was going without breaking twigs or moving stones. Jean-Luc had years of practice and he could move as silently as a man of his size could hope to. The instant he reached the crest he saw the trawler. He stopped and focused the night-scope. She was lying to a mooring buoy in a snug cove secure both from weather and casual watchers. In the shadow of the trees he again used the scope. The ship lay without lights or sign of life. There must be someone around, for a boat was secured alongside. It was a dory; a functional work boat, popular with harbour-masters and yacht yards. He trained the scope on the shoreline. He was not surprised to see a substantial stone jetty, a feature common in Cornwall or Brittany, and sometimes here in Ireland. From the trawler came a bright shaft of light. Jean-Luc shut his eyes. Despite the scope he needed to protect his night vision. He counted to five and risked a quick look. It was dark once more so he guessed the light came from an opening door. Two black figures were climbing into the dory. A mutter of conversation floated across the water, though in what language he could not tell. The engine started and the boat sped away across the gap to the jetty.

Jean-Luc's senses were tuned to full pitch. Somewhere behind him a car was on the move. Instantly he was prone on the ground his ear pressed to the loose earth. A powerful diesel was on the move, climbing the hill from inland. He rolled into a hollow behind a pine tree. Headlights were passing through the trees in front of him; bright beams that forced him to close his eyes again. Then he heard the scraping and sliding as the wheels of the heavy vehicle descended the slope to the shoreline. He heard it slow and stop, the engine still beating as it ticked over. Using the scope he had a quick peep at the jetty. The vehicle was a four-wheel-drive truck. The two men from the trawler climbed into the rear and the vehicle drove off up the hill the way it had come. Jean-Luc lay prone again until it had passed and then he ran to the edge of the wood. The taillights were moving away from him down the reverse slope of the ridge. Using the scope he could just see a cluster of buildings about a kilometre away. He drew a deep breath of satisfaction as the truck stopped alongside them. The engine died and the lights were switched off.

It took half an hour to reach the place. It was a small livestock farm with tiny stonewalled fields that made Jean-Luc nostalgic for Provence. He made steady progress moving over the ground from cover to cover confident he was unseen. Then crawling under a wooden gate, half-rising to his knees a jolting electric shock sent him reeling. Heart racing he lay flat on the ground waiting to see if he had triggered an alarm. No, it was only a cattle fence. As he crawled under it a dozen or so milking cows blew their sweet grassy breath at him.

The night-scope showed a cluster of buildings around a modern stone bungalow. There was a gap in a field wall that gave him a good all round view. Jean-Luc settled down to wait. Three-quarters of an hour and he was rewarded. He heard a heavy vehicle in the distance the other side of the farm grinding up the approach road. Then the loom of headlights until finally a large lorry turned into the gate of the farmyard. Eyes glued to the scope he identified a cattle truck. It drove straight into an empty bay of the Dutch barn. That building was two thirds full of bales. Jean-Luc could see the rear of the lorry, but the rest was concealed.

A door in the farmhouse opened. He heard voices, greetings and a burst of laughter. He could see figures, six of them around the back of the lorry. Then, with a rattle, the long tailboard was pulled down and the men walked inside. Men? He had assumed they were all men but the light inside the lorry definitely revealed five men and one woman. They formed such a crowd that he could get no view of the truck's cargo. He could guess of course, but he needed proof. The light went out and even with the scope he could see little more than shadowy movements. The next thing he heard was the tailboard being raised and locked. Conversation floated across but it was muted; he could comprehend neither the words nor language spoken. The house door opened and the party went inside. Only five people he counted, where was the sixth? He slowly panned the scope. There, the man was sitting on a bale and incredibley lighting a cigarette. What a cretin. Jean-Luc saw the flare of the match as the man bent forward. He also saw the AK47 wedged between his knees. A sentry was only to be expected and it would seem to confirm the truck's cargo. Speculation was no good; he needed a look inside, but how? Even this idiot guard could hardly avoid seeing him. He could take out the man with ease, but that would only tell these people that their cover was blown. Jean-Luc made his decision. He decided to work his way round to the other end of the barn. He would climb on top of the bales and hide. After that he would wait and see.

He began to make his way back on the same line he'd travelled. That was his first and only mistake of the night. He never saw the shape behind the wall. Never saw the man who leapt and pulled him to the ground. Jean-Luc the rugby player reacted instinctively. He scrambled to his feet. Too late; striking out he connected with something solid that gave a grunt. Then Jean-Luc the athlete, for all his experience and training found himself hurled down again and pinned to the ground. Then utter humiliation, as a well-placed kick rolled him over. He was on his back. Someone kicked his legs apart. Then out of the night sky the hard barrel of a gun was rammed into his mouth.

'Mother of God,' whispered a voice. 'It's that Frenchie.'

'You can sit up now – we haven't hurt you.' The voice came from the air above. It was a voice gruff with authority but with a touch of humour.

Mike's head was beginning to clear. He looked along the floor. With relief he saw Clare lying there. Whatever the shock of this capture they had not been separated. He struggled into a sitting position. He still felt sick and his eyes had trouble focusing. They were in the back of an enclosed truck with a bare metal floor and full length side benches. There were four men seated on these benches. They were soldiers: the same sort of men as at St Brigid's.

'What's all this about?' Mike did his best to sound controlled but his breathing hurt and he could feel his heart racing.

'You and the young lady were in a restricted zone. We're taking you to our barracks – there's someone wants to meet you.' It was the same man speaking, presumably the officer.

'Who wants to see us?'

'No more talking.'

Mike glanced at Clare. To his relief she was conscious but she looked pale in the dim light.

'You'd best be sitting on the proper seats now.' The officer's tone was commanding but not unkind.

They drove for an hour. They could see nothing and their guards remained surly and uncommunicative. Then the truck stopped. The officer motioned them to the rear doors. The moment they stepped to earth the vehicle drove off. For a moment they stood bewildered, staring around. They were inside a wired perimeter near a group of wooden huts. The scene was lit with the glare of orange floodlights. It was depressingly like a movie prisoner of war camp.

'Where in hell are we?' said Mike.

'Army camp somewhere,' Clare had recovered her poise and was clearly fuming. 'Bloody cheek, they've no right doing this. I tell you I'll raise some hell in high places and the press when we get out of here.'

'Let's get out first,' Mike muttered. It was all very well for Clare, but it seemed he was in deep trouble in a foreign country where he didn't know the rules.

'And a very good evening to you,' said a voice. A man came out of the shadows of a nearby hut. 'Would you oblige me by coming in here?'

They followed the man into what appeared to be a guardroom. A uniformed NCO saluted and took a position by the door. Mike looked at the man who had spoken. He was an army officer, a captain by his insignia. He was a smart, almost dandified figure, in an immaculate uniform with a Sam Browne belt and polished riding boots. He was the complete antithesis of his special-forces comrades. There was something teasingly familiar about him; then Mike recalled the elegant Irish Army officers he'd seen riding in equestrian competitions.

The officer removed his cap and smiled politely. 'Cap'n Murphy at your service.'

'I'm not sure I ever asked for your services, captain,' Clare rasped. 'Me and my friend have just been kidnapped by a bunch of gorillas and unloaded we know not where.'

'For that, madam, my apologies, but it seems you were in a restricted area during an alert for terrorists.'

'Terrorists,' Clare was scornful. 'I'm not a terrorist. I was visiting my stepfather.'

'You were apprehended while behaving in a furtive and suspicious manner on the property of a government minister.'

'I told you he's my stepfather. I was paying him a visit.'

'Then why creep around his house?'

'Because when I get there, I find him tucked up all cozy with a British spy.'

'Maybe,' the captain's manner was unchanged. 'You will sit down please.'

They obeyed with bad grace. There was a trestle table covered with a grey blanket. Clare and Mike sat one side, while the captain fiddled with a cassette recorder.

'Interview one,' he said. 'The time is seventeen forty-five on...'

'What are we charged with?' Clare snapped. 'Why are we being held by the military in defiance of the constitution?'

'Nobody's said a thing about charges,' the captain replied evenly. 'And correction, madam. We're entitled to detain and question terrorist suspects under a special warrant from the Minister of Justice.' He held up a sheet of official looking paper. 'This is an order to detain Clare O'Dwyer and Michael Walters for questioning on matters that concern the security of the state. There you are, signed by the junior minister, Noel Shaw-Mulligan.'

Clare was suddenly incandescent, almost gibbering with fury. 'That two-faced double dealing little bastard. Didn't I tell you he'd stick the knife in the moment our backs are turned?'

'That's a little unkind. Mr Shaw-Mulligan is only doing what he's paid for.' Murphy seemed faintly amused.

'He's my stepfather – he's family.'

'You have my sympathy, but in this case I think it's a matter of form. We have a right to interrogate in the case of suspected terrorism.'

'We're not terrorists,' Clare scowled.

'We'll see. As I understand it you are Clare O'Dwyer and this gentleman is Michael Ormiston Walters.'

'Ormiston,' Clare giggled. 'You never told me that.'

'I never tell anybody,' Mike flushed angrily. He always found his second name ridiculous. 'How the hell do these people know that?'

'Don't underestimate us, Mr Walters. You may call us a bunch of thick micks, but believe me know everything about you.'

'In that case you'll know all this terrorist talk is bullshit.'

'On the contrary. Two weeks ago you were in contact with Tom Dolan and Peter McManus.'

'Incorrect. McManus was drowned a week earlier while trying to break into my business premises. Before that he'd threatened to kill one of my employees.'

'A young lady who is rather more than an employee I've heard.'

'Well you've heard wrong,' said Clare coldly.

'How very trusting,' Murphy yawned. Clare looked murderous.

Mike resisted taking offence. There was a game being played out here. Murphy knew perfectly well that they had no terrorist connections and his reference to Leanne only proved he was in contact with the CIA. It was they who had invented that smear.

'As for Dolan,' said Clare. 'He and his gang tried to grab my vessel on the high seas. Two days later they lured Michael and me into a trap. It's thanks to Michael that one of that gang was captured by the French police.'

The Captain looked unimpressed. 'How do you explain entering this country at an unrecognized port with an American registered yacht and with a known member of French intelligence among your crew? Where is that man now?'

'He's with the yacht.'

'And where is the yacht?'

'We've no idea.'

'Is that so. We have ascertained that the yacht, *Quadra*, was at Glandore this morning. By four o'clock this afternoon she was gone – why?'

'The crewman had his orders,' said Clare.

'Which were?'

'To put to sea if necessary to avoid a certain person.'

'Miss O'Dwyer, will you please come to the point?'

'Does the name Sam Cassidy ring a bell with you Captain?'

'No.'

'You've never heard of him?' said Clare scornfully.

'No, but I fancy I'm about to.'

'Cassidy's an Australian. He says he represents something called the Irish Australian Cultural Society. The French police are looking for him in connection with the Dolan gang. He's also an associate of the American Professor Anderson.'

'You don't say?' Murphy's tone had changed he was interested. 'This Anderson's in Ireland now. He was thrown out of the North two days ago. Tell me about Cassidy?'

'As I've said, he's Australian. He's two bananas short of a bunch, and a few days back he wrecked my cottage while I was away. So, OK, I've a personal score to settle.'

'You tell the Garda?'

'Yes.'

'You can prove it's him?'

'Yes, he'd been in the village and openly threatened me – there's witnesses.'

'All right, Miss O'Dwyer, I note what you say.' He looked at Mike. 'Mr Walters, I understand that you were born in Eastleigh in Hampshire and you are without doubt an Englishman. What do you say, Miss O'Dwyer?'

'He's English – one of the better examples.' Clare half smiled.

'But you, Miss O'Dwyer, you puzzle me. I understand your father died in our government's service, but he was an American by birth. Can you explain?'

'His father, my grandfather, was born of Irish parents. My father was a Harvard graduate. He accepted a post in our diplomatic service on the invitation of the President of the Republic. My late mother was Irish born, and her great uncle was a 1916 veteran. Captain, I hope my patriotism is not in doubt?'

Captain Murphy gave Clare a shrewd look. Mike's respect for this man was growing by the minute. Murphy was no stage Irishman; he was a skilled interrogator. He had been gently leading them along a preplanned path to where Mike was not quite sure. Of one thing he was certain; it would pay them to tell the truth.

The next question was a shock? 'Miss O'Dwyer, could you tell me something about Delia Lazarraga?'

'Why...why d'you ask?' For the first time Clare was on the defensive and uncertain.

'Because that lady interests me. I understand she's your aunt?'

'You can't chose your relations.'

'Nobody is blaming you for the misdeeds of your grandfather. May I return to your father?'

'He died when I was ten years old. What is there for me to tell?'

'Miss O'Dwyer, please don't get me wrong. I'm not looking to reawake the past or give you pain, but the events of his death were suspicious.'

'I know, I've found out some things.'

'Enlighten me?'

'That he was murdered and Delia had a hand in it even if she didn't do the deed herself.'

'We know your father was working with British Intelligence through Miss Lazarraga who was of course his sister.'

'Half-sister and, Captain Murphy, my father would not willingly have helped the British without orders from our government.'

'I happen to know that he had those orders.'

'Then what's your problem?'

'Why should Miss Lazarraga kill her own brother?'

'I don't know, except it was in Argentina just before the Falklands war.'

'You're deliberately disingenuous, Miss O'Dwyer. Your father was investigating the disappearance of Irish aid workers. His brief never remotely involved the Falklands.'

'I don't care. Delia killed him. I can't prove it but I feel it in my gut.'

'Again, I note what you say.'

'I'll tell you something else, Captain Murphy. I don't think it had anything to do with intelligence work. For God's sake, Delia had only just left college, she couldn't have been a day over twenty. It was one of her first assignments.'

'Why should she kill your father?'

'Pure chance, she found him in Argentina. It was an opportunity too good to miss, so she fixed it for the junta to kill him.'

'What had she against her own brother that she should kill him?'

'Spite, pure spite. She hated him and she hates me. I think she'd kill me too if she could get away with it.'

Murphy paused to check his tape recorder. 'What can you tell me about her mother?' Mike noticed an increase in tension and wasn't sure why.

'Maria has a real grievance against my grandfather. I have to give her that,' said Clare.

'How much do you know about Poz?'

'Who?' Clare looked baffled.

'It's a place in Spain.'

'If that's something to do with Maria, I can't tell you anything. She would never talk about it. Grandfather wouldn't either, only loads of bullshit about his flying deeds.'

'Anyway,' Murphy continued, 'more to the point. If James O'Dwyer rescued Maria, why does her daughter, his daughter as well, carry this spite for you?'

'I can't tell you that. Perhaps you people don't realize the sort of person she is.'

'Once more I note what you say, but I think we have a very good idea of what your aunt is like.'

'You can note some more,' said Clare. 'Who killed that man Clarke in Amsterdam?'

'That's not for me to say, though every investigating journalist in these islands seems to have a theory.'

'I say Delia killed him.'

'No, Miss O'Dwyer, you're wrong there.'

'How d'you know?'

'Miss Lazarraga couldn't have killed Clarke; she was in Limerick that day, and two of my Special Branch colleagues were with her.'

Captain Murphy sat on the edge of the table a mug of tea in his hand. Clare and Mike also had mugs. It seemed their grilling was over and now the proceedings were to be informal.

'As I say,' said Murphy. 'I thank you for your co-operation. The least I can do is return you to your car.'

'May I ask a question?' said Mike.

'Be my guest. It's your turn to be asking.'

'Right, no disrespect intended, but look. Clare says these Special Forces are an anti-terrorist unit. OK, we can vouch for it that they're bloody good.'

'That's nice of you to say so but we can't comment on operational matters.'

'Fair enough, but you say we've been pulled in because we've had contact with Dolan? You say you want to catch him?'

'Sure and we'll get him if he sets foot in our jurisdiction.'

'I don't believe it. I put it to you that if you catch him you'll hand him over to a court who'll let him go the same day.'

'No Michael, not so,' said Clare angrily.

'No, I'm right, it's happened time and time again.'

'Hold on, Mr Walters,' Murphy held up a hand. 'I said if we catch him within our jurisdiction. Believe me if we find Mr Dolan here he'll go to prison for a long time. The cases you're thinking of are extradition to Britain.'

'That's it,' said Clare. 'It sticks in our gut to hand an Irishman to the British whatever he's done. When all's said your justice isn't always that just.'

'You mean the Guildford men?' said Mike. 'All right I'll give you that one – it stank.'

'Captain Murphy,' said Clare. 'What's going on in St Brigid's? Your soldiers and all the Gardai – they were never just waiting for us two?'

'No, they were not.'

'Come on then, you owe us some explanation.'

For a moment Murphy seemed to be weighing his reply. 'No, we weren't concerned with you people although we saw you drive up to the gate. My men radioed a description to Special Branch and they confirmed who you were. Later we monitored your arrival in the hay cart – with some amusement if I may say so.'

'Is it connected with the old priest we met?'

'Could be.'

'All right,' said Mike. 'We saw things as well. We saw that posse of police and all your troops standing in full view. If the IRA were around they'd have run a mile.'

'I imagine that would be so.'

'Then you've made my point – you don't want to catch them.'

'Mr Walters, I'm a soldier, I obey orders. Let me repeat what I said. These terrorists are bad. They're ignorant, deluded people in most cases. God may forgive them but I do not. There are certain times when it is prudent to be wary, to stand back and watch. So, Mr Walters, ask me the same question in six month's time.'

'I'm sorry, I don't understand this country.'

'There speaks seven centuries of Englishmen.'

Captain Murphy was as good as his word. He put them in his car and drove them at high speed through a labyrinth of minor roads before delivering them back to their car. The Morris was still there exactly as they had left it. The gates to the house were firmly locked.

'May I call on my stepfather?' Clare asked. 'That's all I was doing when you grabbed us.'

'I wouldn't advise that now. I would say let sleeping politicians lie – pun intended.' Murphy laughed. 'A word of advice. Find your yacht, put that Frenchman ashore and sail away. Why not go down to the Azores? That's a nice place to be this time of year.' They watched as the car lights vanished into the dark.

'What do we do now?' asked Mike.

'If *Quadra's* gone we'll have to find some place to sleep tonight.'

'I wonder why Jean-Luc put to sea?'

'We'll have to trust him,' said Clare. 'He never says much, but yes, I do trust him. I think you could say he's with us, but not of us – he's got his own agenda, but I don't know what it is.'

'You mean French Intelligence?'

'Yes, but I fancy this time the French are on our side.'

'Anyway,' said Mike. 'He won't wilfully sink the ship. He's a bloody good seaman – one of the best I've shipped with.'

They drove westwards again, this time with Mike at the wheel. Apart from commuter traffic around Cork the roads, by British standards, were almost deserted.

'Where can we stay tonight?' Mike asked.

'Pass me my mobile. I'm going to call ahead and book us into the O'Driscoll Links Hotel and Country Club.'

'What a mouthful?'

'It's every bit as expensive as it sounds, but I'm going to treat us to a night there. It's a real four star place and more important there's a link to our business.'

'What kind of link?'

'Remember Grandfather's list. The last name on it is Newhoffer, Colonel Carl Newhoffer. He has a place over in Galway but he owns the O'Driscoll Links. If he's not there they'll probably know where to get hold of him.'

The O'Driscoll Links Hotel lived up to its title; it was impressive. They had driven along the golf course attached to the hotel. In the moonlight it was a rolling, sombre moonscape ending in the grey glint of the sea. They passed a pagoda-like structure filled with golf trolleys, and there before them in a hollow was the hotel itself. It was a sprawling complex surrounding an ugly nineteen-fifties centrepiece. From this building fanned out wings and annexes, some with folksy thatched roof design. Around them they could see floodlit sub-tropical gardens and palm trees.

Clare pointed at one of the thatched cottages. 'It's supposed to be in the style of a crofter's cabin,' she sniffed.

They parked the Morris. Parked were a couple of dozen cars, some equally shabby, mixed among the Mercedes, Jaguars and BMWs.

'By the way,' said Clare. 'We don't sign in under our proper names.'

'Why not?'

'Because, Michael my darling, we don't want too many questions. There could be spooks checking the register, for O'Dwyer and Walters. And this is Ireland and we've gotta' be married or look like it.'

Mike laughed. 'Not Mr and Mrs Smith for God's sake?'

'Nothing so corny. When I phoned back there, I booked us in as Mr and Mrs Flanagan – so just you remember that.' She turned and put her arms around his neck. 'Mr Flanagan I love you.'

The receptionist was completely indifferent to names though his eyebrows rose several inches as he took in their dishevelled appearance. They escaped as quickly as they could to their room in one of the annexes. Mike fished out his one change of clothing; designer cords, white shirt and a blazer with a yacht club tie.

'When did either of us last have a bath?' he asked.

'I used the last of *Quadra's* shower water the morning you went ashore to see Delia,' Clare giggled.

'I haven't had a bath since we left Peyron's house,' said Mike gloomily.

'No wonder Delia didn't want you inside her place too long – fastidious cow, that one.' Clare eyed him up and down. 'Come on, there's a bloody great bath tub through that door and it's big enough for both of us.'

It was only when they reached the dining room an hour later that Mike realized how hungry he was. They had both spent a day high on adrenaline with nothing to eat since breakfast. They had also been very frightened, but in these sophisticated surroundings they felt detached from the shocks of the day. Clare had changed into her eye catching trouser suit. She had untied her golden hair and it flowed once more over her shoulders gleaming in the lamplight with that tantalizing tinge of flame red. Their eyes met as they touched glasses across the table though both knew instinctively not to spoil the moment with words.

Just before coffee was brought Mike slipped away to the men's washroom. He relieved himself and quickly turned to leave. As he did so he cannoned into a tall tubby man. Recognition was instant and mutual.

'Oh shit!' said Sammy Cassidy.

Mike stood in the doorway rigid and staring. Sammy stepped back two paces and smirked.

'Whatcha' doing 'ere, Pom? You still got yer dirty 'ands on that little Irish girl? Droit de seigneur eh? Still think this country belongs to yer? Why don't yer...?'

Sammy never finished his sentence. Mike had crossed the gap and seized the man by the front of his jacket. Alarmed, Sammy tried to back away but too late. Sammy's fat grinning face had become the focus of all Mike's fears, dangers and frustrations. He grabbed all fifteen stone of the man and crashed him against the door of a cubicle. Sammy's futile arm flailing was nothing. Once-twice-three times Mike slammed the flabby body until it gasped, doubled up and crumpled to the floor.

'You stupid Aussie creep, why do you always turn up like a bad penny when I'm trying to have a quiet dinner with my girlfriend?' Mike's temper had subsided as quickly as it had arisen. Now he was staring sardonically at the ludicrous figure on the floor.

'Cassidy, there's an Interpol warrant out for your arrest. Give me one good reason why I shouldn't ring the police this minute?'

'Hey now, cool it – that'll do.'

Mike spun round to face the new voice. A man had just appeared round the corner. The accent was American; the man himself was tall, thin, sallow, and expensively suited.

'Bernie, this is that fucking Pom, Walters.' Sammy still recumbent was jabbing a finger at Mike.

'I sort of figured that already,' said the American with a faint smile. 'Now Sam, you cool it.' The man dried his hands under a blower and walked across. 'See here, Mr Walters. I guess Sam has things a bit out of proportion where your country's concerned, but then you treated his ancestors shamefully and he's not forgotten.'

'Too right!' Sammy snarled staggering to his feet.

'Mr Walters,' the man smiled. 'I'm Bernard Anderson.'

'Are you really?' said Mike coldly. 'I've heard of you.'

'I'm flattered; may I ask what you've heard?'

Mike said nothing.

Anderson continued. 'You've been told I'm a hate-twisted Irish-Yankee and I want to blow Britain out of the water – so?'

'Something like that,' Mike grunted.

'You're wrong. I can honestly say I have no spite against the English just for their race. It's not what you British are, it's what you do.' Anderson held out his hand and Mike accepted it. It would have been churlish not to. Sammy looked daggers.

'That's all right then,' said Anderson. 'Now, Mr Walters, how say you introduce me to your lady friend?'

Realizing he'd been outmanoeuvred Mike led the way into the corridor.

'Hi there, Michael, you took your time…oh!' Clare had walked round the corner and seen Sammy a split second after she'd started speaking.'

'You!' The venom with which she spat the word startled them all, especially Sammy, who took the full force of it. 'You wrecked my cottage you bastard.'

'Please love,' Mike intervened. The last thing they needed was an embarrassing public scene. 'Please, I've already had a word with Mr Cassidy. At the moment we seem to be on neutral ground. This is Mr Anderson, or should it be professor?'

'Sure, but I'd much rather you called me Bernard.'

'I've read about you,' said Clare. 'Someone told us you'd been thrown out of the North.'

'Correct, the British seem to think my little history talks will overthrow their regime. Would that it were true.'

The hotel bar was almost empty. Mike and Clare agreed reluctantly to Anderson buying them drinks; Sammy glowered.

'I'll tell you where Sam here has things wrong,' said Anderson. 'I've never believed the British were wicked by nature. Say Clare, do you know the story about Pardraig Pearse? What he said to the boys of his school before the Easter Rising?'

'Yes, he told them; "when you've won your freedom, never forget it was the son of an Englishman who led you".'

'Correct, well quoted.'

Clare smiled. 'There's always been some good Brits who've come to Ireland. They say our Saint Patrick was a Brit.'

'Sure, and so's Jack Charlton,' grinned the barman as he delivered their glasses. 'Best manager our football team's had in years.'

'There you are, Sammy,' said Clare. 'How about that?'

'Assholes!' said Sammy as he downed his bourbon in one gulp.

'Mr Walters – Michael if I may?' said Anderson. 'I'm a historian. It's true I fight the Irish cause, but I fight with words and I try to fight with facts.'

Mike was unimpressed. 'Last time I saw Cassidy he was with the IRA.'

Anderson nodded. 'I don't think Sam has the constitution to be a freedom fighter. He has returned to his proper role with our Cultural Society.'

'That doesn't mean the police have stopped looking for him,' said Clare. 'And he smashed my house up.'

'Which was malign of him,' Anderson agreed. 'But I say again, I'm a historian. I have discovered that an important episode in the history of all three of our nations is being suppressed. I resent that, and Michael, I have colleagues who take the British view and they resent it equally.'

'I think I know what you're after,' said Clare. 'You might as well know we haven't got it.'

'I know that, but I think you'd awfully like to see those papers yourself. They're your grandfather's work when all's said.'

'Hey there, I never mentioned papers,' said Clare warily.

'This place is rather public,' said Anderson. 'Would you agree to continue this discussion in my rooms?'

'We'd rather stay where we can be seen,' said Mike.

They had reached an impasse. Anderson glanced around; there was no one within earshot.

'Three years ago,' he said. 'I began a paper on American volunteers in the Irish War of Independence. I always knew there'd been some, including James O'Dwyer.'

'Did you ever meet him?' asked Clare.

'Only once. The man was friendly but he wouldn't talk. Of course he was an old Free-Stater so maybe he thought I'd show him in a bad light.'

'More than likely,' Clare grunted.

'I had my first break a day or so later,' Anderson continued. 'I found an ancient old guy in a charity home. He'd been Colonel Flanagan's driver in France. What he told me was new. I'd never heard it before and it set my ears buzzing.' Anderson's eyes shone with the memory. 'Next day I flew to Oregon and saw Flanagan's widow. Mrs Flanagan was his second wife so she didn't know so much and she was scared. The CIA had been leaning on her and they'd taken some of Flanagan's diaries and letters. I was getting nowhere and then I had my second break. A source told me that one of the leading participants was a Canadian, Captain O'Leary. It was said that this man had written a complete account and that it was lodged in the Canadian National Archive in Ottawa.' Anderson had closed his eyes. Mike surmised these dusty files must be holy grail to a historian.

'I went to Ottawa, but I hadn't been in the archive building half an hour before the police came and I was ejected. It was two days before they let me back and in that time the O'Leary file had vanished and the index entry had been erased.'

'Why did they do that?' asked Clare.

'Someone warned them what I was after. Then I had my third break. I was in a bar feeling real mad when in comes this librarian. He worked in the archive. He said he was near retiring, had less to lose than the others, and he reckoned I'd had a raw deal. I sat the guy down fixed him a drink and this is what he told me.'

Both Clare and Mike had begun listening to this narrative with suspicion. Slowly they began to be drawn to the man and his story.

Anderson continued. 'This man told me he'd been a journalist for the Canadian Army newspaper in 1944. He'd been researching an article on the Canadian forces in the First War. He'd been allowed access to the private papers of David Lloyd George – the British

premier in that war. L-G was still alive, living on his farm in Surrey.
That's where my man was working.'

'He'd been there working, just the odd day at a time, when L-G
died. My friend was told he could finish his work provided he
stopped anyone else helping themselves to papers. It seems they'd
had people trying to steal files – all of them people L-G had fingered,
my friend guessed.' Anderson had a quick look round. Satisfied he
was unheard he continued.

'On my friend's last day a man comes in. He's gotten a written
authority signed by L-G's daughter. He's to be allowed to take away
a file classified; *Flanagan 1919-20.* It so happened my man knew this
file – he'd chanced on it a few days before. I asked him what was in it
but he didn't know. It wasn't his field so he hadn't been that
interested. He remembers the incident because the guy asking for the
file was nervous – real uptight about something. He grabbed the file,
read it; then he shot out the room like he'd won the jackpot.'

'Mr Anderson,' Clare interrupted, 'why are you telling us this?'

'All right, two reasons. One; my friend described the man who
claimed the file. I showed him a picture, a portrait photo from that
time, mid nineteen forties. It was a picture of your grandfather, Clare,
taken from an election manifesto. My Canadian identified him
instantly. That file was taken by James O'Dwyer.'

'Well if he did, I haven't got it now, and I have no idea where it is.'
Clare sounded exasperated.

'I don't doubt you, but I said two reasons. See Clare, I need your
help. I didn't know you and Michael were in this hotel, but it could be
a mighty happy meeting and it's too fortuitous for me to ignore.'

'I've told you, we know nothing.'

'Yes, yes – I know that.' Anderson looked carefully around once
more. 'Look I'll level. I'm not asking you to take sides. I appeal to
you in the interests of truth to help me.'

'But what can I do?' Clare spread her hands in a gesture of
helplessness.

'I know a man who may have some of the answers, but he won't
talk to me.'

'You're the historian. If he won't talk to you he certainly won't to
us.'

'You're wrong there. I think there's a good chance both of you,
Michael in particular, might persuade him to talk. I only know he'll
never talk to me in a hundred years.' Anderson looked at them
pleading. 'Please help me – all I want is the truth of this.'

'Oh God,' Clare sighed. 'So do I – I'll never know my grandfather until I do.'

Anderson stood up. 'Come with me.

He led the way, Clare beside him. Mike followed with deep misgivings. Sammy glowered but remained slumped over the bar.

Anderson left the building and led them across a courtyard to one of the mock thatched cabins. He gave the door a rhythmic knock.

'That you, Mister Anderson?' The intercom spoke with a slurred American voice.

'Sure, O'Rourke, open up – we've company.'

The door opened, inside was a large man dressed in jeans and a polo neck sweater; Mike noted a facial scar and a broken nose.

'Chuck's complanin' about da wine,' the man said.

'What's wrong with it?'

'Says it's da wrong year.'

'Well, send out for the right one.'

'Sure chief,' the heavy walked away towards the main building.

'O'Rourke's a trusty fellow but a mite slow upstairs,' said Anderson. 'I understand that once upon a time he was in the 'Westies'.'

'Jesus,' Clare muttered. 'New York Irish mafia,' she explained to Mike.

They were in a vestibule with a door leading into a larger room. They could see a table still laid with the remnants of a meal. A man sat in an armchair watching television. He was well built, in tweed trousers and an expensive white shirt.

Clare and Mike exchanged astonished glances. Here at last was Charles Venner-Harris.

CHAPTER 33

To Jean-Luc's relief the Irish officer spoke French; very good French with a Breton accent. The special-forces soldiers who had caught Jean-Luc had driven him some twenty kilometres in an off road vehicle. He'd been treated with as much dignity as a sack of olives. Now at last he'd been taken into a mobile operations caravan and confronted with this elegant officer.

'You seem to have abandoned your young shipmates.' the man said.

Jean-Luc shrugged.

'Innocents abroad, I met them myself three hours ago. While I interviewed them my boys fixed a tracker to their car and, 'incroyable', they head straight here.'

Jean-Luc shrugged.

'Yes here, they're staying in the Links Hotel. Now is that not an amazing coincidence or do they know something?'

Jean-Luc said nothing.

'Very well. Monsieur, we mean you no harm. You serve the interests of France as I do those of Irelande. May I suggest that you are here because you suspect the English are about to export some of their troubles to you…n'est pas?' The officer raised an eyebrow, otherwise his face was expressionless.

'Monsieur,' he continued. 'We have known of your presence here since yesterday but we have taken no steps to evict you. Why should that be?'

'Who knows?' Jean-Luc replied quietly. He was at a loss to know where all this was leading.

'It seems my political masters know. Although somewhat put out by your appearance, it seems our government has swallowed pride enough to approach Paris. Perfide Albion – apparently the English are not "playing the game" as they say. Not with either of us.'

'Indeed,' said Jean-Luc, 'what else should one expect?'

'As you rightly say, what else?' The officer looked him in the eye and slid an object across the table. Jean-Luc was startled to see his radio transmitter.

'Monsieur, you left this in the yacht – a little careless perhaps? I suggest you use it to confirm the position, which is,' the officer was smiling now, 'which is that you co-operate with us in the matter of the arms shipment, if and when it takes place.'

Mike was never sure who was the most surprised. He, Clare and Charles stared at each other in shock.

'God, Walters, and er…Miss O'Dwyer.' Charles rose stiffly to his feet.

'Hello there, Charles,' said Clare with a radiant smile.

Mike remained speechless. His jaw dropped as he stared foolishly at his schoolmate. Charles looked much as he had when Mike had seen him last at Cottons Hard. His hair was longer and his face pallid but this apart he seemed in fair condition.

'What the hell are you doing here?' Mike finally managed to gasp.

'I'm not here from choice – believe me. Forcible restraint, illegal imprisonment, contrary to law even in this third world country,' said Charles pompously.

Mike swung round to Anderson. 'What's this about?'

'I told you, Charles is the gentleman with the answers we all want to hear.'

'Charles,' said Clare sweetly, 'do you really know about my grandfather's papers?'

'I've made it completely clear to Anderson. There are certain matters I cannot discuss.'

'Why not?' said Mike.

'I will not compromise the honour of my family or my name.'

'Eh?'

'I would hardly expect you to understand, Walters.'

'Frankly, I'll admit I'm buggered if I do.'

'Quite so, simply attending a good school is not enough to make you a gentleman.'

'All right, Chazz. Try changing the record.'

'Say,' said Anderson. 'Seeing you two know each other I guess you'd like to chew over old times. I'll leave you together to talk.' He gave them a sly wink and withdrew.

'He's really quite a tolerable fellow,' said Charles. 'For an American that is – comes from an old New England family.'

'How do you come to be here, Charles?' asked Clare.

'I was in Limerick. I was in the hotel there due to meet Anderson – he retains my firm for legal services.'

'I remember,' said Mike' 'Irish American Cultural Society. You tried to make Peter Blair write a bogus survey for *Quadra*.'

'Yes, yes,' Charles waved away the comment impatiently. 'As I said, I was in the hotel when Anderson came in with that oaf, O'Rourke.'

Charles had been lured into a car for an alleged business appointment. Once in he'd been seized, handcuffed and blindfolded. The car had driven to a remote cottage where he'd been held prisoner.

'Hey there?' said Clare. 'Describe that cottage.'

Charles gave her a fair account of the interior.

'Holy Jesus!' Clare exploded. 'That's my house that is. D'you know what state it's in?'

'I know, but it's not my fault.'

'All right, but when all this is over you can help put the damage right.'

'Charles,' Mike intervened. 'You do realize the papers have been full of you. I'm sorry to say this, but you've missed your chance to become an MP.'

'Oh, that doesn't matter. I'd have lost anyway. Labour are winning everything at the moment; at least their leader went to a decent school...'

Mike groaned while Charles lent forward with unexpected enthusiasm. 'No, this is much better. I can read the headlines now... "The man held hostage by the IRA – unbowed, unbroken..."'

'Come off it,' said Mike. 'Wake up Charles. Anderson's not IRA, he's a dotty academic with a head full of sawdust. All he wants is information for his thesis. Why don't you tell him what you know and with a bit of luck we can all get on with our lives?'

'No, it's a matter of honour.'

'You can tell us, surely?'

'No, it's confidential matter concerning my family. I will not compromise.'

'Charles,' said Clare. 'What relation are you to Sir Christopher Venner-Harris?'

'May I ask who told you that name?' Charles pomposity was tinged with alarm.

'We were given it by an old friend of my grandfather. It seems, Charles, that this Sir Christopher was a true son of Ireland.' Clare spoke slowly and deliberately while Charles fidgeted uneasily. 'Oh yes, he made a fine contribution to our struggle. Michael and I have learnt a lot about him. I think I might write an article...'

'No! Miss O'Dwyer, please don't do that. It would be most embarrassing.'

'Why so embarrassing? Charles, when you came to see me, you

were full of your Irish granny.'

'I told you, it's a matter of honour,' Charles face was reddening; he was becoming angry.

'I don't know about his granny,' said Mike. 'Looks like his granddad was a spy if he sold secrets to the enemy.'

'Not if he was Irish by blood,' said Clare.

'For God's sake,' Charles burst out, he seemed close to tears. 'The man was my great uncle. Oh, don't you realize he could have been hanged? A Venner-Harris hanged for treason. God, the dishonour, we never spoke of it – it was taboo.' Charles stared pleading at them.

'Charles,' said Clare, 'never mind this Christopher. What do you know about the Flanagan affair?'

'Then you've heard of Flanagan?' said Charles miserably.

'We only know that Flanagan was an American and that he was involved with some conspiracy on the Irish side.'

Suddenly Charles reserve broke and he poured out his story. His great-great grandfather had been the centre of a Victorian scandal. He had eloped and married an Irish girl against the wishes of his family.

'You see,' said Charles, 'she was native Irish, a Roman Catholic, and...and the daughter of a dentist.' Charles voice had sunk to a whisper.

Clare glanced at Mike and rolled her eyes heavenwards. 'Charles, my father was never a dentist, but I would fit the rest of your bill. Michael here doesn't mind, nor I hope will his mother.'

'Walters is not a person of good family,' Charles replied stiffly.

Mike ignored the remark. 'Chazz, I thought your lot came from Cheshire?'

'Our family held lands there but most of the estate's been sold now. My title derives from our Irish lands.' Charles looked mournful.

'That's why you have to earn a living in a proper trade?'

'Profession, the law is a profession, even you should know that, oiky.'

'I thought your granny was a lord's daughter from Limerick?' said Clare.

'Of course, she was a Clarina. I've been speaking of my great-great grandparents. Their sons all married into good families.'

'What was this uncle of yours doing in the Foreign Office?' asked Mike.

'The Cabinet Office,' Charles corrected. 'There was a tradition that the family entered government service. My great-uncle did so though he retained his Irish leanings through his mother.'

'From whence he fed Mick Collins some juicy scraps of intelligence?' said Clare.

'That's why I said Foreign Office. It would be par for the course for that lot,' said Mike.

'Charles,' said Clare, 'Do you know the contents of Flanagan's letter to Collins?'

Charles shook his head. 'All I know is from the account my great-uncle left with his papers. He didn't go into detail, only some rather obscure reference about a pilot and an air flight.'

Clare looked at him sharply and Mike saw Charles wince. 'What pilot. Did he give a name?'

'No, does it matter?'

'It might. Wasn't it risky for him to leave his own records around?'

'Not really, he wrote an account years later but we always knew he was a spy.' Charles looked straight at Mike. He had an expression of hunted dignity. 'I'm not really half such a damn fool as you think.'

'I never said.'

'You didn't need to. I haven't forgotten school. They were so bloody proud of you, Walters. You, from your low-class background and your common accent. I see you've lost that by the way. Yes, scholarship boy rising on your own bloody merits. That's why they made you captain of rugby, head of house. Oh yes bloody trendy to push you and ignore me when I'd been born to lead – expected to lead!' Mike was stunned by this outburst, he had had no inkling of Charles stored up resentment. 'Yes Walters, and much good it's done you. Look at you – working with your hands in a boatyard while I'm a full partner in Dawson-Watts, and a future in politics…'

'You've got to get out of here first, Chazz,' said Mike.

'Patronizing as ever,' said Charles. 'I'll tell you this. Anderson and Cassidy could've tied me down and torn me limb from limb and I wouldn't have betrayed my name, and what's more Anderson knows that. He may be an American with a warped sense of history but he's a gentleman – he understands.'

'All right, Chazz. I know you well enough to accept that too.' Mike held out his hand and Charles took it with mute gratitude.

'How very British,' said Clare, 'and I'm not making fun.'

Charles smiled. 'It's always been my fate to be thought a damn fool, but I'm not such a fool that I can't turn my reputation to my advantage. All this fortnight I've played the idiot with these people and it's paid off.' Charles stopped and listened. 'The fact is I've learned a lot more of their secrets than they have of mine.'

Mike swiftly crossed the room and glanced through the door. Anderson had gone and O'Rourke was dozing in a chair near the front door. Mike went into the bathroom and turned on the shower.

'Come in here, I've read somewhere that running water drowns out listening bugs.' Charles followed Mike inside.

'Charles, we won't push you but now's your chance to tell us as much as you want to.'

'The Provisional IRA are meeting British Intelligence for peace talks at a place called Northovers,' said Charles.

'How d'you know that?' asked Clare.

'The day before we left the cottage Cassidy turned up with an Irishman called Dolan. As for Cassidy – my God! You know I'm not prejudiced, I can put up with Australians in small doses, but that man – awful, simply ghastly.'

'You have our sympathy,' said Mike.

'That first night Cassidy was drunk. They pushed me into another room but Cassidy was shouting so loud I heard every word.'

'Both sides of the conversation?' asked Mike.

'Everything Cassidy said, and some of Anderson and the Irishman. It seemed Dolan was consulting Anderson as to whether Irish-American opinion would support a cease fire. Anderson said yes but Cassidy disapproved.' Charles laughed. 'I gather Dolan's IRA. He got pretty angry himself – said the only time Cassidy was involved in shooting he wet his pants.'

'That I can believe,' said Clare.

'Will you tell us about Flanagan?' said Mike.

Charles looked almost relieved. 'Treachery,' he said. There was complete silence in the room, only the hissing cascade of the shower.

'Whose treachery?'

'Americans, you know how high and moral they like to be. Yes, I'll tell you about Flanagan. In 1918 there was an American army in Europe. They were our allies, our sworn friends...' Charles words ceased in mid sentence. They could all see Anderson by the front door in urgent speech with O'Rourke.

CHAPTER 34

Charles was free. Anderson and his companions had checked out of the hotel and vanished. Something unexpected was clearly happening. Anderson had seemed preoccupied and for the moment uninterested in any of them. O'Rourke the bodyguard was nervous, and although Anderson bid them a friendly farewell he was clearly in a hurry.

Cassidy had been predictable. 'Don't ever show yer face in Oz, Walters. I hate Brits and I've a score to settle.'

Mike was annoyed to find Charles wholly ungrateful. The man refused to divulge a word more about his great-uncle. 'A few more days and I would've escaped. Yes, escaped from the IRA. The press would've made it the story of the month.'

'Well,' said Clare. 'Michaeland I might have something to say about that. Just thank your lucky stars, because if Anderson had handed you to the Provos there's be nothing we could've done.'

They left him to it and walked over to the main building hand in hand. There they had a surprise, and the probable explanation for Anderson's departure. The forecourt was ablaze with flashing blue lights. There were three police cars and several uniformed officers moving around outside the building. One of them walked across and took a close look at them before moving on. Inside the reception area it was the same. By the door were two more gards, and talking to reception was a man in an ill-fitting blue suit. He had that intense look that said: plain clothes cop.

Clare marched straight to him. 'You're too late – they've gone.'

'Who's gone?' the man swung round in surprise.

'Cassidy and Anderson.'

The man looked at Clare with narrowed eyes. In return she gave him a dose of her eye contact that made him wince.

'I'm Chief Superintendent Dowling, Criminal Intelligence. What do you know about Anderson?'

'Only that he's got about half an hour's start on you. He's released the guy he kidnapped.'

'Madam, you're having me at cross-purposes. Who has been kidnapped and who would you be?'

'I'm Clare O'Dwyer and this is Michael Walters. We're staying here.'

Dowling nodded and turned to the receptionist. 'May I use your office? I wish to be private.'

'Sit down the pair of you,' the Chief Superintendent was polite but firm. 'I am aware of who you are. Now when did you last see Mr Anderson and who has been kidnapped?'

Clare told him in a few blunt and succinct sentences. 'I want you to get Cassidy,' she stated.

Dowling consulted his notes. 'Samuel Pardraig Cassidy. Australian national, wanted by the French – is that he?'

'That's he all right. Balls to the French, I want to press charges, he wrecked my house.'

'That's not my province; you'd much better consult your local Gardai. Excuse me...' his radio cracked into life. 'All right, you can tell the boys we'll regroup and move on.'

'It seems,' he said, 'you're right, there is a Mr Charles Venner-Harris. He appears mighty annoyed about something.'

'You didn't use his proper title,' said Mike wearily. 'He's Sir Charles.'

'You don't say,' for the first time Dowling had a flicker of a smile. He looked at Clare. 'Would you be knowing a Mr Toni Constantinescu?'

'Why?'

'Just wondered. And a Miss Annabel de Bouillet?'

'I don't but he does,' Clare jabbed a finger at Mike. 'What've they done?'

'Nothing, she mentioned you that's all.'

'When?'

'In Cork this morning. I would beware of her. The lady made some wild accusations, and she doesn't like you, Miss O'Dwyer.' That was all they could draw from the man. Dowling was in a hurry. He gathered his forces together and drove off into the night.

'What do we do now?' said Mike.

'We go to bed,' she laughed as she put her arms around him.

There was one more surprise. Clare stopped short in the doorway of the main bar, so abruptly that Mike bumped into her. She turned and pushed him back into the main entrance hall.

'What the hell?'

'In there,' she whispered. 'It's Dolan the Provo and another thug.'

'Are you sure?' Mike suddenly realized that though he had twice crossed Dolan's path he still had no idea what the man looked like. At Cottons Hard it had been dark and at Billancourt he had been half drugged. There had been that fuzzy CCTV image that the French had produced, but that could have been anybody. He had a quick peep into the bar and this time it was his turn to be surprised.

'The man he's with, I know him. He's Henderson, Delia's minder.' Mike risked a second look. Incredible; but there was no doubt the two men were drinking together.

'Let's get out of here,' he said. 'Back to our room.'

Once inside Mike locked the door. He paced up and down while Clare flopped on the bed. 'Is this Henderson a double agent?' she asked.

'No way, he'd never be devious enough. He's a not very bright Glaswegian and a Rangers supporter for certain. Apart from both being violent head cases he has nothing in common with Dolan.'

'Too many coincidences,' said Clare.

'In what way?'

'Ireland's a small place – everybody knows everybody. It's still odd though that the whole cast of our mystery seem to be sculling around these parts.'

'Cast?'

'That's right, dramatis personae. Look, first we see Delia and that Dublin man who looks like the missing link…'

'Brogan?'

'The same, then there's Captain Murphy and his heavy mob. Officially they don't exist but everyone knows they do. Next, by pure chance we stay at this place and what do we find? Anderson and that Sammy and they lead us to Charles. Now,' said Clare triumphantly, 'Charles tells us that the Provos are meeting with British Intelligence at some place called Northovers, right?'

'Yes, I'm with you so far.'

'Now, answer me this. Tell me the name on grandfather's list – the man we've still to contact?'

'Colonel Newhoffer?'

'Try saying it as if you came from the Falls road or Shankhill?'

'I can't because I don't, thank God.'

'Listen,' Clare cleared her throat with a grimace. 'Norrhother, that's what Dolan said or rather how Charles heard him. Colonel Newhoffer is an old friend of Grandfather's. What's more important he owns this place, the O'Driscoll Links. There's over three hundred acres including the golf course here, but there's also another hotel and conference centre further up the road – very secluded and private.' Clare was standing, hardly containing her excitement. 'Now if

Dolan's here drinking in public it's because he knows he's got immunity. All those Gardai around here just now and he didn't run like Anderson. If Henderson's here then so's Delia. If there's secret negotiations they'll involve your MI6, our security and very likely the Yanks,' she paused and shook her head. 'If Delia's in charge I dread to think what separate agenda's being cooked up that the politicians know nothing about.'

'Should we try to find out?'

'As I want us both to go on living I would suggest not – but I'd love to be a fly on the wall.'

Rain was beating on the windows and Mike could hear wind buffeting the building. It was blowing out there and he was not where he should be, with his ship. He slipped out of bed and peered through the curtains. It was six o'clock in the first light of dawn and he could see the grey waters beyond the links. There was a nasty swell building out in the bay with visible whitecaps as the westerly wind battered the lee shore they were on. The sky was wall-to-wall low black rain cloud. It had all the makings of a good hard blow. Where was *Quadra*? He was worried when he knew he shouldn't be. Jean-Luc was a fine seaman who could read the signs better than anyone. His experience would have taken him to shelter by now.

'Michael what are you doing?' Clare was beside him. He hadn't heard her so soft was her footfall on the heavily carpeted floor.

They were both comfortably naked in the centrally heated room. She rested an arm on his shoulder and he caught his breath as he felt the touch of her hair.

'I don't like the look of it out there,' he muttered.

'I know,' she said. 'It blows hard on this coast sometimes. There's nothing between us and America – just wind and thousands of miles of sea.'

'I'm worried for *Quadra*.'

'Don't worry, wherever she is she's safe, I know it.'

'I hope you're right...'

His words died as she reached up and pressed her warm body against his and he felt himself arouse to her as they kissed and caressed.

'Forget it for a while,' she whispered. 'Come back to bed.'

Breakfast time came and the weather was unchanged. Thick pulses of warm swirling rain blocked all view of the bay. Charles was leaving.

He stood in his rumpled tweed suit beside his luggage.

'Anderson has paid my bill in full,' he said. 'Most accommodating of him.'

'I should bloody well hope so,' said Mike, 'considering what he did to you.'

'You're going to England, Charles?' asked Clare.

'I intend leaving this afternoon. I've seen enough of your country, Miss O'Dwyer, and I have my political career to attend to,'

An hour later there was a lull in the rain. The hotel lounge had a full-length window with a mount carrying the largest pair of binoculars that Mike had ever seen. He walked across to them and began to scan the waters of the bay. They were on the south shore but at a point where the land swung north towards the town of Glengariff. The shore they were on was taking the full force of the wind and sea while the coast opposite was, by comparison, calm and sheltered. Over there he could see a few small craft moving, and one anchored yacht tucked cozily against some trees. Judging by her lack of motion she was safe enough. He focussed on her. Interesting that she was not a modern production boat; no this was an old'un…

'Clare come quick! I can see *Quadra.*'

Twenty minutes later they had checked out of the hotel and were on the road. Clare drove north round the head of the bay through Glengariff. Mike sat in the passenger seat with his head in the ordnance map.

'I think I've got the position fixed,' he said. 'There's a little cove with some sort of landing and a track leading to it.'

'I know it,' said Clare. 'It's an old fish dock but it's derelict. I sailed in there once when I was at college.'

'If Jean-Luc's aboard we'll give him a call – not that he'll hear much in this wind.'

It was past midday before they found the turning. It was an unmade track heading up a rock-strewn slope towards a belt of trees. On the way they passed a farmstead with a cluster of buildings. At the top of the ridge Clare stopped the car. They were on a promontory with the sea on their right and the little cove at their feet. On the seaward side below them was *Quadra*, clearly visible through the trees. Alongside her was a heavy dory and two figures stood on her deck.

'What's going on,' said Mike. 'Neither of them's Jean-Luc.' He ran forward to have a better view.

'What the hell!' he shouted. 'Hey you, stop that!' His words were blown away on the wind.

Quadra's anchor was being raised and Mike could see a wisp of blue smoke from the engine exhaust. Now she was moving below them. Mike sprinted back to the car. As he reached it he saw *Quadra* again. She had turned to port and was heading down the little creek. At the water's edge was a stone jetty with an antique lifting crane, and moored against the jetty was a sizeable stern trawler. Four more figures were on her deck. Two were seamen handing the mooring lines. Two others standing back were women. Clare and Mike's eyes met. Though the scene was some fifty yards distant recognition had been instant.

'I'd know those two anywhere,' said Clare. 'Delia and mother Maria.'

Mike's instinct was for prudence. They would lie low and watch. The appearance of both Lazarraga women had altered everything. This reasonable British reaction had no appeal for Clare. With a wild yell she was running down the track to the dock. Mike, appalled, made a grab to pull her back; too late, the woman he'd thought he was beginning to know had gone berserk. She was running like the wind, all the time screaming in fury. Oh, what the hell he thought; he sprinted after her. In front of them were both ships and a startled group who had been alerted by Clare's shouts.

'Delia, get off my boat, you thieving murdering bitch!' Clare screamed. She reached the edge of the quay pushing aside a startled sailor in a blue jersey.

Mike ran to stand beside her. The men on the dock were staring at them with blank expressions. Clare was breathing rapidly. Mike was thoroughly alarmed at the sight of her. She stood trembling with eyes glazed and teeth bared.

'Walters,' Delia had come to the rail of the trawler and was staring down at them. 'Walters, what is the meaning of this intrusion?'

'What are you doing with our boat?' Mike replied.

'You've clearly abandoned the yacht and I'm commandeering it in the interests of the state.'

'Whose state?' Clare snapped. 'This is the soil of the Republic of Ireland. You have no standing here. I'm going to call the Garda and charge you with thieving my boat.'

Delia's face was expressionless. 'O'Dwyer, you've always been an embarrassment but now you've become an active nuisance. As for you Walters, you've allowed Charles Venner-Harris to return to

England when I wished to interview him. Mike caught the full force of Delia's venom. The cold black eyes seemed to strip the flesh from him. With a massive effort of will he met her eyes and traded hate for hate.

'You're both in my way at a time when I will not be obstructed.' Delia was staring over their heads to some point behind them. 'Henderson, come here,' she called.

Mike turned round to see the man himself come out of an old Nissen hut.

'Henderson, remove these two out of my sight. Lock them in their own boat.'

'Aye, Ma'am.'

Mike's anger was beginning to burn, but this time it was controlled. He was not going to be pushed around by Delia and Henderson; certainly not with Clare watching. Henderson was striding towards them. This time Mike had a proper look at the man. Corporal Henderson certainly looked the soldier. He was tall and muscular, with short grizzled hair and a military moustache. At the same time he couldn't be a day under forty-five and there was a distinct trace of a beer gut in his ample form.

'Hello Henderson,' said Mike. 'Where's your gun?'

'I dinna' need a gun Jimmie. Ye're ginna' learn respect.'

'I've no respect for you,' said Mike. 'You're rather good at killing apes but I remember you screaming like a pig when the dog caught you – wet yourself did you?'

All the time Mike was watching. He daren't let Henderson come within grappling range. The man was taller and several stones heavier.

'Michael be careful!' Clare was near him tight-lipped and anxious.

He hardly heard her. As Henderson lunged forward Mike sidestepped and drove his fist into the other's face. Mike would never claim to be much of a boxer. It was a feeble jab but by lucky chance it smacked straight into his opponent's nose. Henderson swung round and with a bellow of rage he picked up a length of timber. It was a sizeable piece of what had once been a loading pallet. The man was snarling; his improvised club swinging murderously. Whatever regiment Henderson had belonged to, they didn't use the Queensberry rules. He reminded Mike of a caveman painting.

'Whaa Jimmie – I'm ginna' kill ye!'

Mike watched the other man's eyes. Henderson ran at him with a great shambling rush. There was no fighting back this time, it was self-preservation. He saw the blue eyes flicker as Henderson swung the club; Mike sidestepped. He heard the wood and felt the wind as it whipped past his shoulder. There was a searing pain as the tip caught his ankle. In desperation he hobbled out of range. In the background Clare screamed.

Mike was in trouble. He could no longer run. The pain was excruciating and he felt the warm blood soaking into his sock. Henderson let out a wild whooping laugh as he gathered his club for a final attack. Mike grabbed the only weapon he could see. It was lying at his feet. A four-foot length of straight smooth hazel; part of a firewood bundle maybe?

'Wha' ye ginna' do wi' yer wee sticky? I've got this yin.' Henderson jeered as he waved his club aloft.

Mike shut out everything. He heard nothing he saw only that laughing, red triumphant face. He held the stick in his right hand. The anger had left him; he was icy calm. Suddenly he had a vision, it was no more than a couple of seconds; like an old film clip. He saw Charles Venner-Harris; Charles for the first time a hero to his school-fellows; Charles as Dorset school's champion of epee fencing. 'Traditional sport for a gentleman,' Charles had said, 'It's all in the timing'.

The vision faded, but it was enough. He watched intently as Henderson stalked him. The brute was toying with Mike, enjoying his triumph. The pain was less now. Mike was beginning to be mobile again. The blue eyes flickered as Henderson swung the club. Mike took his chance. Stumbling forward, stick in hand, he lunged the sharp point of the hazel into his opponent's chest, dead centre below the rib cage. Henderson gasped, retched and dropped his weapon. He doubled up clutching his stomach as he staggered just a foot away from the edge of the quay. Mike made his final effort. Ignoring the pain he put his shoulder down and charged. He caught Henderson head on in an American football block. The move born of desperation took the last ounce of his strength. The collision almost stunned him but it lifted Henderson bodily into the air and over the edge of the quay where he fell with a smack and a deluge of spray. Mike walked to the edge and looked down. The big man was in the water flailing wildly with both arms.

'Help, I canna' swim!'

'Well, you'll never have a better opportunity to learn,' Mike called out as he walked away.

'Walters, stand still.' Delia was only a few feet away. In her hand was a small automatic pistol. She pointed it at him; her face as expressionless as ever.

'Stand still for God's sake,' said Clare. 'She's not bluffing, I know her.'

Mike stopped walking; there was real alarm in Clare's voice.

Delia pointed at the trawler. 'Walk slowly to the gangway. Behave and you'll not be hurt.'

They arrived at the gangplank just as two large Spanish sailors were helping the luckless Henderson up the stone steps to the quay. Dripping and squelching the big Glaswegian walked up to Mike.

'I'll say this for ye,' he muttered grudgingly. 'Ye're wasting yer time wi' that boatyard. Aye man a waste – ye'd've made it in the Paras.'

Mike nodded, knowing this crude limited man was paying him the highest compliment he knew. With Delia still behind them Mike and Clare boarded the trawler. Waiting for them was Delia's mother Maria.

Maria positively beamed at them. 'Mr Walters and Clare my dear. This is unexpected, but welcome to both of you.'

Mike mumbled something though Clare maintained a stony silence. Delia waved her gun and pointed across the deck to *Quadra* rafted against the far side of the trawler. 'Climb down onto the yacht,' she ordered.

It was a short fall to *Quadra's* deck. Both of them ignored the boarding ladder and jumped the few feet to their own boat. Another Spaniard was sitting in the cockpit. He stood up and pulled the main hatch open.

'Go below,' said Delia.

Behind them the hatch closed and they heard the click of the lock. Clare sank onto the starboard bunk. Mike had a long look through the deck windows and the side portholes.

'Can't see a thing,' he said.

'What are they up to, Michael?'

'Obviously they're planning something with that fishing boat.'

'Smuggling?'

'It's possible, but is Delia crooked? I don't think so. She's dangerous and mad very probably, but I'd never connect her with ordinary crime.'

'Nor me. No, whatever she's doing it's part of her own nasty little world. What I can't understand is Maria. What's she doing here?'

'I've only met her once and I don't know a thing about her except what you've told me.'

'I've only met her myself three times, but she's always been civil enough, but she's bitter. She's bitter against Grandfather and she's always been more Spanish than English – she was born in Spain.'

'Is she part of the security services as well?'

'Not as far as I know. She's a doctor at a clinic near where they live.'

'Quiet a minute,' said Mike. He stood up and was staring into the open doorway of the forecabin. Somewhere in the bows came a long hiss, then silence except for the wind and the slap of the waves on the hull. Five seconds later they heard a long low human whistle.

Mike ran forward. He glanced briefly into the 'heads', the toilet and shower compartment. Again he heard the hiss but now much closer. It came from the narrow bow end, an area almost filled with sail bags and spare lines. He began to pull these away revealing the access hatch to the anchor chain locker. Again the whistle sounded nearly in his ear. Mike saw the locker door was unsecured and he pulled it open. Inside cheerful but cramped was Jean-Luc.

'What the hell?'

'Is all clear?' asked Jean-Luc.

'Yes, they're all up top – it's only me and Clare.'

'OK, I come out.'

'You've been in there all this time?'

'No last night I leave the ship. This morning, early, I come back. Then come all these Basques. I hide and I see them bring you here.'

'Jean-Luc,' said Clare, 'd'you know what's going on?'

Suddenly Jean-Luc was jabbering in French and Mike was lost. For five minutes he and Clare conversed with Jean-Luc doing most of the talking. Clare's face became grimmer and her terse replies showed she was worried and angry.

Mike could stand it no longer. 'Please what does he say?'

'They're planning to ship guns in the trawler and Jean-Luc's heard them talking of moving a second load in *Quadra*.'

'You mean they're running guns for the IRA?'

'No Michael, it's the other way round. They're taking guns out.'

'That doesn't make sense.'

'Oh yes it does. Didn't I tell you Delia would have a hidden agenda?'

'He knows something, doesn't he?' Mike pointed to Jean-Luc. 'We know he's French Secret Service.'

'That's right, that's really why he's here. You see, half the Basque country is in France, though there's never been so much trouble there from ETA as in Spain. Anyway, the French have somehow got wind of this plot, and Jean-Luc just happened to be here and best placed to do something. He went ashore last night and he was briefed by our people. They've discovered Delia's playing a double game.'

'What's she up to?'

'Delia's negotiating with the Provos, but here's the catch. If the Brits are to give the Provos something of what they want, then the trade is the Provos must give up their guns.'

'Too right, I wouldn't settle for less.'

'So what if there aren't any guns to surrender?'

'You mean if they ship them out first.'

'That's it; Delia's going to broker a ceasefire. At the same time she's giving the Provos the chance to hand one of their arms piles to Maria's chums in ETA.'

'And the French are annoyed?'

'You bet your sweet life they are.'

For three hours they saw nothing of their captors. Clare cleaned and dressed the wound on Mike's ankle. There was a jagged gash where Henderson had caught him with the lump of wood. Jean-Luc cooked a light meal though he seemed the only one relaxed enough to eat much. Mike was surprised to find the VHF radio still intact. His suggestion of a call for help was squashed by Jean-Luc. The Frenchman gave no reason but they suspected he was working to his own plan. Mike switched on the receiver anyway. Bantry Coast Radio was belting out a strong wind warning – force eight imminent. Mike could see little through the windows, though they could hear the wind in the rigging and the patter of rain on the decks.

It was dark before the main hatch was opened. Jean-Luc had already hidden himself forward. This time it was Maria who came down into the cabin.

'Mr Walters,' she said. 'I've come to request the use of your ship and your assistance in sailing her.'

'Not my ship – her's,' Mike jabbed a thumb at Clare.

'Yes, I know that, but you are the master.'

'Are you asking to make a trip with us?'

'I want to charter your yacht to carry a small cargo.'

'Cargo, how legal?' Mike knew very well what this cargo was but it would pay them to pretend ignorance.

'I'll be frank with you. The mission is unofficial but I suggest you are not at liberty to choose. If you refuse I shall have no reason to protect you. I will provide a substitute crew who will, of course, be unqualified.'

Mike's thoughts were racing. Jean-Luc had already told them to play along with whatever was proposed. Mike wanted to tell these Spaniards to go to hell. He knew that if he did that all their lives, Clare's included, would be in danger. Furthermore, Maria's point was a strong one. She needed them to handle *Quadra*. This at least secured their short-term safety. It was unlikely the Spanish deck hands could work or navigate a sailing vessel.

'If I agree to work this ship,' he said. 'I do so under duress. I'm not willingly taking part in criminal activity.'

'I don't accept the word criminal,' Maria replied, 'but I understand what you say.'

'When are you planning to sail?'

'Both ships will leave in an hour, or as soon as the cargo is loaded.'

'You've got to be joking. It's blowing like smoke out there.'

'I'm advised that your vessel is seaworthy and designed for ocean voyaging. I've sailed in her myself in earlier days. However, the bulk of the cargo will travel in the *Juanita*.'

'Will you be coming with us?'

'No, my place will be with the *Juanita*.'

'Miss Lazarraga, if I might give you some advice as a professional seaman. *Quadra's* a damned sight more seaworthy than that stern trawler in the conditions we're likely to meet out there. Secondly, it's downright irresponsible to put to sea in the face of a full gale warning.'

'Mr Walters, I respect your experience but this is an exceptional mission. It so happens these weather conditions suit my purpose.'

'Maria,' Clare spoke quietly. She had been sitting seemingly introspective throughout. 'Maria, who killed that man Clarke in Amsterdam? At first I thought it might have been Delia, but it seems she has an alibi.'

'And what would you know about it?' Maria's face had hardened. Her lips were pursed together and the skin on her cheekbones seemed tighter than ever,

'Grandfather told me to see Clarke. It seems he had knowledge of the Flanagan affair. Next thing we know he's dead, murdered. There was a woman at the scene around that time. The description could be Delia, but if not it could just as easily be you.'

Mike was staring: here was another Clare. Once more the woman he loved and thought he understood was changing before his eyes. Her Irish accent was harder, grittier than he had heard before, and there was a wild light in her eyes.

'I've been learning a lot these last few days, Maria. I've heard tales of Clarke. How he was in Michael Collins' squad, and later in Spain. Now seeing you're Spanish...'

'Basque, Eskadi! Not Spanish never – how dare you!' Maria's smooth composure had vanished. Her eyes blazed her face was contorted as she screamed the words.

'Did you murder Clarke? An old man of nearly a hundred?' Clare's voice was cold. There was stillness in the cabin even the gale above seemed to have been subdued.

'I didn't murder Clarke, I was an instrument of justice. I fulfilled a vow that has been with me all my life,' Maria was speaking softly, barely audible above the renewed noise of the wind and rain.

'But why?'

'Listen, in June 1937 I was three years old. Fascist soldiers came to our village. They were looking for my father. We were warned, and friends put us in a secret hiding place. The soldiers were from Franco's Foreign Legion. There were forty of them commanded by a sergeant – an Englishman some said. Not one of the village betrayed us...' Maria's voice died away. Mike was appalled by the awful expression on the woman's face.

'In vengeance the Fascists killed thirty villagers – men women and little children. When we came out of hiding...into the sunlight...I saw my cousin Pilar. She was dead, hanging by a wire noose. That is my earliest childhood memory.'

There was silence. Again, even the sounds of wind and sea seemed stilled for a few seconds. Mike was mesmerized, but also embarrassed to witness this strange woman's private hell.

'Soon after Bilbao fell – our cause was lost.' Maria's voice was little more than a husky croak. 'Jim O'Dwyer rescued us and spirited us away. Years later he told me he had seen that murder gang and recognized their leader. That Legion sergeant was no Englishman, he was Irish. He was Eamon Clarke.'

'From that moment I swore I would kill Clarke. I was certain Jim knew where he was living. I suppose he thought he was protecting me from myself. He told me things happen in this world – it is life. I must not destroy myself in a quest for vengeance.' Maria's head had dropped, she was barely audible.

Then she spoke again, this time staring straight at them her voice blazing. 'Jim would never understand that such is not the way of our people. I had sworn an oath. I had a duty owed to all those who had died to protect my father. I feared only that Clarke would die before I could reach him.' Maria's face was chalk white, her eyes incandescent.

'Then a few weeks ago fate delivered him into my hands. My daughter was detailed to interview Clarke about the Flanagan document. I went with her. When she had finished with Clarke she confirmed he was indeed the man. I stayed on a further twenty-four hours. I stood opposite the house preparing for the moment. Then two other men went in and one of them I knew. It was Fairbrother of the CIA, and an enemy of our cause. I did not know then that our people had already decided to eliminate him.'

'Whatever had you got against Clarence?' Clare was angry now.

'Fairbrother was an agent of the United States Government. They support the Castilians in the oppression of our country. May I finish?' Maria stared at Clare who said nothing.

'When Fairbrother and his friend had gone, I went into Clarke's room. I carried a steel poker. I killed him, and then I hit him thirty times. I counted each blow, one to thirty. One for each person killed that day in our village.'

Henderson was seasick. The man's face was ashen grey and he was shivering pathetically. He offered no resistance as Mike fixed the safety harness around him and helped him to the lee rail.

'I dinna' like boats,' he mumbled. 'they've na' right sending me out here. My duty's to look after Miss Delia, not help yon dagos.'

'Never mind,' said Mike. 'No disgrace in being sick. We've all been there – just try and keep it off the deck.'

Quadra was holding her own nicely. With the wind just forward of the beam she was comfortable with two reefs and her smallest jib. Despite the gloomy forecast Mike was relieved to find the wind little more than a force seven. The sea state was another matter. There were really nasty waves building. These were not the long sloping seas of the mid-Atlantic, but short irregular waves, potentially very dangerous. Mike looked apprehensively at the lights of the *Juanita* a quarter of a mile to starboard. Much more of this and the trawler could be in trouble. He'd tried to reason with Maria from the outset, but the woman was impervious to argument.

Things could have been a lot worse. Of the two minders Maria had wished on them; Henderson was totally apathetic. The man's hostility to Mike had vanished. It was as if he regarded their vicious fight as some sort of bonding. The rest of the cargo consisted of eighteen metal boxes and a taciturn Spaniard called Carlos. Carlos was not much more of a seaman than Henderson. He seemed interested only in his boxes and was indifferent when Jean-Luc came out of hiding to help with the ship. It was Jean-Luc who now sat at the helm steering carefully up each wave face, concentrating on the breaking crests above. Down below Clare was sitting at the chart table while Carlos lay on a bunk seemingly oblivious to the din and mayhem all around.

Mike spared a quick glance at Henderson. The man was horizontal on the cockpit seat, his head resting on his arm. Mike was sympathetic. He surmised that Henderson had reached that stage where he was too ill to be frightened any more: potentially dangerous because the victim becomes indifferent to safety. Mike slid across the cockpit just as *Quadra's* bow took a green wave slap across the foredeck. A cascade of water engulfed them. Henderson was still lying face down oblivious to the torrents of water falling on him. Mike knelt down, and with difficulty, rolled the man on his side. As he did so he felt something under the oilskin top. Quickly he pulled down the zip and felt inside. Yes, there was a shoulder holster. Mike pulled out an automatic pistol. Bracing his legs he stood up and prepared to lob it overboard.

'Na, dinna' do that,' Henderson croaked. 'It belongs to Five — I've signed for it.'

'All right,' Mike called back. He opened the cockpit locker and pitched the pistol inside snapping shut the padlock as he closed the lid.

At that moment a gust struck *Quadra* laying her lee rail under water for five seconds.

Jean-Luc looked mournful. 'Not finish yet,' he shouted. 'She blow worse before she is better.' The wind snatched away most of his words. Mike mouthed a reply and went down into the cabin.

Below decks the motion was even worse. Timing his moves carefully Mike crossed the cabin and sat down beside Clare. She pointed to the chart. The satellite plot had them fifty miles south of Cape Clear.

'Good,' he said, 'have you spoken to the *Juanita*?'

'Yes,' Clare grimaced. 'I'm worried about Maria, she's acting crazy.'

'How so?'

'She's threatening the captain if he doesn't go faster. The man says he can't. All he can do is try and ride the seas. He says they're taking on water and one of his pumps is broken.'

'I don't like the sound of that,' said Mike. 'The wind's not too bad but there's an evil sea running. Christ…!'

'Michael, what's wrong?' Clare was staring at him. Mike's whole attitude had changed; for the first time he felt perturbed.

'Look at that.' He reached across and tapped the barometer. 'Glass is dropping. That's ten millibars in three hours since I set the pointer.'

'Is that bad?'

'I'll say — that's on a par with the 1979 Fastnet gale.' Both of them knew the significance. The Fastnet disaster had been fifteen years ago in this very area of sea. Mike had heard firsthand accounts from veterans of that night. It seemed he might now be about to face something similar. He glanced at the clock: three-thirty. First light would be between five-thirty and six.

'Come on Clare, we take no chances. I'm going to set the trisail.'

The blast of wind as they came on deck sucked the breath from their lungs. Even Mike was staggered by the change in the last fifteen minutes. The wind was fiercer and the motion even more erratic. The noise from the rigging added a banshee scream to the continuous driving stinging spray. This was frightening enough but the darkness made the seas more awesome. Mike felt puny and very vulnerable. He thanked God for the steadying presence of Jean-Luc.

Mike carefully hooked Clare's lifeline to the jackstay wire that ran the full length of the ship. Whatever happened they must stay attached. Anyone overboard without a line would be dead.

Between them they somehow lowered the mainsail. For five minutes it fought back with all the force the wind could give it. They snatched and fought with the flapping, slippery cloth and finally subdued it. Next they set the trisail. This was a tiny triangle of stout cloth a tenth the size of the mainsail. Mike called Jean-Luc to help while Clare took the helm. As they finished sheeting the sail Mike glanced at her. She sat feet braced against the cockpit sides with the heavy tiller grasped in both hands. Her face was a study in concentration. She had an almost little girl expression as she sucked her lips, her eyes intent on the sea ahead. He felt overwhelmed by feelings of pride and deep love. He resolved then and there that if they came through this alive he would ask Clare to marry him. She caught his eye and smiled . It was a momentary lapse but enough to bring a rogue wave slamming on deck, flooding the cockpit and completely immersing Henderson. Mike and Jean-Luc clung on until the waters subsided.

'OK, it's my turn,' he shouted in her ear. She nodded ruefully and handed him the tiller.

'Jean-Luc,' he yelled jabbing a thumb in the direction of Henderson. 'Get that man below and in a bunk – he's all in.'

Mike gripped the tiller and braced himself. Once more he felt the tremor of the rudder as *Quadra* rushed on towards the next wave. He knew he was sailing in conditions beyond his experience; could he cope? It was not so bad for Jean-Luc; he had sailed in the Southern Ocean and around Cape Horn. Mike gritted his teeth and steered *Quadra* up the face of a wave and through the crest. Good ship, he smiled. Yes, *Quadra* was in her element. Irrational it might be, but he felt the yacht had a personality of her own and that she knew far more of what was needed than he did. The darkness made it worse, far worse. The waves would have been frightening enough in daylight. At night they became huge monsters sucking and hissing. They towered above him, taunting and jeering, offering to crush the ship and send them to the bottom without trace. As for the wind it was beyond anything he had ever imagined. It tore the surface of the sea choking and blinding him with its driving pinpoints of icy spume. Worst of all was the noise. All these things, combined with the darkness, almost unnerved him. He knew now why better men than he had been broken by nights like this.

Suddenly, out of the darkness came the wave. This was no wave within his experience; it was a mountain. It reminded him of a picture of the Matterhorn. Slowly it hovered on the bows as it grew and grew until it towered above the ship. Mike knew fear now. This wave had his name on it. It exuded malice and hatred and it was going to take him down under twenty thousand tons of water. Instinctively he aligned the ship to meet the oncoming sea. Then came the miracle. *Quadra* rose majestically up the face of the wave. As she climbed so the wind increased, the spray blew and the yacht heeled in the foaming mass. Now as they reached the summit the sight was breathtaking. A shaft of moonlight had broken through the low cloud and for a few seconds Mike saw the miles of broken boiling water. It was a vision of hell far truer than pictures of burning fires. Now they were falling, down, down, into the trough and as they fell somehow the wind seemed less intense.

'Good ship, oh, great ship!' This time he shouted the words into the teeth of the wind.

Dawn came and Mike handed over to Jean-Luc. They had arranged that neither would helm for more than two hours. Neither Jean-Luc or Mike commented, but they both knew the wind was still rising even if the seas seemed less fearsome in the early light. Three minutes after Mike released the helm a gust struck *Quadra*. It came from nowhere smashing into them and bringing the yacht close to a knockdown; that dreaded moment when the masthead comes close to striking the sea. For a minute all was chaos. Mike was hurled across the cockpit only to be brought up short by his safety harness. The impact came close to winding him and for one terrible moment he thought his arm was broken. Jean-Luc was dazed. The tiller had torn from his grasp before thudding back into his body. The ship had swung into the wind. The sails slatted, the rigging screamed like a demented string orchestra. Finally the storm jib exploded into shreds. Still gasping with pain Jean-Luc grabbed the tiller and tried to steer the yacht back on course. It was hopeless. A second gust struck home, pushing her down. Jean-Luc dragged the tiller towards him with a ferocious grunt. Mike moved fast. He let fly the main halyard and the trisail came thundering down, billowing away to leeward. Between the two of them they somehow gathered it into an untidy bundle.

They had two realistic chances. They could lash the helm and leave the yacht to her own devices, or they could run before the gale. In the back of his mind Mike still felt concerned for the *Juanita.* He cared nothing for Maria and her schemes. It was a gut feeling that he had a duty to stay near the other vessel. He made his decision. They would lash the tiller and try 'lying to hull', was the technical term, although Mike had never had reason to try it. It seemed Jean-Luc had come to the same conclusion; he was already double lashing the tiller. What would happen now was anybody's guess. If *Quadra* lay broadside to the waves there was a danger she would swamp. Mike really didn't know; they would just have to try it and see. For twenty minutes they sat in the cockpit and watched. *Quadra* was lying to the waves, lurching and rolling, her bare mast arcing giddily against the sky. Wave after wave bore down and gently she rose to each one as the seas sucked and gurgled under her. The wind was blowing harder than ever but Mike was satisfied. For the moment his ship was safe.

Down below was chaos. An inch or two of water was slopping around the cabin floor among the ammunition boxes. The electric bilge pump was working well. The water level was falling, but everything was wringing wet from the bunk cushions to the charts and books. Clare was sitting with the radio microphone in her had. Carlos was watching her.

'*Juanita's* in trouble,' said Clare.

'I was afraid of that – what's the news?'

'She's drifting without power about four miles away. Her captain says they can't hold the water back with the pumps.'

'Has he sent a Mayday?'

'No, Maria won't allow it. She's got a gun pointed at him. She's gone mad.'

'All right I'll talk to them.' He took the microphone and called the *Juanita.* It was her captain who answered.

'Captain,' Mike called. 'What is the condition of your ship?'

'We take on much water. I think soon we sink.'

'Have you a life raft?'

'Yes, raft for six men.'

'Captain, I am coming to your assistance but I cannot be with you before one hour. I suggest you make a Mayday.'

'*Quadra*,' it was Maria's voice. 'I will not make a distress call and I do not want your help. You will hold your course and complete your voyage.'

'Miss Lazarraga!' Mike was angry. 'It's not for you to say. It's your captain's decision.'

'Let me talk to Carlos.'

'All right.' Mike passed the handset.

Suddenly Maria was gabbling in a foreign language. It wasn't Spanish, French, or any other language Mike had ever heard. Carlos was replying in the same language. It was clear he was upset.

Carlos was a problem. He would certainly be carrying a gun. Should they immobilize him? Mike decided not. If they were to rescue the crew of the *Juanita* they would need Carlos's strength to help. There was also something odd going on. Carlos was a different character to the other Basques. To a man they had been surly and hostile. Maria had chosen Carlos to sail on *Quadra*, presumably because he spoke English. At the same time he seemed remarkably laidback and neutral.

Carlos was pulling on his arm. 'She is crazy. Please you talk?'

'Miss Lazarraga,' Mike called. 'We'll be with you as soon as we can. I will require you to fire some flares and please have your life raft ready.' There was complete silence. He only hoped the *Juanita's* radio was still working.

Mike stayed in the cabin just long enough to check the barometer. He stared horrified as he saw it had fallen a further eight millibars. This was no ordinary gale. It would be bad enough riding it out with sails stowed, but now he was obliged to move towards a sinking vessel. On deck he found a surprise and a change of fortune. The wind had veered dramatically. It was now coming at them harder than ever from the north west. They must have passed right through the eye of the depression. This was a bonus, they were now upwind of the *Juanita*. They would have an even chance of reaching her before she foundered.

Mike pressed the starter button of the diesel. The engine responded instantly. Jean-Luc pulled on the sheet to unravel a tiny corner of the big rolling foresail; just enough to help steady the ship. Mike cut the tiller lashings, put the engine in gear, and pushed the throttle to its limit. He was relying on the propeller walk, its natural sideways momentum to help turn the ship before the waves caught her. *Quadra* lurched wildly. Mike felt the pressure come on the rudder and heard the scream of the propeller as it rose above the surface for a couple of seconds. Then slowly but surely *Quadra* was moving again, riding these terrible seas serenely and on the course to take her to the *Juanita.*

CHAPTER 36

Mike knew that the next hour would be a test, perhaps the greatest challenge of his life so far. *Quadra* was magnificent as she started to make headway under her motor-sail combination. Mentally he was trying to estimate how far the *Juanita* had drifted. The trawler's master had given them a position five miles to the south, but she would have drifted some more by now. He was confident that he would find the *Juanita,* but only if her master and Maria co-operated.

Clare was on deck. She sat beside him and yelled in his ear. '*Juanita's* captain radioed. They've taken Maria's gun. He wants us to hurry.'

He shouted back. 'Fetch the distress flares…' He signalled Jean-Luc to take the helm.

Down in the cabin the ship's motion was definitely easier. Mike went to the radio and called the *Juanita.*

'Captain, in five minutes I want you to fire one red rocket.'

'Yes, I do that,' came the reply. 'Captain please come quick – soon we sink.'

'Understood, expect me within one hour.'

Right on cue they saw the rocket some ten degrees further east than they expected. Jean-Luc responded and pointed *Quadra* towards the light that hovered a fiery ball against the sinister black sky. Mike knew the wind would whip the parachute flare some way from the ship, but at least they had a fair idea what patch of sea to head for. Ten minutes later came a second rocket in the same place. Mike snapped the trigger on the red flare and shot it skywards. These Spaniards should see it and it would give them hope. As he climbed down into the cabin again he was beginning to form a rescue plan.

'Clare, we're going to need oil, lots of it – OK?'

'Why?'

'You'll see. There's a spare can of engine oil. See what you can find, even that stir fry oil in the galley will help.' Clare gave him a puzzled frown and started to edge her way across the cabin clinging on to the handholds as the ship pitched and rolled.

'Carlos?' Mike called.

'Yes, Senor?'

'How well do you speak English?'

'Good, I think.'

255

'Right, when we reach the *Juanita* I'll need you on deck. Meanwhile stay on the radio. Tell your captain to have his life raft ready – understand?'

'Yes Senor.'

'OK – get to it.'

Thank goodness the captain of the *Juanita* was a steady character. He had succeeded in keeping his electrical systems working to the last moment. *Quadra's* crew could see the *Juanita* lit up like a Christmas tree from two miles away. The Spaniard had switched on his full display of fishing lights plus a powerful spotlight over the centre of the ship.

Mike assembled his crew minus only the incapacitated Henderson. He had already agreed plans with Jean-Luc. They would use the oil to smooth the sea. Contrary to popular myth very little oil was needed.

The Frenchman took the helm and headed for the trawler. *Quadra* ran downwind towards the stricken vessel with her engine in neutral but with power from a quarter of her foresail. They all marvelled at the speed with which they raced towards their target. Mike tried to focus his binoculars on the *Juanita*. The image rolled in and out of the frame as both ships rose and fell in the waves. The trawler was near to foundering. She showed hardly any hull above the waves. It seemed as if her bridge and wheelhouse were part of a huge raft. Jean-Luc shaped to pass to leeward. Mike yelled at the others to be ready. The *Juanita* was coming at them. They could see her crumbling paintwork and the rivets in her plating.

'Now!' Mike yelled. 'Go...Go!'

The others began pouring oil. A horrible concoction, lubricant, diesel fuel, cooking oil. Would it make any difference? Mike knew the Norwegians claimed a few litres of fish oil were enough to increase the surface tension locally and stop the wave crests breaking. They would soon see.

'Not too fast,' he shouted.

Oil on troubled waters, an old cliché, but did it work for real? Mike glanced astern. They'd shot past the *Juanita*. She was two hundred yards away. This was the moment when they must turn round. Turn *Quadra* broadside to a hostile broken sea then motor back into the teeth of the gale. He saw Jean-Luc put the engine in gear and move the tiller. Mike signalled to Clare. Their job was to roll the foresail before the wind shredded it.

Quadra had completed the turn. The foresail was flapping. Now it was thundering, rending and screaming as the wind caught it. A few more seconds and it would be in ribbons. With both of them heaving on the line the jib rolled sweetly. With relief they saw it disappear.

Quadra under power battered her way back against the gale. The wind seemed worse now than at any time, but the seas were less. The waves were still immense but suddenly they had lost their menace. The crests were no longer breaking. A dollop of spray hit the foredeck and blew back in their faces. It had a nasty chemical taste – oil. The old trick was working better than he'd dared to hope. It might be an illusion but it seemed the surface had calmed as if by magic.

Mike trained the glasses on the *Juanita*. He could see men, black figures wrestling with a square object: the raft. He saw them pitch it overboard, then, bang! The black box was growing, expanding into a round blob with a bright orange canopy. For a moment it stayed dipping and bobbing close to the stricken ship. Now it was on its way as the gale caught the raft and drove it downwind. Jean-Luc moved the tiller and aimed *Quadra* meet it. Mike had a last look at their preparations. Coiled lines were ready as well as a heavier rope with a snap hook. He saw Clare and Carlos tense and waiting. Jean-Luc stared: his face a study of matter-of-fact calm, as he judged the distance between *Quadra* and the oncoming raft. They all knew they must secure it first time before the effects of the oil lessened. The raft was drifting close now, almost under their bows. Now it was only feet away. A man was kneeling in the open door of the canopy. Mike saw him swing an arm. A coiled line swept through the air. It landed on Mike's right hand, the tail catching him painfully on the cheek. Instinctively he caught it and made it fast. They had done it. The life raft was secure.

One by one the Basque sailors were pulled aboard. There were four of them including the *Juanita's* captain. All were close to exhaustion and very cold. One glance was enough for Mike to guess the onset of hypothermia was near.

Clare had one question. 'Where's Maria?'

The captain shook his head. 'She wish to die. We try to make her come, but no good – she stay.'

They bundled the casualties below and Mike began to improvise such dry blankets as he could find.

Clare was sitting by the radio. 'Maria…Maria,' she called. 'Answer me.'

'I hear you,' the radio crackled.

'Maria, why weren't you in the raft?'

'No Clare, honour requires me to stay with this ship.'

'We'll come for you,' Clare pleaded.

'No, stay clear. I am about to complete my mission.'

'Maria, please listen – please!'

'Goodbye Clare.'

Seconds later they heard the explosion. Even inside the cabin above the noise of wind and sea they heard it. Scrambling on deck they smelt the acrid burning carried on the wind along with a smattering of charred fragments. Of the *Juanita* there was no sign.

'Semtex,' shouted Jean-Luc. 'They have many kilos. Maria Lazarraga make it go boom. She go too – crazy woman.'

Back in the cabin Mike looked at Clare. 'Why?'

'I don't know,' she answered miserably. 'I think she staked a lot on this shipment. She was more of a fanatic than I realized.'

'Why kill herself, and for what?'

'That's not easy, Michael, and much harder for you to understand. You never saw the things she saw. You never had your country occupied.'

'I dunno',' Mike sighed. He suddenly felt very low and very tired.

'There's another thing,' said Clare. 'I think she may have died to protect Delia. With Maria gone Delia's in the clear.'

'What do we do about this stuff?' Mike kicked one of the ammunition boxes. He had a quick glance at the Basque crewmen. At least one was unconscious, and the others too oblivious to care. He beckoned Clare to follow him into the forecabin.

'We're not out of the wood yet,' he said. 'Those men are fit for nothing at the moment, but when they recover we'll be outnumbered.'

'Shall we throw the weapons overboard?' asked Clare.

'No, those boxes are too heavy to handle in this sea. I'm not risking anyone getting hurt.' As if to emphasize the point *Quadra* gave a huge lurch. Mike clung to a handhold to steady himself. They must be running out of the oil slick.

'I'm going to talk to Henderson,' he said.

Henderson was in a bunk secured by a canvas cloth lashed to the deck above. The man looked pale and hollow-faced, but the sea-sickness that had crippled him was passing. Some of the humour and resilience of the soldier was returning. Mike told him what had happened.

'Aye, I could see it coming one day. She's a misguided lady and verra' verra' bitter. Aye Miss Delia will take it hard.'

'Was she close to her mother?' asked Clare.

'Aye she was that,' Henderson was staring at the lining of the deck above. 'Aye, Mr Walters. Ye dinna' like Miss Delia, but she's a fine lass. I'd give my life for her.'

'Mr Henderson,' said Clare. 'We've still got the IRA guns aboard and four of those Basques.' She was staring down at Henderson with a touch of menace. 'OK, whose side are you on?'

'I'm na' on the side of yon dagos if that's what's troubling ye.'

'Good man, because sick or not, we may need you to bat for Britain.' She smiled at Mike. 'Is that the right expression?'

'Cricket,' Henderson grumbled, 'that's for the bluidy English.'

'Yes,' said Clare with a rather light-headed laugh. 'The bloody English. Well done Henderson, you and me will get on just fine.'

Mike had a talk with Jean-Luc. It was clear they would not be able to work back to Ireland while the gale lasted. Mike was more worried about the Basques than he cared to admit. The men were professional sailors and obviously thankful for their rescue. However they were connected with terrorists. They might not be bomb throwers themselves but they must have known the nature of their voyage. That man Carlos was a real puzzle. He seemed wholly untroubled and detached from events. Yet here was one fit man at large who might be armed. Mike voiced his fears to Jean-Luc. The Frenchman shook his head. 'Him not make trouble – all OK.'

Mike opened the stern locker and fished out Henderson's handgun. It was an automatic with a live magazine in the butt. He slipped it in the deep pocket of his waterproof.

For five hours they lay hull to while the storm continued to howl around them. Gradually the sky lightened, the sun broke through and solid cloud became masses of fluffy cumulus. The bright sun made the mountainous seas even more spectacular. Below decks Clare reported the Basques to be badly shaken and not inclined to trouble. Carlos had voluntarily manned the galley and was attempting to produce hot food.

As the afternoon wore on the gusts began to lose their sting. The gale was blowing itself out, though the waves seemed as big as ever. At three o'clock they saw a helicopter. Mike recognized it as a Royal Navy *Sea King*. He went below and called to it on radio channel sixteen. The chopper replied at once brusquely demanding their name. Mike answered and reported the loss of the *Juanita*. The helicopter made off eastward. Twenty minutes later a second chopper arrived. Clare identified it as an Irish Air Corps machine. It flew low over them, and vanished over the horizon.

An hour passed and Mike was relieved to see that the waves were definitely smaller. The wind had abated to a steady force five. It was time to make sail. He saw Clare waving from the cabin hatch.

'Radio,' she said. 'I've got the Baltimore lifeboat.'

Mike was surprised. 'Lifeboat, how did they come to be out here?'

'They were standing by a coaster ship and they picked up our talk with the Juanita. They called back but it seems we didn't hear them.'

'Give them my thanks, but they can go home – we're all right.'

'There's something else, Michael. They've been instructed to take the *Juanita's* crew ashore.'

'Who told them?'

'They got the message from that helicopter – the Irish one.'

'They'll have to launch a boat.'

'I know, the coxswain says that's OK.'

'Fine, give 'em our position and tell 'em to come on over.'

The lifeboat appeared on cue, forty minutes later. Mike gripped the butt of the pistol inside his jacket and with Jean-Luc and Henderson on either side he told the Basques they were to change ships. The lifeboat was a big Tyne class vessel, tall and impressive, as she closed to within fifty yards. Her inflatable bounced and corkscrewed over the still turbulent divide and dropped alongside. One by one the men jumped from *Quadra.* They looked a nervous forlorn, bunch. Only Carlos spared Mike and Clare a grin and a wave. As the lifeboat turned away another aircraft roared over them. It was a twin-engine fixed wing type, with French Navy markings. Mike glanced at Jean-Luc who said nothing. Westward the sun was setting and they were sailing again. They were under reefed mainsail and half jib, bumping and banging upwind towards Ireland. Night came and the wind dropped to no more than force three. Mike shook out the reefs and *Quadra* was under full sail again. As always in the aftermath of a great storm the seas were a long time dying. It was a difficult night for those on watch and harder for those resting below. None of them had had proper sleep for twenty-four hours and the motion made it hard to rest. Mike felt utterly drained. Mentally and physically he'd been tested as never before. Maria's death was not his fault but it played on his mind. The euphoria that had gripped him during the gale was gone. He was enveloped in a black cloud of depression. For the moment he was tearful and trembling. With an effort of will he held the tiller and concentrated on the compass.

At dawn they were still thirty miles from the Irish coast. It was Clare who first saw the warship. Mike identified her as a British type 22 frigate. A second smaller ship was pounding up from the east at speed.

'She's Irish,' said Clare excitedly. 'One of ours.'

This second ship was closing on them fast. Soon they could see her stark functional outline and the Irish tricolour ensign. The radio crackled, it was the Irish ship. A polite order, there was no other term for it. *Quadra* was requested to heave to and accept a boarding party. Clare grinned as Mike pleaded with the British ship to intervene. There was no reply.

'I don't believe this,' he said plaintively. 'Arrested by the Irish Navy – I'll never live it down.'

The visiting boat was a grey rigid-inflatable, with a crew of three. Mike caught the line and secured the boat while two of the occupants came aboard. Then the third man, the helmsman, took the boat away. For all his ribaldry about the Irish Navy, Mike looked with interest at the arrivals. Certainly they were Navy men, much the same as seen the world over.

'Mr Walters,' said the first man. 'I'm Lieutenant Delaney and this is Petty Officer Roche.'

'Welcome aboard,' said Mike. 'I'd better introduce you to the owner.' He turned to Clare. She had just unfurled their Irish ensign in its place on the stern. Mike had the feeling he was outnumbered.

'Great to meet you,' said the lieutenant. 'Say, how about putting that kettle on?'

One by one they lifted the boxes on deck and piled them in the cockpit. Lieutenant Delaney sat, notebook in hand, while his colleague opened each in turn. The navy men made a full inventory of the contents. These included ammunition, handguns, grenades and seven AK 47s. The Irishmen became exited over one box; it contained a surface-to-air missile launcher.

'You could knock a helicopter out of the sky with that,' said Delaney.

He turned to Jean-Luc. 'My government and your government have agreed the immediate destruction of these weapons.'

'What about the British government?' asked Mike.

'They'll be told soon enough.'

'How are you going to destroy them?'

Delaney laughed. 'We'll send 'em to the Welsh Government.'

'Eh?'

'That's right, we'll give 'em to Davy Jones right now.'

Ten minutes later the last box had vanished beneath the waves.

'Best place for 'em,' said Delaney. 'Now Miss O'Dwyer, we are going to take your vessel into our dock in Cobh. I am instructed that no proceedings are to be taken against you, but you will be required to sign a declaration of secrecy. You will attend a debriefing. When you have completed that we will release the yacht.'

'What about me?' asked Mike.

'I'm told that you and Mr Henderson are already bound by your country's Official Secrets Act.'

'There you are, Michael,' said Clare. 'Delia's still got you by the balls.'

With all sail set *Quadra* reached Cobh Harbour in the mid-afternoon. Clare was taken ashore while the rest of them were ordered to stay on board. Two hours later Clare returned and reported that they were free to leave. *Quadra* motored the last few miles to Clare's own mooring at Crosshaven. They tidied the yacht as best they could, inflated the dinghy, and landed at the yacht club.

'I want you all to come over to my flat,' said Clare.

Henderson coughed. 'It's verra good o' you, Miss, but I canna' stay. Miss Delia may need me.' With that he vanished into the crowds.

'Come on,' said Clare to the others. 'We've no wheels now so let's be walking.'

Clare's penthouse flat was a modern apartment with a glass-roofed sunroom. She opened the front door and looked around, relieved that nothing had been touched. She showed Mike and Jean-Luc into the sitting room and poured them all a drink. She began to work through the messages stacked on her answerphone. Mike listened with half an ear. They were routine calls mostly: a literary agent, someone selling insurance, and then...!

'Miss O'Dwyer, Clare? This is Peter Blair of Cotton's Hard. I need to speak to Mike urgently. I tried a radio link to *Quadra* but you didn't hear me. If you read this, please find Mike and get him to ring me at once – it's urgent.'

Clare pushed the phone across. 'That's the code,' she said, pointing to his name on a card above her desk. Mike dialled and seconds later Leanne answered.

'Pete's away in Lymington,' she said.

'Do you know what this is about? He said it was urgent.'

There was a pause. He could tell she was nervous. 'I think...I think it's...'cos we've still got people asking questions.' She hesitated and then the words came in a torrent. 'They're weird... Pete's worried, and I'm scared. I've been going home early, and we've still got Benny, but Pete doesn't know if we can afford him, but Benny says Clare's still paying his firm even though the boat's gone. Please, Mike, come back...I'm frightened.'

'All right, calm down. I promise I'll be back on the first flight I can get on – OK?'

'Thanks Mike, I'll tell Peter.'

Mike put the phone down with a sigh. The girl was plainly nervous, almost on the edge of panic. Was it justified or just a hang-up from her experience that night in the car.

'Stupid bimbo, is there really trouble, or just her dreaming?'

Clare looked at him coldly. 'Can't you see that poor child is besotted over you?'

'Rubbish.'

'If you can't see it everybody else does. So when you go home you'll be tactful.'

Mike shrugged. He suddenly had a vision of Leanne, vodka sodden, standing naked and inviting at the foot of his stairs. Thank God that night he'd been too worried to take the bait.

PART THREE

'It'll be nice having my motor back,' said Clare. Her car was where she had left it all those weeks before outside Mike's converted barn flat. It was the afternoon, twenty-four hours after their arrival at Crosshaven. Now they were back where it had all started, at Cottons Hard. Mike was deeply thankful to be home. The gale they had fought off southern Ireland had tracked away north and had been a mere squib here in Sussex. Now the sun was shining again, the creek was full of water, and the channel moorings crowded with smart newly-launched yachts. Only apprehension marred what should have been a perfect homecoming.

'We'll go down to the Yard in minute,' he said. 'I'll take a look inside first and leave our bags.'

He unlocked the front door and took in the remembered scene. The apartment smelt of polish and air freshener.

'Cleaner's been in,' he muttered. 'Let's hope nobody else has.' He walked across the room; Clare followed.

'Nothing's touched,' he said at last. 'But Delia's people wouldn't leave a trace.'

In the end they decided to walk the quarter of a mile to the yard. It was the same creekside route that Mike had followed the night Leanne had crashed her car and drowned one of her abductors. It all seemed so long ago. Much had happened since then and there had been times when he'd wondered if he'd ever see these sights again.

When they had departed on their voyage the yard had been full of laid up yachts. Now it was empty apart from a few long-term repair jobs. He could see a handful of parked cars; yard customers had free parking in summer. One of these cars must be either coming or going. On the far side under the trees Mike could hear the drum of a diesel vehicle.

As they entered the office Leanne leapt to her feet in excitement. Peter it seemed was still away on a refit contract while she held the fort.

'Who are these people you say are asking questions?' said Mike.

'I dunno,' Leanne pulled a face. 'But they're weird.'

'In what way?'

'Asking about you in the pub.'

'What pub?'

'The George.'

'What sort of things?'

Leanne bit her lip. 'I don't like to say.'

'Oh come on, spit it out. Did you hear them yourself?'

'No, but they upset my granddad.'

'Old Wotek?'

'Yes, they knew stuff about our family in the war in Poland.'

'Delia!' Clare almost spat the name. 'That's got to be her people.'

'Who's Delia?'

'She's a relation of Clare's and she's bad news.' Mike had been staring out of the window. That parked car was still there, its engine idling. He badly wanted to talk to Clare alone.'

'Leanne, d'you know whose car that is?'

'Not sure.'

'Whoever it is he's left the engine running, it's a diesel, it could tick over for ever. Slip over and see if there's a problem.'

Leanne left the room and clattered down the wooden steps.

'I don't like any of this,' said Mike. 'I suppose it was too much to hope that Delia would leave us alone.'

'I thought she'd be after me, but I'm much more worried about her trying to dig dirt about you.'

'Are we certain it's her?'

'Yes, I know...' Clare's words died, obliterated by a terrified scream from outside the building.

It was Leanne's voice carrying across the yard and through the open window. They saw her running erratically, sobbing and wailing. Mike raced down the steps as the distraught girl fell into his arms.

'Stay here. Look after her!' Mike snapped at Clare. He sprinted towards the still drumming engine.

The car was a Peugeot estate. From its exhaust pipe ran a length of hose through the driver's side window. Behind the wheel was a man; a dead man. Mike could see the lolling head and the distorted purple features. Even in death he recognised him. Indeed they had parted just twenty-four hours earlier. He was staring at the dead body of Corporal Henderson.

By lucky chance the first police car to reach the scene was driven by Garry, the constable with the missing ear lobe. The same Garry who'd come the night they caught the first intruder.

'D'you know this man?' Garry asked. He looked with indifference at the corpse in the driving seat.

'Yes, I can give you a name. I can tell you who employs him and I can give you an idea where he lives.'

Garry scribbled a note on his pad. He frowned when Mike mentioned the security services but made no comment.

'Look, it's not my place to tell you your job,' said Mike. 'But I think you could have a murder on your hands.'

'Nothing would surprise me where the spooks are concerned – they've done it before. But this looks like a copybook suicide. No, I'd say he topped himself.'

'Will there be fingerprint men coming?'

'Yes, in half an hour or so – why?'

'Garry, I'm not trying to play Sherlock Holmes but I think they should check the passenger door inside as well as out.'

'They'll do that anyway.'

'Fine, I'll tell you why. This car's a mess because I ripped out the hose and smashed the window to stop the engine, but as I did so I noticed something. The gap around the hose was sealed with a strip of linen. That cloth was pushed in from the outside. So to kill himself Henderson must have climbed in from the passenger side and then locked the door himself.'

'In that case our lads will find the prints and frankly Mike, I think they will.'

Garry went back to the police car where his patrol partner was already radioing a report. Clare had walked across and was standing beside Mike. 'Henderson, oh no!' she was pale with the shock of recognition.

'How's Leanne?' he asked.

'She's calm now. I'll run her home presently. Henderson, of all people. Poor man, did he really kill himself, and why here?'

'Clare, I'm sure he was murdered. I think we're being warned.'

'Would Delia kill Henderson? He was devoted to her.'

Mike faced Clare and his face was grim. 'I've told you how Delia killed an ape?'

'Yes?'

'The creature's name was Diamond. I'm not a wild sentimentalist where animals are concerned and this Diamond bit me, I've still got the mark.'

'I know, I dressed the wound again when we reached Ireland, remember?'

'Delia pointed the gun at that ape and it stared at her. It was a terrible thing – their expressions are almost human – like ours. Just before she pulled the trigger it stared at her. I've never seen such an expression of love and trust.'

'I can believe it. The animals in that place are the only living things she has any feelings for.'

'She told me she was executing Diamond for a breach of discipline and as a warning to me. You see, however devoted Henderson was to Delia, it wasn't reciprocated. I think he died because he failed and, like Diamond, he served a double purpose as a warning to us.'

'Do you fancy eating out this evening?' Mike looked at Clare uncertain of her reaction.

'I don't feel like eating anything after what I've just seen. I won't sleep too well either.'

They were back in Mike's flat. Clare had taken a very subdued Leanne back to her mother's house in Midhurst. After a couple of hours the police had removed both the dead body and the car. Garry told Mike, off the record, that the Peugeot had been stolen that morning in Portsmouth. How Henderson came to be in it at Cottons Hard was a mystery.

Henderson's death had shaken Mike as much as anything that had happened to him in the last month. He felt a gamut of emotions: fear anger and, strangely, grief. Poor Henderson, the man was a simpleton, but there was something deeply touching about his misguided loyalty to Delia Lazarraga. Like the poor ape, Diamond, Henderson's devotion was transparent. Yet Henderson had died, not the dignified death of a soldier, but in a squalid staged suicide. Mike was moved by the pathos of it all, and then he felt anger. He made a private vow that if he came through this nightmare alive he would restore Corporal Henderson to the soldierly honour he deserved. The world would know the truth.

Clare was staring at him. 'Why do you want to eat out?'

Mike offered a weak smile. 'I thought we might have a pub meal at the George.'

'Hey, I've heard that name.'

'I know, it's where Leanne's grandfather was asked questions, by whom we know not.'

'But we could make a pretty sure guess?'

'Exactly, I think it's time we had a chat with Mr Wotek Micalczyk. He's usually in there weekdays.'

The George was a large modern pub on the edge of town not far from the coast motorway. Among the regulars was old Wotek, the Polish dustman, raconteur, Eighth Army veteran and Leanne's grandfather. Mike glanced around the crowded bar and smiled; Wotek was in his usual place.

'Hello Mr Micalczyk,' Mike held out his hand.

'Meesteer Walters, is good to see you. Most fortunate – to you I have to speak.'

'I wanted a word as well. This is Miss Clare O'Dwyer.'

Clare gave the old man a dazzling smile and held out her hand. They sat down and Mike ordered drinks. 'You've heard what happened today?' he asked.

'Oh yes, bad business. My son tells me. The man kills himself and our leetle girl finds him – bad business.'

Mike nodded and lowered his voice. 'Leanne says someone's been asking questions?' He looked at Wotek and waited.

'Oh yes, Mr Walters, I say to you be careful.'

'Why?'

'Look, I am Polish. I know what I speak about. See, Great Britain is my country now, but even here there are two kinds of police. There are our true police, our Bobbies, yes?'

'And the other sort?' Clare was staring at him.

'Just so, even in England there are the other police, the one's you never see.'

'What happened?' asked Mike.

'A week ago two men walk in here. They tell me to come outside.'

'What for?'

'They pretend they are the police, the true police, but I do not believe them. They ask questions about you…'

'Oh they did, did they?'

'Mr Walters, please do not be angry with me. I believe not one word of what they tell me.'

'What did they say?'

'They say you make love to my little Leanne. They say for a long time, even when she was not sixteen…'

'Bloody hell,' Mike exploded in fury. Clare pinched his arm as people nearby began to stare.

'Please Mr Walters. Is not true, I know is not true. I tell them so, I tell them go hell!'

'Michael, sit down!' Clare hissed. 'Nobody blames you – this is Delia's work. Mr Micalczyk,' she continued, 'please go on.'

The old man gave a long sigh. 'Then they tell me all about my Uncle Jerz. That he was a traitor and a camp guard for the Nazis. They say I should have reported this and if I do not spy on you I will lose my pension.'

'They can't do that,' said Mike, 'no way!'

'I know, this is Great Britain, we are a democracy. I tell them so, I tell them go hell.'

'Well done, good man,' said Clare.

'Afterwards I warn Leanne and Mr Peter Blair. Nothing happens until this morning. These people come back. They walk into my house without asking and this time I am frightened.'

'What happened?' asked Clare.

'They are the same men but also a woman. It is she who frightens me. You see, I remember…'

'Woman!' Clare snapped. 'What was she like?'

'Very thin, black hair, and face so white.'

'Delia, yes we know her.'

Wotek paused while he drained the rest of his beer. A change had come over him. There was a troubled, far away look on his face. He twice opened his mouth to speak and then shook his head. When he spoke he was at first barely audible above the background chatter of the bar.

'I remember,' he muttered. 'I remember when I was a boy in Poland and I am frightened. Then I say no. Now I am an Englishman and these swine can do nothing. I stand in front of them, my good wife beside me. I tell them how the day before I run away from Poland the Gestapo came for my father. It was winter 1940, there was snow on the ground.' There was a wild look in Wotek's eyes; it was the same look Mike had seen in Maria's face the evening before she died. 'Today I tell the white face, "When the Gestapo came one of them was a woman and she was just like you".'

The whole room was silent. All eyes were drawn to the old man as he sat transfixed, tears streaming down his face. Very gently Clare reached out and gave him a hug. Wotek sat there, hearing and seeing nothing. Clare beckoned Mike to follow. They left the pub and drove home.

Neither of them felt much like eating after that, so they stopped at a takeaway and brought their supper home with them. Mike sat on the sofa, head in hands. Never in his life had he felt so confused. Three weeks ago this had all been a great adventure. Now it seemed more of a dark tunnel with no light and no escape.

'Clare, why is Delia leaning on me?'

'You know too much and so do I. We both know about Maria and the arms shipment, and I would say Delia still thinks I've got those papers.'

'And if we're in her way?'

'She'll rub us both out. She wouldn't have a second thought about it.'

'She can try, but we'll be on our guard from now on. But tell me, why is she persecuting old Wotek and feeding him with all this innuendo about me and Leanne?'

Clare sighed. 'Quite honestly I don't know. I can only think she means to blackmail you.'

'Like hell she will. I'll fight her all the way. It's some sort of justice that she picked on Wotek. He's probably the only person around here who can see her for what she is.'

'Michael, is it safe for us to sleep here?'

Mike grinned. 'No, but I think we have a social duty to fulfil.'

Clare looked at him and raised an eyebrow.

'Yes,' he said. 'We'll take a trip down the road to Eastleigh. I think it's time I introduced you to my mother.' He stood up and reached for his car keys. 'I'll phone from the box in the village. They can listen to our mobiles and they could have this one here tapped.'

They arrived in Mike's hometown of Eastleigh at ten o'clock. Joy, his widowed mother, lived in a council house on a sprawling development. Clare looked around with interest at the cheerless rows of dwellings surrounding a little triangle of green with its children's swings and slides. Forewarned by Mike, Joy was expecting them. She threw open the door, hugged her son, and shook hands warmly with Clare.

'My you're older than I expected,' said Joy. Clare was surprised but couldn't think of a suitable answer.

'Hey Mum, who said anything about age?' It was not like his mother to be tactless and he was puzzled.

'Oh don't worry – it's something I was told that's all.'

'Told,' said Mike. 'You're the first person we've told since we came back to England.'

Joy looked at Clare. 'You're Irish aren't you?'

Clare nodded, waiting.

'That's nice. Kind people the Irish – no side to them – unlike some

I could name.'

'Take no notice, Clare. Mum never took to Annabel.'

'That miss-nose-in-the-air-smarty-pants,' said Joy. 'You're not like that Clare, I can tell.'

'No she's not,' Mike laughed.

'Clare,' said Joy. 'You can have Mike's old room and he'll sleep down here on the settee. That's my rule. Boys will be boys, Clare, and there's always a time to slap 'em down.'

Clare smiled; there was something refreshingly straightforward about this potential mother-in-law.

Joy led Clare upstairs, showed her the room and left her. Downstairs she caught her son's arm and pulled him into the lounge.

'I shouldn't have said that about her being older, it just slipped out. You see, I was told something about you and it's been on my mind.'

'What has?'

'I had a man call in here a few days back – a vicar.'

'Eh?'

'That's right, a vicar. He said he came from over your way. He wanted to talk about you young man.'

Mike stared in astonishment. 'I hardly know my vicar.'

'I didn't say he was your vicar, but you'd better hear what he said while your young lady's out of the way.'

'OK, carry on.'

'The vicar said you were harassing a young girl in your office. The girl is a parishioner of his and he's very concerned for her welfare. Now I like what I've seen of your Clare and I won't have her deceived – right?'

'Mum, I give you my word the girl in the office is eighteen years old. I have no interest in her and any harassing has come from the other direction. Also this is the second time this evening I've heard this rumour, and what's more, I was warned about it by the girl's grandfather and he agrees it's rubbish.'

Joy smiled. 'I believe you son. I can't tell you what a weight off my mind it is to hear you say that.'

'Thanks Mum.' Mike was shaken. This was another of Delia's ploys. Suddenly a distant memory came hazily to mind. 'Mum, this vicar, did he say what village he came from?'

'No, I don't think so – just that the girl was a parishioner.'

'Did he say what denomination he was? You know, C of E, Methodist, RC, which?'

'Oh definitely Church of England. I asked him that and he said yes.'

'Thanks Mum,' he bent down and kissed her. 'You've just confirmed my suspicions.'

'Have I?'

'I'll tell you later when I know for certain. Just take it from me you've had a wind-up – you know a hoax.'

'Who was he then? He looked the part – took me in.'

'There's nothing to worry about, Mum. It was a joke, one in rather bad taste, I think. All part of business rivalry, it's the modern world.'

'I'm more worried than ever now. I think you should tell the police.'

'I might well do that.'

'Mike, you'll be careful?' Joy looked tense and anxious. Mike wondered if he should tell her the whole story. No, that would really frighten her for no useful purpose.

He smiled at her. 'Yes, Mum, I'll be careful.'

He left her and ran upstairs to Clare. He told her what he'd heard.

'Delia spreading more dirt,' she said.

'Yes, but not very cleverly this time. She's not done her home-work. You see the bogus vicar said he was C of E, but I happen to know the whole Micalczyk clan are RC – like you lot.'

Clare did not comment at once; she looked inscrutable. 'I'm trying to work my way into Delia's mind. I've thought about blackmail but it won't wash – it's too crude. Oh Michael, I wish we'd stayed in Ireland.'

'Too late to think that. I had to come home sometime.'

'Michael, would your mother mind if I made some phone calls – I can pay with my card?'

'Of course she won't mind.'

Mike pointed her to the telephone in the hallway and went into the kitchen where his mother was making coffee. Five minutes later Clare came in.

'Michael, I've got to go to London first thing.'

'London?'

'I've an appointment to see Colonel Newhoffer. I rang his place in Ireland but they said he's in London. They gave me the number and I've just spoken to him. He's very insistent that I see him, but on my own.'

Next morning Mike drove Clare to the station and put her on a train for London. By nine thirty he was back at Cottons Hard. Peter Blair's car was outside the office and Mike went to find him. Peter was installing a new engine in a motor yacht. He wiped his oily hands and grinned a welcome.

'Where's the lovely Clare?'

'Gone to London for the day.'

'Good, because I'd like a word in private.'

'Not Leanne again?' Mike grimaced.

'Go easy on her, Mike. It seems you set off to deliver a yacht and you've come back with a wife. The poor kid's not happy, and she's still shook up over that bloke killing himself.'

'Point taken. Is there any news about the dead man?'

'No, the police are being very cagey about the whole thing.'

Mike nodded. 'I've a notion why. I mentioned Leanne because someone's spreading malicious rumours.'

'I know,' said Peter. 'I've had some of it this week. Look, last Tuesday we had a man turn up to look at the books – said he was a VAT inspector. I wasn't here at the time but Leanne showed him the records. He tells her we've been illegally withholding contributions. He hinted you had a hand in the till – wanted to now where you were.'

'That's a bloody lie. The records are spot on and all the cheques have cleared – they're on the bank statement.'

'All right – calm down. I'm sure you're right. Anyway I rang the local VAT office and they know nothing about any inspection.'

'It all fits with what's happening.'

'You'd better tell me.'

'Yes I had. Sit down Pete. I'll tell you the whole yarn and you'd better believe it.'

CHAPTER 38

Clare reached the United States Embassy in Grosvenor Square at ten thirty. She paid the taxi and stood looking nervously at the massive building. All her instincts made her fear this place: a building that symbolized American hegemony. Her student days and her Sorbonne teachers had only reinforced inborn prejudices. However, she had an appointment in ten minutes and she had an urgent need keep it.

She was received coldly while the reception made a long internal phone call. She was taken into a small bare room and given a superficial search by two incredibly ugly women. Then she was led through a maze of corridors, two elevator ascents, and finally into a wing accessed with swipe card and a key code. Through this door was a complex of offices and computer rooms. The whole place stank of the CIA.

Her escort left her sitting on a chair in a sort of waiting alcove. She sat there for ten minutes. Though various people flitted along the passage nobody spoke to her. Beside her was a glass topped coffee table spread with magazines. The one on top lay open at its centre page. It was one of those glossy chat papers featuring the aristocracy, film celebrities and the mega-rich. Clare glanced at it, and then grabbed it from the table. It announced the engagement of Toni Constantinescu to Miss Annabel de Bouillet. The smiling couple was shown posing in full colour sitting on a sofa in some lavish drawing room. It was all a million miles from Cottons Hard. For the hundredth time Clare wondered how her Michael could have become so besotted with this shallow bimbo. Ruefully she also wondered what it was she had seen in the vain and not over bright Toni. In the end Toni would be doing her a favour by firmly removing Annabel from the scene.

Her reverie was broken by a familiar voice. It was a voice she would rather forget.

'Miss O'Dwyer, I'm Jonathan Van Outen. I guess you remember me?' She hadn't seen the man walk up to her. Now he was standing grinning down at her. The tone was unfriendly with a touch of aggression.

'Of course I remember you, you bastard. You broke into my bedroom and tried to blackmail me with a lot of pictures.' She gave him the full force of her eye contact. She well knew the power she had and she made it tell. Van Outen shook his head as if it hurt and took a pace backwards.

'That photograph you stole,' he gloated. 'Don't go thinking it's the only copy. Yeah, little seventeen year old chick, lying naked on that great big bed – nice…'

Clare's temper, held in check for days, finally broke. She stepped forward and handed the man a stinging slap to the face, followed by a deft kick towards his crotch. It was something she had learned in self-defence lessons but never practiced. The kick lacked enough force to hurt, but Van Outen staggered back. He had a look of blank astonishment that hardened into cold anger. 'I'll remember that, you bitch,' he hissed. 'Your grandpa' was a commie and your mother was a whore, an' don't think I can't prove it.'

'Hey, what goes on?' The voice came from behind her. She spun round as she recognized Carl Newhoffer, the man she had come to see.

'It seems this guy has a taste for naked teenage girls.' Clare was feeling both triumphant and vindictive. 'Might lay him open to blackmail, don't you think?' Van Outen said nothing but his look was murderous.

'Clare, it's good to see you again. Come in here and we'll talk.' Newhoffer waved her into a side room. It was a nondescript place with only a table and some stack chairs. Last time she had met this man she had been in New York with Granpapa. That must have been…

'Six years ago,' Newhoffer interrupted perceptively. 'Jim and me, we took you to a show on Broadway.' Newhoffer looked exactly the same as on that day. He was an impressive figure: a man in his mid sixties but still attractive.

'I met that CIA goon in Dublin,' he said. 'What was that about teenage girls?'

'A couple of weeks back he and some others broke into our hotel bedroom in Paris. I was sleeping with my boyfriend. They started asking questions about Grandfather and Flanagan. I didn't know a thing about it, but Van Outen wouldn't believe me. He produced a lot of photographs to blackmail me.'

'How serious?'

'Pathetic. It was when I was in Mexico with Granpapa and Toni Constantinescu. I was only seventeen but I let Toni into my bed because I thought he loved me.'

Newhoffer nodded. 'So?'

'Toni had a camera. He took a lot of pictures of me and some of them were a bit naughty. I wouldn't give a damn normally, but I'm in a new relationship and I didn't want my boyfriend, Michael, to see them.'

'You like this Michael Walters?'

'More than like. We're getting married in the summer,' she paused. 'If only we can get out of this trouble we're in.'

'Now that's where I can help you.' He smiled at her benevolently. She thought, but for Michael, she could easily fall for this man, even though he must be forty years older.

'Can you give us some protection?' She found herself gabbling nervously. 'I've left Michael on his own in Sussex. I'm sure Delia's looking for him. She killed a man in his yard yesterday as a sort of warning we think…' she knew she was sounding hysterical.

'Clare,' he called her to order. 'Cool it, just tell me your story from the beginning and then I'll see what I can do.'

Newhoffer listened for full quarter of an hour, the time it took for Clare to unburden herself. She ended breathless but happier. She no longer felt utterly alone.

'I believe your tale, Clare,' he said at last. 'It fits with everything I've heard. I'll tell you as much as I can. Now first thing – you're worried about Delia and what she might be planning?'

'Yes, I'm certain she's after us. Otherwise why kill Henderson?'

'Assuming it was murder?'

'We know it was,' Clare was adamant. She had to make this man see the seriousness of their plight. How well did he know Delia?

'Clare,' said Newhoffer. 'I will do all I can to help you. Trouble is neither you nor Michael are American citizens. The Brits control their own country though they may not control Delia. I can have a quiet word with someone I know in the Home Office; I guess he'll tell the police down in Sussex something is going on.'

'Is that all you can do? We might both be dead by the time your Home Office friend does anything.'

Newhoffer stared at her. Clare bit her lip and strove for calm; she must look every inch the panicking female.

'All right,' he said at last. 'When we've finished our business I'll drive down to Sussex and be around tonight. If Delia's planning anything it'll be tonight – tomorrow she's due back in Ireland.'

'Thanks Colonel Newhoffer,' she said meekly. Suddenly she felt almost overwhelmed with relief.

'And don't call me Colonel – Carl will do fine.'

'Whose side is Delia on?' she asked.

'Her own mostly, but despite the *Juanita* affair she's just about on the side of the angels. Now look Clare, Delia's opened peace talks with the Provisional IRA. I've been given a brief by the President of the United States to oversee those talks; umpire them if you like. Delia's the only person on the British side that the Provisionals will talk with. The other delegates on our side represent the Republic of Ireland.'

'One of em's that ugly fellow – Michael's met him,' Clare stated.

'Ugly's a subjective notion. D'you know his name?'

'Brogan, Michael said it was.'

'I know, Garda man. The Chief negotiator on the Irish side, if you must know, is your step-father.'

'Noel!' Clare was scornful. 'You really think that Noel Shaw-Mulligan can change the fate of a nation? Carl you are an optimist.'

'You shouldn't denigrate your stepfather. He's a shrewd operator, and as a politician he reminds me of your grandfather.' He looked at her severely and she suddenly felt very young. 'Why this venom anyway? Is it because he's a stepfather? Why, my first daughter is older than my second wife, but we all get on fine.'

'Noel said my father was queer.' That wasn't the real reason she disliked Noel. There wasn't really a reason. It was just the man's attitude.

'He said that did he?' Newhoffer looked questioningly at her. 'Did he elaborate?'

'No.'

'OK, we're drifting away from our purpose here. I want to talk about Flanagan. About your grandfather and Flanagan.'

'Here we go again,' Clare was exasperated. 'I keep telling everyone, I'd never heard of Flanagan before a month ago, and I haven't got any papers.'

'Not physically you haven't,' Newhoffer was weighing his words. 'I've an idea where they might be, but it's you that has the key to them.'

'I haven't got any keys. Anyway what's in these papers? It's about time I knew.'

'No it isn't. That's top classified information. I've only been given the full briefing today. As for keys, there's more than one definition of key. Listen, about a year before he died I met your grandfather in New York. He told me then that he had some documents from way back. They concerned Ireland and he was afraid they might be dangerous if they fell into the wrong hands. I think he meant to tell me more but we were interrupted.'

'Yes, but what has all this to do with me and where does this key come in?'

'Give me half a chance and I'll tell you. Before we parted he said, "those papers, they're safe for now. The key to them's in my boat, if you're smart enough to find it." Just that and I never saw him again. Next I heard he was dead.

'Granpapa talked in riddles,' Clare was definite. 'There's nothing in that boat and there's no keys.'

'Yes, your grandfather talked riddles.' He pulled a wry face. 'No Clare, the answer's something to do with that boat, so,' he smiled now, 'so that alone is a very good reason for me to look after you.'

An hour later they were in Newhoffer's London home just off Chelsea's Sloane Square. Clare sipped her cup of coffee. She felt relieved, so calm at last that she was almost languid. She hadn't slept well last night and twice she had caught herself nodding. Carl Newhoffer was sitting at his desk accessing some computer files. Clare knew better than to interrupt him. It would all be so peaceful here had she not felt this fear. Michael was alone in Sussex, and Delia would not be far away, of that she could be certain. Clare jumped as the mobile phone in her pocket shrilled. Who on earth could be calling her? Not Michael, they had agreed that mobiles were not secure from Delia's listeners. Anyway Michael didn't have the number. Very tentatively she pressed the button and put the set to her ear. She heard the voice on the other end: a kindly Irish voice but with the firm authority of a policeman with a duty to perform. Clare heard the words but for a few seconds she could not comprehend what she was told. Then the dam broke, she dropped the telephone on the floor and she leant forward as the tears flowed down her cheeks and her sobs brought Newhoffer to her side, concern and bafflement mixed in the expression on his face.

CHAPTER 39

Peter left the yard midmorning. He was due to carry out two yacht surveys at Hamble and would not be returning that day. Mike could see Peter was anxious. Mike's story had shaken him badly but he never questioned a word of it. 'I'll stay with you if you want,' he said.

'No Pete, sorry, but I think it'd be better if you left me on my own.' He was firm about it. Peter muttered a little but there was something in Mike's demeanour that stilled argument.

Leanne had left a message saying she was sick. Mike was worried about Leanne. If he was honest he would admit to some manly conceit. That he was the object of her teenage fantasies was a nuisance, but flattering too. There were footsteps on the stairs outside and the office door was pushed rudely open, without the courtesy of a knock. Standing on the threshold was Ricky Lofthouse.

Mike was not pleased. He eyed this intruder with distaste. Ricky was chief reporter of the *South Coast Review.* The *Review,* once a staid local newspaper, had been re-launched a couple of years before as a popular tabloid under the guidance of Ricky and a couple more of his ilk. Targeted at the growing seaside conurbation, it revelled in local corruption, the saucier court cases and pictures of topless girls on Wintlesham beach. Mike would have ignored the rag had it not turned its spite on the yachting fraternity. Sailing, said Ricky, was a pastime of the idle and privileged. Ricky never wrote the word yachtsman without first appending the word wealthy. If the lifeboat was called to some hapless low-budget family cruiser, Ricky would call it misuse of the service by a "wealthy yachtsman".

'What d'you want, Lofthouse?' said Mike coldly.

'Information, squire – straight from the horses mouth. I pride myself on accuracy.'

'What d'you want to know?'

'Are United Marinas buying this place?'

'No, of course not.'

'Don't give me that Walters. I heard lots about you.'

'If that's all you've come to say you can clear out now.' Mike was standing, staring angrily.

'You deny this place is down the tubes?' Ricky sneered. 'Who was that geezer who topped himself out there?'

'I've made a full statement to the police. Ask them or go to the inquest.'

'Look Walters, don't throw your weight about with me. When the receivers come into this office you'll be nothing. Your rich yachtie friends won't want to know you, especially when they hear about the little girl.'

'You watch what you say, Lofthouse.'

'I know the rules, boy – I've said nothing. Tell you though; I went to see the girl's parents. Keen on boats they tell me. Seems she's been helping out here since she was fourteen. Very keen that, very keen. Funny, the moment I mention your name her parents clam up – shut the door in my face. Something to hide eh?'

'I don't believe this,' Mike found himself spluttering. 'You try to taint me, that's one thing, but you've no right to involve Leanne after all she's been through…'

'Leanne eh?' Ricky was triumphant . 'You admit you know the girl. Don't worry, I know that kind of half-foreign floosy – ready for a quick lay…' Ricky choked in mid sentence. Mike had him by the shirt collar as he spun him round and thrust him towards the door.

'Assault,' Ricky gasped. 'Common assault – I'll have you for it.'

'I'm not hurting you. I'm within my rights to escort an obnoxious trespasser off the premises. It's your fault when there's a real story staring you in the face which I might have helped you with if you'd been a bit more civil.'

'What story?' said Ricky.

'One the big dailies would kill for.'

'Oh yeah – you tell me then.'

'That depends on how helpful you are. Come back inside – I fancy asking some questions myself.'

Mike was surprised by his own calm. His temper was under control and already his mind was racing ahead.

'Now Ricky, I'll give you some information about the yard. If you've heard a rumour it's in everyone's interest that I give you a straight answer. First I'm pleased to say that far from going bust, we've just completed the most profitable contract we've had so far. We've rebuilt a classic yacht for a lady who really is a wealthy yachtsman, and she's backing our expansion plans.'

'That's fair as far as it goes,' Ricky at least had the honesty to look disappointed. 'Can you substantiate this?'

'Certainly, I'll let you have details if you tell me who it is that's stirring shit for me?'

'I had a call a week back, private investigator. He wanted press cuttings about you and this place.'

'Did he mention the girl?'

'No, that was later. Now look Walters, the girl's another matter, one of my leg-men got that off a social worker. I believe you about the yard, but the girl's different. I've a duty to my readers. *The Review* stands for decency and family values.'

'I must say I hadn't noticed but I'll take your word. Where did this social worker spring from? He hasn't talked to me or to my certain knowledge, the girl's family. Your turn Ricky – prove you're not lying through your teeth.'

'All right, but for starters the social worker's a woman. She cornered our William yesterday afternoon – he's the one who covered the story when the girl crashed her car in the mud.'

'What sort of woman?' Mike blazed the question and the venom in his voice startled Ricky.

'Funny you should ask that. If she's half what Willie says, you're in for a bad time, Walters.'

'And what does Willie say?'

'She frightened the little sod, had him eating out of her hand.' Ricky looked disparaging. 'Unprofessional that – he should've found out as much as he told her.'

'Did he describe her?'

'Sort of, but she scared him. Nothing to look at, he said: scrawny bird, flat chest, pasty face, all eyes. That's what he kept on about. He said those eyes went right through him like they were burning a hole in his guts. I believed him – the lad's not given to flights of fancy.'

'OK Ricky, I'll give you something in exchange. That woman's no more a social worker than Lucrezia Borgia. Now, do you know anyone in Fleet Street who watches MI5?'

'Are you winding me up?'

'No!'

'As a matter of fact Tony Tulloe's an old mate of mine. He knows about as much about the spooks as anyone.'

'Right, ring this Tulloe and tell him there's some funny business going on in these parts, and the lady your man talked to is Delia Lazarraga. I'll spell that for you.' Mike pulled across a note pad and wrote the name. 'I'll bet good money that makes your friend Tulloe jump through the roof.'

Ricky's mobile face was a study. Excitement, egotism, suspicion, followed in quick succession.

'Why should MI5 be after you?'

'No comment.'

'I won't be made a fool of.'

'Look Ricky, you're an enterprising journalist. I'm certain I'm the target of a disinformation campaign, because this Lazarraga woman thinks, wrongly as it happens, that I've got something she wants.'

'What've you been up to?'

'I'll tell you this much. You've been taken for a ride and not by me.'

'Explain?'

'All right, how much did the police tell you about Leanne's car crash?'

'The same as we heard at the inquest. She gave a lift to one of your customers and the car skidded. The man drowned, she got out, it was an accident.'

'Nothing about a dog being shot and a full scale man hunt on the marshes?'

'That was an unrelated story, we were briefed on that. Prisoner escaped from Lewes jail, they caught up with him here but he got away. We ran the story then it all died.'

'Oh dear, Ricky, I doubt if any of the national papers would've been so gullible. Sorry, but you've swallowed everything they wanted you to.'

'How so?'

'Normally you'd be the last man on earth I'd pour out my troubles to, but this time I'm protecting my back.'

'I don't talk off the record to…'

'In this case you'll have to. If you print any of it we'll both be done by the Official Secrets Act.'

Ricky Lofthouse left in a hurry. Mike saw him clatter down the steps and bustle self-importantly across the yard to his BMW. Mike was satisfied. He had set a hare running that Lofthouse and his minions would be bound to follow. If Delia wanted a dirty tricks war she could have one.

What the hell was the woman playing at? What was the point of it all? He would have no difficulty refuting her allegations. He only knew that the suspense was beginning to work on him, as Delia must surely have intended. She was breaking him down, softening him for the time when she would confront him face to face. He felt chilled; he would rather fight the likes of Henderson any day than face that voice and those all-seeing eyes. No, Delia would come to him and somehow he must convince her that he and Clare knew nothing about Flanagan or his papers, and cared even less.

That was untrue of course. Clare was utterly committed to finding the truth about her grandfather. What was it she had been told? The secret lay in the boat. 'It's all in my boat.' James O'Dwyer's own words. They all knew there was nothing physically present in the boat, but that was to underestimate James O'Dwyer. It might be more profitable to look at the man himself. James O'Dwyer: long surviving politician, self-proclaimed Irish hero and code cracker. Now, there was a thought; code cracker. Was there a clue in the yacht's name? '*Quadra* my real name for her,' O'Dwyer had said. 'Take her home to Ireland. There's a secret in her.'

Mike leant against the desk, head in hands. *Quadra,* codes, anagram; or just possibly something so obvious it had been staring him in the face for weeks. He pulled over the note pad and a calculator. On a blank page he wrote three sets of numbers.

At four-thirty Mike left the office for a stroll around the yard. It was a perfect warm May evening. He stopped to chat with some boat owners he knew and then moved on towards the slipway. There were six young men there grouped around a minibus with two wind surfers strapped to its roof. Mike knew none of them but they were a typical yacht crew of a certain genre. Noisy, dressed in cotton jeans and rugby shirts; city men, brokers or merchant bankers, he would guess. How he wished he could escape his nightmare and be part of that innocent scene.

He left the yard and walked to his own flat on the farm. His resolve was hardening. Tonight he would face Delia. He wasn't claiming second sight. He didn't know why he knew; he just knew. Moreover he wasn't running back to his mother's house. The Secret Service men would be watching there by now and he had no intention of involving her. No, he would face what was to come alone and on his own ground.

The farmyard was empty. In the distance he could hear the whine of a silage cutter. He walked to his front door and entered. All was exactly as he'd left it. He made a pot of tea and turned on the television news. More shootings in Belfast: so much for Delia's peace talks. At six-thirty the phone rang. It was Leanne's mother, Linda Micalczyk.

'Sorry to bother you Mike, but Leanne's not come home from work.'

Mike didn't like the sound of this. 'She's not been to work. She left a message that she was sick.'

Linda sounded alarmed. 'She was fine this morning. Oh, the little madam. I'm sorry about this, Mike, but what can she be up to?'

'I'm sure it's nothing. Look, she's had a nasty shock – it's little wonder that she wants to stay away a day or two.'

'It's still not good enough. She should have told us – her father will have a thing or two to say.'

'You'd better check her friends' houses. I expect she's with one of them. What's that boyfriend of hers called?'

'No I've checked there and they haven't seen her. Mike, I'll admit I'm worried. She's had so much happen to her and those horrible people were back last night – the one's who frightened Wotek.'

Mike swallowed nervously. 'I'm sorry about that. You know what they're saying is rubbish?'

'Of course we do. We'll back you through thick and thin. Wotek says it's nothing to do with Leanne. He says it's all about Poland. Poor old man – why can't they leave him alone?'

'Look,' said Mike, 'if she's not back in half an hour, I should ring the police. She's under a lot of stress, poor kid, and we don't want her wandering around.'

He tried to sound reassuring but inwardly he was alarmed. He had visions of the girl walking tearful along some lonely road. Could there be a worse explanation? Leanne had left a message on the office answerphone. She had sounded sick; the voice was blurred and accompanied by some realistic coughing. What a silly deception – he was annoyed for being taken in by it. Could there be a worse explanation? Could the girl be under duress? The last thing he wanted to do was further alarm Linda. Somehow he didn't feel justified in ringing the police himself. Instead he picked up the phone and called the George Hotel. Could he speak to Wotek? The manageress of the George was apologetic. It seemed old Wotek had left only minutes earlier. He had accompanied a woman and a man she'd never seen before.

Mike's stomach lurched, he felt cold. 'Did he seem worried?' he asked.

'Not worried exactly. He looked strange. It was like that night when the skinheads came in with all those swastikas...' At that moment the line went dead. Not even a dial tone, Mike swore softly.

It was eight o'clock and the daylight was fading. Mike walked round the farm buildings. Behind the thin curtains of the farmhouse he caught the flickering blue reflection of a television. A comforting domestic scene, but it only served to make him feel more isolated and apprehensive. A car was coming up the road from the yard with no lights. It was the minibus that he'd seen earlier. Fifty yards short of the farm the driver pulled over onto the grass verge and stopped. Doors opened and the passengers climbed out. Mike's stomach tightened. These were not the jolly yacht crew of earlier that evening. Here were the same men, but dressed now in dark clothing and balaclavas. Not soldiers this time, not terrorists. These were Delia's men. Mike was sure of it and he knew they would be every bit as motivated and dangerous. Twice in the last three weeks he had been caught unprepared. This time he would be ready.

More traffic; a car was coming in from the other direction, down the track from the main road. He waited as it rounded the corner and pulled over in a gateway. He knew the car: Delia's Ford Mondeo, parked in the same place as last time.

Mike sprinted for his front door. As he passed his own car he suppressed a wild impulse to jump in it and mow Delia down where she stood in the road. No, he was resolved to face her and see who was the stronger.

Inside the door Mike felt the wall below the coat pegs. His groping hands found his cricket bat. He picked it up and slowly flexed it through the air. Then on impulse, he turned on the main light and, standing framed in the open doorway, he waited. For half an hour he strained his eyes trying to see beyond the shadows outside. For a few seconds he was sure he saw people, a semi-circle of dark silent figures. He bit his lip fighting to stay calm. There was nothing there: just shrubs and a row of old staddal stones. He came close to panic then. He wanted to run across to the farmhouse and seek sanctuary with his friends. He could hear his own teeth chattering and his whole body was drenched in sweat.

'Come on,' he muttered. 'Come on you bitch – I know you're out there – why don't you show yourself?' He was yelling like a maniac now, the cricket bat raised murderously.

'Walters,' the voice came from behind him.

Mike spun round, open-mouthed, bat raised. Delia stood in the kitchen door. She was dressed in black except for her usual green anorak. She held a pistol and it had a long silencer.

'Walters, put that thing down, you look like an escaped Neander-thal.' Her finger whitened on the trigger. Slowly Mike lowered the bat and let it fall to the floor.

'That's better,' she said. 'Now will you please shut the front door.'

'How did you get in here?' he snarled.

'As you were giving such an embarrassing performance at your front door, I invited myself in through the back.'

'It's locked.'

'So, I unlocked it.' Delia held up a shiny newly cut key.

Inwardly Mike's spirit sank. Clearly he was no match for these people. He felt calmer now. Delia was here, just as he had expected. For his own and Clare's sake he must face her.

'Perhaps you'd care to come into my sitting room?' His ironic politeness must have sounded hollow, but as he spoke the words he was already feeling better, almost relishing the impending challenge.

Delia nodded and pointed to the door. He walked in and sat down. Delia pulled up a second chair. She sat down facing him a few feet away. She had switched on the angled reading lamp and it lit her face from the side. He could not escape seeing every flicker of her eyes.

'I gave you orders to find Charles Venner-Harris,' she said.

'All right, so I found him. Not that I tried looking, he just turned up.'

'O'Dwyer led you to him, exactly as I predicted. You have yet to report to me.'

'There's nothing to report.'

'Did you give him my message?'

'About his uncle? I didn't need to. The Venner-Harris clan never mention Uncle Christopher – they turned his picture to the wall years ago.'

'Venner-Harris is a fool, but Bernard Anderson most certainly is not. What guarantee do I have that Venner-Harris didn't talk, not realizing the damage he was doing?'

'I can promise you he said nothing to Anderson. Where Charles's family honour is at stake he's unbreakable. Anderson didn't try to beat it out of him. He knew it wouldn't work and you might as well know that too.'

'Very well. Now Walters, we turn to you.' Delia's tone had changed. Her black hair and nondescript features had faded. He saw only her dark eyes reflected in the lamplight. The full power of the woman's personality washed through him; skimming off layer after layer of his self-esteem until there was nothing left to hide. They were all-seeing those eyes, exposing his inner private world, his childhood memories, his teen years, and all those remembered little embarrasssments that still made him cringe. He could never explain what was happening. It wasn't hypnotism – he was not asleep, he still had control of his limbs and speech. He could walk away if he wished. He knew he was being slowly mastered by a personality and a stronger will.

It was his anger and stubbornness that saved him. Without them he would have been destroyed. He stared into her eyes, fighting fire with fire, until he also had broken through the two-way mirror and entered the mind of his enemy. He recoiled from the force of an awesome intellect, grounded from childhood in malice and hate.

'I want the Flanagan file,' she said softly. 'Where is it and where is O'Dwyer?'

'Oh God,' Mike groaned. 'Clare doesn't know where it is. Peyron doesn't know, and the old priest McGee doesn't think the papers exist. Anderson doesn't know where they are and if Charles knows he's not telling. So, once and for all, you're wasting your time with us.' He sat back and slowly, deliberately stared into her eyes. Again those eyes burned into him, sucking at his mind, questing the truth. They no longer held terror. In his turn he stared back, drove out the power and extinguished it as easily as switching off a light.

'Walters, you are not co-operating!' For the first time he detected an emotion; anger.

'I don't know the answers – I can't help you, that's final.'

Delia had moved her gaze and was staring over his shoulder. She gave a curt nod to someone behind him. A man appeared with a burden in his arms. It was the limp body of a girl, her long blonde tresses half covering her face. He laid her down on the sofa. Another man followed; he carried a metal rack with two small cylinders. Delia stood and bent over the girl pulling back the hair to show her face. Mike stood up startled and angry. The girl was Leanne.

'You evil bitch,' he shouted. 'You've murdered her.'

'She's only sleeping,' said Delia. 'Look at her, does she seem dead?'

It was true, the slight form on the sofa was breathing the steady rhythm of sleep. He looked at her face. It had the peaceful look of a small child.

'What've you done to her?' He glared at Delia; suddenly he was shaking again. 'Touch that girl and I'll kill you!'

'Somehow I don't think you'll have the opportunity,' Delia laughed. 'No Walters, you've been a thorn in my side long enough. I gave you fair warning what might happen if you defied me.'

'007, licensed to kill?' Mike sneered.

'No Walters, I won't be accountable for your death. You're going to kill yourself. Such a pity don't you think? Popular young yachtsman, ground down by financial problems and a sex scandal. Yes, so tragic, found dead in the arms of his teenage lover. So sad, people will say – if only we had known.' Delia laughed.

Mike lunged at her, only to be gripped and pulled back by strong arms. For two minutes he fought with everything he knew. He and the man holding him careered across the floor crashing into the table. Delia stepped demurely aside. He was outnumbered, there were two men holding him now dragging him towards Leanne. The third man held something in his right hand. It was an oxygen mask, only it wasn't there to deliver oxygen. As the hand brushed his lips Mike bit hard. It was mind over matter as he drove his teeth into soft flesh and bone. The man yelled in pain and fury. With the hand still in his mouth Mike just managed to duck a clenched fist.

'Don't hit him in the face,' Delia screamed. 'He's got to be unmarked.'

The mask was pressing tight against his skin. He could hear the hissing gas, drowsiness was creeping over him. His grip on the hand in his mouth relaxed. He tried to focus but his vision was blurred. He was so tired...not worth fighting any more...just lie down...must sleep.

Mike was awake. Everything was hazy. Where was Delia? He could move his head and his eyes were beginning to register. He was sitting in a car seat. In front of him was a steering wheel; a soiled and much used steering wheel. He knew where he was. He was sitting in his own elderly Vauxhall. Outside, there were muffled voices. The passenger door was opened. Something was being lifted inside and placed on the seat. It was a person; it was Leanne. They were pushing her towards him. Someone had lifted her half across his body. He struggled to free himself but his limbs were jelly. He concentrated on breathing; deep breaths. At last his head was clearing and with that came the awful realization of what was happening.

Mike struggled to sit up but the sleeping girl was weighing him down. He heard the passenger door shut, then his own door opened. An arm was reaching towards him. A slim elegant arm with a circle of chalk white skin showing above the line of a black glove. He watched mesmerized as the fingers touched the ignition key.

CHAPTER 40

The shabby Austin Montego was moving fast, too fast for the narrow road. It had already alarmed two oncoming motorists and forced a third to take to the grass verge. Teenagers, speculated the other driver irritably. The Montego was travelling along the back lanes that skirted the marshy land to the east of the harbour. To either side were fields; poor, salt-encrusted land fit only for cattle in summer. The car rounded a bend and turned into an open gate. For thirty seconds it bounced over rough ground before slithering sideways in a shallow pool of water.

The driver made no attempt to restart. He abandoned the car, stopping only to pull a canvas holdall from the back seat. He was alone in the field but any watcher would have seen a short stocky man in clothing that merged subtly with the hedgerows. The onlooker would also have noted that although this man moved with an almost wraithlike stealth he had a distinct limp. Within seconds he had scrambled through a gap in the hedge and was standing on the footpath. He fished in his coat pocket and pulled out a charred piece of cork. With it he blackened his face and the backs of his hands. Then clutching his holdall he began to walk, swiftly and with purpose, along the path. He was following the edge of the mud flats that bordered the narrow creek until it joined the main channel at Cottons Hard. The time was seven o'clock.

For the first time Mike had lost hope. He was beaten, outsmarted by Delia at every turn. It was suddenly all so clear. The rumours, the innuendoes, so cunningly sown these last few days. "No smoke without fire," people would say. Yes, Delia would win unless he did something in the next few seconds. Those seconds before the exhaust fumes filled the car with carbon monoxide, the poison that took no prisoners. The gloved hand was turning the key. Mike felt a massive surge of adrenaline as he closed his hand over the slender wrist. With the strength of desperation he twisted the hand. He turned it like a stranded rope, harder and harder, until he felt the ligaments begin to crack. The wrist's owner gave a scream of agony as the body attached to the arm fell to the ground.

'Gas, more gas!' Delia was yelling in pain and rage.

The door was still open. Mike released his grip and tried to climb out. No good – he was trapped by the weight of the girl.

'Leanne, are you awake?' he gasped.

'Yes,' came the faint reply.

'Try and roll off me. If we don't get out now we'll die.'

'I don't care, I want to die.'

'What d'you mean?' Angrily he struggled into a sitting position, pushing the girl towards the passenger seat. He felt her tiny hands clutching at his sweater. He heaved again, but it was no good. He almost panicked. He could hear voices outside, Delia's voice loud and shrill urging her gasman to hurry. What the hell was the kid playing at? Their only chance was to get out under cover of this diversion and run.

'Mike,' Leanne was sitting up clinging to him like a limpet. 'I love you, I love you. I want to die with you…'

Oh God, this was unbelievable. In desperation he lurched towards the open door. His legs were out. Then, climbing drunkenly to his feet, he pulled the girl clear and flung her to the ground. There was a shout. Four of Delia's men were surrounding the car. One of them held the gas cylinders; the others were closing in. It was no good. Precious seconds had been lost. Delia would win. Leanne would get her death wish. Clare might guess what had happened but she would never know the full truth. He was going to die amidst total failure. He felt a profound sense of waste.

At six o'clock that evening, an hour before these events, Colonel Carl Newhoffer was also having problems with the lanes of Sussex. His left hand drive Mercedes filled the entire road as he edged slowly round blind corners regardless of the urgings of young Clare.

Clare sat in the passenger seat, clenching and unclenching her hands. Her grief at the news she had received from Ireland had changed into all consuming fury. How like her grandfather she was, he thought. How very alike in speech and mannerisms. Newhoffer had fond memories of Jimmy O'Dwyer, though that old man had often meant trouble; likewise with Clare. He had a nasty feeling that whatever she had in mind it would be no place for a Unites States Special Presidential Envoy.

'Next turn left,' said Clare. Newhoffer obliged.

'Why do we need to see this old fellow?' she asked abruptly.

'Because young lady, I don't act on impulse. You say the Lazarraga woman was leaning on him. I don't doubt you, but I need to hear his story first hand. I guess it won't take long, then we'll go see your boyfriend – OK?'

The George was not Newhoffer's vision of an English country pub. He could find nothing quaint about the redbrick joint. Wotek was not in his usual place, but they could see him in a phone booth outside the saloon bar. Clare smiled and waved. The old man was every inch the gloomy Pole, thought Newhoffer. Something had seemingly upset him as he hustled over to them.

'Oh Miss Clare – is good you come. I do not like what happens. My daughter-in-law has telephoned me and she says Leanne, our leetle girl, is missing. Not long ago she rings Mr Walters and he says she not come to work this day.'

'Has she done this before?' asked Clare.

'No never.'

Clare tugged at Newhoffer's arm. 'Let's get out of here, you too Mr Micalczyk. We'll talk outside.'

They left the building and stood in the car park. Clare addressed Wotek. 'How long ago did Leanne's mother speak to Michael?'

'Not long, a quarter of an hour maybe – no more. She ring me when she finish with me.'

'Thank God for that,' said Clare. 'Michael's still OK.' She paused while she pulled the mobile phone from the depths of her coat pocket. She walked away to the edge of the car park. The two men watched her as she rang a number, listened closed the line and then dialled again; same result. She dialed a third time, after consulting a number on a screwed piece of paper. This time there was a short conversation. As she spoke, Clare turned and gave them a worried grimace. She replaced the phone in her pocket and ran back to them.

'Michael's in trouble,' she said. 'I rang his house – the line's dead. No ringing tone – nothing, same with his office.'

'Could be a fault,' said Newhoffer.

'No listen,' Clare's voice cut across silencing him in mid sentence. 'I rang the mobile phone that Benny, the security guard uses. Benny says his company withdrew him to another site at four o'clock this afternoon. He can't understand why. He's at Crawley, thirty miles away and he says there's nothing there for him to guard. He thinks there's something funny going on.'

'On the face of it, I have to agree,' said Newhoffer. He looked at his watch. 'It's twenty to seven. We'll get over to this boat yard straight away. It'll be strictly unofficial, because I'm a foreign national, but somehow I don't think la Lazarraga will try any rough stuff if she sees me.'

'No,' said Wotek. 'You go to the boat yard. Me, I will go find our leetle girl.' With that he bowed to them turned away and walked to his car. It was a battered silver grey Montego.

Mike stared around and realized for the first time that he was no longer at the farm. His car was parked next to a boat; they were in the yard. His attitude was fatalistic. If he had only five minutes left on earth, he would make every second memorable. He would go down in the biggest, bloodiest fight he could muster. Delia's men were closing in on him, but his spirits rose as he saw how wary they had become. They were indeed the same men he had seen earlier and taken for a yacht crew. He noticed with satisfaction that the man with the gas had a blooded handkerchief wrapped around his right hand. There had been six men, where were the other two? There, over by the office watching the road. Where the hell were the security guards? Benny and his dog were due back tonight. He prepared for the attack. He was feeling better now; the wooziness was going and his co-ordination was nearly back. The first man to come within reach would feel the full force of his kicking boot.

'Hurry up, what are you waiting for? Gas, use the gas – I want Walters and the girl eliminated and us out of here.' Delia's voice crackled angrily.

A movement in the middle distance caught Mike's eye. Someone had just crawled under the fence by the footpath. The figure was standing now. It was a man, short and stocky, and vaguely familiar.

'Mr Walter! Lie down – now!' It was the newcomer, his voice urgent and commanding.

'It's Granddad,' shouted Leanne.

A gun was shooting; an automatic gun. Mike could see the red flashes. There was a tearing sound. Something smacked against the car. He heard the hiss of a deflating tyre. Nearby a man was clutching his ankle and screaming. By now Mike was also flat on the ground. Three feet away was Leanne. He rolled protectively over her.

'Mike,' she repeated, 'it's Granddad.'

'Wotek,' he muttered. 'It's his voice, but what's he doing here and where the hell did he get that gun?'

Twice more there was firing. Mike heard the crack of the shots overhead hammer into the car. They were short controlled bursts; two seconds at a time, quite unlike the films. Whoever was using the gun was a cool customer and highly trained. There was a shout and the drumming of footsteps. The two men who had been outside the office were running towards them and one had a handgun. The runner stopped and snapped a wild shot. The sub machine gun answered with a short burst. The man spun round and fell over. The second man dived for cover behind an upturned dinghy. At that moment the scene became a pool of light as the heat cell triggered the security lamps.

Mike looked up. Wotek was standing over them and in his hands was a World War Two Sten gun. It was rusty and tarnished and Mike caught the tang of burning dust. He couldn't believe his eyes; Wotek was transformed. The elderly refuse collector and pub raconteur had rolled back fifty years. For a brief moment he was once again the young soldier who had fought across the North African desert to the mountains of Italy.

'Every man will lie face down with his hands behind his head.' Wotek rasped the order. Slowly one by one they obeyed. Only the wounded man remained clutching his ankle and moaning.

Without taking his eyes from them Wotek bent over and spoke gently to Leanne in Polish.

'What's he saying,' Mike murmured.

'There's help coming,' she whispered excitedly. 'They're not to know though.'

Mike strove to stay calm. The security lights would burn for five minutes, then there would be darkness again.

'What can I do to help?' Mike asked.

'Nothing,' said Wotek. 'You must both stay – there is still one of them on the loose.'

Wotek walked slowly round the captives. They lay still, the wounded man occasionally whimpering. 'Where is the woman?' he asked icily. At that moment the lights went out.

Momentarily Mike was blinded, his night vision lost. There was a scrabbling noise near the front of the car. He could just see a ghost-like shape rise from the ground and flit silently away. Above him the gun blazed two shots then silence. He heard Wotek curse and then the click as he fitted a new magazine. There was a patter of running feet fading into the distance. Shortly afterwards they heard the car start by the farm and speed away.

'My fault, the woman she is gone,' Wotek sighed. 'I grow old, once long ago, I would have killed her.'

Mike could think of nothing to say. He tried to blank out his emotions. Their survival still depended on one elderly man and his rusty relic of a gun.

'Mr Micalczyk?' It was one of the MI5 men.

'Yes.'

'You've wounded our colleague – I want to help him.'

'Very well, but you play silly buggers and I kill you – so.'

'I wouldn't try that old fellow. You're in big trouble. You got a license for that gun?'

Wotek laughed. 'So you want to know how I have my gun? I keep her to remember the war. Once in Italy I use this gun to kill six Nazis. Why only six? So, but there were only six there to kill.' The tone was chilling. Mike had a feeling the story was no boast.

'One of you may help your friend,' said Wotek.

'How do we know you've any rounds left?' said another man. The gun replied. Two more shots smashed into the car. The captives lay frozen except for the one who crawled to the wounded man. Mike watched him cut away the trousers around the ankle. The casualty gave another agonized cry.

'I'm going to give him a shot of gas – OK?'

'Very well,' Wotek grunted.

'Mike watched as the man slid the mask over his friend's face. He knew the voice of this man although he had only heard it once before. It was the same man who a month ago had tried to sabotage *Quadra* that night in the yard.

'I've a two hundred pound bill for you,' said Mike. You're the boat vandal. Delia gave you a bad time for that didn't she? Now she's run out on you.' His remark was received in silence.

Mike wanted to do something, anything. What did Leanne mean that help was coming? His eyes were adjusting to the darkness again. The body of the second man still lay where it had fallen. Mike sincerely hoped that Wotek had not killed him. It was not that he cared a jot whether the man lived or died, but after Henderson, another dead body would be more than even MI5 could cover up. At last a car was coming down the track from the main road. He could hear the engine as a car bumped over the potholes. Yes, there were two cars and now a third. Thank God, this last one was a police car, with flashing blue lights. Only he and Wotek were standing; the others on the ground could see nothing – it was a question of waiting and hoping.

The first car had stopped out of sight round the corner of the yard buildings. Now he could hear footsteps, someone was running towards them.

'Michael, Michael! Where are you?' It was Clare. He could see her sprinting along the edge of the water.

'Clare, stop! Keep back!' Mike yelled in desperation.

She wavered for a second too long. She made a muffled scream as the man who had been hiding behind the dinghy grabbed her. She was fighting, screaming, kicking and shouting, but she couldn't stop her captor carrying her down the yard towards them.

'You stop, that's close enough,' Wotek barked.

'Put the gun down and I'll let the girl go. Then we'll leave and take Walters with us.' The man was large, well over six foot and spoke with traces of a Geordie accent.

Wotek remained unmoved. 'In twenty seconds I will shoot the legs of each man until you let Miss Clare go free.'

They had reached an impasse. Whatever else, Wotek was not bluffing. Mike began to count the seconds. Fifteen… fourteen… thirteen… 'Wait, we can talk about this,' said the man on the ground nervously.

'I do not talk to Gestapo…' Wotek's comment remained unfinished. A white light winked at them; for a split second everyone was dazzled. It was a photoflash, and for Mike it was the final shock that almost floored him. The light flashed again and again. The man holding Clare had released her. He had pulled his jacket over his head and was running comically towards the office. Once more he triggered the security lights and at last the whole scene was visible. Mike recognized the cameraman. He was the freelance photographer who worked for the *Review*. With him was Ricky Lofthouse and another nondescript little man in a wax jacket and cloth cap. More people were arriving. Three were policemen and the fourth a tall silver haired man. To Mike's joy one of the policemen was Garry. He was also relieved that Wotek had put down the gun.

'Hi Garry,' said Mike. 'What took the cavalry so long?' With the release of tension he found himself shaking again.

'What the hell is all this, Mike?' asked Garry. 'I was just going off duty when Ricky here reports shooting with a machine gun. Now all hell's broken loose. We've an Armed Response Unit on the road with the Assistant Chief Constable and more senior officers than you can shake a stick at.'

'How does Ricky Lofthouse come to be here?' asked Mike.

'Dunno, seems he was hanging around your place when he heard it. Then we had three other calls from the village and my world went mad.'

'Garry,' said Mike. He fought to stay coherent. He was trembling and he felt he was about to vomit. 'Garry, these people are your Spooks. That one there has had a haircut since you last met, but he's the same character you arrested a month back. They had a bloody good try at gassing me in my own car. If Wotek hadn't turned up I'd be dead.'

Clare was clinging to him tearfully. 'My God, Michael, your car's got a hose through the window from the exhaust.'

'Delia tried to kill me, Leanne too – now she's done a runner. Garry, you people must do something – she's a murderer.'

'They won't touch her, Mr Walters, no chance.' It was the elderly man who'd arrived with the police. His voice was deep and very American.

'Michael, this is Carl Newhoffer,' said Clare.

'What're you doing here, Newhoffer?' It was one of Delia's men and he sounded angry. 'Keep your nose out. This a Five operation. We won't be fucked about by the CIA.'

'I'm not CIA,' said Newhoffer. 'I'm here at the invitation of Miss O'Dwyer.'

'You're a Yank poking his nose in. I warn you – keep off!'

'Eric, pack it in – we've gotta' get out, man.' The big Geordie had rejoined the group and was tugging his friend away.

The Armed Response Unit had arrived. Two vanloads of them, encircling the yard, dressed in black body armour and brandishing weaponry. Their sergeant in command looked mildly disappointed when Garry told him all was now under control. With the new arrivals was a senior officer carrying a megaphone. It was Assistant Chief Constable Rowlandson. Mike had last seen him at the meeting where he had first encountered Delia.

Garry saluted and gave his chief a quick report. Then both Mike and Clare cornered him and began talking at once. Rowlandson raised a hand. 'Wait, we're all going back to the Station. All of us, include-ing you lot.' He turned a hostile gaze on Delia's men who were now a sorry looking group.

'Don't be a bloody fool,' said Eric. 'We've got immunity.'

'Not for attempted murder.'

'You can't prove a thing – anyway we were rescuing Walters. That Polish nutter was forcing him into the car – we all saw him boys, didn't we?'

'You lying bastards,' Mike was burning with rage. Clare was tugging him back but he wanted to close his hands around Eric's throat.

'It's no good, Walters,' Eric jeered. 'You've been messing with that little girl,' he pointed towards Leanne who was being comforted by a woman PC. 'No wonder the old man's gone crazy.'

'Everybody here is coming to the station,' said Rowlandson firmly. 'All you zombies for a start. I shall need to check your IDs. I want old man Micalczyk, he's got a lot of explaining to do. Mr Walters, you are central to all this, we'll need statements from you and the young lady. The rest of you are witnesses. Yes, even you Ricky. This is your lucky day, though I doubt you'll be allowed to print much.'

'What if we won't come?' said Geordie.

'Two of your men are wounded. You're in no position to help them – we've called an ambulance. I gather your leader has absconded. If you want to avoid her name on television and a full scale hunt for her through ten counties, I'd co-operate.'

That was the end of that. The police shepherded the four men into a police van. Wotek and Leanne were put in a second car. Then the ambulance arrived. The man with the leg wound was quiet. The other was still unconscious; blood oozed from his chest as the paramedics hustled around fixing drips and an oxygen mask. 'These gangsters?' asked one of them.

'In a manner of speaking, yes,' said Garry, 'but keep your mouths shut until we talk to you again.'

Clare was clutching Mike's arm. 'Come on, Michael,' she was shaking and her face was wet with tears. 'Colonel Newhoffer will drive us. Michael, I've bad news.'

'What now?' He could barely speak. Reaction was setting in; he was not sure he could take any more.

She clung to him weeping. '*Quadra's* gone.'

'What's happened – where's she gone?'

'I had a call from the Garda in Crosshaven,' she broke down in a gale of sobbing. '*Quadra* was set on fire on her mooring, yesterday evening – there's nothing left. They arrested the man who did it, that's all I know.'

CHAPTER 41

Mike was the first to be called to make a statement. The police station had transformed since his last visit. The corridors were filled with off duty officers called in at short notice. The Armed Response Unit clumped, heavy booted, through the middle of all this activity. 'Cost us a fortune in overtime,' said the Inspector who took his statement.

Mike told his whole story carefully, factually, omitting nothing. The Inspector listened without comment. Afterwards he was shown into a waiting room and left alone. Post-traumatic stress had temporarily unmanned him. He sat trembling, clenching and unclenching his sweaty hands. He hardly heard the door open and a friendly voice call him into the adjacent room. It was Rowlandson.

'You're not thinking of driving home I hope?' said the police chief.

'No, my car's back at Cottons Hard and it's a wreck now.'

'Right, drink this.' He handed Mike a huge tumbler of whisky. It was hardly the thing to mix with Delia's anaesthetic, but it certainly made him feel better.

'I've read your statement,' said Rowlandson. 'You had a close call.'

'I was as good as dead.'

'So I understand. Now, although we allow these people a certain latitude, this time they've gone too far. We're holding all these jokers here until we've spoken to Miss Lazarraga. I have already dispatched an official complaint to London – although much good that'll do.'

'Am I free to go?' asked Mike.

'Yes, you've made your statement but we would like you to accompany us when we talk to Miss Lazarraga. We've agreed to meet her tonight and we think you and Miss O'Dwyer should be there.'

Once again he felt the shadow; that shimmer of fear. He had to grip himself as another involuntary burst of trembling ran through him like an electric current. 'I've seen enough of that woman,' he said at last. 'I don't think I could face her again.'

'That's your decision. Think about it. It could set you free of her for ever.' With a friendly nod Rowlandson left the room.

Shortly afterwards he returned with Leanne. 'We're letting this young lady go home,' he said. 'Her parents are on their way to collect her. She's a brave resilient youngster – wouldn't mind recruiting her to the Force.'

'Oh no you don't,' despite himself Mike smiled. 'We need her at the yard.'

'Anyway think about it young lady,' Rowlandson grinned and left the room.

Mike looked at Leanne. There were smudges on her face and her hair hung down dirty and dishevelled. 'How do you feel?' It was a silly question but he had to say something.

'Awful,' she replied.

'What happened?'

'That horrible woman offered me a lift – said she wanted to ask about you. Then she locked me in a room...'

'Where?'

'Some house in the town, across from the park – near the theatre. I've gotta' help the police find it tomorrow. She locked me in and then I heard another woman imitating my voice.'

'Are you sure?'

'Of course I'm sure. She was pretending to be me and saying I wouldn't be at work.'

'I follow you. Yes, I got that message on the yard answerphone. It fooled me.' Too right it had. Delia must have planned her strike to the last detail. She could never have predicted Wotek. Mike tried not to think about it.

'After that I yelled and kicked the door all day, but no one came. They didn't give me a thing to eat. I've had nothing until the cops gave me a cup of tea just now. God, I feel hungry,' she gave him a wan smile.

'What happened next?'

'It was getting dark and then this bloke comes and pushes the gas thingy over my face. I don't remember nothing else 'til I was in your house.'

'How did old Wotek find out?'

'I don't know. I really don't; he's been ever so wound up by these people. Mum says he's been shouting in Polish about the war and his brother.'

'He was just about in time. We'll have to do something for him. He saved us both and he's in bad trouble because of it.'

Leanne sat silently. She looked utterly defeated and miserable.

'Mike,' she said solemnly. 'I'm sorry about what happened in the car.'

'Never mind, we're both alive and that's what counts.'

'I didn't really want to die, but I meant what I said. You won't...

you won't tell anyone will you?'

'No I'll never tell anyone – it'll be our secret.' He stood up, walked across to her and gave her a hug. 'You heard what the policeman said. You're a very brave girl, and you've a great life in front of you if you take your chances.' He bent down and kissed her lightly on the forehead. He was relieved when a few minutes later her parents arrived to take her home. Mike was doubly relieved that there were no recriminations. A woman police officer had told them as much as it was good for them to know.

When Rowlandson came back he was not alone. With him were Clare, Newhoffer and the little man he'd seen in the yard with Ricky Lofthouse.

'Meet the distinguished author and journalist, Tony Tulloe,' said Rowlandson.

Tulloe was nothing to look at. He was short, balding, North Country speech, sportily dressed.

'You're the one having trouble with our Delia?' he grinned at Mike.

'She did her best to kill me tonight,' Mike replied frostily.

'Mr Tulloe is what is known in the trade as a spy-writer, Rowlandson explained. 'He has a nose for what the spooks are up to. The Government doesn't like him, but he's helped us a time or two.' Suddenly he laughed. 'I think you'll have gathered there's not much love lost between the Force and Five and Six.'

'Where's Ricky Lofthouse?' asked Mike.

'They've just made him sign the Official Secrets Act, but they're letting him keep his photos. He can't print a word, but he could be useful if Miss Lazarraga won't play ball.'

'What are you planning?'

'Miss Lazarraga has agreed to meet us tonight. We've notified the Dorset Force, and they've just confirmed she's arrived back at her house. Officially they'll supervise the interview. I'm going on behalf of Sussex Force and we've invited you, Miss O'Dwyer, and Tulloe as witnesses.'

Delia herself met them at the entrance gate at Tarrant Welcome. Mike looked at his watch – it was exactly midnight. Memories of his last visit flooded back as the headlights lit the scene on either side. The same acres of rolling heather land, with birch trees now in leaf. They swept past the spot where poor Diamond had been gunned down and came in sight of the little cottage and its beautifully tended garden.

Delia parked her car beside another already there. Beside it Mike recognized Inspector Lamont of the Dorset Police. It was little more than a fortnight since Mike had escaped from this place; it seemed an eternity. Subconsciously the scar on his hand began to ache.

If Delia felt cornered, no one would have guessed it. She received them graciously, relieved them of their coats, and showed them into a room with a polished oval table, set as for a board meeting. There were flowers on the table and a tray with a coffee pot and delicate china cups. A log fire burned in the grate and its flames threw a flickering red glow onto the bright chintz curtains and the black and white beams and plaster.

'Colonel Newhoffer,' said Delia. 'Welcome to my house, and you too Mr Rowlandson. The rest of you have of course been my guests before.'

'Including Mr Tulloe?' asked Newhoffer.

'Certainly, I have spoken several times with Anthony, off the record of course. I hope my trust has not been misplaced.' Delia's reply was measured and polite. There was not a trace of antagonism, let alone fear. Despite everything Mike could not but feel some admiration for the woman. Already she had taken control.

'Clare my dear, would you sit here with your friend Michael? Colonel, you sit on my right. Inspector, you and your colleague from Sussex may take notes. Anthony, you sit at the end of the table and absolutely no writing from you. Have you any concealed recording equipment?'

'No,' Tulloe replied abruptly.

Mike was in the kind of emotional state where he was unsure whether to laugh or cry. Delia had quietly imposed her personality on the gathering. Every one of them was obeying her as if they were children with a teacher.

'I'm afraid the coffee is instant,' Delia continued apologetically. 'Things are awry at the moment. I've been busy and I think you all know that I lost my dear mother a few days ago...' There came a subdued murmur around the table.

Newhoffer coughed. 'Miss Lazarraga, I'm sure we will all offer our condolences. We would not be here were we not concerned – most concerned, at the turn your activities have been taking...'

'Ask her what happened to her bodyguard,' Clare's voice rasped. She alone had been unmoved by Delia's charisma.

'Poor Henderson,' sighed Delia. 'He worked for me for five years. Obeyed every command without question and all on a corporal's basic

pay. He was the most cost-effective man in my unit. I shall miss him.
   'Then why did you kill him?'
   'Kill Henderson? I thought he killed himself.'
   'Miss Lazarraga,' said Rowlandson. 'Our pathologists say that Mr Henderson was put in a car under sedation and other evidence points to the engine being started by a second person.'
   'Really, an accomplice perhaps?' Delia replied with the suggestion of a yawn.
   Mike's anger was burning again. 'You killed him just like you tried to kill me and little Leanne.'
   'I think you're over working your imagination, Michael.' Delia's face had the glimmer of a smile.
   'You can't get out of it like that. Everyone here knows what happened. There's all those pictures the press man took.'
   'Indeed, you're telling me all this but I wouldn't know. I wasn't there. As far as I know, all you saw was a mad Pole holding hostage a number of public servants.'
   'Horse shit!' Clare rasped. 'There's a bloody great rubber hose clamped on the car's exhaust.'
   'Quite so, it seems my men staged a timely rescue.'
   'Sorry Michael,' said Newhoffer, 'but you see what we're up against?'
   'Christ man!' shouted Michael. 'You're not going to leave it at that?'
   'No, no, no! Now see here, my boy, I didn't say that. There's ways of handling these things, so let's try some of 'em.' He looked at Delia. 'As you know I'm to report to the President of the United States on the progress of your negotiations in Ireland. More to the point, Clare and Michael witnessed your mother's dealings with ETA and the IRA...'
   'Colonel Newhoffer,' Delia's voice was brittle with menace, 'this is ultra-sensitive material for which none of these people have been cleared.'
   'Sure, sure, but I'm not spelling the thing out. I just say that our people are impressed with your work. I guess it's a pity you couldn't stop at that.'
   'Colonel I do nothing by halves. I do as much or as little as the State demands.'
   'OK, now as I see it your state and my state need you to succeed. I give you full credit – no other negotiator would have succeeded like you have. I want you to carry on with your work unhindered...'

'I also wish to be unhindered.' Delia's eyes were boring into the man. Momentarily Newhoffer looked startled. 'Yes Colonel, the success of my mission is paramount. I will not be obstructed by the likes of Walters and O'Dwyer and when I am I take the appropriate action.'

'Like cold blooded murder?' said Clare.

'All right, young lady,' said Newhoffer, 'just cool it, will you? Now see here Miss Lazarraga. I'll give you my guarantee that as from now these two will hinder you no further. You, in your turn, will guarantee that they can get on with their lives unthreatened.'

'I can't compromise operational needs on the dictate of an outsider,' Delia replied flatly.

'Miss Lazarraga, I ain't dictating nothing. But I tell you…I tell you,' Newhoffer's face and growling voice were within inches of Delia's ear. 'I tell you, if anything happens to Michael, Clare, or to anyone here in this room, including me, no – especially me,' Newhoffer paused, 'I will arrange for a full account of the *Juanita* affair to be sent to Mr Tulloe. He can also make what he can of tonight's episode. That's the deal. You stay within the law and we'll keep our mouths shut.'

'I endorse that,' said Rowlandson. 'Should these people be harmed, I will pursue the Henderson case and I will charge your six accomplices with kidnapping and attempted murder.'

'Good speech, Chief Constable,' said Delia. 'But events have moved on. I have no further interest in Michael Walters or Clare O'Dwyer.'

'Very well,' said Newhoffer. 'Now Mr Tulloe, what can you tell me about the Flanagan conspiracy?'

'This is history, I take it,' said Tulloe. 'In Canada they talk about the O'Leary plot and I imagine that's the same thing?'

'Quite right, not many people know that much – tell us more.'

'Sorry I can't. I only ever heard of it when a colleague was warned off by the spooks and he came to me.'

Newhoffer nodded. 'Colonel Flanagan was the staff officer who organized the return home of the American Army from France in 1919. The man was a total dumbo but he had a head for logistics. It was his job to match units with ships. By mid-1919 he had it all mapped out. The convoys left St Nazaire in France and took a great circle route that sailed them near to Southern Ireland and also close to Devon and Cornwall. Flanagan was an Irish-American and a patriot. Nothing wrong with that in a normal person, but in Flanagan's case his patriotism merged with paranoia. Ireland was engaged in a struggle for independence and Flanagan wanted his part of the action – his place in history.'

'Like John Paul Jones?' asked Tulloe.

'You're getting the picture, 'cept that John Paul's raids were comic book stuff. Flanagan would've created a bloodbath and its repercussions don't bear thinking about. They would've echoed to this day, maybe affected the result of the Second World War. What d'you say, Miss Lazarraga?'

'Perhaps now you understand why I have had to be positive in my actions,' Delia glowered at him.

'For Chissake, Carl, will you get to the point?' Clare was exasperated. 'What did Flanagan do that's nearly got us murdered by this bitch here seventy God knows how many years later, and what's it got to do with my Granpapa?' She ended breathless and staring belligerently at both Newhoffer and Delia.

'Give me a chance and I'll tell you, I probably shouldn't but I guess you've a right to know.' He smiled and then his face became serious again. 'Flanagan knew that many of the drafted men were in National Guard units that reflected their ethnic background. By April 1919 he had found enough soldiers of Irish-American descent to fill two convoys, about fourteen thousand men in all, plus a stockpile of tanks, guns and a few aircraft. Flanagan intended to sail the convoys in one week in May. Convoy One would divert to England and seize the naval base of Plymouth, scuttle the Navy ships there and then retire to the line of the River Tamar. The British would be caught in total disarray, it would be Pearl Harbour times any number you care to name.'

'But this is crazy,' said Lamont. 'The Americans were on our side.'

'Just so, the surprise would've been even greater.' Newhoffer held up his hand. 'Wait, I haven't finished yet. Flanagan had a second convoy: six thousand fully equipped troops destined to land in Southern Ireland and seize the port of Queenstown, that's Cobh today. Tom Flanagan had appointed himself to command and he was going to drive out the British.'

Newhoffer's revelations had reduced the room to a shocked silence. It was Tulloe who broke the tension. 'So that was it,' he shook his head. 'Crikey, you're not telling us this was official – that your government sanctioned it?'

'No way! It was an act of pure fantasy, dreamed up by a bunch of screw-loose romantics. There were less than two dozen conspirators in the know – pure fantasy and it was doomed to failure.'

'Why?'

'Well, to begin with they involved Jim O'Dwyer; he seems to have had severe doubts from the start. More important no one thought to consult the troops. You see whatever legends these men had been fed as kids; well they'd be changing their minds by this time. You see most of 'em had passed through England on their way to France and once there they'd fought alongside the British. They'd been brought up to believe that England was a barren waste inhabited by a devil race and they'd found the reverse. So there you have all those thousands of soldiers on the high seas all dreaming of home. Then suddenly they're landed in some strange place and this madman tells 'em to fight the Brits. No way, never, and of course the real instigator of the plot knew that all along.'

'Not my grandfather surely?' said Clare.

'Oh no, Jimmy had severe misgivings but he wasn't the originator.' Newhoffer looked at Mike. 'I understand you and Clare met the old priest McGee and he told you he'd been a sea officer on the ship *Boston Star*.'

'I remember,' said Mike. 'He said the trip to Ireland was his first ride in an aircraft.'

'Now,' Newhoffer continued. 'There was a twist to this tale, and that's why Miss Lazarraga wants those papers.'

'It's essential the documents are found,' said Delia. 'James O'Dwyer would agree with me were he here, Clare.'

'Having gone this far, may we know what this twist is?' asked Tulloe.

'Sure, McGee's skipper on the *Boston Star* was a Canadian, Captain O'Leary. The *Star* was a troop ship and O'Leary was by way of being the leader of the convoy. The conspiracy was his idea in the first place and Flanagan fell for it.'

'You make it sound as if Flanangan was conned?' said Tulloe.

'An "agent provocateur", that's what Jimmy suspected. You see, he knew a thing or two about O'Leary – about his family background in Canada. So when Jimmy got to Dublin he warned Collins. Collins had Jimmy copy Flanagan's dispatches and they were sent to London to Collins' contact man in Whitehall.'

'Christopher Venner-Harris,' said Mike.

'That's him. Collins had his courier commit the whole thing to memory. He was to deliver the papers, but if the British got on to him he was to burn them and deliver to Venner-Harris verbally. He was a hard guy, that courier. He was the one man Collins trusted not to break under torture.'

'The courier was Clarke,' said Mike.

'Sure, the same old fellow that was beat to death a week or so back. Some reckon the Israelis got him – unfinished business from Hitler's time.'

Mike stole a glance at Delia but her face was her usual mask.

'Anyway,' Newhoffer continued, 'Clarke gave the documents to Venner-Harris and he sent Clarke back to Dublin that night. Two days later Clarke was back for instructions from Collins.' Newhoffer looked round the table and his face broke into a sardonic smile. 'Guess what? Venner-Harris was told to let the British find the papers. Dangerous that, for V-H, because he suspected the Brits were on to him. But he took the chance and left the decoded documents on Lloyd George's desk. You see V-H really was a true Irishman, a gambler.'

'Colonel Newhoffer,' asked Delia coldly. 'How do you know all this?'

'Jimmy met Venner-Harris ten years after the war and V-H gave him the whole story. I got the yarn from Jimmy but I never knew the contents of the papers 'til yesterday.'

'What was wrong with O'Leary, or right with him for that matter?' asked Tulloe.

'O'Leary may've had an Irish name but he was a Canadian through and through. His family had lived on the St John River for nigh on one hundred and forty years. But before that they'd been big land-owners in New York State. That was before 1776 of course.'

'Oh,' said Clare, 'the American Revolution – I think I'm beginning to get your drift.'

'I'm blowed if I do.' said Tulloe.

'Clare's Irish, she understands the way these things are. Imagine, your family is drawn into a civil war on the losing side and losing means just that. You lose everything except the clothes you stand up in. It happens all over the world – look at Yugoslavia.' Newhoffer swept a glance round the company. Clare looked alert but the others were blank and uncomprehending.

'Let me explain. We Americans can be a mite coy about anything in our history that doesn't fit our national myth. It's childish but maybe it's something we caught from you people. We can't take the notion that one third of our people, either openly or secretly, sided with the British in our revolutionary war. Well, these O'Learys were

Loyalists. They fought with the British, they lost and they fled to Canada to start a new life. Maybe it was the Irish in them but they bore an inherited grudge – they hated Yanks. I checked the record, you know there were two O'Learys who died in the war of 1812 – the only time the USA and Canada ever fought a war.

'It was a set up,' said Clare quietly.

Newhoffer poured himself a second cup of coffee. 'That's about it. You see it's 1918. The war's over and everyone's talking about a world fit for heroes and peace ever more – all that bullshit. So there's Captain George O'Leary reading his daily paper. It's all about America taking the high moral ground and teaching democracy to the rotten imperial powers, and President Wilson and his fourteen points for peace. I mean we Yanks don't quite measure up to you Brits in the hypocrisy stakes but we try hard.'

'Colonel Newhoffer,' said Delia. 'What evidence have you for all this?'

'Conjecture ma'am, just conjecture, but it all fits. You see if we don't know the facts it's because the Canadians have been at some pains to destroy the records.'

'That's what Professor Anderson told us,' said Clare.

'Anyway,' said Newhoffer, 'here's my theory. Captain O'Leary is reading this stuff and grinding his teeth, and then suddenly in the line of duty he meets Tom Flanagan. It doesn't take long for O'Leary to size up Flanagan and to hatch his own plan. I believe O'Leary suckered Flanagan into this escapade knowing it would make Uncle Sam an international laughing stock. Not the conventional way to conduct a vendetta, but a darned effective one.'

'But nothing happened,' said Tulloe.

'When Michael Collins found out he pulled the plug. Jimmy said Collins had a talk off the record with an American journalist and a week or so later Flanagan went home under a cloud. The convoy set sail for the States on time with no stopovers, and no Captain O'Leary either. His shipping company transferred him to another command.'

'What happened to Flanagan?' asked Clare.

'He took a drop in rank and a transfer to the US Marine Corps. Probably the price of him keeping his mouth shut. He could easily have been shot, but the government wouldn't risk the reason getting out.'

'Which I presume he did?' said Mike. 'I mean keep his mouth shut.'

'Sure, it's a strange coincidence but both Flanagan and O'Leary died in World War Two fighting in the Pacific.'

'This is irrelevant,' said Delia. 'Do you people realize now how dangerous these papers would be if they came in the public domain?'

'But all this was seventy plus years ago,' Rowlandson intervened. 'What's it to do with us now?'

'Use your imagination, Chief Constable,' Delia replied. 'An American invasion of England; imagine what anti-United States elements would make of that. I saw the original papers in Dublin last week and in them Flanagan talks of forcibly expelling the entire Protestant Unionist population of Ireland to Britain. The term today is, 'ethnic cleansing'.'

'Exactly so,' said Newhoffer. 'If those papers surfaced tomorrow their psychological effect would be incalculable. Either way my mission on behalf of our President would be dead.'

'I don't like facts being suppressed,' Tulloe grumbled. 'Hasn't it occurred to you that you won't be able to conceal something as big as this for ever?'

'See here,' said Newhoffer. 'I don't hold with censorship, but there's enough division in the world. If keeping this old bit of history quiet saves a single child's life in Belfast – then I'm happy to eat my principles.'

Tulloe frowned; he was clearly far from convinced. 'Look I'm not entirely stupid. I take it from tonight's shennanigans that there is a rogue copy of those papers at large and Delia here thinks these young people have them – correct?'

'In every detail Mr Tulloe,' said Newhoffer, 'except that Clare here says she's never clapped eyes on any papers and I believe her.'

'So where are they?'

Newhoffer shrugged and spread his hands. 'I've no idea.'

'But I would guess this Senator O'Dwyer had them at some point?'

'That's right, you see Lloyd George kept Venner-Harris's copy for himself. There's some evidence that he used them to blackmail the United States government – made 'em keep out of the Irish treaty negotiations.'

'So how did my grandfather get hold of them?' said Clare.

'David Lloyd George died near the end of the Second World War. Jimmy guessed the papers were in L-G's private files. He was worried that the Germans might get hold of them. He got permission from L-G's daughter to search the files and he found 'em.'

'I wish he'd told me that,' said Clare. 'Why hide them in a boat?'

'That's where everyone's got it wrong. He said the key was in his boat. Typical Jimmy – he covered his tracks by deception all his life.'

'And now we've lost the boat,' said Clare bitterly. 'Someone's burnt her and sunk her and all for nothing.' She was crying now. Mike reached out and squeezed her hand.

'Is this the sum total of tonight's revelations?' asked Rowlandson.

'That's all I know about it,' said Newhoffer. 'What do you say, Miss Lazarraga?'

'Far too much has been said to these people. I have been put under duress and I don't like that.'

'Madam,' said Rowlandson, 'enough of that. Only your privileged status has saved you from serious charges. I doubt if Mr Walters is feeling so charitable.'

'No I'm not.'

'If that's all then, I think my colleague and I will withdraw.' Rowlandson stood up. Both he and Lamont left the room without a backward glance.'

There was a long pause; so one seemed to know what to say next. From a darkened corner cam a whimper and a scrabbling sound. The four visitors shot round in surprise as the little marmoset loped across the furniture and dropped into Delia's lap.

'This is Papageno,' said Delia rocking the creature in her arms. 'I tell you all my secrets, don't I Papa?'

'Delia,' said Clare, 'who told Dolan to go to St Vaast? They were waiting for us there and only you knew that we were going – I heard Michael tell you.'

'Michael logged his destination by radio to the Coastguard. I imagine the whole world heard him.'

'Oh hell,' Michael groaned.

'The transmission was reported to me,' Delia continued. 'But I've no doubt the *Van Haagen* heard you, she was only a few miles south at the time.'

Mike glared at Delia. 'Are you going to leave us alone? You might as well know that me and Clare are getting married – so I suppose you'll be my aunt-in-law, God help me.'

Delia laughed, it was the same laugh that Mike had heard as he fled from the execution of Diamond: laughter steeped in malice. 'Aunt is it? Is that what she's made you think you poor fool?'

'What's that – what are you saying?' Clare's chair clattered to the floor as she stood eyes blazing.

'I think I'm saying what you have long guessed and will not face up to,' said Delia.

'I can face anything,' said Clare. 'You can't touch me – not any more.'

'Ties of blood. Ties of blood, my dear sister, revealed at last.'

Mike felt lost, he looked round; Newhoffer seemed quizzical but unsurprised. Tulloes's jaw dropped, he was clearly embarrassed.

'Perhaps I'd better go,' he said awkwardly.

'No Anthony, you must stay. You're a journalist and I know you were in Argentina in 1980.'

'Yes but…'

'Then you'll be familiar with the Irish Mission in Olavarria?'

'Hell yes, they vanished. Every last priest and nun and half the poor kids they were looking after.'

'And my father,' snapped Clare. 'She knows – don't you Delia?'

'Your father?' Delia laughed as she cuddled the marmoset. 'Oh come on, Clare. Bobby O'Dwyer was never your father. Bobby, to put it crudely, couldn't have put a bun in the oven if his life had depended on it.'

'What are you saying, damn you?' Clare was clutching her fists in tearful fury.

'I'm saying that Bobby was never one for the ladies. Yes, a deep disappointment was Bobby to his father, but useful in the end, because he solved the problem of Sinaid Halloran…'

'My mother – you watch what you say, Delia!'

'Oh I will, Clare, I will.' The dark eyes gleamed in the lamplight. 'Yes, Michael, Sinaid Halloran was most certainly Clare's mother. It is also a fact that she was the devoted manager of James O'Dwyer's Dublin office.'

'Can you prove what I think you are insinuating?' asked Mike. It was strange, unreal, but on top of all the shocks of the day he felt only excited anticipation.

'Yes, I found a most touching letter from Bobby to his father. It was among the effects we found in his hotel room in Olavarria.'

'So, you did kill him! My…my…'

'Father?' Delia laughed.

'Damn you!' Clare collapsed sobbing into Mike's arms.

CHAPTER 42

Clare sat fully clothed on the edge of the bed, silent and very solemn.

'How d'you feel?' Mike looked at her with concern. The events of yesterday had shaken him but they were as nothing to the effect on Clare. She had left Delia's cottage in a subdued dream world and had scarcely spoken a word as Newhoffer drove them home. All Mike wanted was to take her in his arms, comfort her, and reassure her that he still loved her. His faltering words were inadequate and he was not sure she'd even heard him. That night she'd lain beside him sleepless and anguished.

'Feel – I don't feel anything. There's so much I can't come to terms with.' Again she smiled wanly at him.

'It's Delia isn't it?' He reached out and took both her hands, they felt cold and unresponsive. 'Clare, don't let her win. You don't have to believe any of the things she told you.'

'It's no good, Michael. It's true what she said and I think I've always known it.'

'That your grandfather is really your father?'

'Yes.'

'And that makes Delia your sister?'

'Yes, I suppose it does – half sister anyway.'

'Don't you think you ought to tell me?'

'How can I tell you? I don't want to lose you.'

'Clare darling, I'm the one person in the world you can tell and you're not going to lose me. We need each other more than ever.'

There was a long pause before she spoke. 'My mother married Robert O'Dwyer, but he died when I was ten. Their marriage was a sham but I always called him father, though deep down I knew he wasn't. Then he was always abroad with the diplomatic service and we never went with him. When he died in South America I felt so guilty because I couldn't mourn him. I went to live in America for three years with Granpapa – that's when he took me sailing in *Quadra*.' Clare was weeping: huge tears were cascading down her cheeks.

Mike put his arms around her and she nestled her head on his chest. 'Let it go love,' he said, 'you'll feel better.'

'Mother remarried, she married Noel. I resented him because he knew something. He was always so smug, so patronizing. He knew some secret about me that he wouldn't tell.' Clare was weeping now with anger. 'Then Mam died as well, six years ago.'

'Poor Clare, you must've been all alone.' Mike was moved by the poignancy of her story.

'It was Grandfather who raised me, paid for me to fly to the States for holidays, paid for my schooling in France. I was his favourite and I loved him too…I loved him…I was with him when he died, but you know that.' She was quieter now – the tears no longer fell. 'He was more of a father to me than Robert ever was, and somehow it's kind of right that he should be my real father – it all makes sense.'

'Delia hated him and that's why she hates you,' said Mike. 'I've never seen such hate as she showed last night.'

'She was born to hate. I feel almost sorry for her – she's never loved another human being; only those monkeys and they're just subjects. Pliant subjects of her little kingdom.'

'I wish Wotek had killed her – I'll never feel we're safe while she's alive.'

'No Michael, she'll not touch me now – I don't know why but I know it.'

'It's all wrong though, all wrong…'

'Why?'

'Because right hasn't triumphed. We've exposed Delia and she's still gloating.'

'This isn't a B movie, Michael. It's a dirty rotten world and the likes of Delia know how to ride its dirty rotten currents.'

'I know, Newhoffer said as much last night when he said goodbye. He rang just now by the way – that's what I came to tell you.'

'Yes, I heard the phone ring,' she said dully.

'Newhoffer stayed in Chichester overnight and he's coming round here in half an hour. He wants to talk to me. You see there's just a chance I've cracked this secret.'

'You?'

'Don't look so surprised. I have my moments – I'm not a complete idiot.'

'Sorry, but what've you found?'

'I'll save that for when he comes. I've an idea, that's all. I've spent some time trying to work my way into your grandf…I'm sorry that was tactless.'

Clare smiled. 'James O'Dwyer – my real father. If you're saying you've tried to read his mind. Well nobody ever succeeded in that, I can tell you for nothing.'

Newhoffer arrived at ten am; Mike showed him in. Clare made a brave face but nothing could conceal her red swollen eyes and her greeting was listless.

'Your police chief, Rowlandson, rang me an hour back,' said Newhoffer. 'Those two wounded spooks were sprung from hospital in the early hours.'

'Sprung?'

'That's the word. There were three tough guys with an unmarked ambulance. The man with the leg wound discharged himself and they took the unconscious one as well. Most likely the move'll kill him, but that's their problem.'

'Didn't the hospital raise hell?' asked Mike.

'Not much they could do. The spooks crashed in at four am. The casualty unit was busy and the night staff thin on the ground. They timed it carefully.'

Newhoffer sat down. 'Now Michael, how say we trade ideas. First, I lied to you last night. I think I know where the documents are only I wasn't going to be too forthcoming in front of Delia Lazarraga. What I missed saying was this. Jimmy O'Dwyer told me where the papers are but we're no nearer to getting our hands on them. All that stuff about the boat was hokum. They're in a strong box in the London branch of the Elmer-Bernstein Trust. But we can't touch them without a key. They've been in that box since Jimmy put them there in 1945.'

'Do they belong to me?' For the first time Clare was showing interest.

'I guess they do, but without the key we're no wiser.'

'Is that the key Gran...what he said was in *Quadra*?'

'I understand Michael's got a theory about that. You see in 1945 these boxes had mechanical locks and metal keys. Ten years ago the bank changed the whole system to electronic locks. You need two PIN numbers to access your box. Nobody, but nobody, can open Jimmy's box. The bank don't know the codes either, they're lost in the system. It seems Jimmy took the option to make up his own PIN numbers and it's nigh on impossible to retrieve them.'

'He told me the secret's in the boat,' said Clare. 'You say he said the key was in the boat...'

'Yes he did. He said it in passing once and I never had the chance to ask what he really meant.'

'He was talking a riddle,' said Mike. With difficulty he extracted a piece of paper from the back pocket of his trousers and tossed it on the table. 'There's your PIN numbers.'

'Are you sure?' Newhoffer picked up the paper and looked at it unconvinced.

'No, of course I'm not sure, but I've a gut feeling I'm right.'

'How d'you come by this? Was it in the boat?'

'Not in the boat but of it.' Mike grinned; he was feeling better, particularly as Newhoffer was clearly taking him seriously.

'Explain please, Michael,' said Clare.

'Mr O'Dwyer designed and built his own boat. We've got the plans. He's supposed to have drawn them himself but I would guess the final version was done by a draughtsman. They're signed with the date 1938, although he didn't build her until after the war. On the first sheet of these plans someone's added three sets of numbers. They're written with a modern ballpoint pen so they're obviously more recent than 1938. Remember, Clare, I showed them to you and you confirmed O'Dwyer's writing.' He glanced at Clare and she nodded.

'I couldn't make head nor tail of it at first until I realized they were the ship's dimensions translated from feet and inches into metric and they'd been labeled: a, b, c. Well I thought no more about it for a week or so because we were in Ireland by then. I did wonder why he'd changed the name. Originally she'd been called the *Mary Elizabeth* after his wife. I'm a professional yachtsman and I know that when men name boats after wives it's a gesture – it means the wife hates sailing. Am I right Clare?'

'Yes, Gran hated boats – she was always seasick.'

Mike continued. '*Quadra's* an odd name. I've never met it before but Clare says the old man insisted on the name change as a condition for her taking the boat. I began to wonder if the name itself was significant, an anagram perhaps or a password. Everyone talks about how devious O'Dwyer was, how he was obsessed with codes and number puzzles. Could the name *Quadra* relate to a quadrangle, or what about quadratic? What if the three numbers are just that, the bases of a quadratic equation. I've tried to project myself into the mind of this man and it's just the sort of thing he'd have loved. I'm not great at mathematics, but I used a calculator and these are the final two numbers I came up with. It may be all cobblers but it's worth a try.'

'Well worth a try,' said Newhoffer. 'Whether you're right or wrong, I think Sherlock Holmes would've been proud of you.'

'If Delia finds out she'll try and claim the papers,' said Mike.

'She'll say they belong to the government.'

'No way, they're mine!' protested Clare.

'Only by inheritance,' said Newhoffer. 'But I doubt if any safe deposit would be proof against the CIA or MI5.'

'So we get them out of there,' said Clare.

'Sooner the better. We'll do the responsible thing. You read 'em, I'll read 'em, then we'll all decide.'

'Suits me,' said Clare. 'I'd sooner burn them.'

Mike replaced the telephone and went to find Clare in the kitchen. It was early evening and she was insisting on cooking a meal. Twenty four hours ago Mike had been close to death, today the experience seemed unreal, to have happened to someone else.

'That was Newhoffer,' he said. 'He's just back from the bank. He had to use some special pull to get them to deal out of hours. I was right about those numbers. Would you believe it – spot on?' Mike released a spontaneous whoop and punched the air.

'I thought you had a smug expression on your face.' For the first time in a week she threw back her head and laughed with delighted relief. 'I can hardly believe it after all we've been through.'

'They wouldn't let him look in the box though. It needs you to be there in business hours – the bank people were firm on that. Newhoffer wants us in London tomorrow.'

'What tacky thin paper,' said Clare. She was tipping the contents of the file onto the table.

Clare had driven them to the bank vault and then back across London. Now they were in Newhoffer's house in Cadogan Square, a little oasis of quiet, a few blocks away from the bustle of Sloane Square and the Kings road.

'They called 'em flimsies in those days,' said Newhoffer. 'A lot of official business was on flimsy, saved weight and space.'

'It's only statistics, lists,' said Clare plainly disappointed. She passed one of the sheets to Newhoffer.

'Oh glory be, it's one helluva lot more than that,' said Newhoffer. 'Boy oh boy, what've we here? Detailed breakdowns, unit by unit, shipping list, and all the conspirators by name. Proof positive, no wonder Anderson wanted it, and the Godamm French. I don't care to think what would happen if Ian Paisley ever saw it. Game set and match to Captain O'Leary. My mission would be finished.'

'Your peace negotiations?' asked Mike.

'Sure, I've told Clare a little already. Delia Lazarraga is no ordinary agent. She's British Intelligence's sole link to the military leadership of the IRA. In a few months, a year anyway, they'll stop shooting and to her credit it's Delia who's worked the magic. She's some hold over them, God knows what, but I guess there's more to this than meets the eye.'

'She and her mother did a deal with ETA on the side,' said Clare.

Newhoffer smiled faintly. 'Your crewman, Jean-Luc Chumas reported the whole thing. The French and Spanish are complaining loud and long.'

Mike was lost in the papers. Clare suspected he'd heard nothing for the last few minutes. 'I can't believe this. It wasn't just Ireland – they meant to invade England. It says capture Plymouth, scuttle Royal Navy ships, then defend the line of the Tamar river. Carl – this couldn't happen it's plain crazy – complete fantasy. For Christ's sake why?'

'It's true enough, Michael,' said Newhoffer. He turned to Clare. 'You told me you met Noel Shaw-Mulligan in Cornwall?'

Clare nodded and made a face.

'Did he tell you what he was doing there?'

'He and Toni were on a fishing trip, or so he said.' Clare was still annoyed with herself that she hadn't wondered at the coincidence of Noel's presence. She jumped, startled as Newhoffer released a bellow of laughter.

'Sorry Clare, but I like your stepfather, and as for fishing, that's just what he was on – a fishing expedition. Say did your… sorry I'll rephrase that. Did Jimmy O'Dwyer ever mention a Captain John O'Farrell? Air Service captain that would be?'

'Yes he did, there's an O'Farrell on the list of names he left me, but there was no address or contact – just said Falmouth, Cornwall, England. We never twigged at the time but a few days later we went looking for Noel. Never got to him, the military grabbed us.'

'Irish Intelligence found the man's great-granddaughter in Falmouth. Noel Shaw-Mulligan visited her, charmed the soul out of her, and bought a box of moldering papers for five thousand dollars. The contents meant nothing to the young lady, but she was getting married and was glad of the cash.'

'What was it all about?' asked Clare.

'The maddest part of Flanagan's fantasy world. O'Farrell was to prepare the ground for the Plymouth attack. He was to seek out the Cornish Nationalist movement and enlist their support. It seems there was one, but they were all old ladies, schoolteachers and whimsy poets, and they didn't like the Irish that much anyway. When one of them called the police, O'Farrell went to ground. But it seems he liked the country and eventually found himself a job and a wife. He returned to the States and met Jimmy again, but by that time the depression was on, and O'Farrell came back to England. Seems he'd served in that war with the British Royal Flying Corps, so he had no trouble with naturalization.'

'And nobody ever guessed?' said Mike.

'The whole plot had been covered up. Part of that was an amnesty for all concerned including O'Farrell, Flanagan, Jimmy and, by the British, for Christopher Venner-Harris.'

'And O'Leary?' asked Clare.

'That was a weak link. The Canadian government gave him immunity in exchange for a complete confession of his part in the plot. Canadians have an ambivalent attitude to Uncle Sam and there was always a fear that O'Leary's secrets might leak out.'

'What do we do now?' Clare asked.

She found Newhoffer staring at her and she felt uneasy. 'You're not going to like this,' he said, 'but there's only one safe thing you can do. Give 'em to Delia Lazarraga...'

'Like hell!' Clare felt her temper rise and her cheeks flush. The idea was so repugnant she could not believe what she was hearing.

'Now young lady, you hear me out, huh?'

Clare sat mouth open, her protests stilled.

'See here. Miss Lazarraga wants these documents suppressed and for this once I agree with her. They really are far too dangerous to be in circulation.'

'All right,' said Clare defiantly. 'I say we burn them now.'

'No Clare, in a few days, weeks at most, Miss Lazarraga will learn that Clare O'Dwyer removed a file from a box in the Elmer-Bernstein vault. Could be she knows already. No, with your permission I'm giving those papers to her with a further warning not to touch you folks.'

'He's right love.' Mike squeezed her hand.

'So Delia wins, after all we've been through, and Michael nearly murdered and our boat burned and sunk.' Clare bit her lip and clenched her knuckles. She couldn't take this; it meant defeat, betrayal.

'Delia would kill you to get this file,' said Mike.

'And there'll be no cease fire if those papers get published,' said

Newhoffer. 'Is it worth it – more dead kids?'

'I don't know.'

'You think about it. I'm going downstairs to order some lunch.' He left the room without a backward glance.

'I'll have to give in, won't I?' said Clare.

'I'm afraid so. Remember what you said about Delia riding the world's dirty rotten currents?'

She made a grimace that slowly turned into lopsided grin. 'Michael, I may be James O'Dwyer's daughter but so's Delia. I've his blood in me and it'll be in our children.'

Mike moved across the room and slowly kissed her. 'D'you know the one thing I'll always regret is that I never met him. What a man. I wish I could be half the things he was. War pilot, long distance flyer, code breaker. Then all he did in Spain and putting his career on the line with the Civil Rights movement. And my goodness, he knew how to design a safe yacht. *Quadra* saved all our lives out there.' He laughed. 'To cap it all he fathers a lovely girl child at the age of seventy-two. No, if I could do a quarter of what he did in his lifetime I wouldn't grumble.'

'Well Michael,' she was laughing as well now, 'you'll not be fathering anything at the age of seventy two if I'm around.'

He held both her hands. 'When we get home I've a phone call to make.'

'What now?'

'A call to a timber firm in Bristol – want to know why?'

'Tell me?'

'Because we've a half empty building shed and I've a mind to build a boat in it…'

'Oh Michael, the plans, *Quadra's* plans! You brought them back from Ireland?'

'They're in the office. I've been looking at them. Everything's there: timber list, loftings – the lot. We'll make a start as soon as the first load arrives.'

She threw herself at him smothering him with kisses. 'Michael, you're a genius – we'll call her *Phoenix*.'

EPILOGUE

The Cork Examiner May 12th 1994.

An Australian man; Samuel Pardraig Cassidy was convicted yesterday of setting fire to the yacht, Quadra, at Crosshaven on the afternoon of the 28th April. The yacht was the property of Ms Clare O'Dwyer of Crosshaven.

Cassidy was observed stealing a dinghy and rowing out to the yacht with a 25 litre fuel container. Shortly afterwards flames were seen coming from the yacht. Mr Rodney Wallace of Edgbaston Birmingham, said in evidence that he and his wife had seen the fire from their yacht Ianthe. He told the court that as he came alongside Quadra he saw that the defendant Cassidy had failed to secure his dinghy which was drifting away on the tide. Mr Wallace stated that he called the defendant to jump across to Ianthe. Cassidy refused and screamed abuse of a racial and anti-British nature.

The court was told that Cassidy was taken ashore by a launch from the Royal Cork Yacht Club where he was taken into custody. Gard O'Duggan gave evidence saying that Cassidy had refused to answer questions or give a coherent explanation.

Cassidy refused to plead saying he did not recognize the court.

Judge P Brennan presiding found the case proved and remanded Cassidy for one week for psychiatric tests.

THE SOUTH COAST REVIEW
May 12th.1994

Second World War veteran, Wotek Micalczyk, was charged with possession of an unlicensed firearm and with discharging the same to the danger of the public and protected wildlife.

The court was told that police were called to the premises of Cottons Hard Yacht Services on the night of Wednesday 29th April, following reports of shooting from an automatic weapon. PC Garry Williams stated that the person had in his possession a Second World War Sten gun which was still warm from firing.

The defendant said that he had recently found the gun in his attic. It was a forgotten souvenir of the war. He resolved to hand the weapon to the police but was tempted to try it one more time.

Mr Richard Somerfield defending said that "Mr Micalczyk is a well liked and respected local personality who had given gallant wartime service to his adopted country."

The magistrate found the case proved and awarded a sentence of twelve months in prison suspended for one year.

LONDON DAILY TELEGRAPH
March 2014
NEW HEAD FOR MI6

The New head of MI6 is to be Dame Delia Lazarraga.   The appointment was announced to the House Of Commons by the Junior Foreign Office minister, Sir Charles Venner-Harris, MP. Sir Charles said the announcement was in line with the official policy of open government. In commending Dame Delia to the House, Sir Charles spoke of her many years of devoted service in MI5 counter intelligence. She was a lady with a superb track record of success in the highest traditions of the intelligence services.

THE END

323

Reviews of *The Nemesis File* (continued):

Olympic sailor and coach: Cathy Foster, 11th Dec 2004

Rarely have I read such a racy book! It's carries you along at pace, and holds you fast until the very end. Just then, you think that maybe this is getting far-fetched, but the punch-line pulls you up short, and makes you re-assess the characters and their relationship to events. Suddenly the plot hangs together again in a very satisfactory way, just as good detective stories should.

Instead of long descriptions to 'paint a picture' of all the venues and situations, the writing is succinct and carefully crafted to give the maximum impression for the minimum words. This gives the book its fast tempo, yet nothing is lost because the accurate detailing of locations and action bonds the reader into plot. As a past Olympic sailor myself, I know the sailing venues described in both Chichester Harbour and Copenhagen well, and I can reassure any future reader that the author has definitely done his research. In addition, he's right – you do build life-long bonds with other British athletes and other countries' sailors when you are part of the Olympic team representing your country. It is a pleasure and highly unusual to read a book which describes the joys of sailing and racing so well. Yet it's not a book about sailing, full of technicalities of the sport. Sailing provides the background framework for a story of murder and blackmail where the investigation chases over four countries and three generations of lives. A thoroughly enjoyable read.

Cathy Foster went to the Olympics in 1984 (finished 7th and made history as the first woman helm since the 2nd World War) and competed in two other Olympic campaigns, the last being 2002/3. She's a freelance Coach who specialises in top level racing, including Olympic and Paralympic sailors